Origins of X
Secrets of Sage Mountain

Michael Holmes II

Origins of X
Secrets of Sage Mountain
Michael Holmes II

Published by Remaerd Publishing, St. Louis, MO

Project Management and Book Design: Davis Creative, LLC, dba: DavisCreativePublishing.com
Cover Design: Davis Creative Publishing, DavisCreativePublishing.com
Cover Illustration: Kelly Brasel (front) | Cottrell Turner (back)
Editor: Jennifer Capler

Library of Congress Cataloging-in-Publication Data
Names: Holmes II, Michael, 1990- author.
Title: Origins of X : Secrets of Sage Mountain / Michael Holmes II.
Description: St. Louis, MO : Remaerd Publishing, LLC, [2024]
Identifiers: ISBN: 979-8-9917644-2-1 (hardbound) | 979-8-9917644-3-8 (paperback) |
    979-8-9917644-4-5 (ebook) | LCCN: 2024921685
Subjects: LCSH: Magic--Fiction. | Parents--Fiction. | Enemies--Fiction. | Secrecy--Fiction. | Battles-- Fiction. |
    Survival--Fiction. | LCGFT: Science fiction. | Action and adventure fiction. | BISAC: FICTION / Science Fiction /
    General. | FICTION / Science Fiction / Action & Adventure. | FICTION / Science Fiction / Crime & Mystery.
Classification: LCC: PS3608.049435459 O75 2024 | DDC: 813/.6--dc23

2025

Prologue

Jackson, my best friend, was cracking jokes about how puberty was wreaking havoc on my voice as we walked to the only movie theater in our small town. I turned my head to hide an embarrassed smile as we crossed main street and tried to think of a comeback but was interrupted by the sight of a semi-truck speeding towards us, less than ten feet from my face. I froze like a deer in headlights, thinking about how the truck was moving faster than it should be, and it didn't appear to be stopping. I snapped out of my brief panic-induced haze and pushed Jackson as hard as possible to get him out of the way. When the truck slammed into me, my body shook with the impact as a chorus of screams and gasps rose from onlookers. The cries of the people on the sidewalks roughly contrasted with the deafening squeals of metal violently warping around me. My eyes focused on the sight of smoke billowing from the mangled vehicle's face.

Things only got weirder as my mind raced to make sense of the situation. The semi-truck had hit me dead on where I stood. Instead of flattening my body like a bug, the truck had crumpled around me like cheap tinfoil. The grill had formed a ragged U-shape where we had collided. I say 'we' because, despite the large chunk of my mind reeling from the fact that I was still alive, I definitively knew I hadn't managed to dodge the semi-truck. My mind was spiraling in panic as I remembered we were on a street comprised of the most popular shops and restaurants in town.

I tried to free myself to look for Jackson, but I was completely frozen. In some odd way, I knew I was immobilized more than even the mangled metal would have ensured. I couldn't lift a finger, paralyzed from head to toe, even though every muscle tensed. The driver was fighting a deployed airbag, and out of every building, I could see aghast faces glaring through the windows. All my instincts screamed to flee the scene. Like a vampire with his eyes fixed upon the horizon's imminent dawn, I was supernaturally aware of the townspeople's eyes growing wider and shining brilliantly with cognition of my predicament. The sound of helicopters blossomed in the air.

An odd sense of immeasurable moments later, I was able to swivel my head left to right again only from shoulder to shoulder. I scanned side to side and finally found Jackson picking himself up off the ground across the street from me. I realized I'd been holding my breath in this whole time as a sigh of relief escaped my lungs. My friend came sprinting straight to me once he regained his footing, abandoning the safety of being distanced from this damning scene I was at the heart of. When Jackson reached the truck, I looked around and saw nothing but a sea of accusatory faces.

There was a transformation taking place in the people I had lived alongside amicably my whole life, almost all friends and acquaintances, staring avidly in disbelief as Jackson's hands began to glow. The disbelief was quickly souring as people's faces hardened into anger and disgust, their eyes ablaze with a glowering hatred. Jackson was trying to heat himself up so that he could melt the metal I was entombed in, damning himself in front of the entire town by revealing that he had powers. Being seen using inhuman abilities in public like this was exactly what our parents would crucify him for in any other situation, and for good reason. Jackson was still trying to focus his powers when the first metal bird crested the horizon. In the blink of an eye, several more helicopters were closing in on us. I realized there wasn't enough time for a clean getaway, at least not for both of us.

"Jackson, get the hell out of here. There's no time," I said, earning a confrontational glare from my friend before he followed my gaze.

The imposing government helicopters would be here in no time, and we both knew it. Jackson gave me a terse nod and turned to leave, and I took a moment to feel proud that, at least this time, my voice hadn't cracked when I was trying to sound cool. Jackson was less than five steps away when his mad dash was halted by a golden hammer that came flying out of nowhere and cracked open the side of his head with a sickening crunch. He dropped instantly dead on the concrete as a crew of white and gold hooded men emerged from the nearest space between buildings.

Many of the hooded men held hammers of their own and were cheering and hollering in celebration like drunken frat boys at a toga party. I had the unnatural paired sensations of my heart skipping several beats while my blood began to boil with rage. The gang of Purists came confidently onto the scene, and some even saluted the crowd that was still watching raptly from every angle. Since these hooded assholes were plentiful and local, they normally beat cops to any emergency scene dealing with powered people, and without fail, they seemed to beat the government's special ops goons since it took the federal agency longer to mobilize. They'd killed my grandparents, too many aunts and uncles to count, and now my best friend... who lay bleeding out in front of me. Just for being born different from them. With a Gift. With Power that they resented because their genetic coding meant that they were gifted with nothing exceptional but the purely optional choice to harbor hatred for those that were different.

I froze when I locked eyes upon the dozen or more Purists approaching. My heart and mind slowed as all the dark feelings from my entire life seemed to manifest and rot inside me all at once. The feeling was akin to experiencing the heinous amalgamation of every soul-wrenching shard of negativity I'd experienced, culminating into a storm of blind rage, hatred, pain, fear and loss, all for the first time and simultaneously. The helicopters were right above us now, the wind and lights emphasizing the gruesome horror of the scene more than I had thought possible.

My heart raced as I debated death by Purist or from being a government guinea pig, looking back and forth between the imposing aircraft and the confident killers approaching on foot. Those may have been my last thoughts if not for my vision catching on the growing pool of blood under Jackson's head. Rumor had it that the Purists only ever allowed mutants to be taken prisoner by the government in their presence because the tests and procedures they did were worse than any death that mob justice could deliver.

I had an epiphany that Jackson would be ok right now if he hadn't tried to save me. At the very least, he'd still be alive. More than the threats all around me, I hated myself in that moment of realization, and something inside me cracked. It was as tangibly painful as if it had been all my bones shattering at once. A part of me decided that none of these monsters would live to make the choice of how I died, like they had for Jackson. Something inside me was reaching out malevolently, even though I knew somehow it hadn't broken free of its prison all the way yet, just enough to reach a hand out. Inside me, a wall was being torn thin enough that my instincts kicked in and grabbed ahold of the power leaking through the cracks. I made the tiniest inkling of contact, and everything exploded.

The next thing I knew I was screaming at nothing. I had no idea how long I had been crying out, but I was sure something horrible had happened. I don't know how, but I could feel that I had done something undeniably ghastly. The car was gone, Jackson's body was gone, both the Purist gang and all the innocent onlookers had disappeared. As far as I could see, the world had turned to lifeless ash without even an ember left. The sky was lightly raining ashes and stained a lifeless gray, the approaching airborne helicopters not having been immune to what occurred. I looked around with a lens of bewilderment and growing numbness as an alarm was going off in my ear. There was something crying out for me to pay attention to it. I just couldn't decipher what I was supposed to be paying attention to with what little sanity I had left. What alarm could really be important right now?

Chapter One

I woke up tangled in bedsheets and drenched in sweat. Letting the alarm clock ring out a few more jarring chimes before reaching to turn it off, I stretched out in a vain attempt to release the anxiety and tension from my bones. As I blinked sleep from my eyes, I noticed the Dreamcatcher hanging at the head of my bed had been reduced to a blackened circle overnight, evidence my emotions weren't going to be shaken out that easily. Sunshine was already coming in through my bedroom window full tilt, the multitude of diffused light beams sharply reflecting off the mess of objects on my workbench across the room. The disorganized surface was all the distraction I needed to wake up completely and shake last night's dream from the forefront of my mind. A medley of leftover thoughts from the night before began to bubble to the surface, reminding me of the different ways I could bring the project on the table to completion. With a hearty groan, I tossed the covers aside, reminding myself to get a new Dreamcatcher before tonight, and walked over to my workbench.

I pushed all the dark and cloying thoughts away with the practice of years and reached out with my senses, several that regular humans didn't possess, to the tools on my workbench. Everything but the unworked ores and gemstones I had left out responded to my mind's touch and jumped back to their designated places, which had been a relatively easy enchantment. I pulled down one of the finest chisels I own and a pouch of more delicate carving tools, all of them necessary for my current project. It was a work of magic aimed to be more complex than the enchantment that helped organize my workspace. I had only finished one piece of the set so far, with a copper bronze body and a roughly hewn ruby set into the top, the circumference of which was only a bit bigger than a watch face. As I tapped the crimson stone three times, I felt the enchantment successfully awaken. Then, out of curiosity, I turned it off and on again a few times in quick succession.

I focused on the dregs of my dream, collecting the dark thoughts that lingered and burrowed into the recesses of my mind. As I pressed the stone against my hand, I sensed my magic stir from the core of my being and started to search out all my anxiety, fear, and rage. Like I had practiced the past few days, I focused my intent with both the raw arcane energy and coalescing feelings so that they began to bind and acquiesce into strands of multi-colored light in my mind's eye. The runes carved into both the bronze and ruby glowed softly as the energy left my hand and transitioned to energy stored in the gem. I'd debated with myself while working on this enchantment if I was affecting my internal hormones, neuro-chemicals, or a different physical manifestation altogether that inherently would be attached to the emotions I was targeting. In the end, I could only make the magic work; it was beyond me to connect it with any solid scientific process or explanation. Over the years, my observations had led me to believe that the strongest magic was always fueled by emotion and that, in the end, all the components were truly inseparable. As I purged the last bit of the dream's ilk into the stone, I set the piece of the project back within the larger leather sleeve I'd designed to fit over my forearm and under my street clothes. So far, the armband was set to carry five large stones. The main problem I had now was figuring out which ideas would be best for which gems.

I stood and felt a bit lighter than I had upon waking, even more so because I now started the day with a small triumph. I teleported downstairs from my room to the kitchen and got a small smile and nod of recognition from my Dad as he dutifully read the paper. My Enchanting magic had been denounced as 'unconventional and mystifying' by my Mom, though she had been more excited when my magic started manifesting than my Dad had ever been about my mutant powers. He wasn't a self-hating mutant or anything of the sort, the old man was proud and thankful for his Gifts for the most part. If it wasn't for the striking crimson hue of his skin and the gigantic set of feathered wings on his back, he would've been more excited for me, I think. I still had a year or two before the traditional transition periods for magicians and mutants were solidified. Every day that passed and I remained wingless with my Mother's general complexion, the man breathed a little bit easier.

I grabbed an apple off the kitchen counter and waved cordially before I teleported to the garden out back. The backyard was more my Mom's personal space that we were simply allowed to spend time in. She had potent Earth magic in her veins, which I was showing no real affinity for, to her dismay. That fact hadn't kept her from drilling more botanical lore into me than most people get in a lifetime. It came in handy in some ways, but the plants didn't speak secrets to me or lean out eagerly for my touch like they would with Mom. All seemed right with the green world back here today, as she was elbow-deep in the dirt doing something to a tangled mess of roots. Without looking up to acknowledge my silent arrival, she spoke. I had to wonder if I had just missed the Earth whispering news of my arrival to her. One benefit of growing up here was getting to run around barefoot like her, which I later discovered was due to a deep-seated hope I'd begin communicating with greater elemental forces. To be honest I still ran around barefoot most of the time in hopes the discussion would start any day now, but it wasn't likely.

"You must've had a rough night. What's got you popping into my garden with such heavy feet?" I looked down and realized I had accidentally teleported out here to land with my feet buried deep into the soft dirt I'd meant to end up on top of.

I focused on releasing the last of my anxieties and negative energies and breathed deeply until I felt normal, then teleported out of the hole to stand directly next to my Mom. My secondary mutation showed itself only a few weeks after the first, but sometimes, my emotional state still affected how accurate my aim was. Thanks to what I considered my primary mutation, I'd survived months of falling from great heights and accidentally throwing myself through walls, the most common side effects of a failed teleport. Next to teleportation, the enhanced skin and durability was a great primary mutation, though ultimately impractical for someone who doesn't get out much. The most useful outlets it allowed me to pursue so far were the obviously risky ones to develop, like self-defense skills, acrobatic abilities, and overall mobility training. Things like parkour videos or clips from movies were easier to press the envelope, imitating when you were working with a body that wouldn't break, even if you accidentally fell off a 10-story building.

"Just old dreams Mom, sorry about making craters in the garden. I'm going to weave a new Dreamcatcher tonight, nothing to worry about," I said, and she responded with the kind of general murmur of concern that was uttered whenever she didn't believe me.

"Let me check those abominations; they've got to be why you run through Dreamcatchers like they're cheap talismans!" my Mom said, referring to my tattoos.

They were my first solo magic project, an odd mix of stellar success and a train wreck of failure. Accustomed to the habitual prodding at this point, I pulled my shirt off, stood up straight, and waited as she poked around. I had tattooed five spots on my body with specially charged inks I'd cultivated from the garden, a combination of runes set under a month's worth of full moons, and a few random magical items pilfered from my aunt's collection. The tattoo's presence was often blamed for any bad luck I experienced, although in the case of the Dreamcatchers I couldn't say for certain that she was in the wrong. Although their original intent had been modified from the Native American Ojibwe tribe's cultural aim to help aid me in avoiding my night terrors, a single one woven by an Earth Witch like my Mom should have lasted a lifetime. Last night officially marked the third one I'd burnt through in the past week.

The self-inscribed tattoos were spread so that one laid inside of each forearm, one on each shoulder, and then one over my heart. The situation had earned a more complex reaction of anger and begrudging acceptance than I think would have gone down in most families. She stared hard at the runes I'd harmonized to grant me Speed on my left forearm, shaking her head in both a scolding and impressed way that showed her warring worry and pride. The one on my opposite forearm was for Strength, and it received equal scrutiny as the last one had. With exaggerated disdain she regarded the mark for Healing on my right shoulder and moved on without comment, but things went to hell when she moved to the Growth sigil I had carved upon my left shoulder. The tattoos had successfully imbued me with the enhanced attributes I'd been seeking, however they'd also grown more elaborate with a life of their own. The ink had consistently reacted in an unpredictable way, evolving under my skin until it looked like it was branching out through my veins and into the surrounding muscles. In my defense, there had never been a disclaimer that these tattoos would affect an individual with mutant DNA differently than one who was solely a magician. From what I had been able to glean from my Mom's reactions in the time since I carried out the process, and survived, there had never been a feasible reason to even consider such a warning. This was apparently a type of magic that people rarely used; at least my Mom had never heard of or met anyone stupid enough to try it... before me, that is.

The markings stained my skin and veins with an ebony hue as they grew and evolved like a sentient oil spill moving in slow motion down my veins. I could've sworn I heard her curse under her breath, but she quickly attempted to play it off as if she had noticed nothing wrong before moving on to the last tattooed area. In all honesty I didn't even know if there were any other magic users who were also mutants. There was a long and awkward tension as she studied the layered ink over my heart; I'd meant to use it to enhance my Magical Potency or overall Power. I remember once overhearing Mom say on the phone that she could probably write an entire book on how that rune alone had evolved after being exposed to my system and how it had even grown to form other lesser runes instead of random chaos upon my skin. In a way, it had been a secret source of pride as she talked with my Aunts about the next generation of magic users in the family. With what I could piece together from our family's meager library, and from the lectures I received from her, self-inscribed sigil tattoos were basically guaranteeing death or madness for most magicians.

I groaned, and, with exaggerated slowness, struggled to get my shirt back over my head. When my face popped back out, my Mom had already gripped my left side and was regarding me in what I couldn't help but call a bug-eyed fashion. Her face kept shifting between my chest and shoulder slowly, as if each pass only confused her more. The Growth rune on my left shoulder and the sigil of the Old Ways over my heart had always been the most intricately interwoven, even though that hadn't honestly been part of my plans at all. Approaching the project as if I had been enchanting my own biology meant that my intent in laying out the runes was of paramount importance, so I had just instinctually decided that it couldn't hurt for these two to be close to each other. The shoulder in question held the markings embodying Growth, which I had painstakingly labored to incorporate closest to those over my chest. Above my beating heart were a myriad of runes layered to represent Magical strength, focus, and, above all, acknowledgment of the arcane Old Ways. I'd amalgamated an image from childhood dreams and my Mother's bedtime stories, using both the possibly historical and likely fantastical books I'd read in fascination every day when I was younger. I'd be lying if I didn't admit they'd heavily affected the overall attempt at the tattoo. The Old Ways were a code of conduct for noble and honorable mystics back in the olden days, intact even before humanity became cut off from the other magical planes that coexisted with our own.

"Sometimes I still find myself wondering what in the world you were thinking when you did this Xavier. If you were an Earth Mage I'd have you living in and tending to the garden for the next year, but as things are I'm still not sure what repercussion would fit you best," the older woman said, shaking her head as I took a step back and stretched, allowing my shirt to fall back down.

Although my Mom and Dad were about as far from traditional parent figures as one could have, tattoos were still frowned upon. I'm sure I would've been grounded upon their discovery, but my parents had been at a loss with what to do with me in general lately. I had been more than a bit reclusive after my magic manifested, and threatening an agoraphobe with being grounded is worthless. It was no well-kept secret in our house that my mutant powers had simultaneously saved and ruined my life in a horrifically public manner. It was also no secret that I hated the idea of being the one who messed up, but we got to go make a fresh start somewhere new, leaving behind the ridicule and hatred stirred among those narrow-minded, mutant-hating locals in my wake. When I began to realize that I had magic growing within me on top of the mutant powers, I'd been more confused than resentful of my situation. Every person I'd spoken to, or that my Mom and Dad had consulted, considered this a baffling and unique case.

As unconventional as my existence was, I had been lucky that my mutant Dad had, against all odds, married a witch. After my very public car accident, my mutant gifts followed the traditional chronology of appearing and maturing as most other kids experienced, and Dad was proud to guide me. Apparently teleportation was a rare mutation, so I had to coach myself while developing the skill and work to keep it under control. At first my priority had been centered around not accidentally dropping myself into a volcano, drowning myself in the ocean, or throwing myself into space. From time to time I got to see Jackson and his father for sparring sessions in remote country fields owned by a family friend, who employed my Mom to help keep their business afloat. Guaranteed financial success born of magically flourishing crops apparently bought us enough leeway that if a fireball or two exploded during a fight, destroying nearly half an acre of unused forest in the process, we were still worth putting up with.

As I got older I became almost completely impervious to fire from fighting Jackson, and subzero temperature attacks from fighting his father who we called Blue. No matter how much they had trained and grown together in the months between our meetings I could always reach within myself to become stronger, faster, and recover more quickly than they expected. As if my mutations hadn't been enough of an advantage, my attacks now carried the weight of raw magic behind every blow, and they landed heavily enough for me to win most bouts quickly.

If I hadn't already been paranoid enough about being exposed, my new powers had made me constantly worry we'd have to pack up and move again. Mostly because I knew we were already out of places to run. My folks reassured me that this community was primarily built of people like us who had nowhere left to run, individuals that had already been forced to run from their original homes. After letting me know this I was told never to ask others about their previous lives, and to never discuss ours. Any outsiders looking in would only find a picturesque mother, father, and son. If they tried to squeeze our neighbors for information they would be rewarded with a thoroughly preprepared set of answers, and far more trouble than they had bargained for. Although Purists and government agencies mainly focused on mutants instead of people with magic (because only mutations were biologically detectable through scientific testing), both groups of oppressed individuals had attempted to come together for the first time in history to avoid persecution.

I knew in some loose way that my Mom and Dad had contacts in this modern-day Underground Railroad, where people were quietly moved about in attempts to avoid government captivity or extermination, but I was gently encouraged not to ask questions. So, I didn't. It didn't take a genius to realize that I was now personally one of the beneficiaries of their work. The true danger facing me now, as far as myself and my family seemed to be concerned, was my developing magic. For most people, basic magic appeared and formed along the same timeline that mutant abilities would throughout one's youth. I was done with puberty, and my mutant abilities had solidified, but my magical potency still continued to flourish and grow unchecked and without an end in sight.

"Come on Xavier, time for the basics again," Mom said, effortlessly transitioning down into a lotus-style position and motioning for me to join her on the bared earth.

Grounding was one of the most basic practices that a magic user was trained in, or so I was told, but I still hadn't mastered the process. It involved channeling all the excess energies within yourself, both malignant and benign, and releasing them harmlessly into the earth. The Earth had its own sentience, spirit, and power, and it was capable of absorbing far more energy than I could ever throw at it if I needed help achieving balance. My Mom taught me that, as far back as was historically recorded, learning how to ground was an essential part of every Conduit's training. Conduit was the more modern term of someone capable of letting the raw power of magic flow through them, since many people had grown averse to the old monikers of 'witch' and 'wizard' after their consistent misrepresentations in popular culture. Whereas every mutant is built in a unique way because their individual biology enables and shapes their power, all Conduits' powers are built from the ability to use a similar energy, though there still exists a variation of strength and uncountable predispositions from person to person. I wasn't an Earth Conduit like my Mom, but we could both theoretically use magic energy to cast a lot of the same spells once I learned how to connect with and control my magical energy. My ability to sense the Earth as a magical entity was consistent but was also basically the magical equivalent of sensing which way is up... not very impressive at the end of the day. The real issue was reaching into my own center and connecting it with the Earth's, an act that would be as simple as breathing to a true Earth Conduit. I had been failing so consistently and miserably that my growing frustration had birthed sparks. Literally.

Over the past few weeks, since my Mom had decided I should restart basic training for the magic growing inside of me, part of every day had been spent on what I now viewed as an exercise in futility. I'd grown resentful that I had these powers to worry about and learn to hide on top of my mutations, but apparently couldn't use them properly. She sat less than a foot across from me, patiently resonating in harmony between her own core of power and the heart of the Earth.

"Breathe in deeply. Focus on fortifying your innards against all the negative energy that resides in the world around you and within you. Hold your breath. Sit with the overlap of both reality and imagination, recognize everything holds weight and has effect. All of this can be released. In fact, none of it can truly be held onto." She guided me through the steps of the meditation, saying the same affirmation a million different ways as she guided my breathing in and out.

The tradition passed down from her mother held that the best way to aid your apprentice was for the teacher to display the expertly sustained state to the aspiring Conduit while in close proximity, but I only grew more frustrated every time. The harder I tried to push myself to connect to the Earth, the more my Center refused to follow commands. When I closed my eyes the two felt more adverse towards each other than oil and water, refusing to mix.

Mom's lyrical voice continued to pick at me as she walked through the steps of the meditation, continuing the affirmations as she guided my breathing in and out. As per the instructions for the ridiculous exercise, I breathed in and out and tried to stay positive. I remained open to whatever thoughts and emotions wished to flow through me, which was always where the trouble started. The goal was to observe thoughts and allow them to pass, feeling the pain and sorrow of your life but gaining enlightenment from growing detached enough to rise above it. The practice was meant to encourage a deeper balance within yourself at the end of the session. I breathed in and could smell the cheap beer on the Purists' breath as they hollered in the streets, killing people less fortunate than I had been that night. I breathed out and cringed as if I had been hit by a shotgun at close range.

My heart began dancing erratically and skipping beats as my mind's eye locked onto a mutant child taken away in a cage to be forever lost in the soulless machine of the government labs. My Mother had told me that it was possible I was picking up real-life glimpses into extreme emotional moments others were experiencing. Or that I'd watched too many online mutant-capture videos, along with maybe too many evening news clips, and now my mind was simply regurgitating the scenes. As anyone could imagine, it wasn't reassuring to know that my growing abilities meant I could either be tapping into a live tragedy as it happens or that I was just experiencing echoes of my own anxieties.

"Upon breathing out, you have to let go Xavier. All earthly attachments, your life's regrets, the entirety of your ego. Breathe in and think of the light and all the goodness you can harness." My Mom's voice cut through my psyche, and I attempted to abandon the dark route my mind had begun to walk.

I was luckier than anyone else I'd ever heard of, to end up with parents that not only understood the fact that I was a mutant but also that I had magic. I felt confident filling myself with such grateful energy as I inhaled, but as the tempo led to the exhale, a snapshot from one of my nightmares sprang up to dominate the forefront of my mind. It was my best friend Jackson, bleeding out on the sidewalk. Some part of me knew that he had to be perfectly fine, at most a 6-hour drive away in our hometown. However, the part of my brain that had lived through that dream made its belief vividly poignant concerning what happened to him. Every detail, from the cheaply spray-painted hammer laying against his askew skull to the jarringly vivid edges of blood spreading from his lifeless form, were there as if I could reach out and touch them. I exhaled with that picture in the forefront of my mind, and at first, it felt like my lungs simply weren't responding. Then I realized, no matter how hard I pushed, my lungs weren't deflating. The embodiment of negativity had become like a solid brick within my core. I looked up at the clear blue sky instead of focusing on the Earth and tried to throw the knot of darkness there.

Time froze as I felt an instant release. An explosion erupted and knocked me backwards in astonishment, though a guilty voice in the back of my head admitted it was better than trying to ground. A chill of excitement and relief rolled down my spine involuntarily as all the power inside me screamed out in exaltation, escaping as a pillar of pure light. The world began to feel far away as I inspected this intricate source of pain, rage, and loss inside of me, hoping that maybe, if I could study it closer while actively interacting with it, I could tweak the state into the placid presence my Mom wished I could be. I heard her gasp as the teal lightning bolt sprang into the sky beyond what the naked eye could see. The eruption shook her from the perfectly woven union with Gaia, jumping up and immediately attempting to stop the energy I was casting into the sky. Some part of my mind knew this was ridiculously reckless, but the rest of me was lost in the ecstasy of my new power finally doing something! My sense of time may have been warped by the pure joy of the moment, but when I finally registered the look of utter horror on my Mom's face, it cut me to the bone, and whatever had released the floodgate of power clamped down on that power immediately.

"Xavier! I need you to look at me. Open your eyes and look at me!" Mom's voice reached me like a slap in the face as I finally came back to my senses.

As I focused, I realized the yard was in shambles. As the light show died down, I felt hollow and aching. My kneeling body involuntarily crumpled to the ground and everything went dark.

❧ ❧ ❧ ❧ ❧

As the understatement of the century, my Mom referred to that day as a "learning experience" and focused on teaching me some basic spells and runes. That night I used my mutant power to teleport downstairs and eavesdrop on her consulting with what I considered her "think-tank." I'd call them a Coven, but I don't think they'd ever actually worked magic together or even met in person. The group just shared knowledge and talked over problems safely from afar.

"I have no idea what to do with him. There's an obvious raw excess of power inside the boy, but the way it expresses itself is like nothing I've ever seen. Hell, it's not even like anything I've ever even heard of...." My Mom had vaguely explained to me that most of the contacts she spoke with were distant personal relatives, therefore they were also Earth Conduits.

At that, they were ones we'd never get a chance to meet in real life due to the safety precautions magical families had to take nowadays. Besides those contacts, there were several trusted family friends who were still distantly linked to some part of the family tree or married into it. The most frustrating part of eavesdropping on their conversations was only being able to hear my Mom's side, and knowing that there were only ever Earth Conduit's involved when I obviously needed help from a different type of magic user. I felt more guilt than resentment or helplessness weighing down on me as she broke the silence on her end of the conversation defensively.

"Well, my only real grimoire contains a bevy of Earth Magic lore, more than a lifetime's worth of study for an Earth Conduit, but it's utterly worthless to him, and a basic set of runes. If I had more to work with, then maybe he wouldn't be in so much danger... No, you don't understand, those tattoos on his body are thriving more vibrantly than my garden!... Until I can convince this Sage to come and assess him despite him being... Well, I'm just asking that you spare whatever you can because I know that... Yes, I understand that our position in aiding the Community is of paramount importance, but I also know that if we received any unwanted attention that our son would lay his life down for a stranger at any moment... Even before his magic appeared he would have been willing to protect any of us with his life. I'd like to remind you he is not in question here, I called you all in hopes of aid with... Yes... Thank you all. Blessed Be. Goodnight." My Mom hung up, a dejected and tense aura hanging in the air for the next few moments.

I almost yelped as my Father squeezed my shoulder reassuringly, silently walking past my hiding spot to wrap his wife in a reassuring hug. He was a quiet and extremely intelligent guy; I should've known he would have memorized the spots I most often teleported to around the house.

"You worry too much, dear. Our son is strong, and he's going to be just fine." His deep baritone was nearly a whisper, speaking only loud enough to ensure that the words would carry back to where I was standing unseen in the hallway.

My Dad hadn't used any special powers just now. He simply knew his family that well. I smiled and blinked myself back upstairs and got into bed feeling reassured despite the uncertainty I was facing because my folks were good people and had my back. I may have felt alone, but I had to remind myself that my folks were on my side. No matter what.

Chapter Two

Jackson, my childhood friend, had convinced me to join him for a night out at his cousin's club just outside city limits. It had already become the city's most wildly popular "in-crowd" scene for freaks and freak lovers. I was homeschooled, and even my parents had managed to accidentally endorse the place's utter coolness by warning me not to go near it. In all honesty, Jackson was my only friend. A little older than me, he is the son of my Dad's best friend. In the small town we'd grown up in, we were basically brothers before I had to move away. Both of us ending up with the mutant gene had helped solidify the bond over the years. Unlike me, his parents let him attend public school for high school. I was jealous, but I couldn't question my family's judgment when there were plenty of whispers about my "skin condition" whenever I went out. Since my friend didn't have any visible signs of mutation, it was much less likely he would be targeted or exposed while out in the community.

Jackson's dad had it worse than me in the mutant looks department. The man's skin was pale blue like ice, the style of his mutant power painted clearly on his skin for all to see. Whereas Jackson was a Pyromancer, meaning he had power over fire, his father had a mutation that let him drop temperatures and manipulate moisture to create and shape ice. My physical tells were my black fingertips and the growing tattoos that branched out from where I'd initially placed them on my body. It wasn't quite fair to say they were a result of my mutations because the original intent had been purely magical. The spells I had found were for Conduit enhancements, but in my single-minded pursuit, I had overlooked that the spells were designed specifically and exclusively for a Conduit's body. My Mom was the stricter of my two parents and the only one who knew anything about magic, so I waited apprehensively for a full month before asking her for help. By then, the sigils for Strength, Speed, Dexterity, Growth, and Magic had gone unnaturally dark, while the ink seemed to branch out into the veins around each site.

I wondered what Jackson's mom would think of our unsanctioned outing as I rode shotgun in his truck, watching the outskirts of the city turn into farmlands. Besides the intense backlash I faced for tattooing myself, Jackson was always the one stirring up trouble and getting punished. Despite being a mutant, my friend was a natural ladies' man and a smooth talker. Jackson's parents had dealt with teachers and concerned parents about how he and his female classmates would end up skipping an hour or two of education for a suspicious cornucopia of extra-curricular activities. From a distance, it was hilarious to hear Jackson's take on each incident. If I had a nickel for every time I'd heard him laughingly explain how, "Then they found a burnt outline of a hand on the back of her jeans, and the yelling started," I'd be the richest guy I knew.

My Dad was a strong mutant and my Mom a powerful witch, but my best friend's mom was known for her legendary displays of temper. The woman's anger had always seemed superhuman to us as kids despite her lack of any inhuman powers. Honestly, though, all four parents would lose it if they ever learned of this outing. Jackson had the plausible cover of being out on a date, and even if I couldn't silently escape by teleporting, my folks had gone to a Neighborhood Watch meeting and were sure to follow it up with a trip to their favorite bar. I was too hermetic of a kid for parents to fret over in general.

"You know if you sit and stare off into space thinking deep thoughts in a corner, you won't make any friends tonight? Come on X, you're the smart one and I'm the eye candy, remember?" Jackson had finally broken the silence that had lasted most of the ride.

He lit a cigarette with one brief flick of his fingers and passed me one, which made me think he was just now realizing how nervous I was. My Mom had demanded I learn how to dance when I was younger, and my Father still trained me to fight weekly, but I still knew there was no conceivable way I could survive this trip to a nightclub. The anxiety in my system stirred my Core so much that the energy swirled as if I had a small lightning storm dancing in my gut. I fiddled with my new power dampeners and siphoned a bit of the storm into enchanted repositories.

"As long as you don't singe a handprint onto every girl's dress before I get to meet one, I can pretend to be socially adept. How cheap did your cousin say he could get us in for? We're not gonna make many friends stuck outside the club, either running from Purists or avoiding small talk with kids who want to know why your friend's fingers are dyed black." I joked back at him while wiggling my hand near his face, eliciting some light laughter from my friend.

I tapped the 4 rings on my left hand as he shook his head, a little surge of magic triggering them all into one solid brass knuckle design. I had to wear them all the time now to contain my growing powers. It had begun to be a real problem that my Enchanting skills were barely able to compensate for. After the past few months both hands were fully wreathed in different rings I'd imbued with magic, enabling them to store and suppress my own excess energy. I felt like a gaudy peacock since I'd never worn much jewelry before, but I had no desire to let my Flow get out of control in public. I summoned a flame over my thumb and lit my cigarette off it, smiling as I noticed Jackson watch me work the small magic in surprise.

"Like I told you Spook, my cousin owns the place! He said all we had to do was show up for Freak Night, and we'd get in and drink for free all night... Y'know, once we prove ourselves." Jackson had said the first part a million times, but I had been expecting some small catch to pop up once we were too far out for me to teleport back. My smile decayed into more of a sustained grimace as I tried to reevaluate how awkward of a night I was in for.

"So, the club went from being the new heart of the city's Mutant scene to some spot in the sticks having a 'Freak Night'? How'd we go from the free hook-up to needing to prove ourselves? What the hell does that even mean, Jackson?" I wasn't sure whether to feel reassured or not as Jackson laughed at me, since I was traditionally the voice of caution as he charged headfirst into things.

"OK... I can tell since you haven't already made a split for home, we're far enough out that you can't just teleport there. My cousin is basically human, to be honest. He can glow a little, but you can only see it when the lights are out and you squint with one eye... and don't look out the other. He knows I can do fire like my dad does ice, and promised if I came out and showed him I'm as impressive as the old man we can drink until dawn any night we want! I also knew if it didn't sound like some kind of Utopian society you would've shut the idea down immediately. You *need* to get out of that house! Showing a wanna-be a few fireballs for drinks is better than watching your sullen ass tinker in your bedroom for months on end." As Jackson explained himself it was my turn to snicker because I couldn't stay mad at my best friend for trying to get me out and about. I could go out more if I really wanted to, maybe try and make friends somehow, but we both knew that I wasn't going to take that chance.

I had graduated school early and replaced that time with training, deciding that it was more important for me to work off the growing Flow instead of slogging through Math and English. I self-consciously tapped the rings on each hand and thought about why I'd really been a hermit as I felt the energy get absorbed, letting out a relieved sigh as the contraptions reliably reacted without exploding. I still hadn't really explained my blossoming magic to my best friend. He can shoot fire from his hands, feet, and mouth, but that was a part of him that was scientifically explainable. We'd both been trained to control and accept our mutant powers since we were kids. Despite what the government was saying, magic wasn't as scientifically based as mutations, and only a third of the power I was manifesting was hypothetically understandable. Jackson would undoubtedly be excited to see how much my fighting and acrobatics had improved now that I was saturated with the awakened Conduit powers.

I couldn't fly or use telekinesis, but my limitations were constantly changing. I was beginning to feel like I could leap over any house in a single bound. I can perceive my Flow affecting the world around me more and more on an instinctual level. Outside of how the energy inherently seemed to enhance my body, though, my powers were far from even the deep ends of normality. The months I'd spent holed up experimenting, I had gone through my Mother's grimoire a million times. Mainly it highlighted how her powers were different from mine, but I was able to adapt some of the material for my own uses. The longer I studied her grimoire though, the decipherable runes and sigils of magic became a vibrant and living language that I found I could apply to enchanting. I went from making rocks into multicolored lanterns to animating the garden gnomes so that they patrolled Mom's gardens at night and kept critters out that loved her immaculate supply of vegetation. The magic had birthed the slightly worrisome side-effect that the little men now mooned visitors when they thought no one was looking, but I was close to fixing that. I tapped my middle finger's ring nervously, letting it absorb the excess Flow and anxiety, a movement that has become a somewhat consistent twitch now.

"You know I can't stay mad at you, Sparky. You're right, I would've ditched, and I'll even do a small trick or two if it means free drinks. Since we might be walking into the lamest party ever, then I might as well give you the gifts I made now. You know how people fawn over you when we get in public." I reached into my pocket and pulled out a bag of candy and a red aerosol spray can. I could already hear the wheels turning in Jackson's head for where to start with the plethora of jokes waiting to be made by such an odd display.

"So, we all know you smell like an angel, despite spending a good amount of time literally ablaze. However, I figured you weren't going to wear one of the fire-proof outfits my Mom spun for you years ago, because they were all 'ugly as sin' I think were your exact words. Two sprays of this over your body, and the heat won't burn your clothing for about 48 hours. I won't tell you how annoying it was to test that since I'm not actually invulnerable to heat. Don't eat the candy yet! Just a bite of one should help recharge you if you're running low on firepower, and suck on a couple at once if you're injured. You won't be as resilient as me, but I figured if things went south tonight, I've gotta keep my ride home alive." I jerked to grab the wheel as Jackson pounced on the new toys.

He'd always said magic made him itch most of the time, but I guess I had found the exception by making him personalized presents. As I'd expected, he popped one of the candies in his mouth immediately, causing his eyes to glow like stoked embers as he made a face exactly as if he had just swallowed a lemon whole. I quickly rolled down my window as he hollered in excitement and slammed on the gas pedal; the temperature had quickly gone up 30 degrees in the tiny front seat area.

"Wow! Sorry, had to try one out. Finally, some hocus-pocus I like! That was like eating a bomb wrapped in a cookie. I'm guessing your mom put together some kind of healing plant mojo? My joint pain's completely gone! Remind me to kiss that woman!" He slowed the car down from one hundred to sixty and stretched leisurely, rolling down all the windows after noticing I had broken out into a sweat next to him.

Just like my body built up Flow, Jackson's fire was fueled by a naturally produced mix of enzymes and hormones that had the regrettable side effect of chronic aches and pains. My Mom had used all kinds of herbs and poultices to help the chronic joint pain Jackson had developed the same time as his powers.

"Spray yourself down before your pants catch fire. You can only trick me into a club with you half-naked if I'm already drunk at the start of the night. I actually whipped both up by myself. Turns out I'm going to be a mutant and some kind of magician after all. Mom said the magic kicking in late was probably because of my mutant DNA, but that I'll probably be stronger than her one day. That's what she says, at least, and I've actually been immersed in nothing but hocus-pocus the past month. I'll show you some stuff I've built when you drop me off." I realized it was the first time I had really spoken about the development out loud with anyone but my parents.

My Mom had called half the Conduit family tree around the country, bragging as if I had just gotten accepted into MENSA or Harvard. My Dad appreciated the way the Flow had let me float above ground at times since he'd always hoped that I would grow wings like him. Neither my Mom or myself had the heart to tell him I was doing so purely on accident. Jackson regarded me with a mix of surprise and what might have been newfound respect before giving his outfit a few liberal sprays from the small bottle I'd given him.

"I figured it had to be some kind of heebie-jeebies weirdness going on. Your pops is a great man, but he's a terrible liar." Jackson's smile became more genuine as I chuckled at the term "heebie-jeebies" that he and his father were prone to using. It's what they called all magic beyond the blends and ointments my Mom had made for him since we were kids.

"He couldn't even come up with a full lie, X! At first, he said you were just stuck in the house for a while, and then gave up making that lie stick and gave the phone to your mom every time I called. By the way, she might be a bit mad at me. I fell into a fit of laughter on the phone when she told me that you'd caught mono. You've never been sick once in the years since your powers showed up! You can shake off any ice my old man lays on you, and burns that would hospitalize normals are as good as gone in less time than it takes to grab a bandage. In the end I figured you were either painfully lying in bed growing a tail or getting some other new power under control." Jackson brushed off the situation while he spoke with ease.

He seemed to handle everything life threw at him. I smiled at the picture of my parents struggling to come up with lies to feed him, though I shuddered openly at the thought of growing a tail. We'd both successfully made it through all our "mutation manifestation" years without any major detriments, especially compared to the only other young mutants we knew around our age that couldn't present as Normal anymore. One girl had eyes that were basically lidless glowing orange discs, a boy who could fly and shrink but had hairless purple skin, and another who'd developed gills and had webbed hands for feet.

The conversation abruptly ended as we turned off the narrow backroad and crossed a set of train tracks. Past a half-dead cornfield on our right, I could see an isolated warehouse the size of a small airplane hangar. Even from how far out we were, I could see people hanging out at the entrance, which had minimalist lights and no sign above the door. There were enough cars parked out front for there to be a party, as far as my limited experience could judge. I only ever really went in public for movies, family birthday dinners, and the local library. Each location was actually run by an old friend of the family, so there weren't as many gawkers at Dad's hidden wings or Mom's rare slip-up with magic.

"Remind me why your cousin's club is in the middle of nowhere? Wait, first remind me why the club is inside an abandoned warehouse again? At least we're guaranteed to meet all new faces." I was sure my anxiety was overblown but cautiously fed more energy into the rings.

I didn't exactly have a fear of crowds as much as being utterly unsure of what to do with myself inside of one. We were parking near the back of the gravel lot when my friend tried to help banish my social doubts.

"Come on man, the party is already next level inside. You will probably meet more people tonight than you have in your entire life! My cousin said we're on the list, so we can just skip the line and go in if that's what you're worried about. Would you really feel safer if all the Purist douches and every other hoosier with

an inferiority complex knew where a bar like this was? Let's just go party for once!"
Jackson was right, as usual.

It did make sense to have a business like this in a remote and low-key spot. I
hopped out of the car and fell in step next to Jackson, ignoring the line of 20-some-
thing people trying not to look pissed off at having to wait outside. We had barely
taken 5 steps from the car when Jackson grabbed the back of my coat and gestured
for me to wait.

"Let's drop the tourist route?" he proposed quietly while looking around. I
followed his gaze before I realized this was probably the first time in our lives it
wouldn't matter if anyone was watching.

"I'll aim for behind the doorman. You know I'm not gonna taxi you around
all night though, right?" I responded with my traditional bit of griping but leaned
towards my friend so our arms were touching.

Instead of stepping forward I envisioned us standing directly behind the
doorman. I narrowed my vision in on the older guy sitting on the stool with his
clipboard simply because it helped me to orient myself after a jump. I waited to
hear Jackson inhale and then teleported us from the parking lot to the club's door.
The act of blinking from one spot to another is nearly instantaneous as far as I
can tell...one moment I'm in one place, and the next, I'm where I aimed to be.
This time though, I felt a tinge of apprehension as we landed in front of the club.
My reflexes kicked in, and when our feet felt the ground, I caught a meaty fist
thrown towards where my head had just materialized. Without thinking, I kicked
the stool from where the sitting bouncer had launched his off-balanced punch,
using his own momentum to take him to the ground. I held him in an arm bar and
dropped my knee to his shoulder to thoroughly pin him to the ground in the blink
of an eye. I took three or four shaky breaths before I realized what I had done.

"Well, shit. Did you knock him out? We must have startled him when we
popped up behind his stool. Wait... he's coming round now!" Jackson yelled theatrically. "My friend is gonna let you go. We weren't trying to pull anything on you,
I promise. My cousin is Antoine, he invited us to come out tonight. You're good
X. Let's try this again."

Jackson was standing behind me now, looking like he was trying to hold back from busting out laughing as he spoke to both me and the guy pinned under me. I teleported 5 feet away from the bouncer and started slowly walking back towards Jackson and the gruff-looking man wiping the dirt off his shirt angrily. The older man seemed to be getting increasingly pissed off as his eyes focused on me and took in the reactions of the people in line that had happily broken ranks to watch the spectacle. I wasn't sure how badly I was blushing, but I could tell this was like Christmas to Jackson, enjoying my mortification almost as much as the people watching seemed to get off on the nervous excitement of the moment.

"I could smell you right before you were there... didn't make a damn sound though. Come here, kid." The man was half grumbling to himself and half explaining to Jackson and whoever else was in earshot how it wasn't his fault this gangly kid had gotten the upper hand.

This close up to him, I could see his enraged eyes were feral with cat-shaped pupils, and his ears were as pointed as his elongated canines on display at the moment. Jackson pretended to look away but rubbed his chin in my direction as a subtle warning I was about to get punched. I braced myself for impact and thought about trying to warn the man about my other mutation as I continued to walk closer, putting my hands up to emphasize that I didn't want to fight. Without completely knowing how this would play out, I began contemplating the long series of jumps it would take me to get home. It had been enough of a strain to bring the two of us across a parking lot. I wasn't drained completely, but the act took significant energy.

I was painfully aware of all the eyes on us as I came within reach of the bouncer, who'd crossed his arms and waited for me while muttering angrily to himself. The feral man smiled at me and threw a wild punch so clumsy and untrained I decided to not even react. A loud crack rang out as he connected with my right cheek, and I did my best not to laugh like most people did as the guy yelped like an alley cat and fell to his knees. The brass knuckles he had slipped on while his arms were crossed had cracked, and by the way he cradled his fist, he'd probably broken a couple fingers.

I looked nervously at the club's door, noticing the shocked and curious gathering of people outside the club. This moment was quickly becoming one of my greatest fears. For years I'd mulled over what could go wrong if I visited my town's only bar or any other social event since I'd gotten my powers. Jackson was just shaking his head and smiling amusedly, walking to stand between me and the crowd while dialing a number on his phone. He casually raised a pointed finger in the universal "hold on a second" gesture, and, as always, his ridiculous confidence and social grace somehow seemed to placate everyone. I relaxed slightly as he laughed boisterously at the voice on the other end of the line and said something quietly before looking back at me.

"My cousin said to relax, the look on your face is cracking up all the staff members that are watching the security cameras. I call the next fight, though; you have no idea how hilariously easy you just got off. Stop worrying, man!" He hung up the phone and considered the broken bouncer cradling his mangled hand before saying to me, "So there's one last thing I've been meaning to tell you."

Before he could continue, the door opened, and three men walked out towards us. The first two were identical albino twins with long pale dreadlocks that looked like characters straight out of some cliche B-list movie, wearing matching sunglasses that made it impossible to tell where they were looking. The third man pointed and giggled openly at the doorman, who promptly flipped him the bird with his good hand. This new guy proceeded to walk over to Jackson and gather him up in a big bear hug.

"How's my baby cousin? Can't even wait to get inside before you cause trouble! Your little friend here just gave these people a free Freak Fight. I should charge them extra to get in now! Is this the mystery kid you grew up with?" Jackson's cousin was a greasy-looking older guy with long slicked-back hair.

Maybe it was the tone he spoke to us with, but all his features seemed like a knockoff version of the classic good looks that ran in my best friend's family. He had the same air of charming confidence and panache that made socialites like Jackson stand out, but unlike the Firestarter, there was a strong aura of slimeball thrown into the mix. I looked away towards the bouncer and saw the albinos carrying him inside; he'd gone completely limp somehow when I wasn't looking.

"You know my dad, Antoine, he's just a private guy. Now, this mysterious man who accidentally beat up your jerk bouncer is X. X, this is my cousin Antoine. He's actually the club's "Special Talent" scout for the brawls. You'll love it; we get to meet all types of people and strut our stuff in the open! I'd say what you saw over the cameras gets my friend his first drink, don't you, cuz?" Jackson had kept his arm tightly around his cousin's shoulders as he turned the taller man to face me, using the moment to give me his best "please play along" face while the other man couldn't see.

That face had gotten me involved in every crazy scheme we'd been through since we could walk, and as my half of the tradition went, I attempted to ignore the sense of dread the situation invoked. Antoine stuck his hand out to shake mine, a gaudy set of fancy rings and bracelets catching my eye.

"I'd say he gets one, but that means you're in the ring first! I got you somebody better this time, a real beastly guy from out of town. He just took out the rubber man from a few hours north, that bum could throw a punch ten feet away but couldn't take three to the head! Before we go in though, what do you do, kid? Jackson's got a classic name, 'Flame Fist.' I'm not even sure what your powers are." Antoine's hand reached out awkwardly in the air to shake mine as he spoke. My dread ramped up a few notches and I fought to ignore the sensation.

"Look at the black tips man, he's not much for handshakes. I don't think X is fighting tonight, just watching to get comfortable with the scene for next time! You're in for a treat though, my boy can do everything from…"

I teleported directly in front of Jackson and his cousin, just close enough that my raised finger was set perfectly to shush Jackson mid-sentence. I didn't want to ruin things, but I just wanted to drink and go home. There was no way I was going to let Jackson's big mouth explain my strengths and weaknesses to the resident "Freak Fight Promoter."

"Just call me X. I'm not here for trouble. I do what I can, when I have to. Jackson meant to ask if we could come in and have that drink he owes me." As I spoke Jackson picked up on my souring mood and shifted demeanors fluidly, moving his cousin towards the door and covering for my lack of social graces with different conversation.

I was painfully aware of everyone's stares while I followed the two inside, but as I stepped through the front door, a smile crept over my face despite myself. I was, without a doubt, in the single most impressive place I had ever seen. Loudspeakers were blasting some kind of catchy electronic song I'd never heard, and the crowded dance floor at the center of the room was wild, with people moving to the sound. Jackson and his cousin headed towards the bar on the left side of the room, away from the main crowd. I could see modern-looking couches and tables on the opposite end of the dance floor set up just far enough from the music for people to talk. The bar itself almost extended the entire length of the warehouse wall, with four different bartenders working along the line. I noticed one guy slinging drinks flamboyantly with four arms, working efficiently on at least three orders at once for the group in front of him. We walked down the length of polished wood until we approached the four-armed worker I'd noticed. The bartender shook hands with both Antoine and Jackson at once before looking me over thoroughly.

"What can I get you gents?" He chirped happily after the brief moment of assessment; his gaze continued to come back and linger on me unabashedly every few moments as he spoke.

"Just three glasses and a bottle of rum, Hicks. We got two new Champion Freaks in the house tonight!" Antoine shouted boisterously, causing me to cringe slightly.

It was fine when Jackson and I were calling each other Freaks or my parents said it because there was always a kind of conspiratorial compliment behind it. My best friend, reading me like a book, filled up the two glasses and handed me the bottle with the same "please play along" face that had gotten me to walk through the door. I tried to relax and took a harsh swig straight from the bottle, and we began back down the length of the bar more leisurely this time.

I caught myself smiling again as I noticed there were more mutants here mingling with normals than I'd ever seen. I saw a girl with wings like my Dad's on the dance floor, having just enough room to flit around while being fawned over by three guys. Further down the length of the bar, a guy with scales was taking shots and hitting on a girl who had mismatched glowing violet and crimson eyes.

If the place was as mixed as it seemed at first glance, at least one out of every ten or twenty people in the club was flaunting some kind of mutation, and everyone was acting like it was normal!

Maybe I owed Jackson more than I thought. This was more of an open setting than I'd ever dreamed would exist in my lifetime. My parents always thought being in the open like this would take at least three or four more generations of change, when somewhere around half the normal humans in the world would be giving birth to mutant children (except for the magical bloodlines). I heard my Dad's voice of reason in my head, arguing this had to be a setup to collect unregistered mutants in a government raid, throwing everyone on the dreaded government's Mutant Registration and Surveillance list. I stomped out the little voice and wrote off the idea as overblown paranoia. My old man was always looking out for government traps after living through a childhood where he had to go to great lengths to hide his mutations daily.

Feeling much more relaxed after sipping on the bottle and eyeing the crowd, I realized Jackson and Antoine had led us to an unmarked door at the end of the bar. I'd been walking behind them silently this whole time as they talked and sipped at their cups, but now they were shaking hands excitedly and laughing about something I hadn't caught onto. I decided I had enough rum warming my stomach to start talking again.

"So, what's downstairs? This place is amazing, Antoine," I said, stepping forward to take advantage of the break in their conversation. After seeing the club, he seemed slightly less slimy by association, so I listened eagerly when he drained what was left of his glass before answering.

"Upstairs is only one half of the show, my friend. Jackson said it'd be better for you to just see things in action, so he's going down first to put the lights on and get everything running while I show you around up here." He waved Jackson towards the door as he spoke and reached up to put his arm around my shoulders, leading me towards the stretch of tables and couches instead of the bar. I looked back over my shoulder in time to see Jackson flash me a mischievous smile and a thumbs-up before disappearing through the door.

"Alright, Mysterious X, let me introduce you to the best band of misfits you'll ever meet." Antoine led us straight towards the crowded couch area and began the first in a long chain of introductions with almost every mutant in the club.

Taking shots and cracking jokes seemed to be as natural to Jackson's cousin as breathing while we worked our way around, meeting at least a dozen different groups of people. Everyone lit up at Antoine's approach with a smile and didn't even blink when he introduced me as his new friend "Mysterious X" instead of an actual name. I felt like a mix between a VIP and royalty as people laughed and cheered while Antoine told the story of how I floored the doorman to almost every group. Apparently the guy had a solid reputation as a jerk who loved picking fights with people. It made me feel less guilty over the whole incident that he seemed universally hated, which made me feel slightly guilty for feeling better about it, but the bottle of rum helped quell the internal struggle.

On top of the story painting me as a hero, I made sure to keep in mind how walking around with the club's owner was affecting the way that everyone was taking an instant liking to me. After visiting a table with three girls fawning over a guy with no visible mutations, Antoine made a point to assure me that, secretively, the guy was only getting attention because he could generate enough electricity to power the whole club. Antoine looked at me with a wolfish grin and asked the time. Without waiting for a response, he rushed us across the club back to the door leading downstairs Jackson had taken.

Chapter Three

I'd finished over half a bottle of rum and was ecstatic over having met more people in an hour than I had in the past decade. Antoine gave me a conspiratorial nudge as we approached the door that led downstairs, putting his arm over my shoulders for the first time in a while. I balanced myself against his sudden weight, realizing that my head was swimming with liquor.

"So, X, now that you've seen what the top half has to offer, it's time for your tour of the basement. This upstairs is a Sanctuary for the enlightened, a chance for everyone who understands that humans and mutants are meant to coexist. A safe place for everyone to let off steam and fly their Freak Flag openly. Now... the basement is equally beautiful in sentiment if not presentation. It holds an insane amount of potential for both Jackson *and* you. Jackson's earned a couple hundred bucks while we've been shooting the shit up here, probably in less time than it took you to get into the club tonight." He started walking down the stairs now, dragging me with him as my mind began sluggishly processing what Antoine was saying.

"Wait... Jackson's been in one of your Freak Fights this whole time? For fuck's sake, Antoine, you know who his Dad is, right? He'll kill all three of us if anything happens to Jackson." I pulled away from Antoine and started carefully down the stairs as fast as my inebriation would allow, but his next words stopped me in my tracks.

"Look, kid, what Daddy Ice doesn't know won't hurt him. This is Jackson's fourth fight, and so far, he's barely gotten touched! Those albinos you saw out front earlier are the best healers I've ever seen, anyway. The doorman you beat up? He's been back at his job, good as new, the entire time we've been inside. You couldn't use the extra money? You're signed up for the bout after him already! It's either you or him stepping into the cage in ten minutes... regardless of how you're feeling. If you can just calm down and think about getting 300 bucks in hand, the entire place keeps treating you like a king. Or, wuss out and be a nobody while your friend reigns supreme and gets your payday." Every hint of slime ball on Antoine that I'd repressed noticing during our walkabout resurfaced with his well-practiced speech. Had he said the same things to Jackson?

I reached the bottom of the steps and was faced with a black wooden door, and for some reason, I noticed I was less freaked out about the scenario than I would've been at the start of the night. The fact Jackson had already fought and won several times was at the forefront of the calm. If he was getting big cash this easily, why shouldn't I? The place seemed safe enough, they had healers at the ready, and I had never lost a fight against Jackson during our time growing up together. Maybe I'd even fight next week. It could be fun, and I could definitely use the money. No business in town would hire a mutant, and with a couple hundred dollars per bout, I could get a lot of stuff for my enchanting. Maybe even save up to buy a car at some point.

"Ok, Jackson can fight all that he wants. We both know I couldn't stop the hothead if I tried. Tonight, I'm just gonna watch from outside the ring, though. If he signed me up, then he can handle two rounds by himself. I just want to see how things are run before I step in the ring." Antoine smiled at my response and patted me on the back before opening the ominous door.

"That's what I like to hear. You'll come around, I promise you that much, X. The crowd will be chanting your name just like they do Jacks-..." Antoine was suddenly speechless, heading into the crowd without another word to me.

I stuck close behind him as I took in the open room, it seemed bigger than the upstairs somehow, even though the crowd filled the seating tightly. The entire place was set up so that there were tiered rows surrounding the basement's centerpiece, a giant stage with a barbed wire cage. The crowd was going wild, and as I followed Antoine down into the madness, nobody paid us any mind. I finally caught the full scope of what was going on at the same time I could make out that the people weren't screaming Jackson's name.

"Stone Fist", as the fans were calling him, had without a doubt done more than just get a punch or two in. One of Jackson's arms hung limply from the shoulder in a way that suggested dislocation, his left eye was swollen shut, and his shirtless torso was mottled purple and blue in a dozen places with bruises. It felt like time slowed as I processed the scene in horror, and Antoine was quiet for maybe the first time in his life. The two of us remained standing like statues as an uninjured mutant turned towards the crowd and pumped his arms up and down cockily, conducting the cheers into a crescendo of blood lust. Jackson had a pronounced limp as he moved to lean on the cage wall and catch his breath since the fighter with cement gray skin and milky white eyes was all but ignoring him right now.

I watched with a mix of disbelief and mortification as the fighter stopped showboating and turned back towards my friend. I knew from personal experience that Jackson never admitted defeat until he was knocked out cold. The stone-skinned mutant strutted across the ring to his wounded opponent and almost lazily raised his right arm, theatrically closing his open hand finger by finger to make a fist. Jackson lifted his good arm to defend himself, letting loose a pained battle cry as the football-sized fireball shot from his fist to explode against the golem-like man. Stone Fist casually covered his eyes as the attack barely caused him to stagger backwards a step before relaxing his posture. Meanwhile the flames around Jackson sputtered out. My best friend was wobbling on his feet when the final blow came, knocking him back into the fence before falling limp to the ground in one fluid motion.

Rage bloomed like a small bomb in my gut, and my magic responded to it with tendrils of Current sparking to life around my clenched fists. I grabbed Antoine and teleported us next to Jackson with barely a thought. My heart began beating like erratic thunder in my chest as the smell of blood and stale sweat overwhelmed me.

"Whoa! What the fuck was that? My lungs are burning!" Antoine doubled over and kept up a constant string of complaints that I tuned out.

I might have felt bad about it if I wasn't still debating kicking his ass. Teleporting without air in the lungs didn't do any real damage, but it definitely felt like your lungs got left behind the first few seconds.

"I need to get him to a hospital. We're getting the fuck outta here." I said before bending down and lifting Jackson's head, checking that he was all right.

I reached to pick him up while Antoine ran to open the rusty cage door behind us. I could feel the vibrations before I heard the heavy pounding footsteps heading my way from within the ring.

"So, you're the Flamer's boyfriend? My cousin heard that rag doll in your arms telling the whole club about you sneaking up on him. You think you're hot shit? Ganging up on the bouncer to make a name for yourself? I'm gonna have to teach you some respect, whelp. Just 'cause Antoine helps run this place doesn't mean shit in the ring!" Stone Fist's voice sounded like he was gargling gravel in his throat as he spoke.

I looked up to see the barrel-chested mutant had stopped a few feet away from me, and his little speech only further fueled my fury. The guy was around my parents' age, and his gray head stood a good six to nine inches taller than me, meaning he had to be around seven feet tall. Up close, his beady eyes looked dead in their milky whiteness, and his thick stone skin had streaks of black soot showing where Jackson had tried to burn him. I laid my friend's head back down to the floor gently and stood to face the condescending voice as people continued to scream and cheer this jerk's name. Before I could respond, Antoine ran back into the cage with a microphone in hand, ignoring Stone Fist and me as he addressed the crowd.

"Are you ready for more action? Our new champion, Stone Fist, has just decimated the undefeated Flame King. Now he's hungry for more! The next challenger looks like he's out for blood, but is he strong enough to squeeze blood from the stone? Let's hear it for our newest fighter, Mysterious X!" The crowd went wild as Antoine's voice boomed out from a PA system with speakers set all around the basement.

I stared daggers at the bastard as he ran excitedly up to Stone Fist and had a quick whispered exchange that ended in an emphatic handshake before he approached me with a cheesy smile that was anything but charming.

"Ok, X, look. Jackson's in no shape to go to a hospital, and the nearest mutant-friendly one is hours away at best. The good news is that Stone Fuck over there just agreed to go double or nothing. You do this, and I'll have the twins fix up

Jackson before you're even done duking it out. Plus, you'll win 800 bucks! How 'bout it, buddy?"

Antoine delivered his pitch like a desperate salesman trying to convince a man that his handful of shit was a nugget of gold. The grin on his face disappeared as I tapped a ring on my right hand and whispered the words to a small cantrip I'd been working on. The power stored in the ring manifested like a pet eager to please its master. Antoine's arms snapped down to his sides, and his legs went stiff as wood, the magic making his muscles freeze up against their will. I grinned wickedly in gratification at his panicked gaze as he fell face first, with almost comedic slowness. The crowd started up a light booing as I picked Jackson up and carried him towards the identical brothers, who were waiting around with decidedly apathetic demeanors by the cage door.

"If he's not better by the time I look at him next, you'll spend the rest of your lives trying to heal each other," I promised to the duo in somber tones as they nodded agreeably, reaching out for Jackson.

To my relief, as soon as they made it down the stairs, the brothers set his beaten body down and began to tend to his wounds at the side of the ring. As I turned back around, I saw the big oaf timidly nudging Antoine's prone body, looking freaked out by the display of power.

"Hey asshole, ready to get the beating of your life?" The venomous words escaped my lips without thinking.

Raw magic burned inside me as I slammed the cage door shut behind me. The crowd picked up my challenge due to carefully aimed mics hidden all around the cage and erupted into cheers. Stone Fist walked haughtily to the center of the ring and raised his hands, smiling like he'd never been offered such a sweet deal before. As the people around us reacted with shrieks of support, my opponent waved me to come at him.

"Don't try any of that tricky shit on me, Princess! I'm gonna lay you out like a real man does, with my fists!" The arrogant whine of bravado was back in his voice, even as his body language was discernibly uncertain about what was about to happen. I suddenly wished I had hit that bouncer much harder than I had and that I'd get an excuse to do it again.

I realized I may have drunk more than I'd thought, but the liquid courage helped me block out the crowd while the adrenaline sharpened my mind a few notches. I knew my mutated skin was tougher than any rock I had encountered, but that wasn't a great reassurance against my opponent's mutation since he only looked like stone. I squared up and settled into a ready stance as the hardened giant started at me, practically foaming at the mouth with unbridled rage. I waved him forward repeatedly to keep him coming with one hand, purposefully leaving myself exposed a little too long. Like I'd hoped, he launched a meaty jab over my lowered hand to strike at my face. My Father had always drilled me extra after sparring matches because he realized my enhanced skin made me careless when defending. That extra training came in handy now that I was drunk, letting me easily lean back out of the way of oncoming blows that were decently quick. The steady onslaught mixed with the libations in my system was challenging, but I saw each move clearly enough so that when Stone Fist wound up for a particularly wild uppercut, I decided to take a gamble. I could have avoided the blow but instead angled my forehead at the last second, interrupting the oncoming attack and adding my weight into the movement. The resounding sonic boom birthed as his superhuman blow met my mutant flesh and silenced the tumultuous basement arena.

The moment of silence stretched eerily as I grudgingly gave the guy some credit; he'd probably managed to bruise my lip. Stone Fist was cradling his right arm, staring down at his hand in disbelief. Though I'd mainly shrugged off his attack, from the look of things, he was going to be feeling it for a long while. Chunks of stone flesh had gone flying when he took his cheap shot, exposing a bloody mess of pink flesh underneath. I noted the unnatural angle his forearm now formed, betraying that the bone underneath had broken as well. The brawler shakily raised his good arm, earning scattered applause among the steady stream of awed murmurs. His dead eyes made his face harder to read than a normal person, but I could tell he was barely masking his pain with every movement. The spectators began to call out sporadically to encourage the injured behemoth to keep fighting, the crowd regaining their prior rowdy bloodlust. Stone Fist raised his uninjured arm again to wave me onward, copying my earlier taunt.

"You haven't won yet, Princess! Stone Fist is gonna lay you out just like your worthless friend." The man taunted me while pumping his remaining fist emphatically as if confident he was about to finish me off any moment.

I couldn't help but wonder if a lifetime of boxing injuries may have finally caught up to the guy. I paused to mentally tap into all the Flow I could safely reach around the dampeners. Thanks to his seemingly boundless bravado, it was hard to hold onto any reservations about kicking his ass. One thing the excess magic could be used for was magnifying the powers of my Enchanted Ink. Right now, I mustered my willpower to push all the energy into the tattoo for Strength on my forearm. Though I didn't have mutated muscles to overcome the size differential between the hulking sentinel and me, the enchantment let me bolster certain physical abilities with raw magic. A battle cry erupted from Stone Fist's lips as he threw a hammer fist blow directly over my head, aiming to crush me like a barbarian. With little effort I caught his fist mid-swing with one hand and spoke to him over the sounds of the arena.

"What kind of corny dumbass speaks in the third person?" I chuckled darkly. His eyes widened in disbelief before I hit him with all the power coursing through my body.

The crowd went wild with laughter and cheers as my opponent collapsed backwards like a ton of bricks. Without looking to see if he was ok, I turned towards the exit of the cage and began walking, almost tripping over Antoine's frozen body on the floor. I knelt and tapped one of my rings, specifically built to help absorb my excess Flow, hoping it could pull my Energy off of him since I didn't actually have a counterspell prepared. My Mom said that was the issue with using magic in anger; it was too easy to do things in the moment that weren't as easily undone later. To my relief, the sleazy fight promoter jumped to his feet like he'd been electrocuted and ran from the ring, shouting incoherent apologies over his shoulder. I let out a breath of relief I hadn't realized I'd been holding when the albino duo stepped away from Jackson. My friend was still unconscious, but his injuries had been mended beyond what was humanly possible. The battered pyro's dislocated arm was set back in place thanks to the duo, as well as having greatly healed all the bruising he'd accrued. I stopped to quietly thank the two healers, then unceremoniously hoisted Jackson over my shoulder and made a beeline for the door that had led me down into this bloody cesspool.

All the spectators were on their feet and chanting "*X!*" as we passed, patting me on the back and spouting inebriated phrases of endearment and encouragement.

I couldn't explain why exactly, but it sickened me to the pit of my stomach to have their approval. Maybe it was because I was literally carrying a dear friend that the same people had gleefully watched beaten to a pulp, but that was just a guess. I looked back at the macabre stage where we people with Gifts beat the living shit out of each other for the entertainment of normal people, the normals I'd been ecstatic to walk among and be accepted by who automatically praised the name of whatever Freak caused the most damage. My souring mix of emotions continued to churn as I spotted Antoine through the crowd, holding the door leading upstairs open.

"Listen, you gotta promise me Jackson's dad won't find out about this. My boss knows the old man and that he would throw a major wrench in how well business is going. She's willing to do *anything* to keep that from happening, and the way you're storming out makes it pretty obvious you're going to run straight to him." Antoine plead, keeping his eyes pointed at the ground.

The only reason I didn't stop to knock him out was because I felt a tinge of guilt for leaving him paralyzed on the ground earlier. The slimeball had completely deserved it, and maybe he deserved worse, but testing out my magic on him without thinking could've ended up horribly. Taking the stairs and Antoine's veiled threat in stride, I waited until I was at the top of the steps before I called down to him.

"Fuck off, Antoine. Collect your blood money and have a good night. I have a feeling we're not coming back anytime soon." I heard the twerp curse loudly before I opened the door at the top of the stairs, club music washing over me.

Knowing what lay underneath the colorful scenery before me, I found the atmosphere took on an almost cartoonish nightmare vibe. All the frivolity and endearing abandonment of social norms was built upon the shedding of blood for money just below the surface. I ignored the mix of curious and hostile glances that I received while continuing to head for the front door. To my dismay, the same feral-eyed bouncer was waiting for me as soon as I stepped outside. There was no real indication of how much time had passed except that the line of people he watched over had greatly diminished compared to earlier, less than two dozen hopeful faces.

"Look Mr. Big Shot, you need to slow down and talk shit out with the boss. You know you won a fat stack of cash just now, right?" The bouncer yelled in my face, but I blatantly ignored him. About ten paces past him, I turned back, maybe because I felt bad for hitting the guy earlier or maybe because part of me hoped the night could end on a slightly less awful note.

"Keep the money, man. Split it between Stone Fist, your ass, and everybody I met tonight for all I care. Your boss has nothing to worry about from Jackson and me. We're going home, and I don't ever want to talk about this shit show with anyone, especially our parents. Have a good life," I said, waving over my shoulder as I turned back to the parking lot.

Chapter Four

While doing my best to ignore the guttural snarls and curses the feral doorman was throwing my way, I got the distinct feeling I was being followed. A group of subtle presences barely registered on the periphery of my consciousness, making the hair on the back of my neck stand at attention. Whoever was following me knew how to stay out of sight, but I couldn't figure out what they were waiting for. If the big bad "Boss" was trying to stop me from leaving then wouldn't it have made more sense to attack me inside the club? With every row of cars I passed without incident, my anxiety rose. Once I reached the halfway point to Jackson's car, the eerie silence of the empty lot weighed heavily on me. I knew that an opponent with patience was dangerous, and the subtle confidence in this group's approach made them completely different from people like the doorman.

My instincts screamed to stop and take stock of my surroundings, but I brushed off the feeling and kept walking. If they'd stayed out of sight this long, then I wasn't going to gain anything by stopping to look around; at most, it would just encourage them to pounce. With a limp body still slung over my shoulder, that scenario was far from ideal, but with every few cars I passed, I worried about what the stalkers were waiting for. Of course, with my luck tonight, some idiot would manage to sneak up on me with a gun in hopes of stealing prize money I hadn't even taken. It may have been the adrenaline wearing off or the liquor still in my system, but while I carried on, I began to feel a little unsteady. The shakiness began around the same time Jackson's car came into view, giving the odd juxtaposition of relief and unease. I considered that I was just being paranoid and that there was nothing but the regret of a bad night hanging over me. I stopped trying to figure it out as the passenger side door of the car finally came into reach. I fumbled to open it, gently sliding Jackson's body into the passenger seat. Only after closing the door did it occur to me that we hadn't left the car unlocked. The cement ground seemed to wobble under my feet, making me lean against the car until the swell of vertigo passed. I had to reassess if I was fit to drive us out of here.

"Excuse me, that was a hell of a fight!" A polite voice piped up behind me. I jumped at least a foot in the air with surprise, teleporting to stand on the driver's side of the car before turning around. Across the hood of the car from me I was facing a startled middle-aged woman openly gawking at me.

"We were wondering about that little flitting thing. What kind of power is that? Sorry for the scare, Jackson never did end up telling anyone your name. Do you really go by X?" While she questioned me, the diminutive figure put on a practiced smile that didn't quite manage to reach her eyes.

She was dressed in a conservative gray pantsuit more akin to what you'd find in an upper-class business office than a night club. I refrained from answering her questions when I noticed the healer twins approaching casually from the direction of the club. It didn't seem likely that a fan of Jackson's would know which car was his and be waiting nearby for us or that this particular woman would make a habit out of approaching mutant cage fighters alone... unless she was extremely dangerous. I was trying to process everything when the girl with violet and crimson eyes I'd met earlier tonight approached with a jovial spring in her step, emerging from between the row of cars opposite the truck. I vaguely remembered Antoine had called her Fluoric as she stopped on the empty pavement between us.

"I took quite a few bets on it, honestly... your power has to be super speed or teleportation, right? It's so hard to tell sometimes!" Fluoric giggled and started to slowly close the distance between us. Admittedly I'd been enamored with her just hours ago, but now any desire to become further acquainted with her was replaced with dread.

"To be honest, I'm just a guy who hates surprises," I lied, backing away from all three parties.

Hopefully, they were just meeting this far away from the club to do drugs or something. To my dismay, each of them shifted trajectories and continued to walk towards me, except the middle-aged professional. She seemed to be the one doing the least to hide their true intentions out of the four people approaching me. The twins had covered an alarming amount of ground while the ladies distracted me with their probing statements.

"Jackson is well enough now, guys. We're heading home so he can sleep it off. Y'all did a great job, though," I called out as I reached the rear of the truck.

To my dismay, the albino duo's faces didn't even seem to register I'd spoken at all. The spritely girl with the manic demeanor waited by the car's front door until the two men reached us, one standing patiently behind her as the other moved to the opposite side. I cursed under my breath and tried desperately to think of how to talk my way out of this. The harder I thought about it the more immersed in confusion I got, like my brain was a well-oiled engine sinking in a tar pit and still trying to run. The club girl started meandering towards me with the healer maintaining just enough distance to be respectful. She moved with both hands outstretched so that her fingertips lightly touched the cars on either side and at first, I bemusedly chalked it up to inebriation. However, after her first steps, an audible hiss and crackling sound caught my ear. Even from this distance I could see that everywhere she touched the metal it was violently bubbling and melting away.

"What the hell do you people want?" I finally choked out, retreating a few steps as I noticed the businesswoman had joined the other pigment-deficient guard.

The creepy duo approached slowly in silent steps, and I realized belatedly that at least they seemed to have no interest in Jackson. I wished he was awake to throw some of his classic smooth talk into the situation; I could barely even talk. I could barely even... I cursed at myself in revelation.

"What are you people doing to my head? There would be no need to ask questions if one of you were a telepath," I demanded, earning a smile from both women.

Forming complete thoughts grew increasingly difficult as the profession-al-looking woman frowned and furrowed her brow as if she was focusing intently on a problem. Fluoric laughed wildly and then grew abruptly quiet as her female counterpart growled at me and spoke.

"It's really quite impressive how coherent you are right now. I'm not exactly telepathic... but when I'm close enough to a target, I can confuse them. In a sense I can mix up the wiring in anyone's brain. With how much effort I've put into sabotaging your brain, I can't tell if you're an exceptionally high-functioning idiot or...." The rest of her diagnosis was cut off when I made a few quick strides forward and threw my fist directly into her face.

Since I was operating completely off instinct, I followed up with a punch to her gut, and when her body naturally crumpled forward towards me, I stepped into her momentum and launched my knee into her nose. One of the albino twins caught her unconscious form and began dragging her backwards, and it was like a cloud bank immediately dispersed from within my skull. I felt an instant pang of guilt, but all I'd been able to comprehend when she spoke was whether she could read my next move or not. When the businesswoman said she wasn't a telepath, I stuck with the idea her powers were still what was messing with my mind. The simplistic plan of attack was mostly acting off muscle memory from sparring techniques I'd had drilled into me by my Dad. If my mind had been clear I never would've torn into the woman so violently, but I took a little solace in the fact that she'd fallen directly into the hands of a healer. Before I had time to process the situation further, a small figure hopped on my back and squeezed me with a playful giggle.

"Holy damn! That was awesome, X! She won't be down long because of the healer, but you still seriously wrecked the Boss up. Where was that ferocity in the ring?" Fluoric seemed genuinely excited by the violence as she clung to me.

Remembering how her gentle touch had corroded metal earlier, I debated staying still versus teleporting to try and surprise her. I hastily dismissed the idea, though, because she'd still be on my back and might cling tighter in response to the move, and I needed to get her off. Plus, if her power was triggered by her fight or flight reflex, like many mutants, she'd hold onto me as well as try to melt me in half. I turned my head to the side to try and get a clear look at her and found her luminescent mismatched eyes sparkling as she smiled at me.

"Talk to me while you can, don't be boring like the glow worm guardsmen! Once they get her back on her feet, you'll be too stupid to be any fun. Do you need some incentive, big guy?" the spritely figure teased as she clenched her legs around my torso and moved to slap the side of my head. I easily caught her small hand and was struck by searing pain a split moment after.

"Freaking pixie acid shi..." I let loose a string of curses as every place her skin touched mine ignited as if she was stabbing hundreds of tiny needles into my nerves.

I looked at my hand in stunned agony and saw that her skin was secreting a glossy off-white acid that was getting all over me. With both arms wrapped around me and skimpy raver shorts allowing Fluoric to press exposed thighs and calves to my body, I was covered in the stuff before I had a chance to move. The pain was worse than being hit with fire, ice, or a car, for that matter, but it hadn't broken through my skin anywhere.

"Oh my god, what are you made of? Now this is exciting!" She burst into a fit of ecstatic giggles as I worked on centering myself and pushing through the pain.

Though the rings I was wearing acted as dampeners, my magic was still within reach. If I concentrated properly the agony could even help me fuel more power into my tattoo for Strength. I could feel it working when the rush of energy hit my veins like lightning, the power tempered and routed by the network of runes forming the tattoo. It gave me enough of an edge to send her petite poison-spewing body off me, accidentally tossing her into the front window of an expensive looking smart car. Fluoric's motionless form instantly began melting the hood and glass beneath her, but I felt confident she would be ok for some reason. Before I could turn away from the scene, I received a blow to the back of both legs at once with almost surgical precision. I fell to the pavement in a heap as an unfamiliar voice addressed me.

"Thank you for the moment of relative silence. Please don't judge too harshly. My brother and I are currently employed here, but you'll see as you get older that the job market for mutants has gone to shit. Nothing but blood money to be made, even for healers. The Boss will be conscious soon, and I will resume pretending to be a mute." He looked at me with something like pity in his eyes as he stood above me. "You're humble and kind kid, so unlike your friend, you don't really belong here. Believe it or not, that matters, even in a place like this. The Boss is only out to gather info on you, but with how much that info is now worth, she'll go to any length to get it. So, stop holding back and end this game quickly, as if it's life or death. Stop holding back, kid."

The albino's smooth baritone voice was empty of emotion. I would've ignored him, but it felt like the hip joints where he'd struck had come undone, my femurs dislocated from my pelvic bone. His brief speech reminded me of a guidance counselor who'd been stuck giving out unheeded advice for a few too many years to really care about anything anymore. He'd leisurely strolled past me towards Fluoric while he monologued, allowing me to army crawl towards the nearest car. When I reached the rusty gray SUV, I did some not-so-graceful rolling and wiggling until I could prop my legs up against the back bumper. The inelegant move sent shocks of pain through my body that made my vision blur. This time drawing on my power was harder; the rings could barely hold the Current in check with my emotions this unbalanced. Instead of releasing my restraints, I used my remaining willpower to clamp down on the bucking energy, taming it like a wild animal.

As my vision came back gradually in small patches, I ushered the agitated Current towards my tattoo for Healing, adding my desperation and pain to help fuel the magic. Normally, fixing a dislocated joint without help is hard to pull off, and I'd never even seen someone attempt to fix a dislocated hip before, but I had to try. With the Current in place, I slammed my feet against the car bumper, pushing to straighten both legs, and almost passed out from the friction. It was like hot railroad spikes were being hammered into me, but I could tell everything was back to being functional, at least. Somehow the healer's touch had been able to damage my insides, completely surpassing my mutated skin. I was going to have to make sure one of them didn't sneak up on me again; the healing magic didn't make me impervious to pain. I made a mental note to leave an IOU to whoever now had two sizable foot shaped dents in their bumper as I took stock of my surroundings. While extricating my legs from the back of the car I saw Fluoric was already beginning to stir. Even though the albino was avoiding touching her directly, he was still able to help. A few choice curses silently escaped my mouth as I stood up and my favorite shirt fell to the ground, just rags and scraps after whatever acid girl had attacked me with. So far, I'd seen her touch-melt metal, fabric, and burn my skin badly enough that I'm sure a normal person would've been killed by it. I checked the direction I'd last seen the Boss get dragged towards, and a chill ran down my spine to see the empty space where the healer and she had last been.

I stood perfectly still, trying to not just listen but also feel the space around me. The process was almost like echolocation, releasing my Current out lightly into the environment and then trying to discern details about the objects it encountered. Since I'd been focusing on Enchanting for so long, the inanimate objects around me resonated more clearly: the asphalt, the cars and their components, beer cans, and other discarded items. The cacophony of responses made it difficult to process, but it was possible to suss out where the living bodies were. Soon two heartbeats thrummed vibrantly against the backdrop, and I could tell where they were like flies buzzing against strands of a spider's web. I focused on their locations, each three cars apart, and shook off the odd double-vision sensation that using my Sight like this sometimes caused. I could barely manage to pull off the trick, let alone use it and fight at the same time.

As I ran stealthily towards the nearest figure, I realized one of my shoes had been left behind in the busted-up car's metal. I hastily pulled off the other shoe and tried to think of a strategy that could help separate the Boss from her ivory guard. Without being able to distinguish who was who while using my Current, I lined myself up to intercept the nearest adversary. There was a tight space between two cars they'd have to pass through to rejoin the rest of their group. I wasn't proud of the strategy as I lobbed my sneaker overhead but gave a silent cheer as it hit the car between the two crouching bodies. I held my breath until the sound of a fleeing body was only steps away, then jumped out and clotheslined the unsuspecting figure, sending his long locks flying as he went head over heels before landing in an unmoving heap. When I stepped out from my hiding spot, I saw the diminutive Boss scurrying back towards the rest of the group, only looking back once to see what had become of the fallen member of her crew. I crouched down to check on the man and saw he was still breathing but had gone limp as a noodle.

This fight could go on forever if the two healers kept revitalizing every opponent I struck down. Looking at the prone body of one of the duo, I realized it was also likely his brother would heal him or that his powers might help him heal faster than normal. I closed my eyes and focused on feeding a tendril of magic to the sigil for Strength and turned towards the car behind me. I took a second to slowly choke off and stop the active Flow before reaching out, which honestly involved a lot of gracelessly slapping at my set of rings and deep breathing at this point. If it wasn't for these enchantments I'd spent the better part of a year perfecting, I wouldn't be able to use my magic. Even controlling Current in the basic ways I'd done so far, I still had far more energy than I could control without them.

The car I was facing was one of those ridiculous mini smart vehicles, where four of the things could fit into a single regular-sized spot. I grabbed the handle and pulled, taking the whole door off the car's frame by accident with a screeching tearing sound like thick tin foil. I lifted the door in astonishment, barely straining as I experimented with raising and lowering the mass one-handed. It felt like nothing more than a heavy bag of groceries, though I could feel an unnatural burn as the magic manifested in my muscles and fueled them to new heights. With my other hand I reached down, trying to be gentle, and tossed the seemingly weightless healer in the back of the car. My gentle attempt to jam the mass of metal back in place worked, if only in the sense that I was sure the car's occupant wouldn't escape through the mess of bent metal and shattered glass I'd created. I silently hoped the car owners I'd inconvenienced tonight had good insurance and ran back towards my remaining opponents. During the short jog, I tried to drain the excess magic from under my skin, realizing if I hit someone this juiced up, I'd probably shatter bones, rupture organs, or maybe even accidentally kill them.

Every time I tried to make sense of this nightmare, I was regrettably inclined to believe what the pretend mute had said when we were alone. If these people were trying to kill me then someone would have brought out a gun or at least a knife by now. All mutant powers aside, bullets were still considered more efficient than nausea, acidic burns, or dislocating joints. If they were really trying to learn the full extent of my powers, then it was in my best interest to show them as little as possible.

I felt my fatigue get stomped out by adrenaline when I saw that all three creeps were waiting in the open lane behind Jackson's truck. I broke into a sprint when I was still about 30 feet away from them and braced for impact. The bastards would see me coming after the racket I'd made gave my location away, but I didn't think they could stop me. With the healer on one side of the Boss and Fluoric on the other, their leader waited unconcernedly until I was only a few feet away before raising both hands ominously. With her gesture the world unceremoniously turned upside down. I felt myself stagger and then stumble as I tried to orient myself, feeling my hands and knees contact pavement as my stomach did flips. My disorienting momentum only halted when I hit yet another vehicle, though the world continued to spin as I failed to orient myself against the wall of over-whelming vertigo.

"Yes! Now lay it on him thick Fluoric, I want to see how tough he really is," the Boss said triumphantly, surveying the state her power had left me in.

I tried to judge how far away they were, but the attempt brought on a fresh wave of nausea before I could even begin to act. As I failed to assess my environment, the girl with glowing eyes hopped onto my chest as if straddling a horse, briefly knocking the wind out of me. Every bit of flesh she was touching birthed an awe-inspiring blaze of agony as the poisonous moisture poured from her body onto mine. I gritted my teeth and involuntarily let out a quiet growl in defiance, realizing I could use the pain to orient myself against the sickness holding me down.

"Wait, Fluoric! I need to see those tattoos clearly. And you! Make yourself useful. Take care of his arms." I heard the Boss addressing both of her underlings but remained focused on the mismatched eyes of the sadist above me.

Flouric grabbed my wrists almost playfully, and if it hadn't been for the violent-ly-dripping acid on her hands, this would have been the most intimate moment of my life. As instructed, the remaining albino brother heeded the woman in charge, approaching from behind and delivering a solid kick to each shoulder. Just like last time, each strike caused an explosive reaction under my skin escalating the pain level of the already excruciating experience. Not only was skin burning every-where Fluoric was making contact, but now each rotator cuff felt ripped open and blown to bits where I'd been struck. I was reasonably sure the pain had grounded me enough to throw the giggling freak flying, but the world was still spinning too damn fast. I readied myself to endure the torture and wait for a better opening to present itself.

"The tattoos... some of these are Witch Symbols. He might not even be a mutant, he could be some kind of experiment... I bet those rings he's been playing with are enchanted! Fluoric, melt it all!" the Boss exclaimed excitedly.

My heart skipped a beat as I saw her studying my skin, eyes widening at how the runes covered different parts of my body. At the thought of losing the power dampeners, I bucked wildly but failed to dislodge the body on top of me. I'd waited too long, and Fluoric was expecting the move now, moving with a wild smile to weave her fingers between mine, and soon I could feel sharp jolts of magic begin to ricochet around my system as the protections I'd painstakingly constructed liquified. The sudden release of power hit me like bolts of lightning inside my fingertips, carving a painful path up each arm, stomping around my skull, and then thrashing against my heart and belly like enraged pterodactyls. I hadn't gone more than a few seconds without wearing some kind of inhibitor in almost a year, when I'd cobbled together the first functional version of the idea. The more I worked on them the more intricate and effective I'd made each version, trying to keep up with how my powers were growing. There were less than three rings left between my two hands when I decided to warn these bastards that I was going to lose control without them.

"Please... don't... I can't..." I uttered, failing pathetically to speak.

As soon as the first word had passed my lips, the Boss cranked up her power and all words eluded my grasp. The vindictive freak on top of me seemed to only get excited to new heights upon hearing my broken pleading, pumping out more of her personal poison. I felt like I was going to explode from the menagerie of horrific sensations warring inside of me. I could feel another ring disintegrate between our hands, and I realized the pain from the acid was dissipating even as the mutant remained where she was, visibly dripping more acid on me. The minuscule relief made room for all the rage and helplessness that had built up over this entire shitty night and set my blood boiling. I closed my eyes and held onto all those ugly emotions, and as the last ring melted away, I realized I was screaming. Then... I think I exploded.

Even with my eyes closed, the blast of light left afterimages that stubbornly refused to go away while I tried to steady myself. I sat up with ease, the body that had held me down now nowhere to be seen. I realized the pain had disappeared as I moved to stand, the released Current in my system mending my injuries seamlessly as the Healing Tattoo reacted without prompting. The last globs of acid on my skin were being burnt away before my eyes by dazzling cerulean flames that I had never seen before. The light danced painlessly over my skin and engulfed my hands everywhere that had been saturated in Fluoric's poison. As my vision cleared, it dawned on me that every car in a thirty-yard radius had been cleared away by the blowback of what had occurred. I felt more relieved than I'd expected when I discovered Fluoric's body beneath a dented jeep at the edge of the cleared space. When I shook my flaming hands, I could still feel a slight tingle from the pain she'd inflicted, but seeing that her chest was still rising and falling was reassuring. I kept an eye out for the Albino and his Boss while trying anxiously to disperse the light from around my hands. With every push to suppress the power, it sprang back up involuntarily like magical heartburn.

I felt the Boss's presence before I saw her, a touch of dizziness running like a shiver down my spine. The disheveled woman and her employee huddled between two cars that had been knocked on their sides. The dread-head was checking her neck for a pulse while the other hand rested on her shoulder. I thought of how he had spoken openly with me earlier and I raised my glowing hands as a halfhearted gesture of peace.

"Leave her be for now. She's squeezed more than enough info out of me tonight. I haven't wanted to fight all night and now I can't even control how hard I'll hit. Once I get out of here, by all means, fix everyone up." My plea must have come out sounding more reasonable to his ears than I expected because he stopped immediately.

Maybe it was more that I now, obviously, had the upper hand, and it was wreathed in arcane flames. The pigment-less healer put his hands in his pockets and began walking away without a word. I waited to make sure he was really leaving and then let out a long breath of relief before trying to figure out where Jackson and I had parked. I only got five steps away before an impossibly annoying whine of a voice called out behind me.

"I didn't say I was done yet, young man." The Boss was back on her feet, although I was pretty sure she wouldn't have been able to do so without leaning heavily on a car at her side.

"What the hell is wrong with you? I'm done with whatever this whole fight was about, and you need to sit back down before you hurt yourself." I stepped back towards her as I spoke, frustration flaring at her bravado. I audibly groaned in frustration when she unsteadily moved to stand without the aid of the car, staggering towards me.

"That's going to be a bit of a problem, Mysterious X! No one is done fighting… until I say they are!" She spat the stage name with a contempt that seemed to help steady her, and at the end of her declaration, she pointed both hands at me again.

This time, however, the uninhibited magic loose in my veins rose to combat her powers. I couldn't help but smile at the look of utter confusion on her face as I stood unfazed. At this point, the gaining momentum in my system had become heady and intoxicating, more potent than any liquor I'd ever tasted.

"What the hell are you?" she asked in honest consternation, abandoning her steady march forward.

The rush of unfamiliar energies building inside of me ratcheted up bit by bit as I started walking towards the disheveled Boss of the Freak Fights. I noticed the rips and dirt on her as she visibly strained with effort to stop me, but all I felt was my own magic. When I was only a few feet away from her, an oddly pleasant chill shook me from head to toe. I'd never experienced so much raw energy at once in my life! I lifted my hands from my sides and watched with detached curiosity as the azure flames turned black as the night sky above us.

As she studied me, the Boss's already pale face turned an ashen shade of ivory that I didn't know living flesh could emulate. I started repeating a steady mantra of "please don't kill her" in my head while closing the distance between us, noting that my opponent's seemingly indomitable aggression had finally died out. With great care, I placed my hands on either side of the Boss's face. With this nearness, I could see the green pupils of her eyes dilate madly until they were two eerie black orbs, and I felt countless tendrils of magic seep through the skin and furrow into her body. With a push of effort that felt like little more than snapping my fingers, I shut down everything inside of her that I could reach. I jumped back as she fell limp to the ground between my hands. I spent a split second hoping she hadn't just died before the entire world disappeared into a numb blackness all around me.

As if waking from a deep sleep I slowly came to my senses outside Jackson's truck. My hand was still on the door handle, and to my relief, I could see him lying blissfully unconscious in the seat. Looking around, there was no evidence of the horrific battle that had just occurred, nor any hint of the opponents I had faced. I debated the possibility that I'd just experienced an immaculately elaborate hallucination until I realized a clammy hand was wrapped around my ankle. After checking my hands were flame-free and realizing I still wore every ring I'd started the night with, I bent down to look at whoever had grabbed me. Lying flat on her stomach was an unconscious body that almost exactly matched the woman I'd mentally monikered the Boss. Her hand fell limp to the concrete, and I realized she must've waited under the car until the exact moment I stood still at the door so she could grab me. My mind flooded with questions as I timidly dragged her out and placed her safely in a nearby exposed trunk bed. The woman had the same face as the Boss, undoubtedly, but was even smaller in stature than I'd thought. Most notably, she was no longer dressed to blend into a Fortune 500 board meeting. What had really happened after she grabbed my ankle like some kind of guerrilla warfare specialist?

She looked pale as death, and I had to work up the nerve to check her pulse, but once I felt the weak throb of life in her veins I bolted into Jackson's car and started the engine. The machine growled to life and a bit of tension left my body as I floored it like the devil was on our tail. I tried to ignore the club's entrance as we passed, but three bodies on the ground outside the front door caught my eye. Fluoric and the twin healers were being watched over by a growing crowd, which only strengthened my resolve to get away at top speed. From what I could tell in passing, none of them had even the slightest sign of damage from our confrontation. Equally confusing was that the parking lot showed no sign of the battle I was starting to feel aches and pains from. As my adrenaline began to ebb, I guided the excess energy into my rings, inexplicably still whole on my hands, and began the long drive back home.

Chapter Five

After almost a solid two hours of speeding down the empty country road I spotted a reassuring figure on the horizon. My Dad was flying low and fast over the highway, crimson feathered wings on full display for the first time in years. As I caught sight of him, he deftly landed in the middle of the road ahead of us. If he'd flown here from home, then he must have begun heading this way before I even escaped the club's basement. To my surprise, when I stepped out of the car, the old man wrapped me up in a spine-crushing hug. Dad held me there just long enough that I had to reevaluate how much trouble I was really in.

"Alright, son, I'm going to need to hear everything. Blue filled me in, so don't try sparing any details to cover Jackson's ass. Are you good to drive?" the old man said, looking me in the eyes and assessing me head to toe.

Without waiting for a response, he furled his wings and hopped into the back of the truck, too large to fit inside the front with Jackson and me. After hopping in and starting the engine words just began to flow out of me uncontrollably, talking through the open windows to him. It took maybe half an hour to tell the whole story, and to my Father's credit, he didn't tell me to slow down or interrupt with questions once. I trailed off after recalling how the bodies of everyone I'd fought outside the club had ended up in different places than they should've been when I left. My old man finally cut me off when I began questioning my sanity because I hadn't honestly figured out how half of it was possible.

"Let me fill in some blanks for you now. Even though the location is new, the same people have been running the Freak Fights since I was your age. The woman you pegged as the Boss goes by the name Pasithea, well, at least she is this year. Your Mom informed me it's the name of a Greek Goddess, just obscure enough that she'd feel hip and witty using it. With a touch, she can trap people in a shared illusion, and the only way out without her permission is to kill her in the vision. The other powers you were saying she displayed.... maybe she's kept them secret over the years? I'm not sure, and that bothers me. Her skill set made her more desirable for management positions than to dazzle an audience in the ring. I can't believe she's still hanging around the fights, but Blue warned me to expect her hand somehow. Don't bring it up, but they used to date way back in the day." My Dad paused for a long time before speaking again. The world became quiet to my overwhelmed system until there was nothing left but the road, the rumble of the engine, and a light snoring that came from Jackson.

"Blue used to be a big-time champion in the underground fights. As we got older, he realized how corrupt the system was. The two of us brokered a kind of peace treaty between the Underground and the Inhuman Mafia to avoid all-out war. Those of us who wanted to stay safe and secret would remain off-limits. On the flip side, anyone who wanted to make money and a name for themselves could use their Gifts in the fights. You said earlier that Antoine was a big part of the night, right?" Dad laid it all out calmly like we were discussing how I'd recently thought about joining two rival sports teams. I was reeling from all the information but nodded in affirmation about Antoine. My boring Dad and his childhood best friend had apparently been key in shaping the way things worked for everyone like us, and I'd never had a clue.

"For the most part, the accord keeps both sides out of the other's way. However, this was so long ago Antoine was still just a toddler... and hadn't developed any powers when the initial lines were drawn. Blue told me that some faction of the Mafia had recruited Antoine about a year ago, and neither he nor I could hold it against him. After his parents were publicly ousted and killed by Purists, he had trouble making a living. Most people won't hire a suspected mutant. Until now I hadn't been sure Pasithea was the one to bring him in, but he was an obvious target to snare: raised among the Mutant families on our side long enough to make connections and eye potential fighters, rarely barred from places most Mafia recruiters can't go because of his family ties. That gray area is why our hands were tied when Jackson first started fighting, since you're both of age to pick a side of your own," he explained to me, and most of the pieces seemed to click into place.

I had only been vaguely aware of the tension between the Mafia and Underground before now, but the politics going on between the two factions had apparently influenced most of my night. Our conversation had lasted the rest of the long trip back to town. At the start of the night, I would have bet my life that my Father had never been involved in anything akin to brokering a treaty with the local super criminals, but here we were. I looked over my shoulder at him with a newfound respect and wondered how many other epic secrets he was keeping from me.

"So, I'm literally the only one who was unaware of the Mafia fight club? If you'd warned me about it, I never would have gone!" I yelled indignantly over my shoulder. The thought that I could've avoided this entire experience was both incomprehensible and infuriating at the same time.

"Trust me, I never thought in a million years that you'd get mixed up in any of this. When I first heard Jackson had entered the ring, it came as a shock. It was even harder to believe that his parents were willing to let things naturally play out. Most people don't find their way out like Blue did, but he said that Jackson would have to learn the hard way. Since you hadn't left the house in months, there was never a right time to fill you in." The regret in his voice was palpable, and I knew I had no real right to be angry.

"How do you tell a kid with both superhuman and supernatural abilities that they have to avoid the one place they can go to publicly show off? If we handled it wrong, wouldn't we make you more likely to go looking for the club?" His frustrated tone resonated with me as he spoke the questions aloud. It wasn't as if they'd forgotten to tell me out of pure negligence or apathy. It was new territory for me to question the way I had been raised. Even more worrisome was how much my Father's tone matched my own uncertainty.

"It was a given that eventually Jackson would be put up against someone he couldn't beat. That's how the people running the show make their money. First declare a Champion, set them up to dominate for a few weeks, and finally throw them against a Ringer. A fighter miraculously happens to be a terrible match up power-wise for the current Champ once everyone knows they're a winner. The Mafia then sits back and collects the stacked bets when the Champion falls. Stone Fist is no regular mutant floating through town. When somebody in the Mafia wants to send a message or mess somebody up so badly that they never hop in the ring again, he gets called. I can even think of a few times where he killed opponents in the ring for money, but anything that happens on Mafia turf is out of our hands. It's even further out of the hands of the cops, that is if they could be forced to care," Dad said with a familiar resignation that I couldn't help but agree with. As a large, dark-skinned guy in a small town, I'd always been wary of the police, even before I had powers.

"Thankfully, the news that Jackson was going into the ring with him reached us while the neighborhood watch was still together. Our informant also told us that Jackson had another mutant with him, which led to your Mom nervously looking for you with magic. In all these years, she's never once successfully found you through scrying, but for some reason, it worked tonight. Scared her half to death, but also confirmed enough that I started heading your way. If I'd let Blue drive out here in a blind rage, then the treaty would be dead. We would have gone to war. Jackson has already fought of his own free will and accepted profits from working with the Mafia. I agreed with Jackson's folks, he'd see how corrupt the fights were. Eventually he'd renounce all Mafia ties of his own volition. But I wasn't willing to let Antoine try to trick you into a contract. It would've been all my fault. You've been going through your own problems, the magic stuff, so I've neglected telling you about certain things. I'm proud of you for not falling for it. If you'd accepted that money from the fight, you'd be cut off from the Underground's resources... which we'll need now that you're famous. Your Mom and I are calling in every favor we can get to keep you safe." While he spoke, I found myself playing catch-up with my outdated pecking order of dangerous forces in the world.

"I'm not famous, it was just a basement full of drunks. Plus, I don't think anyone could have seen what happened in the parking lot, even if they'd tried to," I replied, shuddering at the thought of losing control of my magic like that again.

"They tape the fights, Son. Between that footage and whispers of you single handedly taking on that psycho's entourage outside... there are probably fighters across half the country drooling over who gets to challenge you to another match. Did either Jackson or you give out your real name? Any details on how our families are connected?" My stomach dropped as the questions hit the air. In the heavy silence that followed I went over the night again slowly in my head.

"I told Jackson to say my name was X at the start of the night. As far as I know he left things at that, but we were separated for a while. My stage name was 'Mysterious X' if that helps," I answered with an inward groan. My head was spinning with the possibility of causing my family to go into hiding. I still felt overwhelmed by guilt for making the family pick up roots and move when my powers first appeared. Had I really made the same mistake again so ridiculously soon?

"The problem is that they can discern that you're semi-local and that you're connected personally to Jackson. Most importantly, you performed better than every Gifted they had and walked away unscathed. That makes them look weak. If Pasithea can convince even one person that it was because you're a mutant who can use magic, just one person, it'll change the way that everyone thinks," my Father explained, which did nothing to soften the apocalyptic nature of the news.

"So, what's our next move? She has no proof. Maybe they'll think that she's trying to cover for her failure. Wouldn't they have to respect the truce if they realize that I'm your son?" I asked him, a bit ashamed to try and cop out of the situation in such a way. We were almost to Jackson's house when Dad finally responded.

"If anyone even loosely believes Pasithea's story.... Your Mother and I are the only Mutant and Conduit couple that I can think of on this half of the country. Back when we first got married it caused a bit of a stir. It won't take people long to connect the dots. Your Mother can use Earth Magic to hide you from most scrying, but now that you can be found by magic.... We'll figure out our next move together. That's all that matters," Dad explained as the truck reached Jackson's street. There were cars I didn't recognize parked along the curb in front of the familiar brick house as we pulled into the driveway.

"There was a bit of a frenzy among the Neighborhood Watch when Blue found out his son was being set up against Stone Fist. He wasn't the only one who wanted to head to the club and put those assholes in check. I knew you'd protect him, though, even if nobody really understands how strong you are yet. The only thing I worried about was that people are going to start trying to guess how powerful you're really going to become. I've seen the world from both the Mafia and the Underground's perspectives, and I'm certain they'll go to war to procure power that can upset the balance in their favor. The treaties mainly survive through promises of mutually assured destruction." Dad explained as I cut the engine off. I couldn't help but stop and mentally give thanks to the old truck for not dying on us during this hellish night, and the engine gurgled a vaguely positive sentiment in return as it rattled heartily and died.

As I got out of the truck, I instinctively went to the passenger side door and draped Jackson over my shoulder. It might take a while before I stopped feeling protective over him after everything that had happened. Picking up on this, my Dad gave me a wide berth while I retrieved his limp form. For his sake I hoped Jackson was still knocked out, so he wouldn't have to face his parents until the morning at least. My Dad led the way to the humble two-story home, and when we reached the front door, he barely had time to knock before Jackson's mother, Maria, wrenched the door open. Her eyes were red and puffy, belying hours of tears as she took a moment to look me up and down from head to toe. Maria wrapped me in a tight hug despite the circumstances and then stepped out of the doorway so that we could enter.

"Thank you for bringing him home safely. I'm so sorry you got wrapped up in all of this, Xavier," Momma Maria fretfully muttered to me.

I didn't know how to respond, having grown up with her as a second mother, so I just gave her a quick one-armed hug and gently moved Jackson's body off of my shoulder. Now that he was in reach she began fretting over him instantly, looking over every bruise and scrape. The sounds of heavy footsteps heralded the approach of Blue and at least half of the Neighborhood Watch as the front door closed behind me.

"I'll take him now, Xavier. Thanks for having his back," Blue said as he approached.

The six-and-a-half-foot frost blue-skinned mountain of a mutant lifted Jackson from my arms like his son weighed nothing. His eyes grew steely and cloudy in the silent moments that he surveyed the damage done to his only son. The temperature in the foyer dropped at least ten degrees before my Dad walked over and put a steadying hand on his old friend's shoulder.

"We know it could've been much worse. Your boy is going to be ok, especially now that he's never going back to work for those people again," my Father said, trying his best to be reassuring.

The reaction wasn't immediate, but there was a collective sigh of relief when Blue nodded his agreement and walked from the room with Jackson in his arms. Momma Maria followed her husband, and together, they stoically climbed the steps towards Jackson's room. I took my time looking at everyone left in the foyer and recognized most of the Gifted people present as my parent's friends or close acquaintances. Tonight, it seemed as if most of them were looking my way with a new sense of admiration, which was a foreign and somewhat awkward sensation. Thankfully Dad's demeanor openly stated he wasn't interested in going over the whole story just yet.

As he headed towards the kitchen I happily followed on his heels while the crowd split for us to pass. We passed most of the remaining people in the house before finally reaching the living room. My Mom and the oddball of a man I'd come to call Uncle Operator were sitting on the living room couch and speaking in hushed tones. I noticed an open laptop on the table in front of them with a series of repeating images. As we got closer, I realized they were close-ups of my face. My Mom jumped up and looked only slightly less worried and puffy-eyed than Jackson's had. She grabbed my shoulders and eyed me up and down like parents do when they seem to expect to find a limb missing or a massive hole to appear in one of their kids. I think I even felt her switch spectrums to study me with Conduit's Sight rather than just staring me down. Before I could say anything, she slapped me, which didn't hurt much but made her recoil in pain after connecting with my cheek.

"Owwwwww!!!!" Mom groaned in pain before breaking out into laughter and wrapping me in a hug. I laughed and whispered an apology to her as I returned the awkward hug.

"Ok... we're happy you got out of the house, but no more drinking. You're a mean drunk apparently... and the internet is proof!" she chided me lightheartedly, sitting back onto a nearby couch and allowing me to theatrically inspect her hand for injury.

"Does it not show him beating Jackson to a pulp before I got there?" I asked sheepishly in an attempt at forming a defense. To my surprise I was answered by a voice from a cellphone instead of my parents.

"They edited the fights to look as if they were unrelated, and I doubt most people can tell that much. They used a couple of different camera angles to really try and sell the upscale in brutality. If you know what to look for, you can see that Stone Fist is pumping the crowd up with you standing behind him and waiting to fight twice out of sequence. The video also cuts around the portion where you'd normally sign their contracts, maybe a silent admission on their part that no one but us would care about. What happened, kid?" the familiar digital rasp of Uncle Operator's voice asked.

I knew he was using his Gift, allowing him to interact with technology in ways only he really seemed to understand. The laptop screen he gingerly rested a finger on was flitting through different images faster than any human eyes, or my own, could keep up with. It switched between the pictures and intricate pages of coding, and his voice had come out of the cellphone sitting on the table next to his computer. It was a nifty trick, the phone having turned on by itself and transmitting his voice without visibly moving a muscle. I'd always considered my unconventional Uncle a badass in his own realm and easily one of my favorites among the odd extended family I had in the Neighborhood Watch. We called them the Neighborhood Watch because Agents of the Gifted Underground didn't quite roll off the tongue. It also would have probably gotten them killed or arrested if anyone heard the title being used. I spoke to the computer's screen rather than his body instinctively, I guess because I knew he was more in the hardware than his body at the moment.

"Didn't learn it was a fight club until Antoine was trying to convince me to hop in the ring. I'd said no already but then lost my cool when Jackson got beaten to a pulp. Antoine said if I fought we would be free to leave... and apparently, I'm a mean drunk," I admitted. After tonight, I would try to avoid leaving my room for at least another year.

"I knew you were too smart for this shit. Antoine is the variable I hadn't considered until now. He must have signed on as a Recruiter with the Mafia, which means he'll end up responsible for failing to make you legitimately contract-bound before throwing you into the mix. Technically they have no justification to come after you, especially once they realize you're Underground Affiliated. Your emergence is going to have everyone wanting more troops, and old Antoine might lose a finger or two for messing up tonight's business," the laptop's speakers chirped as he processed the scenario out loud. We were accustomed to his odd habit of talking to himself through a multitude of devices while thinking. If it hadn't been for my Dad opening up on the car ride over, I wouldn't have understood most of what he said.

"Do you think they can connect Jackson and me? They only knew me as X," I asked weakly, knowing the question needed to be addressed.

"The only face not blurred by their technician is yours. They'll be tapping all their resources to see if anybody recognizes you. Even if you hadn't been 'Mysterious X' it would only be a matter of time before they ID you." My parents exchanged worried looks while the TV delivered his sentiment this time. I couldn't help but smile at the sarcastic way he said the uninspired stage name; it really was beyond awful.

"That sounds about right. Any way you can delete the video or something?" Dad asked stoically, but I knew it couldn't be that simple. An indecipherable static came from the phone, probably a sigh of frustration or a burst of bitter laughter.

"Once it's out there, it's out there. I'm trying to hack and edit most major sites the video popped up on, and I can blur his face wherever I can't crash access. It's all a momentary bandage at this point, though. If someone really wants to hunt down an unedited copy that shows Xavier's face, they can eventually find it. He needs to stay in a safe house for now, and you two need to head home." The blood drained from my face as Uncle O spoke. I berated myself silently for thinking that this nightmare was over; things were worse than I'd imagined.

"No way. We'll all go to the safe house. We are not splitting up," Mom said adamantly, looking at me and my Father for support.

"We've got a plan. Anansi is going to come with you two back home. That way when they send someone to your house, she can implant a memory of meeting your son, who, it turns out, looks nothing like the boy in the video," Uncle Operator explained.

When I turned around, I saw the grinning face of Anansi staring expectantly at us. As far as I knew she could manipulate memories, though I was thankful I'd never witnessed her power personally. At least not to my knowledge, which was the scary thing about her. If she did use her powers on me, how would I ever know?

"It will be easier to implant a new memory of Xavier if I don't have to remove a real one first, which is bound to happen if he's there. So just to be careful, Xavier should wait things out in the safe house. Just until the heat dies down," Anansi explained, easing some of the tension in the room.

I could tell my Mom still wasn't thrilled about the plan, but she didn't object because she knew it was the best one we had. My parents had known Anansi and Uncle Operator almost as long as they'd known Blue, and all were integral to keeping the Underground alive and running.

"Our house is already being watched. If Xavier teleports quickly from here to the safe house on a back alley route, they won't be able to track him. Especially if they're busy watching you two drive home with Anansi in the backseat as a decoy," Blue said as he walked into the room unexpectedly, earning a fraternal punch in the arm from my Dad and slugging him back immediately.

"Is Jackson going to be ok?" I asked hesitantly, earning a half smile from my best friend's father.

"Thanks to you, he'll be fine, until he wakes up at least. I think Maria might actually kill him this time," Blue said with the slightest hint of a smile.

"Which safe house are we thinking? There's no way Xavier can make it to anywhere in one leap," Dad said hesitantly, ignoring the outraged glare my Mom threw his way. To everyone's surprise, Uncle Operator stood up and answered him while casually stretching the stiffness out of his body.

"It's best if you don't know yet. We don't know who the Mafia is going to send out as part of their search party. After you three have drawn attention away from the house I can direct Xavier with this burner," Uncle Operator said, tossing me a clunky disposable cellphone from his pocket that was still in its cheap plastic package.

"Sounds like the best option. I'm in," I said quickly, preemptively cutting off the objections of my parents.

This was what the Underground excelled at after all: hiding and protecting people in trouble. Besides, this was the only way I could think of to avoid making my family have to pick up and move because I had screwed up tonight. With only a bit of stubborn grumbling, it took less than ten minutes before my parents left the house with Anansi in tow. I'd given her my hoodie to mask her feminine figure and face, and Blue had lent me a spare shirt and blue jeans to change into. I had to keep away from the windows but heard the general murmur of concern in the house as two cars with tinted windows began tailing them out of the neighborhood. The drive would take at least an hour to get back to our house, so I waited twenty minutes before starting on the route Uncle Operator had laid out. I'd be sticking to backyards, alleyways, and abandoned buildings. The entire ruse would become worthless if I was spotted in the area while people needed to believe I was in the car with my parents.

Executing the plan was easier said than done. Teleporting took a light toll on me that I normally didn't pay much attention to, but the long point-to-point leaps that the map was demanding were much farther apart than I was used to. By the halfway point I had to stop and catch my breath, crouching down behind some overgrown hedges in a part of town I didn't recognize. The long-distance jumps were beginning to worry me, and not just because they required more energy. I had to take the chance of landing in places that I couldn't see and knew nothing about, making each blink a stressful leap of faith. The gene for teleportation is rare but there were still plenty of stories about how so-and-so had blinked into the middle of a bank wall, or the bottom of the ocean, or even the Earth's upper atmosphere. I knew Operator must have taken the dangers of teleporting into consideration, but if even the slightest thing was of out of place from what he anticipated, I could end up exposed or even injured. With my breathing under control, if not my anxiety, I lifted the small screen and oriented myself against the crude digital map.

Before long, I was in a dilapidated building where the only real claim to being shelter was a thick set of boards covering the windows and doors. I doubted anyone else would want to chance entering the rotting shack; it looked like the whole place could be knocked over by a strong breeze. Soaked in sweat and dead tired, I gratefully made my way to the basement. Uncle Op had sent a text when I neared the location that my family was almost home safe, and I reread the message reassuringly as if it would keep them from harm.

After using the weak light from my phone to find the stairs, I reached for the light switch and froze just before flipping it. A chill ran down my spine as my senses told me I wasn't alone anymore. There was a tension in the air and the barely distinguishable sound of someone moving about in the darkness below. I flipped the switch and hastily jumped down the dozen or so steps, hoping to take my opponent by surprise. However, my wobbly knees gave out on impact, so I clumsily turned the momentum into a forward roll. Instead of gaining a strategic advantage I found myself crouched opposite from a stranger, sitting with a look of awkward surprise on her face. She was a wiry figure with olive skin who immediately seemed completely relaxed despite the circumstances of my sudden arrival. Despite having waited in the dark for me, the stranger didn't appear to need time to adjust to the harsh fluorescents I'd turned on above us. In fact, she didn't even move to stand as I adjusted my stance, waiting for her to make the first move.

"Well, you're a spirited one. I like that. Y'know, I barely beat you here. That was an extremely confusing route you took. My name is Pixie. I'll be your ride to the interview." The bubbly voice that came out of her seemed out of place in this grungy basement. I considered her for a drawn-out moment and decided to remain in a fighting stance. Reaching for the phone in my pocket crossed my mind, but if she'd followed me here then calling Uncle Operator probably wouldn't help anything.

"You can kindly tell the Mafia I have no interest in starting a fighting career. I didn't accept any of the money or sign a contract with Antoine. Please, just leave me alone," I said, attempting to be polite and diplomatic as a default since I didn't have much experience with these situations. Pixie burst out into heartfelt laughter, bending over double and even snorting a few times like people do when they're really tickled by something.

"I saw the uncut version of your fight! It was great! Honestly, I was cheering for you. That's not why I followed you through town to this subterranean shit hole, though. Your dear ol' Dad set it up so that when he died, you'd get to come to Sage Mountain like he did at your age. If you're having trouble with the Mafia, I'd say he kicked the bucket at the perfect time. They can't touch you if you're with us," the enigmatic figure said, switching fluidly between bubbly and calloused tones as she spoke.

"I have no clue what you're talking about, lady. My Dad is alive and has never been to the mountains. Are you with the Mafia or the Underground?" I asked skeptically, hesitantly accepting that this night was, in fact, getting weirder again. It didn't seem like she was trying to trick me, but just because she believed what she was saying didn't mean that I should. Pixie cocked her head to the side quizzically, and after a long moment, she seemed to decide to take pity on me.

"Those are really the only two options you see in life right now? That's pretty bleak, kid. We didn't know you existed until right after your biological Pops croaked. I guess it's kinda our fault for assuming that you'd know anything about him or us. So... to catch you up on things: First, your Dad is dead. Second, he made sure you had a full ride set up to come study at Sage Mountain. And third, we aren't affiliated with the Mafia, Underground, Purists, or the government. And as far as I can tell, we're your best option right now." She laid out her points in a clinically detached manner as she spoke.

My mind reeled at the implications, though I still tried assessing if she could be a Mafia agent trying to trick me. Did her news mean that my parents got hit by the Mafia agents when they got to our house? Mom and Dad were both strong, but they weren't invincible. I stepped back towards the stairs and pulled the phone from my pocket, keeping my eyes on Pixie as I began to call home. It was unsettling to see that whoever Pixie was, she genuinely seemed unbothered right now because if she was lying, this phone call would clearly dismantle her claims. An icy vice grip encompassed my heart as the line rang three, then four times before a familiar voice answered.

"Xavier? Is that you? Are you ok?" Mom said eagerly. The feeling of foreboding that had built up relaxed tenuously as I thought of how to respond.

"There's a stranger here at the safe house with me. Is Dad ok? Are you ok?" I ventured a step towards Pixie as I chastised myself for believing her.

"What's going on? Who's there with you? Your Dad, Anansi, and I are fine. We just got home, and nobody has even come to the door yet. Is she the one that left the package in our living room?" Mom sounded about as concerned and skeptical as I felt. It was reassuring to know that my family was safe, but now I had to deal with Pixie and whatever her agenda was.

"Did you leave something at my parent's house? What are you really doing here?" I demanded, feeling my hostility bristle anew at the thought of someone breaking into our house. Pixie shook her head calmly and seemed a bit bored by the events transpiring.

"All I've done is follow your trail to this rank basement. My intel is never wrong. So, either they haven't told you the truth, or they don't know who your real Pappy is either! It's probably no coincidence that there's a package waiting there just like there's one waiting here," Pixie said, nodding towards a pristine mahogany box sitting to the side of the stairwell's base I hadn't noticed. It was immaculately clean and polished compared to the layers of dust and neglect that blanketed the rest of the basement.

"How am I supposed to know you didn't deliver both?" I attempted to examine the box while keeping the odd woman in my line of sight. Pixie sighed theatrically and, with a barely perceivable whoosh of displaced air, disappeared from the chair in front of me and reappeared next to the box.

"Are you always so skeptical? If you don't object, I'll happily open your little mystery present," Pixie said, tenderly kicking the wooden container with her steel-toed boot. It must've been lighter than it looked because her gentle tap sent it sliding across the room towards me. She giggled and looked at me expectantly, but I didn't move right away. Just because it hadn't blown up after getting kicked didn't mean its contents were safe. To my surprise Pixie grew impatient with my caution and made a little game out of kicking the box around the room, grinning like a toddler with a new toy.

"Mom, are you still there? My uninvited guest says her name is Pixie and that Dad is dead. She also keeps talking about some place called Sage Mountain.

Should I try and lose her?" I whispered, turning my head discreetly away from the distracted woman. To my surprise Anansi's soothing alto replied.

"I've met Pixie before, she's a bit crazy but not with the Mafia. Your parents decided to open the box. You need to get ahold of yours and come home immediately. If Operator calls you, tell him we're going into Blackout Protocol. Bring Pixie with you if she's willing, we could use her perspective on things," Anansi said, and I could hear my parents arguing loudly in the background. The line abruptly died, and I stood there dumbfounded until the dial tone hit me like a brick. I stared at the childlike character still kicking the package and chasing it around the room.

"You know Anansi?" I asked in disbelief. Pixie stopped kicking the box and cocked her head to one side in contemplation.

"Anansi… I remember that cutie! Well, as much as she lets me remember, at least. We've contracted her to do odd jobs at the Mountain before. So, are you going to open the mystery box, or do I get to do it?" Pixie said, seeming happy to have the focus of events brought back towards her. I hesitantly walked over and picked up the box, thinking about the sound of my parents arguing. I'd never heard them fight like that in my entire life.

"I need to get home. Anansi said to bring you along if I could. Are you in?" I asked bemusedly, earning a wide grin from my new companion. I was beyond confused and felt like I could sleep for a month straight, so if she declined or needed any convincing, I really wouldn't be up to the task.

"I thought tonight was going to be a boring pickup. You seem interesting so far, so I'm in. Plus, I'd love to see Anansi again" she replied while closing the distance between us. I briefly wondered what the history was between Anansi and Pixie, but I really had bigger mysteries to solve at the moment.

"I don't think I can teleport us both all the way back to my house. We'll have to figure something else out," I said worriedly, wondering if the Underground had a beat-up car sitting near the safe house for emergencies.

"How do you think I followed you here, kid? I can see the traces you leave behind whenever you blink, and I can teleport too. Mine works differently than yours, but I'll get us there. Just grab my shoulder and focus on the house, then picture every detail of one of the rooms: windows, floor, furniture, everything," Pixie instructed, shocking me into obeying.

I'd never met another Mutant with one of the same Gifts as me, and I'd never thought it was possible to visually track my movement. I tucked the box under my right arm and reluctantly grabbed Pixie's shoulder. I felt an odd pressure building around us as I pictured the two story brick house, then the living room on a whim: the crimson carpet, the couch, Dad's recliner, and the TV that was only ever touched by him. My ears popped right as the ground shifted almost imperceptibly beneath us. I tensed in anticipation but felt relieved to see I was home in my living room, exactly as promised. Pixie smiled at me for a moment before our attention was captured by angry shouts in the kitchen.

"They've got the neighborhood surrounded! If he stays here, he's dead! Or worse!" Anansi yelled more aggressively than I'd ever heard her speak in my life.

"Just because he's not our son doesn't mean we'll ever stop protecting him!" Mom shouted back vehemently.

What did she mean by not our son? I turned the corner into the kitchen, and the look on everyone's faces said that, yet again, my night had gotten worse.

Chapter Six

I stumbled and found myself blinded as Pixie and I abruptly arrived somewhere new. A split second ago I'd grabbed the mysterious woman's shoulder and said I was ready to leave. It was the first time I'd ever had someone else teleport me, and I immediately made a mental note to apologize to Jackson for ridiculing his complaints about the process.

My ears popped from the altitude change and I gradually began to take in how the night had turned to day. The midday sun revealed a lush green valley that filled my nostrils with scents of wildflowers and the deep woods. A cool breeze blew past us, and I began to note that there were pockets of people spread out all around us.

"Welcome to Sage Mountain! You stay here and get acquainted with some of the other Apprentices. I've got to blip over and tell the others we've made it," Pixie said, punching my arm playfully before disappearing with the slight pop of air.

The abrupt sensation of being alone in unfamiliar territory spread through my gut like a hot blade of anxiety. My first time leaving the house after a year of seclusion had ended up setting my old life on fire in ways that I could never have guessed in my wildest dreams. If I had really had a choice in the matter, I'd be back in my bedroom tinkering with some frivolous enchantment, and the world would never have seen my face again. Instead, I was here, in the lush depths of a forest, at the foot of an unknown mountain, with no real clue as to what this place was. Fidgeting with my power dampeners helped quell the rising panic attack until my heart was only beating an aggressive staccato instead of painfully thundering away like a jackrabbit on meth. After a few long minutes stretched on I finally relaxed enough to grow fascinated with the events going on all around me.

A group of maybe half a dozen people stood in a circle to my right. A group of spectators sat in the grass around them, some appearing as if they were waiting to join while most appeared content to just watch. One member of the inner circle stepped forward with a mischievous smile and plucked a few blades of grass from the earth with a flourish. Everyone waited patiently as he whispered to himself, and he focused so intently on the object that veins in his forehead and neck began to visibly pulse. I smiled as the blonde-haired boy suddenly cried out in triumph, a subtle whisk of smoke escaping his clenched fist before he triumphantly held up a small rock for the others to see.

Nods of approval and calls of encouragement broke out as he playfully tossed the stone to the girl next to him in the circle. The short brunette raised the grey sphere up for everyone to see and then cupped it in both hands, blowing into them and shaking the stone vigorously like a gambler would do with lucky dice. When she halted the motion and opened her cupped hands, the rock had been made into an uncut diamond, reflecting the sunlight in a plethora of rainbows from every facet. As the young woman raised the gem for all to see, I realized they were collaboratively using a type of magic I'd only read about. Transfiguration spells, sometimes called Mutagenic magic, allow Conduits to turn one object into another for a time, which my Earth Witch Mother had been vehemently opposed to in principle.

The spectacle evolved as the next woman in line snatched the diamond from its previous owner's hands. Instead of clutching it tightly, she held the diamond out on one open palm, leaving it for all to see as her free hand manically gesticulated and pulled at the air above the precious stone. All that I remembered about this discipline of magic was that it was based around coaxing matter from one form to another. The further from an object's natural state of being the Conduit was aiming for, the more raw Current they'd need to supply as a catalyst.

The memory furthered my interest in the spectacle as the space around the diamond grew hazy like hot air wafting above concrete in the summer. The different facets of the diamond began to stretch and distort as she kept the effort up, elongating the gem and refining its shape till it distinctly resembled a blade. She stopped for a moment to wipe sweat from her brow pointedly with one finger and then carefully wiped the liquid from the tip of the knife to its hilt. She whispered something under her breath as she moved, and the gem seemed to shake in her grip. The transparent diamond darkened rapidly until she held a metal blade with a crudely shaped hilt and pommel.

This feat made the crowd go wild with applause and cheering as the knife was carefully passed to the lanky boy next to her. He closed one eye and peered at the dagger from different angles, probably using his Sight to assess the layers of magic already placed before using his own. Finally, he shrugged his shoulders theatrically and got down on one knee, stabbing the ground with the blade and leaving it there. Putting both hands palms down over the knife, the stubble-faced Conduit started speaking a complicated incantation that contained pops and clicks as part of the dialect. I could tell he was repeating the same thing over and over until both his hands and the hilt glowed a soft pink.

As if pushing against heavy resistance, the boy shakily raised both hands, grunting with effort when he clapped them together overhead. He held the pose as the light shot like a sunbeam from between his hands down into the weapon. Once his hands were empty of light, the boy lowered them and began a complicated series of hand signs, none of which I recognized. The moment he stopped, the glowing blade began to collapse in on itself unnaturally, undulating like a blob in a lava lamp. The glowing matter disappeared under the dirt for a few moments, then applause broke out as an arcane, bizarre-looking, blue and purple bonsai tree bloomed in its place.

The two guys left standing who hadn't participated yet took lengthy turns looking at the unique vegetation before admitting defeat. I thought the spectacle would end there, but the group then began debating who had done the most impressive casting. I would've stayed to see who won, but during the lull, my attention was grabbed by a game of football that had started up in a different part of the field behind me.

Compared to what I had just seen, the sports match seemed ridiculously mundane at first. As the two teams lined up and the QB got ready to receive the snap, I realized all the players were probably Gifted. The match erupted into a storm of movement and collisions as the play came to life along the central line of players. I quickly picked out one player pushing against their much larger opponent with telekinesis instead of their hands. The next oddity became apparent as a pair of players squared off together above the ground, seeming less concerned with the fact that they were flying than with grappling their opponent fifteen feet in the air.

Both sides seemed evenly matched in those first moments until a girl to the side of the QB deftly ran by and was slipped the ball. She ducked down low and slipped under the gap left by the two linemen fighting too far off the ground to block her passage. Once through the defensive line, she morphed in quick spasms, exploding into a hulking biped of monstrous muscle at least three feet taller and 300 pounds heavier than before. Her skin was stretched unnaturally over her new form. I could see each massively enhanced muscle fiber moving like steel cables as she knocked three guys off their feet and out of her path with a wave of one titanic hand.

Before she could run the rest of the field to score, however, the earth in front of her churned and shifted like it was coming alive. I saw a member of the opposing team with one hand dug into the ground and her eyes squinting with effort as thick walls of earth erupted in front of the hulking giantess. Instead of trying to dodge the barriers, the mutant ran straight through them, effortlessly smashing the first two constructs with her strength and momentum. After the next two walls, she began to show signs of fatigue though, her power drained from the effort of punching through the walls one by one.

Three walls later, the mass of muscle labored for breath, slowing down and raising a veiny fist to smash another earthen wall. She succeeded in taking down the obstacle, but to my surprise the smallest guy on the field had caught up to her, using the momentary pause to hop onto her back. The giantess barely noticed his presence at first, moving forward with hardly a glance spared to what must've felt like a flea on her back. I blinked and realized a second boy identical to the first had also latched on. By the time she reached the next wall there were four more desperately clinging on. I could see a slight shimmer ripple over the boys before twelve more identical bodies appeared to try and weigh down their opponent.

She wavered as the young boy kept multiplying, and I quickly lost count of how many were clinging to her arms, legs, back, and head. With a ground-shaking crash, the giantess toppled, and I saw one of the tiny figures strip the ball from her before sprinting the opposite direction down the field. I jumped and turned away from the game as someone I hadn't heard approach tapped my shoulder. A sly smile and intense blue-eyed gaze awaited me, both managing to belie a mischievous excitement.

"Welcome to the party! You're a pretty big fella, aren't you? Call me Mal, the Mutant Apprentice extraordinaire." The fair-complexioned boy reached his hand out to shake mine, and I only briefly hesitated before shaking it.

"I'm X, nice to meet you. So... you're the official welcome wagon around here? I don't quite know what to do with myself," I confessed, feeling something off about the encounter but still trying to be courteous. After all, this was the first person that I'd met here besides Pixie. Mal's smile seemed well-practiced as he continued to stare me down, and I couldn't help but be reminded of Pasithea.

"You could say I'm the UN-official welcome wagon, for the Mutants at least. So, what are your gifts? This year we've made a little tradition of show and tell among us Freaks of Nature," Mal said, his statement tailored to cut off the refusal he'd seen forming in my mind before he'd even stopped talking. The sense of déjà vu to being back in the club's parking lot intensified as I fiddled with my cuffs uncomfortably.

"Why are you so certain I'm a mutant and not a Conduit?" I asked, looking around for a way to casually escape this conversation.

To my dismay I noticed several kids from each game slowly turning their attention towards where the two of us stood. Only two or three people were coming closer though: an attractive girl from where the Conduits had been competing and a boy wearing glasses who had been on the sidelines of the football game.

"Oh, come on, we've got to respect tradition. I didn't make up the rules, but it's kind of fallen on me to uphold this one," Mal explained, slowly stalking closer to me. I said nothing and resisted the urge to back down from the creepy flaxen-haired weirdo, turning to keep him in front of me as he casually meandered around the space. He seemed to take the silence as some type of nonverbal consent to move on to his next topic.

"Your parents help run the Underground back home, right? I wouldn't expect you to have heard of me... but we're actually from the same state, believe it or not. The rumor mill is on fire right now about the kid that has command of both Mutations and Magics. Even at Sage Mountain, nobody has heard of someone like that really existing," Mal said as he began an exaggerated set of stretches and warm-ups. I watched warily and waited for him to explain more, and apparently, he read the silence well enough to decide on explaining further.

"People are pretty split down the middle about believing it. The Conduits are so sure that you aren't what people say you are that their top guy isn't even going to uphold tradition and challenge you. I think that's a piss poor attitude to take, so here we are." Mal was almost lecturing at this point, and my heartbeat quickened as other students from all over the field decided to wander over and watch us expectantly.

"I don't want to fight, Mal. You seem like a nice enough guy, and I've had a rough couple of nights. I'm not much for fighting," I pleaded, telling both a truth and a lie to try and dissuade the charismatic Mutant. To my surprise, the guy laughed heartily at my statement with genuine amusement in his eyes, stopping his warmups to address me.

"We've all seen the video of your fight at the club. I was surprised to find out that the taboo mixed couple of the local Underground had managed to have a kid in secret, let alone a kid that could demolish a mafia goon without breaking a sweat," Mal explained in a matter-of-fact way like he was stuck explaining something to a particularly slow child.

"You're telling me that you're from..." I began to ask, but Mal interrupted me with a loud yelp and outstretched hand.

"Woah, woah, woah buddy! You never know who you'll end up fighting against once we all graduate and go back to the real world. You can go by X if you like since that's the name we all know from the video. Anyway, you ready to go?" Mal asked, raising his fists now that his warmup and speech were over.

My optimistic fantasy of having arrived at a carefree and friend-filled haven died as I let my bag drop to the ground and got ready to fight the stranger who'd come to both greet me and beat me up. A couple of people clapped, and one or two even cheered, but I felt my spirits plummet as Mal started to close in. I pushed the rising Flow, exacerbated by my adrenaline rush, into my dampeners and began to critically analyze my opponent's stance and movements. The guy obviously knew how to handle himself, a wary confidence behind every move.

Mal's first attack was a feinted jab to the right side of my head, followed up quickly by a wide-thrown left hook. I didn't react to the feint and had plenty of time to lean out of the way of the real attack. The crowd cheered with more enthusiasm this time, and Mal narrowed his eyes. If things remained strictly in the realm of boxing, I was already sure the match would go my way. As if to test the thought crossing my mind, the Gifted attacker unleashed a wild series of blows, some thrown more as overreaching grasps or swipes than actual attacks.

I easily stayed out of the street fight-style onslaught, trying to move as little as possible but having to raise my arms several times to block the blows coming my way. Even considering my enhanced skin, I felt like most of his blows didn't land, like I hadn't shrugged off expected contact as much as avoided it altogether. The crowd that had grown rowdy went silent. Mal hopped back out of the reach of my long arms. I cocked my head to the side and met Mal's eyes, apprehensively studying me. I raised my fists anew in confusion, expecting that now he'd unleash the Gift that had made him the top fighter of all the other mutants around us. The cocky blonde stood with hands behind his back, with a baffling smile of confidence that matched the growing gleam in his eyes.

"I noticed you fidget with these a lot. First in the video and now you've done it repeatedly since arriving. Are these how you fake doing Magic? If so, then I'd rather just see who was born with the superior Mutation," Mal announced in a stage whisper so that everyone could hear him. To my growing horror, he then raised a hand holding one of my power dampeners, and then, with exaggerated gravitas, he revealed his other hand containing the second bracer of the set. After fighting Fluoric I'd thought dampener bracelets around my wrists would prevent scenarios like this from happening.

"Please, I need those. They help dampen my powers! We're not safe withou-" I tried to explain, but my words got caught in my throat as Mal began juggling the enchanted items. My two bracelets became airborne, along with several random rocks he must have pocketed before the fight with this exact plan in mind.

My opponent seemed to take my continued lack of a counterattack as proof I was no threat without the stone accessories. I felt my Flow rising and heaving around my insides like electric bile trying to find an outlet to escape through as the crowd laughed and cheered Mal on. It took several agonizingly long heartbeats before I could force some of the energy to be manageable, and I fed all of it into my rune for Speed. Focusing on my breathing and Mal, I could tell I hadn't been able to amass a fraction of the power I could safely martial with the dampener's help. If I overreached into the core of my power, I could easily lose control while attempting even the simplest things.

It was hard to not be at least a little impressed with the guy's juggling skills. With the world slowing down a fraction at a time as the magic enhanced my system, it was only more obvious how effortless the feat was for him. I took a deep breath and made a straight dash to close the distance hanging between Mal and me, eliciting a clear surprise written across his fair features as he registered my approach. I was, unfortunately, still slow enough that he had time to abandon the juggling and throw a hasty fist in my direction. Ignoring him I focused on catching the bracers, getting close enough that I could pluck my belongings out of the air. Turning my head down to face him I realized we were only inches apart, which was about as awkward as it sounds. The triumphant smile that had spread across his face met my confused glare until a burning sensation exploded in my chest, all the nerves and muscles in my body seizing uncontrollably. There was only a split second to look downward before what felt like a small bomb threw me flying backwards.

Gradually coming back to my senses, I managed to sit up and rub my temples. A quick stretch revealed I wasn't injured anywhere, so I hopped to my feet and looked around to figure out what the hell had just happened. Though I was only a few feet away from where the ring of spectators stood, I had landed outside the circle. Half the people were watching me with mixed shades of shock and confusion. With the festive mood dissipated, I pushed my way through the crowd and came face to face with a scene that made my stomach lurch. Mal's pale white face was drenched in sweat as another boy cradled his head in his lap, and after a moment's debate, I began to head closer.

While fretting over the fact that I wouldn't know how to heal the damage I'd done, I froze mid-step. The guy holding Mal had shifted to the side, giving me a glimpse of his mangled arm. It was mainly held aloft by the bizarre angles that the broken bones formed, unlike any injury I'd seen in person. I realized it was the arm he'd thrown a punch with mere moments ago and cringed as my mind made the connection. Had I done this to him somehow? Scanning the crowd didn't lead me to think anyone had somehow hopped in to stop the fight last minute. As I searched through the pack of faces, I realized all eyes were now firmly planted on the two of us. Things didn't stop being uncomfortable when Pixie chose that moment to appear next to me with a loud pop.

"Awww, how sweet! You kids have obviously already met, and I'm loving the synergy. Why don't I hear any clapping for the winner? Looks like I'll have to ship Mal to the Healers... again. Somebody be a dear and show the new Champ to the dorms?" Pixie said, patronizing the entire crowd with ease before she disappeared with Mal's unconscious body. The spectacle seemed to be officially over as most of the crowd broke off into smaller groups and left.

"Well... it's about time someone put him in his place," someone grunted as I walked to grab my bag. When I turned to face the speaker, I realized it was the same person who'd been cradling Mal's damaged form.

"Is he ok?" I asked, focusing on the features of a guy seemingly the same age as myself. He was a head shorter than I was, with a loose crop of chestnut curls on his head, along with a pair of shaded glasses that looked more geared towards function than style. Nobody else seemed interested in doing more than staring at me or pointedly ignoring me, so I found myself thankful someone had decided to speak to me.

"Mal's a great guy, but he's picked a fight with every single Mutant Apprentice that arrives. You're the last person they're letting into our class and one of the first to beat him. The healers here are literally magic, and a few even better ones that are Mutant, so don't worry about our resident kleptomaniac. He'll be back up and causing trouble in no time, though it'll be a longer time before Pixie stops giving him shit for how you just shut him down. They call me Justus," he declared, sticking out a hand for me to shake.

To my credit, I only hesitated for about five long seconds before grasping his hand, going over at least a dozen different powers or spells that could sucker punch me through the physical contact. I flinched slightly upon contact but relaxed when nothing happened. Maybe it was the momentary lack of being assaulted, or maybe it was the fact I was determined to have at least one friend in my new life, but the guy's open demeanor seemed genuine. I felt some relief at the news that Mal would be alright, though that worry was almost immediately replaced with the realization I might have to fight someone else now. As if reading my mind, Justus started walking towards the far edge of the field and motioned for me to follow.

"Mal's power is intangibility, which makes him feel invulnerable, even though everybody but him knows the two powers aren't the same. If I was able to walk through walls as a kid, I'm sure I would've turned out the same way though. He's even learned to use it as an offensive power by making himself solid while he's mixed up with something else. The funny thing is that he can't really explain how it works, just mumbles something about his cells overcharging whatever solid mass is mixed up with his." Justus explained as our stroll took us from the field and onto a well-worn path among the trees.

I would have worried about some kind of trickery, but it seemed like most Apprentices were also trickling down this path as the sun began to set. Most people went out of their way to give us a wide berth, but a few smiled and nodded at Justus as they passed our lazy pace. I was holding back a million questions but made a mental list of them to find answers to later. The guy had silently volunteered to show me around when no one else seemed willing to take the job; I didn't want to annoy him by trying to discover what the other students probably considered common knowledge by now. I appreciated Justus's efforts to fill the awkward silence so much that I wouldn't interrupt him unless there was something I thought that only he would know.

"Yona and I are pretty sure that he only discovered the trick by blind luck. He would never have purposefully risked losing so much as a pinky. You'll meet her before long, she'll be the angry girl whose attitude is too big for a human body.

Anyway, I love the guy, but he only takes risks that he's certain will work out in his favor. You flipped the script on him today, though, and the Conduit champ isn't likely to bother you. The witchy folk were as obsessed with the moronic fighting as we were, but she probably won't try and mess with you... at least not today," Justus explained at length, and I found myself content to follow him through the forest trees as the path seemed to curl towards the base of the mountain. There was a lull of silence that lasted for a few minutes before I decided he was politely waiting for me to enter the conversation.

"I get how he stole my bracelets now... so it won't work a second time. I'm guessing you and Yona are Mutants too?" I asked, fidgeting with my dampeners and wondering if another attack was imminent.

I was looking at Justus apprehensively when he took off his shades, my gaze locking onto his unnatural silver eyes. It felt like he was trying to look through me and into my soul, though not inherently any more unpleasant than excessive eye contact with strangers normally felt. After an unnaturally long period, he blinked first, shaking his head vehemently before looking back at me.

"I'm a Mutant, but the real question is... what the hell are you?" the perplexed man asked, putting the thick glasses back on his face as he spoke. I thought of my parents and found a thick lump in my throat, blocking the way even if I'd known what words to say.

"Sorry man, that was rude of me. You're an Apprentice like the rest of us now. Let's get to your dorm," Justus said, recovering from the momentary awkwardness as he resumed leading me down the path, becoming increasingly populated by other students.

My unofficial tour guide informed me that I was lucky that I'd arrived on one of their days off, which were given out at random compared to traditional schedules. The Sages conducted classes and exercises at their personal discretion, whether it be day, night, weekend, or holiday. The class size apparently ranged from almost the entire class to only three or four people, solely depending upon what subject matter was being taught and who could benefit most from it. I was surprised to hear that classes weren't inherently separated based on Mutation or Magic, though plenty of Conduit Apprentices still carried a superiority complex over their fellow students. Justus explained that he attended more classes than almost any other student because his Gift involved mimicking other Mutant's powers, which immediately set me to asking questions I'm sure he got all the time.

"That's an amazing power. How does it work?" I asked as we passed a group smoking and trying to look bored. They didn't make eye contact with me, but I could tell their interest was piqued as we passed the strong stench in the air.

"Well, in simplest terms, when I lock eyes with a mutant, my genetic code adapts to copy the other person's ability. If the person I focus on is human or a Magicia... er, Conduit, I just drain their energy. A few random people got hospitalized after my power manifested, to be honest. Everyone was released with varying incomplete medical explanations that boiled down to 'acute fatigue.' My control has improved a lot since then, but I still wear these shades most of the time." He smiled as he tapped his glasses, making me wonder if he had enhanced vision somehow in the dwindling sunlight. I also noticed his attempt at censoring himself to call Magicians by the preferred term of Conduit, even though I hadn't confirmed or denied what I was.

"So, do you have my powers in your arsenal now? Do all those Gifts just accumulate inside of you? It's hard to imagine all that power in one person," I said as we began approaching the end of the path. A random spattering of students was waiting there, so my impromptu guide stopped before we reached them to respond to me.

"That's actually part of why I was so weird earlier. Normally when I mimic someone's power, it kicks in immediately and only lasts a few hours. I couldn't glean anything off you, though, not even the bit of vitality I can normally pull off humans or Conduits. People around here are expecting big things from you, and so far, they're probably not disappointed," Justus admitted a bit guiltily before nodding towards another random patch of Apprentices that were pretending not to notice us.

"I didn't know I was coming here until last night. What do you mean that people are expecting things from me?" I asked apprehensively, the hair on the back of my neck standing at attention. To his credit, Justus seemed to go deep in thought before he responded.

"You've never met a precog before, have you? I know I never saw one before coming here. As a rule, they mainly keep to themselves, or else things can get really creepy... even for Sage Mountain. The seldom times we do get to mingle with them, they only ask odd questions and give incomprehensible warnings. Being able to see the future at the same time as experiencing the present or uncontrollably experiencing mixed pieces of the past, present, and future... well, you can guess why their conversation skills are lacking. One thing they made sure to share with us was that a being, both Mutant and Magic, was coming... the first of its kind. Since you're officially the last person joining us, we're all a little bit impressed that you're prophecy-worthy. The witches and wiz- I mean Conduits, might try and act unimpressed but it's just because everyone here is so competitive. One of the Sages will probably show up soon and lead you to which house you've been placed in. It was nice meeting you, X," Justus concluded with a smile, and I made sure to shake his hand before he left. It felt like he was the first person I'd met in a long time who'd been willing to lay all their cards on the table. Hopefully, I'd meet more people like him.

As if on cue, Pixie appeared from nowhere in front of me, the slight popping noise not taking me off guard for once. However, what did surprise me was the luminous neon purple glow radiating from her eyes, which was stunning in the dim light of the forest. The Sage cocked her head to one side and stifled a laugh.

"If you leave your mouth open like that, you'll catch flies," she said with a wicked grin. As a warm blush worked its way up my neck, she laughed openly. I moved my hand to cover my mouth abashedly while averting my gaze. It wasn't a mean or vindictive laugh, but I still felt embarrassed as she continued chuckling.

"The other Sages are waiting for us. Take my hand," Pixie said, stepping towards me so that we were close enough to touch. I was still debating how she could have hidden that glow all this time when I blinked and found we were somewhere else.

A room full of creatures surrounded us now, and I use the term creatures because there were several obviously inhuman beings in the congregation. At least two people in the room of half a dozen were members of races I hadn't even considered could be real until now. The first person to approach had alabaster white skin that legitimately appeared to be hand-crafted stone, and they wore a swath of fabric that covered the top of their torso and hid their face from sight. Their long legs bent backwards at the knees, ending in enormous three-toed feet that were at least as long as my forearms. Not wanting to be rude, I reached my hand out and could see a toothy ivory smile as the manhole-sized fist carefully closed its three fingers around mine and shook. The massive living statue didn't say anything but awkwardly turned to shuffle its bulk to a different corner of the room, revealing a proportionately massive set of wings protruding from their back.

I had read voraciously on the subjects of gargoyles, golems, and similar constructs even before I began showing an affinity for magic. It was fascinating to me that such potent and ancient beings were within grasp of the modern world. Of course, my enthusiasm was dampened upon discovering how often such constructs ended up killing their creators.

As if in an effort to top my current sense of bewilderment, my attention was drawn to a person I was trying to convince myself couldn't actually be a vampire. She wore a long and elaborate Gothic dress that seemed to float over the ground to match her unnatural grace, and the woman's short crop of red hair only accentuated the pallor of her skin, being a few shades shy of a corpse. When her eyes met mine, I felt a jolt of adrenaline, knowing in some instinctual way that I was in the presence of a predator. The woman didn't reach out to shake my hand but nodded silently, breaking the tension that had built as we stared each other down.

"Interesting... very interesting. A pleasure to meet you, X. I am Lilith, and this is Sage Pious. She likes you, and we both look forward to working with you," Lilith said with a lingering smile, showing off elongated canines that retracted as she moved to stand by Pious.

The next person to approach looked utterly ordinary in comparison to the first two. A middle-aged man who had an unruly mane of red hair similar to Lilith's, but his was long and pulled into a ponytail. His face grimaced a tight smile that didn't last long as he grasped me firmly by the forearm. I instinctually returned his grip. He released a light pulse of magic from his body, so subtly and efficiently that I didn't have time to react before my exposed tattoos flared to life and writhed visibly in response under my skin.

"Well met, Apprentice. Call me Sage Atticus. We have much to discuss," he said abruptly, cutting off my chance to respond by releasing my arm and lifting a sleeve to show a familiar tattoo representing the Old Ways.

It wasn't exactly the same as my own, but distinctly akin to it. Atticus turned on his heel and strode purposefully across the room from the first two Sages, and I suddenly couldn't tell if I was imagining tension between the room's occupants or not. As if sensing the same animosity, the next three teachers approached me at the same time, conveniently placing themselves between the two parties.

"I am Marequin, the Sage in charge of General Combat Studies. This is Solomon and Alpha, whom you may study with later on if we deem it prudent to your growth," Marequin said with a raspy voice. The last members of the group simply bowed in my direction instead of interacting with me, which I was ok with since I was already overwhelmed. I barely had time to meet their eyes and awkwardly return their bow before Pixie grabbed my arm. The world shifted before I had a chance to get out of the clumsy gesture, so when I stood up, I realized we were somewhere else.

"I hate Marequin. He looks down on all us Mutants like we're little universal accidents," Pixie declared in frustration as she began walking.

I reoriented myself and realized we weren't at the same place that she had picked me up from as I'd expected. The building we'd appeared next to looked like a hodgepodge of the most durable materials that the architect could integrate without regard for style. There was only a front door, which was made of some durable looking substance that was neither wood, stone, nor metal, and sported no doorknob.

"I'm putting you in the Shield Quarters. Thanks to the future-seeing collective, we knew the right number of beds to put in before the year started. I don't know if you've heard, but the other Apprentices have been here for almost a month now. Tomorrow, we'll test you and find out where you stand," she explained ominously, moving us with another teleport to the front steps of the architectural oddity.

I immediately removed my hand from Pixie's shoulder, and without any warning I could feel enough Current buzzing from the walls to know that this was no ordinary house. Now that I wasn't the one piloting the experience, it was decidedly undesirable. Questions were running through my mind too quickly for me to voice any one of them in particular as we walked into a spacious stone-floored entryway. I started trying to organize my thoughts, weighing what seemed most important to learn while not knowing if Pixie was really my best source of information. I fell in step behind her, stoically climbing a set of wide stone stairs until I realized that Pixie abruptly wasn't there anymore. She was easily one of the oddest people I'd ever met. Reaching the top of the landing, I took stock of my surroundings while the sense of abandonment washed over me.

A monstrous chandelier in the entryway worked in concert with intermittently spaced fixtures to bathe a long corridor of closed doors in soft light. There weren't names on the doors, but I assumed that every closed one that I was passing had to have been claimed by another Apprentice, since Pixie said I was the last arrival they'd planned for. I noticed that the walls and floor in this area seemed to be shaped from one solid piece of gray rock. I wondered if Magic or Mutation had been used to build this place, and there was no way of telling if it was somehow built from the mountain or just a giant slab of random rock. As I made my way to the end of the corridor there were two doors left open. Of those two doors, the one closest to me had a light on that spilled out into the hallway. Assuming Pixie had hopped ahead to leave the light on for me before leaving, I turned the corner into the room and ran into the last person I expected.

"The King is dead. Long live the King," Mal said cryptically, hopping spryly out of bed despite the arm I'd injured earlier being resigned to a sling and cast. I stepped back hesitantly towards the door to the room and bent my knees enough to be ready to move if he came at me. The smaller blonde figure raised his uninjured arm in a gesture of surrender.

"You already sent me to the healers once today. I'm in no rush to head back to them. This house is for people with Defensive Mutations and… well, whatever you are. To keep me from robbing my housemates blind, they put me in charge of the place and, by proxy, protecting the Apprentices in it," said the woefully familiar face smiling at me. I still didn't feel inclined to let my guard down.

"You caught me by surprise earlier. Why should I trust you now?" I replied, racking my brains for ways to defend against intangibility. Mal gave his first unmistakably genuine smile at that, more of a wicked grin that made me think of the Cheshire Cat welcoming me to madness.

"If any member of Shield House suffers an invasion or confrontational offense... then it reflects poorly on me. There is no stronger motivation for alliance than that of mutual self-preservation. Any foundation under other pretenses is foolish," he explained casually, lying back down and putting his good hand behind his head.

"Besides, there isn't anyone to witness how impressive I would be if I won Round Two right now. I only pick fights that I stand to gain from, that will enhance my standing. Your room is next door. Get some sleep, New Fish. They've got big plans for you, as far as I can tell." Mal closed his eyes after that.

A few long moments of standing there watching him was all it took before I felt stupid enough that I went straight to the next room. I was still skeptical enough to put a lazy enchantment on the door so that it couldn't open without my willing it and laid down in the bed. Worrying about the nightmares awaiting me, I lazily slung a Dreamcatcher over the bed post and was asleep as soon as my head hit the pillow.

༄ ༄ ༄ ༄ ༄

We waited. As the final streaks of day bled away into night, we ached with the scent of power growing around us. I could feel the darkness burning within me, stronger after every hunt. I could taste its call, echoing in the yearning howls of the others around me. The powers driving hunger began to boil my blood, from the shaking contractions of my strained heart to the raging flames flooding my fingertips. This was only my third time, but leaving the Dark to hunt felt like it was my whole life. I waited by the Leader's side, his cold strength emanating thick enough to bind us from moving, despite the pack's palpable excitement. He was our Master.

The very air was screeching under the strain of our might, a melody so utterly pure we couldn't help but howl even harder. There was nothing to do but give in, feel it build, and wait. So, like the stars we burned, every second of its passing tortured our heightened senses. I started pacing in circles, every nerve in my body screaming for release. The building resonance reached so deep into our souls that we died and were reborn in this moment that lasted an eternity.

85

The moon had risen. Even without looking, we knew that he had given the signal, and it was as if a weight beyond worlds had been lifted off our shoulders. It has begun. The sweetest bliss imaginable was ours. We bounded out through the tree line, down into the streets, down to our prey. I could barely feel the foreign concrete underneath me, the alluring pulse of life thrumming at the heart of the city already overwhelming my every sense from this distance. It drew us closer with its promise of life, of food. I ran straight towards it, the pack all around me.

We gained speed until the Master's voice cut through my mind. Stick to the outskirts, sniff out stragglers. As one, we turned our gait from a mad sprawl directly towards the city into a single file beeline curving about its edge. The timing of our formation shift left me at the lead. If it hadn't been for His voice breaking my concentration from the intoxicating aroma at the heart of the city, I never would have caught it. The nearby smell was glamoured to reek like a dog or some lower animal, but in that moment of distraction, the masking faltered for a split second. I tasted the trail in the air for what it really was. I smelled the scent of a witch.

As soon as I knew it in my mind, the Master knew as well. I could feel his cold smile somehow. Without looking back, I could feel him reaching from behind the tree line, fixating on the scent intently. Immediately I could tell that he was touching it from afar; the flaws in the fabric of the spell started to tear larger as it was unwoven. The smell was, without doubt, that of an animal when the glamour was running, but it left a strong tang in my nostrils that was too potent to be natural. The spell was recklessly fueled, almost like the witch was burning fur to cover her own less potent smell. The rest of the pack behind me absorbed the knowledge as we ran; their howls of excitement rang throughout the streets like the melodies of twisted bells in a hollowed church. The scent grew stronger with every corner we took, leading us deeper into the lifeless and decrepit section of the outer city.

It didn't matter how far she went or how cleverly she thought she had hidden herself. The taste of her was filling my nostrils. Then I saw her. She was seconds away, sprinting towards an abandoned house with boards covering all the windows. I was filled with the taste of her fear, dancing in it as I closed the space between us. She was fast, but we were so much faster.

She was ours. I ran beside her playfully. She couldn't see me, but I knew she could somehow feel me. She could sense the darkness here to take her. For a moment frozen beyond time, I was trapped, admiring her beauty. The sweat raining down her neck, the primal fear adding a grace of desperation to her run. Her face was young, with angular cheekbones and a strong chin displaying shock and disbelief along with her fear. She looked out of place for the city, different than normal prey her age. Her pants and shirt seemed to be handmade, and the cloak she wore over everything was thick and rugged, red hues the only dye used on the entire ensemble. I could see the glisten of her soul's aura laced with golden flecks of her false scent charm still clinging to her. Master had torn the glamour to bits by now. One step closer, and I was taken over by the hunger: the Pack swarming right behind me, waiting for me to take the first taste.

I moved into her path and put my hands on her shoulders, stopping her and pulling her against me. I looked into her brown eyes, grown large in terror and apprehension. There was no reflection of her death, there was no hope, only blind fear. All her muscles tensed, her heart going cold and slowing as I began to feast. There are no words for the ecstasy that engulfed me as I drowned in the taste of her soul. I felt the rest of the pack join in around me as I ate. I could feel her coursing through my veins now, her spark part of my darkness. All too soon, nothing remained, a silence absolute and deafening where a heartbeat had once been thundering. We were left buzzing off our new strength in the silence. A human is good enough to help sate the constant hunger, but a witch yields so much more. We were left brimming and nearly uncontrollable.

We still wanted to hunt, not due to pure hunger anymore, but because the spirit and yearning we had at the beginning of the night was now imbued with a drunken fervor. The sounds of my brothers' howls of joy and desire filled my senses, but every few moments, I heard a haunting and foreign sound ring out. I couldn't decipher its source at first. The mirthless laughter of our Master rang in my head, and I knew on some level what the sound meant. Yet it felt like his mouth mutated the sentiment unfathomably. I had never heard him laugh before.

I couldn't decide if I liked it. He felt me listening, and a chill ran down my spine as another icy smile was pulled in my regard. Then he said three simple words that meant the world to us.

"Go, free hunt."

Without thought or even full collective acknowledgment, we were gone. Towards the city; Towards the life. Towards more prey than we ever could have imagined. A free hunt night.

Chapter Seven

I bolted upright at the sound of someone banging on my door. I sat confused for a few groggy moments before I remembered where I was and why. After hopping out of bed, I dispelled the protective magic with a touch and wrenched the door open to find myself face-to-face with one of the Sages from yesterday. He wore dark blue robes embroidered with intricate black swirls, and his well-groomed beard was just long enough that the bottom drifted into the patterns. The Sage's brown skin was a few shades lighter than mine, but his milky white eyes were such a harsh contrast that made him appear darker somehow.

"Good morning, Apprentice. Ready for testing?" Marequin's scratchy voice caught me off guard as it was coupled with a wide and inviting smile. I gave a weak grin in return and noticed he had two sets of canines instead of the usual one, not a vampire but also decidedly not human.

"As ready as I can be, I think. What exactly is involved in this process?" I asked, hurrying to fall in step behind the Sage. He'd begun walking away before I even responded, and in my hurry to catch up, I reached the stairwell before I realized I'd left the door unprotected magically. I guess I'd find out one way or the other if Mal was true to his word about protecting the house now.

"We'll only be going over the nature of your Gifts and their qualities. It's not so much an actual test as it is an assessment, a session of observation and evaluation," Sage Marequin said, not slowing his pace as he began heading down the stairs. Although I was a few inches taller than the older man I realized he covered ground a lot faster than I did.

"What if I don't have full control of some of my Gifts?" I probed hesitantly, checking the power dampeners on my wrists subconsciously. Marequin gave a raspy but polite chuckle before answering.

"There are many people here trying to attain mastery of their abilities. The testing field has been reinforced with shielding in progressive layers since before you were born, both magical and mundane. Do you have any other questions?" the Sage asked, and from his neutral tones I couldn't tell if he was taking my paranoia seriously or mocking me. I was too uncertain and anxious to risk asking which it was, and thankfully the Sage seemed content with my silence.

The buildings we passed as we walked were all fascinating in unique ways, and no two looked much alike. Some were the size of huts, while others were more akin to mansions built out of bizarre materials. The only thing that was consistent as we walked on the lush grass was that no structure impeded the natural growth of the land around it. Vegetation sprouted all around us, and there was no distinct pathway cleared out as far as I could tell. Vines claimed most of the brick surface of one building we passed, and another had a banyan tree that seemed to have grown into and around walls built of a pink, coral-like rock. Next to that, even more alien constructs stood in defiance of all logic, except for universally being placed to minimize impedance on the forest's natural growth.

"I can't help but notice you don't seem to take after your father much," Marequin said after a stretch of prolonged silence.

The statement took me so completely off guard that I stopped walking and subsequently had to run to catch up with the surprising Sage. I knew my apparent father had wanted me to come here, but I hadn't met anyone who'd spoken as if they knew him.

"You knew my father?" I managed to squeak out, reassessing the Sage as a possible source of vital information. We walked in silence for a while as he seemed to ponder how to respond.

"How much do you know about him?" Marequin queried, annoyingly answering my question with another question.

Unconsciously I put my hand in my pocket. I'd slept with a letter from the man in my pocket the past few nights. Pixie had assured me that the other Sages knew more about my situation than she had. Apparently, they all knew my Mom and Dad back home weren't really my parents, well, at least not my birth parents as I'd thought. The boxes and several other letters provided irrefutable proof of that nightmare and worse. The dead man who had abandoned me used ridiculously powerful magic to make a kind, young, barren couple believe they had conceived a miracle child. My entire life, so full of love and affection, had been unwillingly coerced out of the two people I love most in the world. Despite hating the guy for that, I was equally curious as to *why* someone would do such a thing. The fact that my only leads seemed to rest here at the school he'd arranged for me to attend had been one of the main motivators to come. It didn't have anything to do with the haunted looks of realization in my family's eyes. Definitely not.

"Nothing, except that he wanted me to come here," I said, feeling both timid and frustrated with the situation.

The Sage remained quiet long enough that I assumed the conversation was over for now. Hopefully, other Sages would be more helpful than my current companion, though I doubted any of them were used to getting such awkwardly personal questions from students. A few minutes later, we came upon a large open valley that hugged the base of the mountain. Sages Pixie, Pious, and Solomon were already there waiting for us. Pixie grinned so broadly I could see it from a distance, and then she appeared less than two feet in front of us.

"You're finally here! I was getting bored. Are you ready for this, X?" she asked, almost bouncing with excitement. Unsure how to respond, I just did my best to smile and nod.

"I'm sure you know we're here to look at your abilities. We wanted to have both Conduit and Mutant Sages here today so we can come up with a comprehensive plan for how you should spend your time here," Solomon said as he approached in a more reserved manner. The slight tingling sensation from having magical Sight directed at me fluttered across my skin as the Conduit Sage quickly studied my aura.

"How many people with both Magic and Mutations have you all taught before?" I asked, remembering what Justus had said the night before. I knew I was the only hybrid my family... well, my *adopted* family knew of. That didn't mean that there weren't others like me out there somewhere. The Sages exchanged uncomfortable glances all around, a process that seemed alien with so many confident personalities gathered.

"There are a lot of abilities that seem to walk the line between Magic and Mutation. However, despite that fact, every Gifted person ultimately falls into one category or the other," Pixie explained excitedly, and I noticed a slight frown crease Pious' chiseled features.

"Why don't we just get started? Tell us about your Gifts as you understand them, Xavier," Marequin asserted tactfully.

I hesitated before responding. I wasn't exactly a big fan of this place yet and didn't have much reason to trust these people, but I needed to get stronger. There were major forces in the outside world that I'd have to try and stand toe-to-toe with eventually, and right now, I was no real match for them.

"Well, I can teleport, though only short distances compared to Pixie. I've got enhanced skin too. I don't know if I'm bulletproof or anything, but more durable than humanly possible." As I answered, both Solomon and Pixie began to move in response before I finished speaking.

Solomon reached into a pouch at his side and pulled out two pairs of thick glasses that were covered in runes I didn't recognize. With a slight pop of air, Pixie disappeared and, with a loud cracking sound, reappeared with an entire table of weapons. My heartbeat quickened at the sight of guns, knives, swords, and miscellaneous instruments of battle. Solomon picked up an insidiously curved scimitar from the center of the table, and as he inspected it, the blade was engulfed in ruby-red flames.

"Both of those abilities can often be mistaken for Mutations when they're actually just part of how a Conduit's power is showing itself before maturation," Marequin explained as he took the second pair of enchanted glasses that Solomon had produced and, to my surprise, expertly hefted a two-handed stone hammer from the table over one shoulder. I briefly considered the notion but was almost completely certain that my mutations were separate from my magic.

"Tell us about your Conduit powers as well?" Pixie prompted. I noticed that she and Sage Pious were tactfully ignoring the small arsenal and found myself happy to take a few steps towards them.

"I was raised by a woman who came from a long line of Earth Conduits. I've been working on enchantments, but outside of that, I can't do much. Hell, I almost blew up the house just trying to ground last week," I explained, earning intensely inquisitive stares from both Conduits wearing spectacles.

"You're unable to ground? At all?" Solomon asked in disbelief, and I felt the heat of embarrassment flush across my face.

"Why don't we focus on one thing at a time guys? Can you teleport halfway across the field for us?" Pixie interjected, nodding towards the open field in front of us.

I was thankful she'd cut that inevitably awkward topic short, so I focused and blinked myself about thirty yards out towards the center of the open valley. Looking back, I saw all the teachers staring intently at where I'd just been. Without any direction I only waited a few moments before teleporting back to the same spot.

"Now *that* is unique," Pixie mused, studying the air around me for an awkwardly long time without any explanation.

They had me go back and forth a dozen times until I'd broken out into a light sweat. Marequin signaled to halt and began tossing a few different powders in the air over where I'd been repeatedly appearing, chanting under his breath. I kept my mouth firmly shut as I noticed small bones were in more than one handful and noticed that only the magical Sages were interested in this part. I wiped sweat from my brow as that particular series of mystical tests finished, and both men removed the special goggles and exchanged long and inscrutable looks. This lasted until I began to wonder if they were talking telepathically somehow, especially when they wordlessly stopped the silent exchange and turned towards me at the same time.

"Alright, young man, step up to the table and let's test this enhanced skin of yours," Sage Marequin said as he, Solomon, and Pixie each claimed weapons off the table.

Pious surprised me by gently grabbing my hand and holding it to the table, and I realized the others were spreading into a loose circle around us. To say my anxiety spiked as the group prepared to assault me would be akin to saying a volcanic eruption is Mother Nature sneezing. Marequin approached slowly from my right, making heavy eye contact as he raised the steel hunting knife.

"Brace yourself, boy," The Sage said as he stabbed the blade down vehemently. I closed my eyes instinctively but only flinched reflexively at the quick jab of impact. There was no pain. When I opened my eyes, the Sages were all staring at the broken blade in Marequin's hand.

"Now things are getting interesting," Solomon said while raising the sword I'd seen him choose earlier, fire rippling along the razor-like edge and following in its wake as he struck.

This time I felt the blade's edge as it broke on impact, and though it stung a little, my skin showed no sign of being burnt. Pixie gave a small cheer and began appearing and disappearing around me, kicking at my shins, first gently and then with increasing strength. The childish antic made me laugh in surprise, unbothered by her steel-toed boots as they bounced off me harmlessly. While I was distracted, Marequin jabbed me in the back with something, and suddenly my body was seizing spastically from what I guessed was a supercharged taser. I fell to the ground, and for a few moments the burning ache was in my every muscle fiber. I forced myself to stand and glared at the Sage for a moment before I could stop myself, remembering I had technically signed up to be attacked right now in the pursuit of academics. Did they have to enjoy it so much, though?

"So, you're not invulnerable. Attacks that don't rely on breaking your skin have a greater effect. Knowing your weaknesses is one of the most important parts of...." Marequin's mini-speech was cut off as something hot and hard slammed into the back of my skull, making my mind swim for a few breaths.

I've heard a concussion technically happens when your head gets hit so hard that your brain is slammed against your skull, and suddenly, feeling like an expert, I decided that was exactly what had happened. I was unsteady for a long moment but managed to stay upright, even catching the glint of surprise in the eyes of the Sages as I eyed them warily. Unconsciously, my magic began to flood my system, and through the haze, I could direct the Current towards my healing glyph tattoo. I instantly felt better, my mind clearing as the energy went to work patching up the damage.

"That hammer was 300 years old! It was, until now, considered indestructible," Solomon said, looking me up and down with renewed interest as he adjusted the odd bifocals that he'd reequipped. The antiquated hammer he cradled like a hurt puppy looked like its top half had been bitten off, the runes layered into it now incomplete as I realized the missing chunks were on the ground surrounding me.

"A strong enough blow can have effect under his skin and negatively impact organs and maybe bones as well," Marequin chimed in excitedly. I grimaced slightly as I turned to consider the opaque-eyed Sage, his enthusiastic attitude towards my pain a little creepy.

"Was all that at once really necessary?" I asked, but the Sages ignored me.

They began a whirlwind of conversation where they all seemed to speak at once and somehow understood each other perfectly at the same time. I tried to decipher the exchange briefly but then gave up, seizing the moment of reprieve to heal. Nothing was seriously wrong with me, but my nerves were shot, and I wished that I had anywhere in the world to be besides this bizarre cloister of freaks. I knelt over the remains of the warhammer and considered what enchantments it may have been imbued with.

"Think you can play follow the leader for a bit?" Pixie asked, leaving the huddle of Sages to stand next to me.

Pious also slipped away and had a slight smile on her face while Solomon and Marequin began fiddling with their goggles intently. Pixie's playful energy was contagious, and though I made sure to keep my defenses up this time, I smiled when she disappeared and reappeared halfway across the glade. I focused in my mind and appeared next to her, smiling at the simple task.

"That's nice and all... but how about this?" the dubious Sage taunted before disappearing again. She appeared next to a tree about fifty yards away at the heart of the valley, then double that distance to its opposite edge. When she appeared in front of me again, only a heartbeat later, she had a fire in her eyes.

"Can you catch me?" Pixie asked, disappearing as I reached out to grasp her. I watched as she cycled randomly and rapidly between the three spots of varied distances in the valley. I had never tried to coordinate this Gift for speed or accuracy like she was displaying, but I felt excited butterflies as I tensed my muscles and focused to try.

"Ready or not, here I come!" I shouted gleefully before blinking to the spot I was sure Pixie would appear in next.

She flashed me a wicked grin as she appeared just out of arm's reach and had time to casually blow me a kiss as I failed to grab her. Outside of my late-night dash to the safe house recently, I'd never had much room or reason to teleport repeatedly, let alone become adept at the way Pixie seemed to link her coming and going so effortlessly. This was the place to push my limits, though, and I needed to give the chase a real try. I began jumping faster and more frequently until the constant reorientation started to make me queasy. If I could have used my power like Pixie, then almost the entire nightmare night at the club could have been avoided. I quickly became drenched in sweat, attempting to anticipate and act on the Sage's movements. My accuracy and speed improved a bit upon focusing, but I was still nowhere near close to catching the elusive mutant. I raised my hands in a gesture of defeat after she began pretending to play on her cell phone, and she jumped up and down in excitement from the opposite end of the field in celebration. I was unashamedly panting for breath as I called out to her.

"I give up. I can't catch you, Pixie. Want to go back to hitting me with stuff?" I joked, though I realized both Sage Solomon and Marequin were sporting new weapons from the selection at the table when I blinked back towards the congregated teachers.

"Nobody expected you to catch her, though it was fun watching you try. We were mainly studying the oddities around how your teleportation Gift works. I'm personally not even certain that you are teleporting, but we'll figure it out," Marequin explained, tapping the thick goggles for emphasis.

"Your skin and teleportation are assuredly Gifts granted due to mutations. When that hammer rattled your brain, though, you used Current to heal the damage. Though Mutations sometimes present as Magic and vice versa, we took special care to verify which is which in your case," Marequin continued slowly as if I was a particularly daft child.

"Your Blinks are unique, though, and I can't wait to work with you. There is absolutely no displacement of atmospheric gasses as well as no discernible discharge of energy in the traditional sense, like a flash of light or smoke when you move. With practice I can probably even coach you to narrow the scarring of space-time that all teleporters leave in their wake. The only thing more valuable than our movement is untraceable movement," Pixie said with more seriousness than I'd ever heard from her so far. The space-time scarring she'd referred to made sense when I considered all the science forums I'd studied ravenously over the years. There were always ongoing debates about how the teleportation gene, and others, worked.

"If we can move on to assessing your Conduit side, I'd prefer to start before dark," Marequin interjected, pulling out my bag of belongings and shaking it playfully. I made a note to myself that apparently, Mal wasn't much protection against the Sages before reaching out to accept the bag I'd definitely left tucked under my bed this morning.

"Ow! What the hell is that?" Marequin said as he dropped the bag and cradled his hand as if he'd been bitten. I realized that may have been exactly what happened and pulled the tiny writhing figure out of the pouch.

"Good job, buddy! You can relax now, these are friends. Why don't you grab some sleep?" I cooed, putting the garden gnome into its inert state with a focused thought through our bond. I noted that his pitchfork had a bit of green blood on it and suddenly wondered what species Marequin was again. I looked apologetically at the Sage, who was more intrigued than angry upon seeing the enchanted figure.

"I made a whole set like him to help protect my Mom's garden. This little guy left the rest of the group behind and has been protecting my things for me since we left home," I proclaimed proudly while holding the eight-inch-tall porcelain figure up to the group. Pious' mouth was hanging open a bit while both Solomon and Marequin eagerly grabbed the little bearded guy from my hands.

"Does he have a personality? Or is the little guy more of a miniature automaton?" Pixie asked quietly, sounding reserved for the first time since I'd met her.

I realized why when I turned from the two male Sages pawing at my creation to see her gently scratching Pious' back in placation. The Sage's intricately carved stone face and hollowed eyes were somehow clearly locked on the garden gnome with a sense of horrific recognition. I wondered yet again what kind of creature Pious was, if they'd been born or created, though I guess the difference didn't matter much to me in the end.

"The gnomes all developed distinct personalities and became part of the family before long. Rex is my little friend's name. He's fiercely loyal and loves to chatter about the clouds looking like animals or plants, which is apparently often. I genuinely consider him a friend. Hopefully, this type of magic isn't frowned upon. Would you like to meet him, Sage Pious?" I ventured anxiously, feeling like a guy who shows up to college and is embarrassedly trying to explain his stuffed animal collection to new friends.

My mind was reeling from the implication of how intricate and evolved a construct like Pious must be to act and be recognized as an autonomous Sage. I felt worse when the stone-hewn Sage declined, and not just due to the gentle giant's obvious discomfort. I couldn't help but be fascinated by the idea of learning Enchantments powerful enough that I could one day bring something like Pious to life.

"If you produced something this complex with household supplies and a novice book of runes, I think we're going to have a lot of fun working together. Now why don't you remove those dampeners and show us a few simple spells?" Sage Solomon asked pleasantly, filling the awkward silence as if he hadn't noticed it. I took a step backwards instinctually and shoved my hands into my pockets.

"If it's ok, I prefer to keep them on at all times. I never got the hang of any spells outside of Enchanting, because I could never get past grounding. My... the Conduit who raised me didn't think learning anything else was prudent until I could ground properly," I stammered nervously as all eyes seemed to focus on me. I'd known this point would inevitably come up, but it still filled me with dread.

"In order for us to know more about what we're dealing with and how best to help you grow, we're going to have to see you without them on," Solomon said with a practiced patience I could tell didn't come naturally to the man. I looked from face to face and could tell they'd all heard students say similar things often enough that any further warnings would fall on deaf ears.

"Sometimes in... in the past, when I failed at grounding... I kind of exploded," I admitted sheepishly. This earned renewed looks of interest from the Sages, although maybe some were looks of concern.

"Well, now I *have* to see it!" Pixie exclaimed, bobbing up and down excitedly before checking how the others were reacting.

Though their responses were a bit more professional, they all seemed to agree that I should show them, whether it led to an incident or not. For safety's sake,

Pixie and Pious watched from a distance while the two Conduit Sages drew elaborate warding circles around me. Both of the latter used a mix of sigils and runes that I was unfamiliar with, but they reassured me that they were only to protect myself and the spectators.

"Are you ready, Xavier?" Solomon asked, finishing a last layer of softly glowing symbols with a flick of a finger. I sat on the ground in the center of their magic and could feel it close around me like an invisible layer of bubble wrap. I gave what I'm sure was an unconvincing smile while handing over my dampeners and the Sages stepped back only a few paces, much closer than I would have liked them to be.

"Alright, let's begin," prodded Marequin. My stomach churned as I accepted that I would have to show them what was essentially the magical equivalent of wetting the bed.

"Ok, I'm connecting to my core," I narrated in a self-conscious tone. I knew Solomon and Marequin could tell using their Sight, but I wasn't sure about Pious and knew Pixie definitely couldn't.

Without any dampening enchantments on me, Flow began to build momentum, running aggressively through my entire body. With its leash unhooked for the first time in a year, my power responded to my hesitant call like a feral beast racing to feel out the limits of its cage. The energy ricocheted around inside me and tested the borders of my ability to restrain it, birthing teal sparks that crossed over my skin in random places. With sheer force of will I tried to master and temper the flood of power, controlling my breathing as best I could. As the energy resisted and bucked against my intent, I reached down into the Earth below and tried to connect the two forces. If I was successful, my excess energy would come out through my center and be absorbed harmlessly by the ground. My senses could make out the underground ley lines power below the mountain, a position of naturally occurring supernatural energy. As I feared, the power within me refused to acquiesce into the earth to dissipate harmlessly. The bubble wrap protections started to press and buckle against my skin as the pressure of my magic grew wildly. The freed power wanted to act, to escape, to shape the world, and it was willing to break through anything that stood in its way.

All the Sages watched quietly as the warding circles broke in quick succession. My panicked efforts towards pushing the power back down and calming it were useless. I might as well have been using my bare hands to try and stop a volcano. My vision began to go white at the edges as the power exploded from my body and tore into the open air. All my muscles contracted at once so violently that I missed the stun gun from earlier, magic tearing through me and out of me in an upward beam. Part of me relaxed in some small corner of my mind as I registered that the explosion wasn't aimed at any of the Sages, at least.

Numbness and apathy flooded within me as the last of my will to hold back the Flow sputtered out. Just like in the garden, a solid beam of energy escaped me, but this time it didn't go harmlessly into the sky. I stared in disbelief as the blast of crackling light shot through the tip of the mountain and continued out of sight. My body went through several stages of brightening and fading before the true tail end of the explosion came through. I felt weak and rubbery as I fumbled to put the bracelets on again.

My heart skipped a beat as my eyes fixed on the mountain again, its imposing shape hanging over us all. The landmark now had an unnatural hole bored through it about three-fourths of the way up, like a giant had taken a perfect bite out of the stone. The wound was perfectly cylindrical, and the plume of smoke that trailed off it was made more drastic by the midday sun shining through the absent stone. A sudden blow came out of nowhere and interrupted my musing, a small body tackling mine and sending us rolling in the grass.

"That was shit storm crazy! I've never seen such destruction up close. How'd you pull it off?" Pixie gushed excitedly, chattering blithely as she sat on top of me. The more stunned trio of Sages still standing in place had their eyes fixed on the mountain in a mix of disbelief and awe.

"It was an accident, I swear! That's why I didn't want to take off the dampeners," I pleaded worriedly, picturing what my life would look like if I got kicked out. A homeless Freak living exposed on the streets wouldn't last long.

"Don't worry, Apprentice. You aren't the first to hit the Mountain, though you may be the first to put a hole in it. Can you do it again? Maybe with a little less Current?" Solomon asked, and I relaxed at his academically inquisitive response to the situation. Both Marequin and Pious remained silent, though their eyes obviously shifted back and forth between the newly renovated mountain and me.

"I've never done it on purpose before, can I try with the bracers on?" I replied hesitantly. Pixie hopped off me with surprising agility, and I sat up slowly, reaching inward to check on my Core. Astonishingly enough, I wasn't as drained as I remembered being after the first explosion. Though I'd used up a ridiculous amount of energy, the remaining power was still too much for me to confidently control. A slight tingle in the back of my mind signaled that someone was scrutinizing me with magical Sight again.

"Are those sigils worked into your skin?" Marequin interjected, squinting his milky white eyes as he spoke. I flinched at his incredulous tone but rolled up my sleeves to expose some of the ink before responding.

"My Mom... I mean the woman who raised me, had very little in the way of grimoires or magical literature in general. Due to my lack of control, I was drawn to working with the runes and sigils that were in her books. Even with poor control, I can manage to use my power by working through them. I just never considered the fact that the magic might work differently with my Mutant physiology. They've grown and spread under my skin over time, but they work," I explained as all four Sages came up close and stared at my handiwork.

"Atticus is going to lose his mind when he sees this. By all rights you should be dead," Sage Solomon murmured as his gaze followed the black ink up and down my forearms and shoulders.

"Why would he care?" I asked, feeling uncomfortable as Marequin pushed my sleeve up even further to study how the ebony veins spread outwards.

"Sage Atticus is a Druid, in the classical meaning. The Druids were renowned for markings of power earned during training. I can make out some of these symbols, but the way each central rune spreads into smaller intricacies... not even Atticus' tattoos are this elaborate," Marequin explained, his face only inches away from my shoulder as he spoke.

"I've heard of the Druids, how their lineage of Conduits communed more intimately with the Earth than any other. If he could give me some advice about the situation, I'd really appreciate it... To be honest, I only did the five centrally marked areas. The rest grew out on its own," I admitted, sighing in resignation as four sets of wide eyes refocused on me in bewilderment.

"This marking for Healing on your shoulder has at least four supporting runes branching out of it. How do you operate them?" Marequin asked curiously, his face still only a hand's length away from my skin.

Taking a step back subconsciously so that I no longer felt his warm breath on me, I decided to demonstrate the process for them. Before beginning, my hands found their way to fidget with the dampeners, and the way their collective gaze tracked the movement was unnerving. It was obvious how much I relied on the enchanted tools, but a quick glance at the smoking mountain reassured me that they weren't a frivolous precaution at least. A tendril of Flow responded to my mental pull, flooding the sigil over my heart for the Old Ways. A familiar rush came over me, and I decided to brave a glance back at Marequin and Solomon. Big mistake. Marequin's mouth actually hung open, and Solomon dropped his goggles in surprise, so apparently I'd done something freakish again. It was upsetting to be faced with the fact that even these so-called Sages were unfamiliar with how my powers seemed to work. Apparently, my worries weren't just my paranoia; I was a freak even in this place so far removed from the regular world.

"That will be all for today, Apprentice," Solomon said tersely, striding towards me confidently.

"Wait a minute, am I the only one considering that this kid isn't human at all?" Pixie interrupted, instantly filling the air with an odd tension.

"What exactly do you mean? I guess you're right in a way. I'm half mutant and half magic," I offered hesitantly, earning a pitying glance from most of the teachers.

"Well, what if that's just what you were led to believe, kid? We know your father was a powerful Conduit. A lot of what you're doing isn't normal for a Conduit, though... Do any of us know anything about who or what his mother is?" Pixie asked, speaking openly to me as well as the other Sages.

My heart missed a few beats as I felt the emotional wound tear back open at the thought of my recent family developments. It wasn't that I hadn't already begun obsessively wondering about my Mother's identity. What hurt most was the inevitable thoughts of the two people who'd raised and loved me due to being under a spell. I hadn't gotten to say a proper goodbye. I wasn't even sure they'd be interested in talking to me.

"You were there when he found out, Pixie. The Baron left no information on his biological mother, and we don't know what kind of people he associated with these past two hundred years. We learned a lot today, and I don't understand all of it yet. There should be no dispute that he remains at the Mountain, though, in my opinion," Solomon said while placing a supportive hand on my shoulder. I kept my eyes firmly planted on the ground as the other Sages more or less grumbled their assent.

"So, what happens if we find out that my Mom was Inhuman or whatever?" I pushed myself to ask. Marequin spoke up first this time.

"It depends on what race or species she is. There are some who are happy to coexist with us on this plane. Many prefer to keep to themselves, though, and certain age-old treaties would require us to send you to their realms," the Sage explained matter of factly.

"You're about as Elven as my butt cheeks, and the Dwarves would let you roam free as you please. The question had to be asked, but I sincerely doubt you'll need to worry about politics, Xavier," Pixie said offhandedly, and I hoped she was right. An uneasy feeling still hung over me as we dropped the matter, and our group headed back from the open field.

Chapter Eight

I woke up gradually to the sound of a man mumbling to himself. The fast jumble of words ran on, incoherently washing over me as I pushed the haze of sleep away. My body snapped to attention as my brain caught up to the fact there shouldn't have been anyone in my room.

"Well, at least you woke up. If I was a genuine intruder, you'd be dead or robbed blind by now. We can address that later; I'm your Sage for today. Please rise and meet me outside immediately," the tall stranger said as I tried to teleport out of bed. To my embarrassment, I appeared behind the enigmatic figure so entangled in my blanket that I only managed to slip and fall to the ground.

"It's good to see you have spirit as well as talent." His gentle voice remarked amusedly before stepping over me and leaving the room.

In the awkward silence that followed, my still sleep-addled mind raced to analyze the one-sided interaction. Any student would have bragged about the successful intrusion and a real enemy would have attacked while they still held the advantage. The abrupt dismissal the man gave me before leaving the room served as further evidence that he was just another eccentric teacher. With that realization, it only took me about forty-five seconds to throw on some clothes and meet the enigmatic figure waiting patiently outside my door.

"Can you teach me how you broke through my wards?" I asked as the man began walking away wordlessly.

"If I decide you're worth the time," he replied curtly. "First, we must go into the forest. I am the Druid."

With that said, the barefoot man began walking out of the building at a brisk pace. His legs covered the ground with impressive efficiency. I was a good two heads taller than the man but had to hustle to keep up. By the time I was fully awake, we'd left the menagerie of buildings behind and were hiking through a section of the forest that held no manmade trails to follow. The Sage visibly relaxed as we left the hub of activity behind, and we settled into a different silence than before, more comfortable somehow.

"You may call me Atticus. Welcome to one of the oldest sacred forests left in the world," the Sage said as he slowed his pace considerably and gestured around us with the wave of a hand.

I was breathing heavily from the morning hike but felt compelled to take in our surroundings anew. In contrast to the clearing that I'd been led to by the Sages yesterday, I felt pleasantly engulfed in the wilderness. As if sensing my acquiescence, the older man stopped, barely a bead of sweat on his head compared to my drenched shirt.

"Drop the pack, lose your shirt and shoes. By all that's holy, weren't you raised under an Earth Conduit? Was she some incompetent hedge witch?" Atticus prodded as I reservedly followed orders.

Almost all basic Earth magic worked better with direct physical contact with the planet itself, and I'd spent countless days barefoot trying to emulate the woman who'd raised me. I eagerly hopped out of my sneakers but hesitated to remove my shirt, and in the short time it took to overcome my awkwardness, I found myself facing the Sage stripped down to a purely ornamental loin cloth. My eyes lingered over the elaborate tattoos that knotted from his navel to his neckline. Upon scrutiny, I found that the ink wavered like smoke clinging to his body, making it hard to discern anything outside of the sigil for the Old Ways near the center. In contrast to the rest of the design, the recognizable mark thrummed stalwart and steady with power over Atticus's heart. Noting my gaze, the Druid made what I guessed was small talk in such bizarre circumstances.

"Although there are many Earth Conduits left in the grand scheme of things, there are none outside my sect who should be able to bear this mark and live. You recognize it?" the Sage began to speak again as I split my mind between tearing the sodden shirt over my head and thinking about the magical rune.

"It's almost identical to mine, but at the same time, I can tell they don't have the same functions," I responded confidently as I balled up the shirt and threw it on top of my other belongings. Ever since my Magic manifested, I would occasionally know how certain building blocks of Enchantments worked or would react to each other intuitively. The Druid's face became a neutral mask as his eyes avidly scrutinized my exposed skin.

"Where did you learn these? The woman who raised you would not have… in fact, she literally could *not* have created these. I need answers about… all of this," he said, gesturing vaguely towards all of me.

I could tell by how his eyes had lit up with sudden intensity that he really meant my Old Ways tattoo. It took a long minute for me to respond, swallowing a lump in my throat to suppress the emotional bomb the repeated mention of my Mom/Not Mom set off.

"I did them alone, there's no way my family would have approved of me getting tatted. In fact, they were furious at first. I mixed and enchanted the ink on my own, then over time the markings grew out unexpectedly on their own. We had a family grimoire that went back about two or three generations. Most of the Earthen lore was unusable for me, but I memorized that book cover to cover anyway. I got obsessed with the different ways a small set of Runes could do big things. I was raised on stories of brave Druids protecting the Earth. The way she would speak about those that upheld the Old Ways was a mix between honor-bound samurai and an order of tree-hugging monks." My explanation elicited a wry smile from the stoic Sage, though his eyes continued to steadily analyze my tattoos.

"I think I'm going to like you, kid. An honor-bound tree hugger is hilariously close enough to how I try to operate, in spirit at least. So, your childhood bedtime stories inspired your tattoo choice?" he asked with a surprising lack of judgment, and I found myself a bit relieved.

My perception of the man improved immensely when I realized that there was genuine amusement and intrigue affecting his reactions to me. In my mind, that was infinitely better than the awkward stunned silences and pitying looks I'd been receiving lately.

"The stories also said the Old Ways sigil was worn by those who aspired to a code of conduct. Their cornerstone pillars of kindness and morality existed to keep them from becoming the monsters they fought. Things were complicated sometimes back home, and I was worried all this power would make me into a monster...." I trailed off, and Atticus nodded slowly, comprehension of my unspoken sentiment quickly dawning on him.

"You knew from your bedtime stories that this Rune is used to kill evil," the Druid concluded aloud with a somber expression, and I relaxed further when he didn't admonish me or pass judgment. If I had been some kind of demon or objectively any type of undeniably evil entity, the rune would've snuffed my life out.

"Now, walk me through those four. Say what you think they mean, and then explain what benefits you thought slapping them on your body would yield," he said, seemingly unwilling to let the silence grow awkward. I was thankful to not dwell on the subject, so starting with my right side, I pointed out what I considered the markings for Strength and Healing. The Sage's eyes widened at where the tattoo for Strength on my forearm drifted down towards my hand and led into black-tipped fingers.

"Why Healing? I've heard you have a rather formidable defensive mutation that would've existed before your Conduit abilities," Sage Atticus asked animatedly, his eyes going in and out of focus as he observed me in both the regular and magical spectrums. I hesitated only for a moment before deciding this was the only Sage that I'd truly clicked with upon meeting so far.

"I'm durable but not invulnerable. I haven't found anything that can break my skin yet, but my bones and organs are only protected to a certain extent from that. Seems like a rookie mistake to not have healing if I could ever need it," I explained, earning a discreet chuff from the older man that may have been either a laugh or a note of approval.

"How many can you control at once?" he asked, leaving me feeling naked and stupid in a way that had nothing to do with my lack of clothing.

"Everyone was so surprised I lived through spelling my body this way that I never explored controlling more than one at a time. How much of that can you activate at once?" I responded, taking a turn to vaguely gesture at his body as the teacher had mine.

Without hesitation, the Sage drew his long hair back into a bun with a practiced motion, then visibly began relaxing his muscles from head to toe as he sank into a light trance state. I trained my vision to the magical spectrum and found myself bewildered by Atticus' shifting aura, which became so bright I quickly became blinded. My eyes stung as I turned my head to the side and tried to make out details on the glowing figure in my peripheral vision. It wasn't the Druid's energy itself that held such overpowering radiance, but the countless points where his shroud of power mingled with the world all around him. As my Sight adjusted, his entire collection of tattoos had stopped wriggling and were rotating slowly around his torso like a map of celestial bodies, radiating a full spectrum of golden hues. When the Sage opened his eyes I flinched in surprise, facing a pair of solid gold orbs staring back at me.

"Here, each piece has a unique purpose, too complex to explain to a novice. I can tell you that I am never more powerful than when connected to Nature and in balance with myself," Atticus explained slowly, as if it took extra effort to both experience and explain the state of being at the same time.

I made frantic notes in my mind while attempting to comprehend the collections of intricate magical symbols lit up before me. As if they weren't impressive enough, the way the Druid seemed to operate them with ease was a feat I couldn't even begin to aspire towards.

"Once you've learned more, I'll be happy to work with you. The art of Enchanting, or Inscription Magic in general, is potent and damned useful if you don't get yourself killed. One thing my tattoos do is enhance my senses, and it's plain to see that vicious binding spell anchored around your soul. Hurts my head just to look at it, and you've got power leaking out in every direction as it falls apart. The Baron must have used his life force as part of the power source that has held the binding together over the years," the Druid explained, blinking slowly for a few moments as the last of the honey-golden light receded from his now perfectly normal eyes.

"Did you know him? My father?" The words slipped out before I realized I was forming them.

"We never worked together or anything, but I taught many a student aiming to replicate his spell work. You know he was a Necromancer, yes?" he asked, eliciting a fervent nod from myself as it was the *only* thing I knew about my biological father.

"Well, the type of energy that Necromancers and Druids work with are related in the sense that they're at almost exactly opposing ends of the magical spectrum. Some naively think that means Death Magic is evil, but those views are limited by superstition and ignorance." Atticus explained everything to me calmly and evenly, and I realized the Druid had probably been working up to addressing this subject all along.

"Since it has become increasingly rare for truly gifted Conduits to be born, Necromancers are nearly extinct. The same is unfortunately true of Druids and many other types of magic users, but Necromancers were never plentiful to begin with. The most powerful among us can use a variety of magical frequencies, but we'll have no real idea about your potential until the Baron's seal is gone. Your father was gifted, excelling at almost everything he tried. Still, at his best, I know he didn't have the raw amount of Current you will soon wield," the Sage said, and I caught a hint of something like admiration in his eyes. There was a pattern I was starting to notice among all the Conduits, and I finally felt like I'd found the right person to ask.

"Everyone keeps talking about how rare it is for powerful magic users to be born nowadays. Are we going extinct or something?" I tried to pose the question with a lighthearted tone, but the tension in my voice remained. The older man nodded slowly in recognition of my question and avoided my gaze for a few long minutes before answering, obviously taking his time to pick his words carefully.

"You grew up in a rare environment, which may work to your detriment now. There isn't a single other Apprentice who grew up seeing Mutants and Conduits working together as equals," Atticus said gently, though his body language was somber.

"Part of the hostility you perceive is that while Mutants face hostility from the government and are demonized publicly, the birthrate of those with mutations is on the rise. You may have meant it as a joke, but many people believe that Conduits are going extinct, and with the present decline of our population, they estimate that the age of magic will be over in just a few generations. As often happens with humanity, those in power quiver at the concept of becoming the minority." The Sage stood as he finished speaking and began to put the rest of his clothes back on.

My mind was reeling from... well, from everything at once, I suppose. There was something akin to culture shock upon finally hearing reasons for the tension between the two groups, casting my alien nature as a member of both parties in a new light. If the people who raised me had known any of this, they must have decided to keep me in the dark about it. A nauseating wave of anger, guilt, and homesickness hit me all at once like a bout of food poisoning. My whole life had been a lie to keep me hidden and create a bubble that kept me from the real world. Guilt won out and seemed to clench around my heart as I scolded my own thoughts. The plain truth was that this Baron character had stolen almost two decades of my parent's lives with mind-bending powerful magics. What kind of monster does that to people? What kind of monster did that make me?

"Don't forget to breathe, young friend. I will personally begin teaching you at some point. Until then, I need you to do two things," Atticus said, derailing my emotional spiral with his calm and confident tenor. I mustered up all the strength I had left to pull myself together. The last thing I wanted was to seem an unstable wreck in front of one of the Sages. That would likely be the quickest way to get kicked out of this place, and the more I learned, the less I felt ready to leave on my own.

"First, there are two tomes in the library I will authorize you to check out. You will not share them with the other Apprentices for any reason," The older man instructed me as he finished pulling on his robes. "Second, and this is the more pressing matter, get dressed so I can take you back to the dorms," The Druid said with a smile, and the tension burst as his laughter caused me to realize I'd never redressed.

After taking a moment to laugh at myself, I pulled my shirt back on and we began the hike back through the woods. Coming back took less than half the time it'd taken us to head out, increasing my earlier suspicions that the Druid's magic was active as we traveled. Atticus slowed when the first familiar buildings came into view and turned to me.

"So, have you thought much about what your mother was? The biological one?" the Sage asked lightly, as if he was inquiring about my favorite color or if I was feeling peckish.

For the second time today, the powerful swirl of emotions opened viciously inside of me. I breathed deeply and funneled as much energy as I could into my power dampeners. The tingle of the Druid's Sight focusing on me didn't help my anxiety, but I consciously allowed myself a few moments to quell the storm inside of me before responding.

"I've thought about it a lot. Did you know her?" I risked asking, watching Atticus' face intently for a reaction. To my dismay, the man's face seemed earnest and open when he replied.

"No clue in the world, to be honest. Baron put a lot of effort into your unique binding and clandestine upbringing. Seems doubtful you'll know more till you can see more of yourself. Have you thought about breaking the binding?" the Sage suggested, leaving me dumbstruck in the midday sun.

"You can do that?" I queried, failing to hide the mix of desperation and astonishment in my voice. The Druid's eyes took on the same honey-gold hue as his probing gaze had earlier while he studied me up and down, seemingly calculating details about myself that I couldn't yet fathom.

"It will be dangerous. Your body, spirit, and powers have grown around the binding in place for a long time. Done improperly, the procedure could likely kill you. I'll consult with the other Sages and get back to you," Atticus said solemnly, and before I could ask anything further, he turned on his heel and went back to the forest.

The sudden quiet left me feeling hollow after enjoying the odd man's company, and only then did I realize that, at some point, my hands had begun to glow with dark blue energy. It took a solid ten minutes of deep breathing and fumbling about with my bracers before the awakened power receded. Maybe more power was the last thing I needed, even if it was my only clue to follow.

Chapter Nine

My mind was so overwhelmed trying to digest the day's events that my body began to wander aimlessly. The thoughts were too heavy to be discarded and my problems too complicated to face head-on yet. Soon, I managed to reclaim a slice of sanity through the art of placing one foot in front of the other, then repeating as necessary. It didn't matter that I was utterly lost on a path of unfamiliar dorm buildings, the day was still gorgeous and mine to enjoy.

The crisp mountain air was still new and invigorating compared to the stale air of life in the suburbs, and the sky was clear but not overly hot. Changing directions for possibly the hundredth time, I came across a portly fellow distractedly mumbling in frustration to the book he held closely in front of his face. With how absorbed in the pages he was, I almost felt guilty to interrupt him for directions, but we seemed to be the only people hanging about this part of campus.

"Excuse me," I began, having approached the last few yards unnoticed as the stranger remained focused on the literature. He jumped in surprise and dropped the book, but to his credit, the round-faced blonde hadn't yelped out loud.

"Sorry about that, I'm a bit lost here. Can you point me back towards the dorms?" I finished awkwardly, realizing the hodgepodge house defied convenient descriptions.

Upon further inspection I noticed the stunned guy's book was some kind of grimoire, and I hurriedly scooped it up and handed it back to him. If it had been a family relic or something, I didn't want to appear both lost and rude. The young man's waspy complexion was complimented by an expensive haircut that hung over round cheeks rosy with effort, and the disgusted sneer he was giving me was almost picture-worthy.

"I was beginning to think the spell wouldn't work. Where the hell have you been?" His nasal voice snapped at me haughtily, like a servant who'd be receiving no dinner tonight. My mood began to sour as I saw him look the book over closely as if my touch had made it dirty.

"The wretch was probably getting another round of special treatment from the Sages, Kenneth. Aunt Crowley said they would never have admitted such carnival trash in her day." A shrill voice dripping with venom came from nearby, and every time I tried to look at the speaker, my eyes slid off their glamoured form. It was a common enough stealth spell that worked by keeping people's gazes from clearly focusing on an object or person. I didn't have enough control over my own power to cast it but could usually see through others using it with little effort.

"Now Ophelia, mind your tongue, I rather enjoy a good circus. This... change-ling stains everything we stand for as Noble Conduits," the pompous boy said, making a hot rage flush through me.

I found myself using magical Sight instinctually and saw Ophelia cringe as I openly took a moment to stare at the duo eye to eye, letting her know I could see her. Ophelia was a gaunt girl-woman around the same age as her companion, with a classic tanning bed bake and excessive makeup combo that somehow was more off-putting than usual in the ancient forest. They both had healthy, thrumming auras of Flow, though paltry compared to the Druid's earlier display. Together, they amounted to quite a bit of magical power. While Ophelia's Flow was lightly wrapped around her figure with a spell that would make her go unnoticed, the pompous boy's power was slowly rescinding from the stone path between our feet.

"So, you used some kind of bootleg summoning spell just to sneer and talk down to me? I don't get why inbred rich kids always end up thinking they're royalty." I assessed them darkly, losing my temper a bit but feeling justified. I turned my back on the duo and walked away briskly. I made my way around the first few forks in the road without a real sense of direction, simply aiming to get some distance between myself and those douches.

"My dear Kenneth, did he think we'd really let him get away after talking to us like that?" Ophelia asked in amusement.

I looked around me in utter confusion. Inexplicably I'd wound up walking right back to the self-proclaimed noble Caucasians. Her question apparently a rhetorical one, she immediately began weaving an intricate web of visible magic with both hands held overhead. After a few stunned moments I realized the spell that led me here was still active, somehow making any path I chose lead back to them. I couldn't tell what she was casting, but nothing good came to mind. Kenneth was choosing from an extensive assortment of wooden rods stuffed into his coat pockets. With my Sight focused on them, I could tell they'd each been imbued with different flavors of power, though I couldn't discern what kinds from here. Justus' remark about not being challenged by the Conduits anytime soon seemed to ring mockingly in my ears as I tried to think of an impromptu defense.

"I've been here less than a week, and I already have two stalkers? Is this how the Conduit Champion conducts business?" I said as bravely as I could manage, deciding to try and knock them off their game.

Kenneth's face began to turn purple in rage at the insult as he whipped out a wand and fired a bolt of dark magic at my face. I teleported at the last second, barely dodging the inky trilling blob and appearing between the duo. With a quick jab to the back of his head, I knocked the fledgling mage to the ground, making his collection of enchanted weapons go sprawling wildly. Unfortunately, Ophelia was perfectly poised to strike as I moved, and the sickly yellow strands of her magic wrapped around me in quick spasming jerks. A curse escaped my lips as my arms snapped to my sides, and the mucous-like cocoon restrained my hands. I could teleport again but knew the binding spell would stick with me easily.

My active Flow was held back by the dampeners, but power still coursed into my tattoo for Strength easily enough as I focused. Trying not to be too obvious, I used my enhanced muscles to begin nudging free from the shackles bit by bit. The cocoon held long enough to allow the recovering Kenneth to scoop up a new wand. I knew he'd chosen one because a crack like a gunshot rang out, and the explosive force struck my gut and doubled me over. The surprise of the blow had gotten me more than the strength of it, and when I straightened, I caught a flicker of concern on Kenneth's face at the speed of my recovery.

A predatory snarl escaped my lips, and I pulled harder at the ochre restraints, seeing dark cracks form while Ophelia grimaced with exertion. Her brother let loose a volley of attacks, expertly firing at least half a dozen bursts of the kinetic-based magic. The weapon was a poor match-up for my defensive mutation, to his dismay, and I was able to shrug off most of the blows that I couldn't avoid completely.

The battle fell into a one-sided rhythm as the cold and calculating part of my mind took over. My Flow rumbled inside of me as it reacted to the violence. It felt like any moment, the pent-up power could lash out of its own accord. For once, I welcomed the sensation, counting on the outpour of power. A modicum of relief came over me when I could verify with my Sight that all the jerk's weaponry I'd thrown about was imbued with a relatively similar level of power to what I'd already seen him use. I teleported to avoid another shot and could see in the magical spectrum that the wand in his hand was almost spent.

"Ophelia, would a little help here really be too much to ask?" the boy implored, drenched in a sheen of sweat that hadn't been there just a few minutes ago.

His request fell on deaf ears, however, and I noticed the strain had melted through at least three coats of Ophelia's alabaster paint. With all the Flow coursing through my body I was impressed that the spell was still holding up. With how strong I felt, I could've torn up police cuffs like tissue paper. It was only a matter of time until she ran out of juice, and I could deliver my emancipated fists to their faces. My lack of fancy equipment and narrow spell repertoire were embarrassingly obvious, but fighting back still felt good.

Kenneth's reliance on the wands was verified when he left himself completely open to attack, scrambling hastily to find a new one on the ground. Taking a chance, I charged straight at him, my blood pumping loudly in my ears. He was expecting the move, though, and quickly scrambled into a low dueling stance. Unfortunately for him, I'd pulled up short to stand among a pool of the fallen wands on purpose and just in time. A grin split my face as the almost pleasant blue flames flared into existence around my hands, eating through Ophelia's spell and spreading all the way up my shoulders like a flamethrower had gone off.

"Know what, Kenny? These look expensive," I said with mock solemnity, cherishing his shocked face as I picked up one of the weapons.

The enchantment fizzled out while the gemstones and wood blackened and became ash between my fingertips. I shaped a funnel for the bounty of anger and confusion inside me, then began to feed the emotions to the azure energy.

Holding my intent in the front of my mind, the flames changed into pulsing coils of electricity, making my arms look like overbrimming Tesla coils. My magic could sense the resonance of the enchanted items at my feet, like some kind of syncing and overloading of frequencies. Jagged teal bolts shot from my hands and fried every wand on the field between us, providing a brilliant glow that illuminated the looks of devastation on both Ophelia's and Kenneth's faces as they took in their neutralized arsenal.

"Well, I hate to humiliate and run, but...." My triumphant parting words were cut short as strong hands clamped over my face, surprising me into inhaling a fistful of acrid powder. I broke out into a violent coughing fit as the hands retracted and my mouth and lungs burned.

The blue magic flared harmlessly around me as my vision began to darken and my limbs grew leaden. A deft kick from behind swept me off my feet, and I caught a glimpse of someone that was neither Kenneth nor Ophelia. The figure strode past my paralyzed form and said something in a foreign language to the pale duo. My struggles to move on the ground grew more feeble every second as the powder cut me off from my magic and my body. Still able to see and hear everything, my stomach churned as Kenneth retrieved a dagger from the small of his back.

"Looks like the monster needs to learn his place. Think that just because you chipped their shitty little mountain that you're one of us? Magic users are the only real players in this world!" Ophelia worked herself into a zealous fervor as she preached.

Not wanting to interrupt, Kenneth took deliberate care, picking his way closer to where I lay. The blue eyes above his bloodied nose danced with a maniacal ardor, conveying his deep hatred louder than any words. My eyes fixed on the dagger, never having seen its like before. The metal seemed to pulse organically, almost like a beating heart, and glowing eyes bubbled seamlessly in and out of existence across its surface.

"Since you're an orphan, I thought I'd be kind enough to show you one of our family heirlooms. A touch of greatness like you've never seen before." With a satisfied grunt, Kenneth knelt next to my head and dangled the twisted weapon inches above my eyes.

Beyond the obviously damned situation I was in, I hadn't truly felt scared until now. Something inside the dagger, or maybe one of its eyes, was calling out to me. The voice turned to honeyed whispers that came from everywhere all at once and inside my head. Kenneth's wild eyes drank in my reaction and his smile seemed so wide it was painful to behold.

"You lost this game before you even got a chance to play" he guffawed, raising the blade above my head reverently before stabbing down.

◣◢ ◣◢ ◣◢ ◣◢ ◣◢

My senses came back gradually as someone held my hand and others spoke. With momentous effort I managed to crack one eye open. If I could have, I would've leapt out of my skin. A bear's snout less than a foot away from my own seemed to chuff in amusement at my reaction before ambling away. Looking around in alarm, I saw Justus had knelt to check my wrist for a pulse as Mal watched dispassionately.

"You were right. I can't believe those nut jobs really pulled this crap," Justus said, speaking over his shoulder. Mal shrugged in response.

"My info is never wrong. He's just lucky Yona was willing to track him down before opening ceremonies. I think that spell was meant to hold him here overnight," he replied flippantly, seeming bored with my predicament.

"What do you think, Yona? Can you set the big guy free?" he asked the lounging mass of muscle and fur.

The bear stood on its hind legs, easily over seven feet tall, and then began to visibly shrink. To my surprise, fur turned to clear skin, snout and fangs formed a dimpled smile, and in less than a minute, a simply dressed woman with Native American features stood with us. After assessing me silently for a bit, she reached out a hand and trailed a set of intricate swirls over the mustard-colored magic Ophelia had used on me for the second time today. Her magic felt like the first chill wind of winter washing over me, and I sighed in relief as the binding spell began to crack and chip away. Our eyes met briefly when I sat up, and I thanked her awkwardly, shaking off the last bits of magic like a particularly nasty spiderweb.

When I stood and tried to stretch out my stiff muscles I couldn't help noticing her eyes lingering on my forehead.

"So, are you guys really going to make me be the one to point out the bloody dick on his forehead?" Yona asked amusedly, and everyone but me burst into laughter.

Chapter Ten

"Today, we celebrate for many reasons. Some celebrate because we have gathered at these hallowed grounds, others do so in acknowledgment of the rich traditions we hold so dear as Gifted Peoples. I embrace this celebration personally, looking forward to the growth and progress of you all, our valued Apprentices. We give thanks and honor to how each truly unique being will go out in the future to shape our ailing world." Sage Solomon paused, taking time to stare deeply at the students gathered.

"Each of you must make the most of your time at the Mountain. I've been here... well longer than I'd care to admit, and the only thing that remains the same is that time moves in unexpected ways. Hit the ground running this year, always do your best, and paramount above all, cherish this time. Few places in the world remain a safe haven for those with true Gifts." Solomon smiled magnanimously, and the assembled crowd cheered and applauded his words.

"Now that the year has begun, we'll be reaching out to make individual schedules. There will be countless opportunities presenting themselves for students to take advantage of, but much of your time will be in your own hands," Alpha said, her deadpan tone contrasting Solomon's but carrying just as well in the large crowd.

"Every year, this inevitably leaves just enough time for people to get into trouble. Outside of House-based rivalries, we must make one rule abundantly clear. Fighting is allowed... in fact, it's encouraged. This must be done in the proper way, however, as all-out anarchy could become catastrophic. Formal duels require the presence of two dorm heads, or one Sage, and go until one figure taps out or is rendered unable to continue. If these restrictions are ignored, you will find that our disciplinary practices have not been updated for several centuries." Lilith finished with a sadistic smile emphasizing her teeth, effectively stabbing the festive atmosphere in the neck. There was a general stir as everyone seemed to absorb the information, but the greater ripple of excitement came as hundreds of plots were birthed at once within the crowd.

"It's no secret the world is screwed up right now. Many of you will be feared or hated just for having been born. We are here to make you strong enough to face that world. Able and empowered so you can carve out a life of your own, on your terms. Now get out of here and enjoy your last day before classes," Marequin said, dismissing the crowd with a flurry of whistling arcane fireworks that shimmered all the colors of the rainbow.

Pixie was a cackling blur as she teleported through the crowd, standing still just long enough to shoot a confetti cannon or throw glitter bombs at people. The festive combination did wonders for my mood, and a smile crept over my face as the confetti and glitter turned to bubbles and dancing lights. Laughter and cheers carried through the air, and, for a bit, my heavy heart felt lighter taking in the spectacle.

As if on cue, my gaze locked onto some of the only faces untouched by the mirthful atmosphere. Ophelia and Kenneth stood with a closely gathered clique of maybe half a dozen richly dressed students. Every one of them seemed to be doing their best to stare daggers at me so intensely that I dropped dead on the spot. Mal must have noticed me glaring back at them because he promptly flipped the group a rude gesture with both hands, and Justus put a reassuring hand on my shoulder. I couldn't keep living here if I was going to get jumped by these assholes on a daily basis. So, I began to plan.

⸎ ⸎ ⸎ ⸎ ⸎

"Whatever he is, it doesn't matter. The official assessment is that even if he's meant to be a threat, the boy is too little too late. That comes from our highest authorities," Sage Atticus said, the finality in his voice silencing the assembly before him. His fiery red mane and related demeanor put him in stark contrast to the dozen others in the room. Soon, their concerned rumblings began anew despite the Druid's reassurances. Various world leaders, politicians, criminals, and general faces for shadow organizations had gathered. A man with a honeyed baritone raised his voice to be heard over the others.

"The abomination destroyed a magical arsenal that cost me a literal fortune! He even survived a direct blow from an infernal Thyrsus blade... and broke it." The mix of indignation and astonishment crescendoed as the short statement incited another wave of uneasy murmurs.

If this man's children had been successful, the seed of a willing spirit would've been implanted in the young Apprentice, like had been done with all of those present. These were people used to being in utter control of every situation. If they didn't outright own all the pieces on their respective chess boards, they had intimate power over the hands that moved them.

"Do you truly wish to draw more attention to the incompetence of your family?" The chilling tone that Atticus used cut through the crowd like a scythe through wheat, bringing a suffocating stillness to the silence that followed. The question was purely rhetorical, however, as the Sage continued.

"I can overlook the fact that you clearly ignored the order to leave the abomination, as you've dubbed him, alone. Admittedly, I even received some modicum of enjoyment watching him beat the shit-eating grins from your offspring's faces. Do you know how lucky you are that they didn't expose us? What pride you must have felt... sending the pair off to ambush and murder their unsuspecting classmate. Your sense of honor is truly breathtaking," he finished with venom. A new speaker came to the forefront as the spurned father chose to keep his mouth shut rather than defend his actions.

"Not to beat a dead horse, but the boy bested a team of Enforcers at one of my night clubs. That was without being able to control his magic. Why don't you just kill him?" a woman's voice implored from the crowd.

"The argument can be made that killing any number of our students would be better than building them up. The same discussion was had about your generation, and the one before that, and so on, going backwards further than most of us can count," Pixie chimed in, appearing next to Atticus without pomp or pretense in the meeting. "Do you really think we've forgotten how the Baron was stronger than all you lot put together?" She challenged, grinning wolfishly at those who'd voiced their doubts. "Just as was done with each of you, we will find a use for this Apprentice or dispose of him at our discretion."

Chapter Eleven

Taking the time after the opening ceremony to hole up in my room, I went into a tinkering frenzy that put my past efforts to shame. Maybe it was the sudden estrangement from everyone and everything I'd ever known. Maybe it was the fact that the Mafia apparently either wanted to kill or forcibly recruit me. It could even have been that I'd been attacked twice since coming to this school and apparently now had enemies on campus who hated me just for existing. Whatever the catalyst, I was fed up with being attacked and my pride was more than a little bruised at being humiliated in this most recent ambush. With the new books the Druid had dropped off, several exclusively for Enchanting, and a belly full of rage, I was ready to begin building an armory. Almost.

Unlike back home where I could order supplies online or run to the hardware store, now I found myself at a hidden mountain base. After a ridiculous amount of debate, I gave into the obvious route and found myself outside my neighbor's door. Surprisingly classy jazz music vibrated through the wooden door as I knocked. Less than ten minutes later I was back to work, laughing to myself about how Mal had seemed offended it had taken me this long to approach him. The prodigious kleptomaniac already had more bulk supplies from dubious sources than I could've guessed and enough random inventory that he would soon run out of space. In exchange for the components I needed, he'd told me to figure out some kind of magical solution to his storage problem. After that, I managed to impress myself with what I was able to accomplish with a long night of tinkering.

One of my biggest problems had been solved by the official start of the school year. It seemed unlikely I'd receive more unannounced challenges with the official declaration of school rules by the Sages. It wasn't impossible, but with the threat of retribution now possible from the Sages I hoped it was less likely to happen. Since the last attack had been three-on-one, it was difficult to discern if it was driven by the Conduit Champion's ambition or something more sinister. Learning that neither Kenneth nor Ophelia were actually the Conduit Champion had been more than a little upsetting, guaranteeing that I would need to be ready for a fight when I saw the duo in the future. Everything I put together would likely be for fighting until I could deal with the troubling siblings or at least feel reasonably safe from them.

Neither of my adopted parents had been proficient with weapons, unless you counted the old shotgun I'd never actually seen my Dad touch. Despite that fact, when Mal showed me a chest full of pilfered daggers, swords, and other miscellaneous implements of battle I greedily dug in. I wasn't eager to make a fool of myself in this oddball crowd, where many people would likely be proficient, but I couldn't resist the chance to make an actual magic sword.

The morning sun rose, and I still hadn't finished testing out new ideas. The vocabulary of runes and sigils I'd had experience with had more than quadrupled thanks to the new books. It was a safe bet that I'd only touched on about a third of the content over the night's session, and I was rueful to stop. The process was akin to learning two new alphabets, then mastering the languages, and finally speaking the different tongues well enough to mix them fluidly. Otherwise, the magic didn't flow properly, and the symbols were more akin to scratches on a page than magic. I figured it was technically a good thing enchantments were so difficult, or every graffitied wall and shifty tattoo parlor would be a small library of arcane power.

I could vaguely hear the bustle of other students moving about the house by the time I left my room. A few guys nodded amicably as they waited in line for the lavatory, not hiding their interest as they stared, and I couldn't blame them. By the time I'd waddled down the stairs and followed my nose to the kitchen, I'd decided I was trying to carry too much gear at once. Mal and a few others sitting with him at the head of the table abandoned their spread of cereal and pancakes to watch.

"Holy shit, man. Did you even sleep?" Mal asked, looking at the ridiculously extensive arsenal I was displaying. The genuine intrigue in Mal's eyes turned fiery with greed as the cornucopia of gear continued to take up more and more space.

"Can everybody but Freq and Viz give us the room? We've got to talk to our new brother here," Mal said calmly, and like in an old gangster movie, everyone cleared out silently except the two he'd mentioned by name.

The small pile of wands and rings I'd begun to display grew as I emptied my pockets, removing the superfluous layers of gloves, coats, necklaces, et cetera. Thankfully, the other guys seemed content with Mal's outlandish demands and took loaded plates and cups with them. The two mutants the House Leader had ordered to remain with us silently closed the doors behind the departing company as if they'd done it a million times already this year.

"Nice to meet you, X. I'm Johnny, but everybody calls me Freq. This gorgeous specimen is Viz, and you just might be nature's answer to Mal's ceaselessly sticky fingers. You've made his magpie collection of pickings into sellable bits," Freq said jovially, his laid back and complimentary manner easing the tension I'd begun to feel in the room.

Freq's short and brick-like build moved from the doorway and plopped into the seat to my left. After placing the last few products on the table I stopped to shake his hand, taking in how the jet-black curls covering his head contrasted his unnaturally mercurial eyes with pupils that seemed to constantly shift hue. They rippled between a vibrant emerald and rich crimson as he moved between assessing the items on the table and myself.

Viz spoke in low tones to Mal that I couldn't make out until seeming to come to some conclusion. The boy seemed half feral as his scrawny frame refused to stand still, assessing everything constantly with minute and economical movements. I waited a few awkwardly long moments before realizing it was one of the rare occasions I was dealing with someone as socially inept as myself. With a blink I teleported to stand between Viz and Mal. Both jumped but, to their credit, neither cried out at my abrupt movement.

"My name is X. I'm guessing you're a friend of Mal's? I didn't mean to hijack everyone's breakfast time," I said, my joke falling flat as the gangly pale boy froze and stared at my outstretched hand.

"Sorry X, Vis is a bit skittish. Not big on handshakes, but almost as good a thief as me," Mal interjected, and Viz flashed a quick grin before disappearing.

I blinked in surprise and looked around the room, wondering if he'd teleported like me.

"So, I'm thinking your intent is to use some of this scrap to even our debt?" he continued as if his friend hadn't just vanished into thin air. Continuing to look about with careful disinterest, I finally noticed a torn-up pair of shorts floating in the air where Viz had been standing before and smiled.

"Come on, Mal, are you really claiming to be a better thief than the local Invisible Man?" I quipped, earning a genuine smile from Viz as he faded back into view. Mal gave me a begrudged chuff of a laugh and went on as if I hadn't posed the question.

"I could nickel and dime you for supplies all year, X, since enchanting seems to be one of your passions. I'd make a pretty penny too. However... there's a better option for all of us," he finished cryptically, stalking around the table to stand by Freq.

"How are things looking, bright eyes?" Mal said to the other mutant, whose vividly shifting red and blue orbs had never left the table.

I wondered if the mutant had some affinity for magic like me as he took another few moments to assess the goods in depth. I'd kept all but three of the daggers and swords Mal had been willing to part with. Several pairs of gloves, a half dozen rings, two cloaks, and a smattering of other random items were laid out for potential sale. It had been a much-needed catharsis to get lost in the creative process I used to make new enchantments after recent events, and if this went well, I would likely be able to do a lot more. Each successful enchantment not only bolstered my confidence but also showed me how I could make the same effect more efficiently in the future.

"Remember those sticks that Kenneth was bragging about? I clocked those as ranging from an average of three and the highest as six. These are all a solid five or higher, even including the smaller bits like the gloves and rings," Freq said, not taking his radiant gaze off the table.

"Are you a Conduit too?" I asked curiously, earning a shocked glance before wry chuckles passed around the room. The numbers he'd referred to didn't match any kind of magical rating system I'd ever heard of, but the numbers seemed to imply my work wasn't half bad.

"No, you're the only one in the house as far as I know. I can see and interpret the world differently with my mutation." The young mutant winked at me and began pointing to different items on the table. "The amount of power poured into each shows up as different hues and vibrancy to my eyes. I'm not quite familiar enough to guess what the different items do, but I'm working on it," Freq explained, his eyes fluttering between a feral yellow and crimson as he faced me.

"Did you really burn Kenneth's stuff?" he asked, with a mix of disbelief and admiration in his voice. I hesitated briefly before deciding there weren't likely to be any in the room who would begrudge me for the matter.

"You mean when Kenneth and Ophelia jumped me for no reason?" I declared more than asked, letting the anger show through in my tone. "I turned a good bit of his fancy toys to ash. Of course, after I did, their third fighter came from behind and dosed me with some kind of knockout powder," I grumbled, fingering several pieces I had on me meant to deal with those specific assholes next time we met. When my attention returned to the room, each of the three seemingly hardened mutants was staring at me like wide-eyed boys.

"About that... could you recount the tale for the fellas? The details are a little hazy for me, except for finding you with a dick drawn on your forehead, I mean," Mal asked, pouring on false charm so thickly that it almost smothered me. It wasn't that he'd forgotten, but Mal was the type of misfit who wasn't beyond lying to make a tale more entertaining. I figured it would be better to tell the truth of things, as it was almost guaranteed that the Conduits I fought wouldn't do the same.

"Mind if I ask why first? I'm a little wary that apparently there are rules around fights for students... since none of the people who've attacked me here have seemed to follow any," I replied, with only a bit of genuine resentment towards Mal.

Compared to the magical attack I'd faced, the confrontation between the two of us had been downright friendly. Amused chuckles accompanied Mal's deferential apology, and I smiled to show that I was only half serious. To my surprise, Viz spoke up next from where he leaned casually against the kitchen counter.

"The rest of us have been here almost a month now, big guy. Fights were pretty much anything goes at first. The magic folk think we're scum, and we think their heads are so far up their arses they're stuck looking out of their belly buttons," he explained with a slight lilt of an accent that I couldn't place. The shock that had initially come over me regarding all the social tension between Mutants and Conduits was quickly becoming a prominent theme.

"I have to admit you're the first one of us to get the three-on-one treatment. Have to consider that they've been posturing and crowing all this time, then you come in last minute with the best of both worlds. Not only do you blow them all away, taking a bite out of the school's mountain, you challenge their claim to genetic superiority." Viz's hazel eyes seemed harder than steel as he laid his thoughts out. The overall intent wasn't unfriendly despite his demeanor. In fact, I felt warmed by the odd sense of camaraderie I'd been extended.

I broke into a quick rendition of events after leaving the Sage and we'd all finished eating and had a good laugh by the time they'd heard everything. The brutal end to the fight and the unsettling nature of how things had ended only inspired a reserved silence at the end.

"I think that's enough of that, killer. What we need to hammer out right now is business." Mal seized on the lull in conversation naturally. Anyone so effortlessly charismatic as him always tended to put me on the defensive.

"Kenneth bragged about those wands before you arrived. Said they were worth a fortune that the likes of me could never imagine... and that no Conduit would ever sell to mutants." The head of the household swept his arms vaguely about the kitchen at those gathered.

"So... yet another thing they'll hate me for would be breaking their monopoly on magic items?" I interpreted hesitantly, making purposeful eye contact with each of them in turn. Mal and Freq met my glare with open smiles, while only Viz seemed to really acknowledge any gravity in the situation.

"I've got three conditions, and I'm in," I said with a smile, earning a salute from Viz using his glass of OJ while both Mal and Freq hooted their approval.

"Well, let's hear it, we've all got classes today," Mal said flippantly but merrily enough. I pulled out some paper and made a loose contract with the other three Gifted entrepreneurs before we parted ways. It looked like I had a part-time job of sorts already.

"First condition is nonnegotiable. I get a rematch. An official one. In front of everyone," I said, going into my plan among a chorus of jubilant laughter.

Chapter Twelve

"For the record, I am an undead predator generally referred to as a vampire. Those unaware of this simple fact need to embrace that every myth, whisper, and legend you have ever heard is likely based on distorted fact," Sage Lilith said candidly, with a relaxed tone that most teachers would employ when discussing something as basic as the syllabus on the first day. Looking around, I saw a few faces of shock, but most people didn't seem to bat an eye at the news, and those who were surprised tried to hide their reaction quickly.

"With my tutelage, you will learn fact from whimsy. The distinction will hopefully be enough to keep you alive when you need to face those of us who go bump in the night," she assured with a smile to the small handful of students.

As I looked around again, I wondered for the hundredth time today how our teachers went about choosing the students to attend each class. The fact we'd met in a chapel that no one had seen had been creepy, but apparently, things being a little creepy would be part of the class. The only thing that was more off-putting was the fact that most of us were sure the space had been empty yesterday.

"Have any of you wondered why there are no supernatural Apprentices at the Mountain? No young Fae, fledgling therianthropes, or other species? Only Conduits and Mutants?" Lilith began to pace as she looked for an answer from the crowd.

"Most of those groups have an established hierarchy of leadership. The best mentors and structures for learning are often already within their own communities." Yona surprised everyone as she spoke up. Her short body's large presence took up the entire pew, except where I had graciously been allowed to perch. With one foot kicked up and her laid-back posture I'd thought she wasn't even listening until now.

"Correct, young lady. If memory serves... you have a unique experience with the subject matter. Would you mind sharing with the class?" the Sage prompted with a coy smile that told me she had hoped things would play out exactly this way.

"I was adopted by Regulars, nice people though. My ability to shift came at a young age, and instead of killing me or calling the cops, they took me to a local werewolf pack. Every group of shifters like them have set hierarchies, lots led by an individual called their Alpha. This particular Alpha realized I was a Conduit who's therianthropic, which is why it manifests differently than people who get the ability from biological lineage," Yona explained with a total lack of enthusiasm before becoming engrossed with picking at her nails. I thought her story was fascinating but couldn't help hoping that the Sage wouldn't try to make my family background into a teaching aid.

"Thank you, very illuminating. Among a typical pack of shifters, the Alpha's word is law. The benefit to that is that every kid born into their pack is trained to master that Gift from a young age so that they can be a productive part of that community. North America has many packs that mainly govern themselves as well as each other. Many claim that's why they haven't been outed fully to the public by the government yet," Sage Lilith continued, picking up her lecture without missing a beat when Yona trailed off.

The ability to self-govern and stay out of trouble was often brought up by Conduits to explain why they were less targeted than Mutants by those controlling law and public policy. With a blur of inhuman speed, she moved from the front of the chapel by the lectern to abruptly appear standing at my shoulder.

"Now why do a bunch of misfit mages and mutants need to learn such details?" Lilith asked, causing the whole class to split their focus between her new position and my flustered face.

"I... well... she's immune to silver and can cast magic? If the biological shifters are allergic and can't work magic, I can see the value in learning the difference." My answer came out accidentally as almost a question, but thankfully the Sage gave a small grin that seemed to purposefully not put her fangs on display.

"Knowledge is paramount in this field. If you show up to a zombie uprising with silver bullets and wooden stakes, you're going to have a bad time," she surmised, earning chuckles from around the room. "Members of this class have been chosen to receive what some may call aggressive hands-on experience with supernatural beings. It is not a required course. If anyone is uncomfortable with inherently... bloody work...." She paused for emphasis, and I saw more than one face pale considerably.

"Then you will not be penalized in any way. Know that there is no substitution for this particular experience. After completing this course, students will qualify for several coveted positions of employment around the globe." The Sage looked around the room at this, and I took note of the many pairs of eyes that avoided hers, which held the light of a challenge and a sparkle that promised violence.

When her gaze met mine, I found myself instinctually rising to meet the challenge. Some part of me knew this was necessary, and I had to trust my gut. Without a family to go back to, nothing sounded better than a place to belong and earn a living after graduation. I saw the flash of fangs again as Lilith smiled warmly, acknowledging my reaction.

"Be here at sundown tomorrow for the real introduction to our subject. You are dismissed," Lilith said, her words causing a flurry of movement as the more frightened students ran unashamed from the building. I waited a bit for the rest to clear out, carefully waiting to catch the Sage in relative privacy.

"If you wait any longer people are going to start thinking we're lovers, Xavier. Come tell me what thoughts are racing through that marvelous head before you explode," the Sage said mockingly without looking up from the papers she'd begun packing up from the lectern. Despite her words, the overall tone had been warm and friendly, so I wasted no time in teleporting to the front of the room.

"So do you already have some magical way of knowing who'll come back tomorrow?" I asked nervously, trying to think of how to frame my real question.

"In a way... though I'm not a spell caster or anything extravagant like that. Vampire senses are acute enough that individual heartbeats ring like tiny bells to my ears when they're racing." She paused, watching me for a few brief moments to assess my response.

"Your heart rate increased, but not nearly as much as most. There's also a distinct change in a person's scent when they're afraid, a bouquet of adrenaline and other hormones. Yona and you seemed refreshingly... undisturbed," Sage Lilith concluded, her pauses made all the more disturbing because she never seemed to blink. It was a bit unnerving to think that one of my teachers could essentially smell emotions and listen to my heart like a polygraph. It was time to change subjects.

"I was hoping you could clear up a few questions I had? There are some finer points I'm unfamiliar with because of my... sheltered upbringing," I ventured, earning a curious glance from Lilith.

"Those that seek to educate themselves about what they are ignorant of are my favorite. If you are similarly free after our scheduled class periods in the future, I will endeavor to give you a crash course on the many species you've been kept ignorant of," the Sage proposed, tossing me a book offhandedly as she spoke.

As I reached a hand out to catch the book, her lithe form blurred in a burst of supernatural speed. Lilith caught the book near the end of its arc across the room towards me and smoothly stepped forward as if the display of power was nothing. Flipping through the pages and ignoring my stunned expression, the vampire placed a bookmark within the pages with a delicate touch and held the book out for me. I couldn't help but smile apprehensively as I made a show of poising myself to try and snatch the book.

"I forgot to mark a starting place for you, cheeky boy," she tittered, shoving the book at me and shooing me from the room.

"One last thing, Sage Lilith. I could make a living doing this? It could be a life after school here?" I whispered, knowing her enhanced hearing would catch every word.

"There are already people hoping you'll choose this life. You'll have time to think on it, Apprentice," the teacher replied, her eyes shining again with the promise of challenges and violence.

Less than an hour later, my first class on enchanting revealed I wasn't nearly as knowledgeable as I'd considered myself. Not that my creations up until now were any less impressive, but they were such unusual products that they were barely comparable to standard enchanting. Thankfully, Sage Marequin managed to spare me from any serious public humiliation by catching me on the way into class before things got started.

"The small menagerie of creations you've hobbled together thus far are amazing but utterly unconventional. The baby steps of this discipline will be of great benefit to you. Also... you may not want to make *all* of your enviable skills public knowledge," the wooly bearded man had said upon seeing me.

I nodded and hurried to find a seat, receiving more curious than hostile stares from those who'd overheard. The hour-long class passed in a blur from there, my hand cramping to near immobility as I took intricate notes. I was astounded when I realized how much convoluted lore was attached to something as trivial as a generic Activation rune, used to turn an item on or off. From what I'd learned today I could infer how the smallest embellishment would change the way an entire piece worked.

As jarring as the direct focus of the lesson was, learning how many facets of enchanting I wasn't even aware of had been the bigger takeaway. The concept of imbuing different segments of runes with precise amounts of power was revolutionary. I'd always maxed out the capacity of each finished character to full strength. The concept of permanent versus temporary use enchantments had also never occurred to me, but I was determined to master creating both.

My mind voraciously ate up every new fact and tried to sort them into a coherent pedagogy of lore. Maybe the biggest reveal of all was how few Apprentices were even interested in the subject. Apparently, most of the Conduits who were powerful enough to imbue runes and sigils properly were also from rich families that considered the work beneath them. Why take a labor-intensive course like this when you could just buy the pre-made items? Since I'd spent my entire life without access to the magical markets that existed, their mindset baffled me. Some Apprentices even retained limited access to the shops now, and I made a mental note to have Mal get me some kind of access.

Chapter Thirteen

The day wasn't even over and I already knew we'd made a profit selling the first round of items I churned out recently. Most mutants jumped at access to magical items, and there had even been a fair number of Conduits interested. Apparently, my style of enchanting was ultimately so impractical that there was nothing like it in the major markets, and my business partners had made it a point to grab interest by emphasizing this. Viz had been waiting for me outside of class, stoically letting me know that they had held up their end of the bargain. I had another fight on my hands, but at least I had picked it this time.

Mal spent most of our walk trying to stoke my anger to new levels. I gave the occasional grunt and nod of the head but felt a million miles away. Like a twisted therapist, he tried to rip open my insecurities and enflame them for potential profit. Yes, I'd been picked on and branded a Freak most of my life. Mal eloquently wove all the details he knew about me into the ugliest tapestry possible. Not really a Mutant or a Conduit: just some outcast who was abandoned like trash as a kid for being both.

I was growing familiar enough with the school's layout to note that my new friend's tactics subtly began to shift as we got closer to our goal. I tuned out even more as Mal's rhetoric changed to weaving how now was the once-in-a-lifetime moment to seize the narrative for the better. I could have given the speech for him at this point. Eternal sunshine, roses, and so much more awaited if only I would rise above and change my life! It wasn't any special dedication to pessimism that made my nose wrinkle indignantly at the words. I had the same instinctive reflex when faced with politicians or Army recruiters. Sometimes there was often no way to weigh all the pretty words people threw around, to tell if their speech was worth the time they took to say it.

When we began passing other students, I picked up on the now familiar mix of hushed silence and furtive whispers that had followed in my wake since arriving.

There were a few huddles of mutants giving waves and shouts of support, but I did my best to ignore them too. It all began blurring together as I turned inwards, dichotomously a neutral observer and true source of the tumultuous emotions threatening to bubble over.

Before I realized it, we'd arrived. We were stomping up a pair of rickety wooden stairs to an old stage that was reminiscent of a Shakespearean play. There were three people already on the wooden platform, seeming small in comparison to the large crowd gathered. My heart thundered against my rib cage as my eyes locked with Kenneth's blue orbs less than a dozen paces away. The blonde oaf was prancing about the stage animatedly, fencing an invisible enemy with a gaudy rapier. With a final thrust to vanquish his imaginary warmup foe, the self-absorbed prick flourished the thin blade about in a slow circle before sheathing it and turning his full attention to me. I turned my Sight on briefly and wasn't surprised that the heavily bejeweled sword was verifiably packed with enchantments. I felt the hint of a wicked smile, imagining how his face would look when I put my fist in it.

"Are you alright, man?" Mal asked, discreetly bringing me out of my fugue state.

I nodded and tried to give him a reassuring smile but found my muscles were so rigid from anger I probably just twitched. Now that my vision wasn't solely latched onto Kenneth, I became aware of Ophelia and Atticus also on stage. The Sage stepped forward and raised his hands for silence, and the crowd quickly acquiesced.

"Alright, everyone, we've got an odd occurrence here. First day of classes, and we've got our first official duel of the year to conduct. To reiterate the rules, you need a formal challenge to be submitted and a Sage to preside over the conflict. Gentlemen, think you can wait long enough to put on these rings before we start?" The fiery haired Sage seemed almost cheerful at the prospect of the first day having some extra excitement.

Walking to the center of the stage, Atticus produced a wooden box from somewhere inside his cloak and ceremoniously held it up for all to see. I strode towards him as the lid lifted to reveal a matching set of clunky grey rings hewn from stone, nestled in a rich velvet fabric.

"Every year we face the same problem: our students possess breathtaking powers and the vigor of youth. How do we keep all these brats from killing each other?" Atticus quipped earnestly, chuckling good-naturedly along with the crowd.

"Well, my solution is archaic but simple and effective. In the past these rings were imbued with the power to mystify audiences, allowing olden-day actors to cause deadly harm to one another with unparalleled realism. A pair can fight to the apparent death, have their rings removed, and be none the worse for it in time for the next act." The Sage explained the magic as Kenneth and I claimed one of the rings and hurriedly shoved them on a finger. An unnatural shudder ran from my toes to my scalp, and I felt a vague awareness of the same power flashing over Kenneth.

"Now that that's settled, a few basic rules. The duel goes until someone taps out or is incapacitated. No need to hold back. Are we ready?" Atticus asked, a gleam of excitement in his eyes. To everyone's dismay, Ophelia boldly stepped forward, addressing the crowd as if they'd gathered there for her speech.

"Are you ready to see this mutant put in his place?" she said enthusiastically, getting a surprising number of cheers from the crowd. "A mongrel so desperate to prove himself that he blemished the mountain that gives our school its name?" she cried, damning me with her words and a pointed finger at the now irregular silhouette.

The same people that had cheered now booed me directly, like this was a bad children's show, and I may have briefly flipped the crowd a rude hand gesture. To my surprise, and everyone else's, Mal casually used his power of intangibility and walked directly through Ophelia to stand in front of the crowd. Though apparently unharmed, the shocked harpy's eyes went wide in astonishment, and she began sputtering wordlessly, too angry to make a coherent statement.

"Just because you're a rich witch doesn't mean you have to be such a cliche bitch, Ophelia. Why not tell us how you and Kenneth lured this strapping young hybrid to the edge of camp with a summoning spell?" Mal pitched his voice to appear calm but carry clearly out over the crowd.

Genuine laughter mixed with shouted questions bubbling up from the crowd, and I realized I couldn't care less about the popularity contest that had become part of the event. The prospect of getting randomly jumped by other students wasn't a laughing matter to me for some reason. After letting Mal go on a while longer, I wordlessly walked past both him and Ophelia to face a surprised-looking Kenneth.

"Enough talk. Let's do this." I said quietly, my voice quavering with tightly restrained rage.

Without preamble and quick as lightning, the pompous boy managed to whip out the thin blade and jab at me in one fluid motion. Knowing that he could stab at me for days without breaking my enhanced skin, I didn't even bother to dodge the blow. This turned out to be a large miscalculation on my part. At first, I looked on impassively as the rapier's length bent drastically when Kenneth leaned into the stab fruitlessly.

I could feel the enchantments trigger and hear a boom like thunder before I was tossed head over heels. The acrid tang of smoke tickled my nostrils as muscle memory kicked in, turning my fall into a roll that ungracefully brought me back up to a ready crouch. I'd been stubbornly prepared for the expensive-looking metal toothpick to deliver a devastating blow, and the look on Kenneth's face belied he'd expected the same. A dark grin split my face as my opponent blanched. I had years' worth of experience withstanding explosions from Jackson, making this seem like child's play.

I pushed my seething Flow into Speed easily but didn't go for the kill yet. As my body and mind sped up, it became as easy as skipping rope to avoid the rapier's spiral-shaped attacks and increasingly obvious feints. I began a slow and deliberate march towards the object of my amassed fury.

The thin sheen of sweat on Kenneth's face grew into a drenching downpour and his eyes slowly grew wide with apprehension. With a single-minded focus, I drank in every detail as I closed the gap. When I was only five paces from the flailing duelist, I stopped bothering to avoid his blade and moved the magic into Strength, abruptly letting at least half a dozen wild blows land. The explosions were deafening but didn't faze me this time around.

Instead of being knocked backwards I pushed forward. I easily got inside my opponent's guard when he flinched from the backlash of his own attack. The thrill of the fight climaxed as my hand found and latched around Kenneth's throat, and I squeezed until his face began to turn from pink to an almost royal purple. Chubby little fingers tried to claw at my hand while I lifted him off the ground with my magically augmented muscles. With a small clatter, the rapier fell to the stage floor. Kenneth made another effort to attack, pulling out a handgun from the small of his back.

As I'd thought, without all the fancy wands, the element of surprise, and his sister's immobilizing spells, the pompous boy was no real match for me. I easily smacked the gun from his grip but wasn't able to stop the power I felt him building up while I was busy doing so. An involuntary growl escaped my clenched teeth as Kenneth's power washed over me from head to toe, like having a bucket of battery acid splashed over me.

Unfortunately for the Conduit, the stab of pain only made my grip tighten, and I could feel he was drained of power. With savage efficiency and almost carnal delight, I reared the fist holding the limp figure back and slammed him into the ground. His shocked face grew bloody from the impact, and his nose broke on the first punch. I found my fists flying until his skull was unidentifiable pulp.

As the bloodlust released its hold over me, I didn't bother meeting anyone's eyes. This hadn't made me happy; it was simply necessary. A warm ripple of magic washed over me as I took off the school's enchanted ring and dropped it on the stage. For Kenneth's sake, I hoped the Sage hadn't been exaggerating the healing power of the set. Some small part of me would regret it if I'd genuinely beat him to death in front of the entire school.

Chapter Fourteen

The next day, I walked the trail to class feeling self-conscious but a bit more confident. Seeing Yona wave me over to walk with her and a group of other Apprentices raised my spirits even further, and I quickly found myself comparing first days with her. We stuck primarily to which teachers and classes we'd had and avoided the obvious matter of the duel.

The path we followed seemed to have been haunted by a lunatic sculptor at some point, having left progressively intricate works aside the dirt walkway. Yona made a point to stop and admire each piece, even though they quickly vacillated between the magnificently macabre and whimsical. We ended up so enthralled we lagged behind the rest of the group to study the more intricate work just off the beaten path.

There was a tree carved out of an alabaster bonelike material that was so well done we were left speechless. It had been rendered as if lightning had struck the trunk, cleaving a raw tear down the center mass. The right side of the tree was vibrant with every elegant trace of life displayed. Half a dozen entrancing flower blooms vigorously stretched their petals outward, flushed with hues of every natural flora I'd ever encountered. Even knowing they'd be stone, I squeezed several hanging fruits that my imagination made seem plump.

The other half of the tree was embroidered with decaying fissures, and small animal skeletons hung like wind chimes or enmeshed with the wood itself. The only mighty branch left in the equation held an empty noose that seemed to have flowers growing upon it. A shiver ran down my spine as I traced my fingers over the artist's mix of tree bark and squirrel bones. Out of the corner of my eye I caught the gentle movement of the noose swinging in the wind. It took a good thirty seconds before I realized what was nagging me about the scene and I jumped back in surprise. Yona looked over in amusement, still admiring the more vibrant patches nearby.

"Do stone nooses normally swing in the wind?" I asked, immediately regretting how the question sounded like some half-baked goth poetry. I was saved the embarrassment after a loud pop caused us both to turn and find Pixie watching us.

"That's what's holding you two up!" she shouted enthusiastically. "It always amazes me how few people notice these sculptures. No more dawdling, though… class is starting," Pixie said, taking a moment to appreciate the arboreal art in a way that said she'd come here often.

Before I could ask about the statue or its sculptor, the Sage put a hand on Yona's and my shoulders and the scene disappeared with a pop. The first thing that struck me about our new surroundings was the smell. It had been almost a lifetime since I was last in a gym class. Even in the large open-space environment, the smell of sweat and stain was overwhelming. There were a myriad of grunts, cries of victory or pain, and the distinct smack of skin on skin as Pixie dragged us forward.

Around us, people had been set to doing all sorts of odd and inscrutable tasks. One girl we passed was practicing a dance that appeared half classical ballet and half Muay Thai in front of an abnormally large mirror, trying to match her moves to an out-of-sync reflection. The girl in the mirror seemed to have a stronger mastery of the fighting style but also stood amongst a succession of bloody battles.

Another student we passed was ringing an odd set of silver bells with kicks that trailed a near-neon light in their wake. From what I could tell, he was trying to make a song with the striking rhythm. Lastly, before reaching the head of the structure, we saw a mass of puffed-up tough guys arm wrestling. Their struggle caused the stone table to shatter, and, to my surprise, the other students immediately shoved a new table between them. Even craning my neck, I didn't get to see a winner crowned before Pixie pulled me away. At the far end of the unconventional assortment of activities, I finally caught sight of the actual teacher of the class. Sage Pious was silently engaging three Apprentices at once in a sparring match, and Pixie indicated excitedly we'd be stopping here to watch.

Amazement overtook the crowd as a ferocious exchange of blows took place between the Sage and three Apprentices. One of the guys' blows rang out like gunshots as Pious blocked them, somehow shrugging off the enhanced attacks with little effort. Another had a luminous burgundy aura visible to the naked eye, weaving his body through the battle as if his hands and feet were bladed points. Most impressive of the three attackers, however, was the lethal woman attacker's rubber-like mutation. She could make her fists the size of my head and throw haymakers with accuracy and speed from fifteen feet away. The Sage was easily more awe-inspiring than those three combined, their stone body constantly flowing between stances with an efficiency I'd never seen before. The mass of stone could transition between fighting on all fours like an animal and standing on their back legs seamlessly, using the ability to throw off each opponent's normal battle rhythm.

"That is one badass stone man-beast," Yona said aloud as we watched the match. Pixie growled at her comment almost immediately, and the surprised Yona looked back at her with an eyebrow raised in question.

"Pious is a giant, sentient, ancient creature with a wisdom and willpower that has outlived entire civilizations. The Sage, like the rest of us here to varying extents, aren't traditional human beings. So, what makes you think they're a man?" Sage Pixie's voice had grown increasingly hostile as she made her point, dropping to a deathly calm when she finished with a question.

"You're right, I'm sorry. What does the Sage prefer? Neutral pronouns?" Yona said in response, facing Pixie fully with a sincerity that I respected. She fluidly accepted her part in the situation and sought to learn how not to repeat it in one deft movement. This displayed more social grace than I'd ever shown in my entire life, and Pixie nodded approvingly.

"They/them, or just Pious. And to be honest, they're less caring about the matter. Very few can communicate directly with the Sage, so I've grown accustomed to pointing it out for them as if it were my own identity in question. Also, the main reason I help them run this class, yours truly here talks enough for two Sages," Pixie bragged humbly with a grin, already returned to her typically bubbly mood.

The thought that Pious couldn't verbally communicate with people on their own made me curious again with how autonomous the being really was. Turning back to the intense sparring match, I realized there was likely no substitute for the experience I could gain from directly going up against Pious.

"Do we all get to spar with Sage Pious in this class?" I asked hesitantly, and from Pixie's surprised face, I wondered if I'd come off seeming more eager than I meant. Yona cracked her knuckles and then slugged me in the shoulder.

"Exactly! Where do we sign up to throw down?" she asked with a devilish smile that I wished I couldn't help but return. It was hard to deny that I was itching to punch something. My anger felt too raw for sparring, though. Shying away from the feeling, I focused on Pixie's response instead.

"Pious or I will call you in personally for both group and individual sessions. Those three were chosen to spar at this point because of a mix of factors we were able to scout out ahead of the school year's start, not least of which was how developed their powers are and how well they've been integrated into unique fighting styles," Sage Pixie said in a placating manner. "Yona, as one of our shifters your training curriculum will differ a bit from Xavier's. You'll be over here with the others for now," she said, leading us over to where a small group was already huddled together. Pixie held me back with a hand and waved Yona forward, leaning in conspiratorially to whisper to me.

"Don't want to get too close, they're in for a hell of a day with that wild man in charge." I craned my neck to see but was pulled away while the students still obscured the unknown Sage from view.

"Why can't I train with them?" I asked ruefully as we left Yona with the other therianthropes. Pixie chuckled like I was a spoiled child begging for ice cream.

"That would be a waste of time… or maybe get someone killed. Take your pick," the wild Sage said in an offhanded way that still managed to convey sincerity. "So far, we've seen you fight at the club and in your duel with Kenneth. While impressive, there are a few concerns to address," she laid out, stopping our stroll through the crowd to face me directly. I felt distinctly uncomfortable as the capricious woman stared me down for several moments.

"What kind of concerns?" I asked hesitantly, feeling my apprehension swell up like a balloon in my chest. Before responding, her sharp gaze swept around us, seemingly assessing the passing students before responding.

"What would you have done if you could've killed Kenneth for real?" Pixie asked the question in a carefully neutral way. "What happens the next time you throw a punch that can shatter someone's skull?" She let the silence stretch until it was obvious I didn't have an answer. "Part of your studies here will focus on developing nonlethal options to dangerous situations. The best person to teach you how... is ironically the deadliest Sage we've got."

"You know I don't care for your flattery, Pixie," an exasperated voice called out from the trees behind us. "He must be a real mess if you've brought him to me this soon. Has the school year even started yet?" A tall and lithe figure strode towards us. We'd walked right past her, none the wiser. Long black hair in an intricate set of braids reached from her head to her hips, and she wore a sturdy-looking jerkin and matching pants.

"I knew you'd find us eventually," Pixie retorted amusedly with a smile. "This is Xavier, the punk who defaced the mountain. X, this is Sage Alpha, your personal tutor." I blinked in surprise while trying to process what was happening. Apparently, my competency had been found so inadequate that I required remedial lessons of some form. From the way the woman's eyes looked me over head to toe, she obviously found me lacking and made no effort to hide the fact.

"So we've got a killer on our hands? I've seen worse," the Sage said with a slight sneer. Pixie grinned widely at me with false cheer and patted my back.

"Well... that sounds promising. I'll pop off now and let you two get started. Don't die, Xavier!" she piped cheerily before teleporting away. There was an awkward silence after her departure that stretched until Alpha sighed resignedly and sank into a lotus position on the grass.

"Come on then," she said in way of invitation, patting the ground next to her. "Might as well get to know each other a bit before the work begins." The tension eased out of me as I joined her. An unfamiliar accent made the teacher's words seem clipped short in a way I was unaccustomed to.

"So, what are your particular gifts then?" she asked, casually pulling a concealed dagger out from her jerkin and cleaning her nails with it. I wondered if she was the only Sage not involved with admitting and testing Apprentices or if I'd run into more as the year went on.

"I can teleport and have extra durable skin, essentially. I've also got some magic, but my Flow isn't really under enough control to be useful," I explained bashfully, wilting a bit under Alpha's intense glare.

"Your skin doesn't look mutated. Well, except for... is that some kind of infection? We should murder whoever used a syphilitic tattoo needle on you." The Sage cocked her head to one side and gestured at the black veins she could see on my arms. I explained my tattoos and found myself having to take my shirt off for an inspection yet again, which was hopefully a trend that wouldn't last all year long.

"Not Enochian... touch of Druidic there, but maybe inspired from Mimir's Well here? Not quite African or Germanic OR Chinese here," Alpha muttered to herself as she took the sight in. "How far can you push these body enhancements? Does the one for Speed amplify enough to outpace your short-range teleportation?" The rapid-fire questions were mostly expected but took me a moment to respond. The last inquiry was one I'd never considered before, and I wondered the best way to test my different powers.

"I'm not really sure how to answer either of those questions. Never had the opportunity to test my upper limits back home. Mostly had to keep things under wraps," I explained with a wave at the dampeners on my wrists.

"On to your weaknesses then. You must learn your limits before overcoming them. I have no magic, but I can teach someone with your... condition well enough. Besides the curse and living with your powers in secret, is there anything else? Weakness to sliver? Iron? Peanut allergies?" she asked, in even faster succession than before.

I'd never heard anyone refer to the binding as a curse, but it made a certain sense, so I decided not to contradict her. Would that mean my biological parents cursed me? Or had I been such an ugly little ankle biter someone else did the deed? Realizing I'd gotten lost in thought I shook my head in the negative to her questions.

"Alright then, we'll discover more of them together. What kind of training do you seek?" The fact that she'd asked this last question was likely the most endearing thing she'd done since we'd met, so I tried to respond as honestly as possible.

"I want to be the best I can be with what I can do." My reply made me wince as soon as it came out of my mouth. I did not want to come off as a total cliche but had spouted off what was likely a line written in every self-help book on the market.

"I have to be strong enough to not just guarantee my personal safety and freedom. With all the help I've been given I should protect those who can't do what I can. Strong enough to avoid being anyone's plaything." The explanation came out in a jumble and still ended up feeling inadequate. Thankfully Alpha had been watching me like a hawk and appeared to see something she approved of.

"As a type of non-fey changeling, I think you'll need that drive. I am old, Xavier, older than almost any other I know of. There was a time no one would begrudge you for being either Conduit, Mutant, or both. Now you'll need to work harder than your peers to succeed. We will test your will and hone your might." She smiled, and I had the uneasy feeling I may have signed up for more than I bargained for.

Chapter Fifteen

A type of dual-faceted momentum built up as I leaned into my studies and life at Sage Mountain. With pure force of will I attempted to avoid the implications of my past by spending all my time pursuing potential fruits of the present. There was, of course, plenty of time to be spent on thinking about my family and what the word *family* meant. However, I much preferred spending time studying and training. The fact that it helped me put off fully dealing with my unresolved issues was only part of the reason I spent every waking moment doing so.

Whenever I wasn't in my room studying or enchanting, I was either in class or training with one of the Sages. Not at the top of our class but in good standing, measurable progress became my main focus. Towards what? That was still a bit uncertain. There weren't traditional grading systems in place, but I was still able to set goals and monitor my growth in other ways.

Each Sage seemed to be grooming me for a different path. Marequin suggested I make a living as an Enchanter, either independently or as part of a larger company. Without any real connections in the industry, I felt uncertain about making a career that way though. Besides that, there would be an ingrained bias against any half-mutant working in the magical industry.

Contrary to my pessimism about the future, I was currently making decent money by crafting magically enhanced items. My business-minded housemates were able to take things like fireproof clothing or pens that took notes for you and turn them into profit. They also seemed to be the campus suppliers for cigarettes, alcohol, and marijuana, but I wasn't part of that venture. Not because I thought it was immoral or anything; I just didn't have a way to contribute to their supply and distribution at the moment.

Justus kept trying to convince me to join his plans to work with the government. Apparently, they'd begun integrating Gifted People into their ranks, licensing them to use powers in an official capacity. At first, I thought he was joking. Not only because of the open discrimination policies the government imposed but also because of the job title. He assured me that U.F.O.'s, or Unidentified Field Operatives, were the real-life James Bond secret agents of the USA. The idea of being paid to fight terrorists or human traffickers appealed to me on a visceral level, but the potential to be misused as a pawn of some crooked politician seemed too great. If society only learned to accept those who were different because we are doing their dirty work, wouldn't it only make things worse for the Gifted in the long run?

Despite these reservations I did most of the training requirements prescribed by the Sages to help prepare for the career. A standard résumé wouldn't do much good, so we focused on developing different combat proficiencies, marksmanship skills, and even becoming familiar with modern laws surrounding the Gifted communities.

If given the choice, I found myself leaning between being either a Ley Line Guardian or a Sentinel. Yona had been the first to tell me about the former, and it was most likely what she'd end up doing after graduation. Like the vein of power that ran under the school, ley lines wove around much of the planet. On top of enhancing and generating magical energy, the cocktail of forces they held was a natural lure and food source for a myriad of entities. Left unchecked, an area of converging lines could be harnessed for negative intent or used as a weak point to tear a hole in reality. One answer to this vulnerability was the Order of the Guardians, tasked with traveling and protecting areas of concentrated power.

Yona was particularly interested in regions that overlapped with indigenous reservations and holy sites. With the waning of magic worldwide, it felt all the more important to her to protect these spaces. She had access to divination magic and rituals that I did not, so when she said big changes were coming, I believed her.

The job openings for Ley Guardians were few and far between, and while I worked alongside Yona to qualify, it seemed clear who in the class would be chosen. The people skills needed to help communities around the ley lines maintain equilibrium was one of many things that clearly eluded me. We'd run countless practice scenarios where different factions operated in the same area. It was often essential to build trust with the leaders of opposing sides, building up allies and tactfully handling enemies. I lacked the social awareness and charisma to skillfully navigate such encounters most of the time. Far too often, when I was in charge, tensions would spike, and all-out war would end the scenario. Conflicts on ley lines were dangerous because the open power source would fuel both sides and could cause a chain reaction that spread like wildfire to neighboring areas.

The Sentinels seemed like a more natural outlet for my skills. They were tied to the Mutant Underground I was familiar with through my adopted parents. I vaguely remembered that Anansi may have been a Sentinel at one time but had no way of checking. Bastions of the Mutant community, Sentinels came in both stationary and nomadic varieties, basically operating however would be most effective as they went. The agents were best known for protecting ousted Mutants and guarding people during relocation efforts.

Unlike with Ley Guardians, Sentinels were often targeted as high-value criminals for their work by the government. Since people with mutations were being targeted, it was commonplace that the job of helping them remain free was the most vilified of official positions. Trying to keep families out of cages and standing off against Purists on a regular basis fit more with my skillset than observing and manipulating local politics.

The only bit that made me balk was not knowing if my adoptive parents were still active in the Underground. I'd still had zero success in drawing a response out of the times I'd written home by now.

Pixie assured me there was always work to be had for a teleporter in the ranks, though, especially one that could fight. Since the end of the school year was still a ways away, I hadn't decided between the differing paths yet. The Sages coached us and helped us talk through plans, but their official assessments would be saved for the end of the year. More than one student had gotten in trouble trying to indirectly view the meticulous notes that were being kept on each Apprentice's progress.

※ ※ ※ ※ ※

"You could always come stay with my family over break," Yona offered, and to her credit, I knew it wasn't out of pity. We'd become much closer to friends than acquaintances as the months flew by since our arrival.

"No, I'll probably just enjoy having the run of the Mountain to myself. Thanks for the offer, though. Maybe over the summer I could visit?" I returned genially, genuinely meaning the last part at least.

"Still no response to your letters?" she asked tentatively, and the cringe that ran through me was more obvious than I would've liked.

Since the year started, I'd lost count of the letters and packages I'd sent to my adoptive parents. Pixie had assured me they'd each been delivered, and I'd done my best to not think about them since. I would need time to process, too, if I found out the teenager I was raising wasn't actually my son.

"Who's up next?" I asked, trying indelicately to change the subject.

The sparring class around us was buzzing with activity, mostly with people preparing to fight or jockeying for a better position to watch others fight. Sage Alpha had been adamant that I attend all of Sage Pious' classes despite not being allowed to participate yet. She had taught me many things, not least of which was how to learn from observing my opponents. The whole world was a sea of enemies in that particular Sage's mind, but their wealth of experience was invaluable.

"Justus is taking Ratri, have you met her yet?" Yona replied, deftly going with the shift in topic.

Including herself, there was only a small handful of friends that I'd discussed my family with, and luckily, they were pretty understanding. It wasn't uncommon among Gifted students to have family issues, especially if you were the first with Magic or a Mutation. Without knowing the memories they'd gotten back the night before I left, my mind could only run wild with scenarios about my parents. They'd said they still love me, no matter what, and I'd decided early on that that was all that mattered. Now I was just doing my best to not think about it most of the time.

"Ratri? Wasn't she a specialized Conduit?" I asked halfheartedly, trying to refocus on the upcoming bout.

I had a journal filled with notes about the strengths, weaknesses, and general information I'd gleaned about everyone in the class, but it wasn't something I was supposed to advertise. This fight would probably be one of the few I couldn't confidently predict the outcome to beforehand. Specialized Conduit was a term that had emerged as many magic users focused on one particular application of their Gift rather than trying to be a mediocre, all-around magic user.

"She's the one they're calling a Shadowmancer. I think odds are in her favor at least five-to-one. They haven't seen Justus fight in class since the two of you began sparring," she explained, her tone a bit sour at the end.

Sage Alpha had brought Justus in to offer a different opponent than herself and the other Sages for me to go up against. After absorbing her ability to heal, I'd found Justus an even match for my own skills almost every time. I waved over at Viz, who was making his way through the crowd merrily, taking bets from most of those gathered.

"What's up you two? Trying to place a bit of cash on the action?" he said, vibrant eyes constantly shifting hues as he studied the crowd around us.

It turned out Viz had little to no control over the shifting kaleidoscope of colors, but his mutation was well worth it. Viz's sight was better than any microscope, telescope, or other imaging tools currently possessed by humankind. On top of that, he could perceive frequencies and energy, both mundane and magical, in ways that were hard for anyone else to wrap their head around.

"How are the odds so far for the Boy Scout?" Yona asked with a smile, the use of Justus' nickname earning a small chuckle from the amateur bookie. The trend had started because Justus was the only one at the school concerned with underage drinking or the general boundaries of illegality for the Gifted.

"This is going to be brutal, eh? Right now, the crowd is favoring Ratri at straight nine-to-one odds. Everybody loves a bit of blood sport," he said mirthfully, eyes a mottled purple and emerald as he took the scene in.

I reached into a pocket and took out all the money I'd saved up from the last few months of work. It wasn't much in the way of straight cash, but I had a few hefty gemstones and other baubles that were also an accepted currency around these parts.

"Put it all on Justus to win," I said confidently, enjoying the way the Apprentice's orbs bulged in surprise. Yona looked at me questioningly, and when I didn't respond, she hesitantly drew out a few crisp green bills.

"Might as well, then," she declared, scrutinizing my poker face one last time before Viz began to recover. Hiding his shock wasn't easy, but he quickly stashed the small fortune in a coat pocket before marking down our bets and moving on.

"You know Justus hasn't fought in Sage Pious' class in the past month, right? The last match he was in, he ended up needing weeks with the healers," Yona pushed, never having seen me place a bet before.

"What does everyone think he's been doing with the time?" I asked evasively, grinning as Justus came into view.

The area was set up so that a waist-high fence of sturdy wood outlined the actual sparring space. It was a 30 x 30-yard enclosure of meticulously manicured grass, nurtured by a mix of blood, sweat, and magics. Without pretense or arrogance, my friend entered the center of the enclosure to an indifferent crowd, beginning a basic warm-up routine familiar to all from basic lessons over the year.

Unknown to the rest of the class, after his last defeat Justus had done brief but intense training with Sage Alpha and me. With his ability to leech her healing powers, he'd not only recovered on the same day he was injured but had also been subjected to extended training sessions with the Sage and myself. The regeneration rate he could gain from Alpha meant that he could recover from any overly powered blow I could dish out.

My hand-to-hand fighting proficiency had almost doubled during our time together, as he had totally different instincts than Sage Alpha. Honestly, the most brutal part of our time working together had been when we fought not each other, but Sage Alpha as a team. There was no discounting how valuable the experience against such a seasoned opponent was, but there was also no discounting her brutality.

"Since he wasn't fighting with us, everyone's assumed he was still on the mend... maybe in remedial lessons? Everyone knows how his power works, so it's pretty easy to tell when the matchup isn't in his favor," she explained, and my smile widened wolfishly, knowing Yona probably undersold how weak everyone thought our friend was. Justus had asked me to not share about our joint training before today. He was far too morally upright to bet on himself, or gamble at all honestly, but I knew he had plenty of motivation to prove himself in the ring today.

"I think you'll be glad you bet on him, Yona. That's all I'm going to say," I spoke, while locking my focus onto the appearance of the Shadowmancer.

Ratri was using part of her Flow to darken her aura as she entered the sunny clearing, lazy umbral whips floating ominously around her like octopus tentacles. In contrast to Justus' plain white clothing and tactical gear that protected knees, elbows, and head, Ratri wore a gorgeous crimson and black silk saree wrapped around her frame. I'd always found the form of dress elegant, but she seemed lithely ready to strike as she took a stand across from her opponent.

"You know I hate that nickname, Changeling," Yona said with a playful punch to my arm, using my least favorite moniker in turn. Even with my mutated fortitude I hissed at the sting of the blow. She didn't need to shift into a bear to display superhuman strength after all.

"I hope you're right though. At nine-to-one odds, my twenty bucks would be...." She trailed off, doing math in her head. "That can't be right," she said with a questioning glance at me.

I only smiled and turned on my magical Sight as the thrill of the gamble amped up a few notches. I wasn't much for gambling or the lottery, but I noticed that most of the time the odds were fairly predictable around the class's schedule.

"This is the only time we'll be able to get odds like this. Need to make the most of it," I assured her, nodding at where Viz stood taking a small mob's worth of money, eager to bet on Ratri.

After hearing Yona's assumption of events, I relaxed, assuring they'd have enough money from the losers to dish out my winnings in the end. Justus' mutant Gift wasn't the easiest to adjust to and turn into a strength, but I had faith that he was up to the task. Sage Pious came flying down from the skyline and landed with a ground-shaking thump between the two competitors, the glow of magic about her compensating for the lazy way her sculpted wings flapped like moving through molasses.

"Don't die Boy Scout!" someone called from the crowd, and Pixie appeared with a gentle pop of air displacement next to Pious as laughter rippled through the crowd. Ignoring the taunt, the match proceeded undisturbed.

"Today, Apprentices Justus and Ratri will go head-to-head. This is one of the last sessions before the Battle Royale, so anyone caught not trying to learn and observe will see their actions reflected in their final grade," Pixie warned, making eye contact with all of those in the circle before teleporting out.

Every match began more or less the same in this class, and both Apprentices walked to the opposite corners of the sparring space in anticipation. Studying each party with unyieldingly stoney eyes, Pious lifted their hand and began to count down with three outstretched fingers. Justus tossed his glasses to the ground, and I felt a swell of pride in my friend.

The moment Pious' count reached zero, three things happened all at once. Unsurprisingly, Pious quickly backed far enough away to referee but not impede the battle. Ratika's aura seemed to swell with power, and the umbral presence around her sharpened and grew with malevolent intent. Finally, Justus began shuffling backwards in a slow jog while staring down his opponent with an infuriating smile. I shared his smile discreetly as people around us booed at what seemed to be an act of cowardice to pull away from the fight. Soon, he was dodging limbs of shadow every other step, an immeasurable rhythm to his movements as tentacles lurched out from the ground. The so-called Shadowmancer stared him down boldly like a cat playing with their hard-earned mouse.

"Did you make him some of your equipment?" Yona ventured, watching my continued cheeriness as Justus was tripped up by the umbral attacks launching from his own shadow.

He had easily taken half a dozen glancing blows by now despite avoiding all the truly devastating strikes. I was wearing a heavily worked set of leather armor under my street clothes and Yona knew I had made items that had swayed the outcome of several fights among our peers. The armor I'd made for myself had changed a lot over the past few months, updated whenever I wasn't drowning in work on other people's items.

I had made a lot of progress in my enchanting but found I needed to specially cultivate a lot of the components I needed to create the kind of effects I wanted. I could make a shirt fire-resistant in my sleep now, but for something like a set of armor that would change to fit both human and animal forms? I had a lot to learn to truly overcome the gaps in my knowledge. Not only had I begun delving into blacksmithing, but also into tailoring, tanning, and general cultivation of source materials used in my crafting products.

"Don't worry, you're still first in line for my custom orders," I reassured her, never taking my eyes off the fight.

Now that the first few minutes had passed, Justus had gone from evasive to less conservative defense. No longer invested in keeping his opponent at a distance, he danced closer, not initiating any attacks but following up blocked blows with precise counterattacks. Normally, absorbing this many hits would have left an enemy on their last leg and one good thump away from crumpling. If I hadn't trained with him recently, I never would've noticed the myriad cuts and bruises that had healed visibly on Justus' body as he soaked up the blows.

As the blood and body armor still covered most of him, the first thing visibly evident to the crowd was how quickly Ratika seemed to be losing her stamina to continue. Practically bouncing with energy, Justus began to close the last stretch of distance between him and his opponent, her aura seeming to lighten visibly as it shrank inward. Justus' ability to leech power and vitality from other Gifted took time to kick in, but he'd bought plenty of that while letting his opponent attack.

The light beating that the Shadowmancer had just doled out paled in comparison to the tempering Sage Alpha had conducted. While Justus could "borrow" the Sage's healing mutation, and one of my tattoos helped facilitate my own recovery, she had often merrily declared that it was only logical to try and break us. In the few weeks Justus had joined Alpha's and my private sessions, we'd gone through a cornucopia of tortures to strengthen the body and mind. Something Sage Alpha had decided early on was that my nearly unbreakable skin was inhibiting my fighting reflexes, and, unfortunately for me, she knew many ways to make the mutation essentially negligible. Alongside Justus, I'd been burnt, frozen, and even electrocuted to build a pain tolerance. We'd spent hours together, healing our shivering and shaking selves as watchful eyes pushed us to recover faster. Worse than that were the torture racks, specialized hammers, nails, and mallets Sage Alpha had used to shatter bones, tear muscles, and inflict general internal trauma.

"You've got to be kidding me. He wouldn't have lasted ten seconds against her at the start of the year," I heard someone call out, knocking me out of the unpleasant memories.

Rather than contending with her shadow tentacles, Justus was now engaging the Shadowmancer directly in hand-to-hand combat. Though they seemed to be an even match at first, I knew she had already lost the fight. With a punch that fell short of its mark and a missed block or two, the witch began taking heavy blows to the head and body from her unwavering opponent. As the fight seemed to be sucked out of her, the shadows seemed to grow restless at Justus' feet and climb to wrap about his shoulders and fists.

"With how much he's improved, Justus could probably go toe-to-toe with any of us now," Yona said, a touch of admiration in her voice. She wasn't an easily impressed person, and her praise elicited another touch of pride in our friend's progress. The memories of getting our asses beaten side by side as we fought Sage Alpha seemed almost worth it now.

As Justus moved in to finish the match, I couldn't help but assess and critique his technique, vastly different from my own. The evasive maneuvers, soaking up damage like a punching bag, and every facet of Justus' fighting style was meant for this exact outcome. Keep the opponent confident, keep them throwing out attacks, but above all: keep their eyes on the target. This fight had been over in my mind once I saw how Ratri stared down her opponent loathingly. Given enough time, Justus could drain the power out of almost anyone.

In the last match the class had seen, he had gotten pounded into the dirt because he tried to rush things. All the martial arts training he'd done up to then may have helped him compete with other's inherent Gifts, but the simple fact was that superhuman powers outweighed such skills. Therefore, Justus had dedicated himself to pursuing the best of both worlds, evolving his fighting style to complement his mutant Gift. Buying time and keeping a foe busy gave him enough time to look into their eyes and make their power his own. I barely needed to watch the rest of the match. In the blink of an eye, the Shadowmancer lay unconscious in the center of the ring while a victorious Apprentice stood calmly looking down at her.

A chorus of cheers and outrage rang out as Sage Pious walked into the ring, lifting Justus' fist in acknowledgement of triumph for the crowd. The most vehement outcry was clearly from those in the crowd who'd just lost all their money.

I wondered how Viz, Mal, and the boys had bet, but the only safe gamble was knowing the House always wins so I was sure they'd be fine.

Yona and I waited patiently as both Freq and Viz made their way through the spectators, the duo fastidiously collecting debts and consoling other Apprentices. Without being an expert on how probabilities and betting worked, I knew that Yona and I were likely the only people out of nearly one hundred students to have chanced the long-shot odds.

"What are you going to do with all your money? I might save mine until I can blow it all over the holiday," Yona said, speculating animatedly with her back against the fence as people dispersed. A grin split my face as I considered my options.

"I'm going to bet it all, just one more time." As I said it, I couldn't help but feel joy at the shocked expression the statement yielded. Of course, that was also the moment that Freq and Viz finally decided to join us.

Where Freq and Yona were in average street clothes, both Viz and I wore what we'd taken to calling our "Sunday Best" or battle-ready gear. For Viz this meant sparse skintight straps of clothing that only needed to meet two requirements. Firstly, they were all non-reflective material, so as to not interfere with how the mutant bent light while invisible. The second condition, and more important fact if you asked him, was that each strap concealed knives. Lots and lots of knives.

In contrast, my garb covered head to toe if I had my hood up. Since there wasn't any armor plating available stronger than my own skin, the outfit supported me in other ways. Elbows, knees, and feet were weaponized rather than reinforced, and enchantments I'd hand-carved into the metal plates over vital areas could produce a variety of nasty surprises for my enemies. My brass knuckles had evolved to the point of nearly being gauntlets, the weave of cloth, metal fibers, and gemstones woven from knuckle to elbow.

Instead of throwing knives, I had a set of razor-sharpened metal bands called chakrams adorning each forearm that I'd grown proficient with using for a distance weapon. Anyone else attempting to use them would find themselves bloodied as the projectiles were honed to the point that only someone mutated like myself could safely handle them. On top of that, the circular shape lent itself easily to enchantments compared to average darts or kunai. People who worked with magical tailoring materials were more prevalent than general enchanters, so I'd found a simple hoodie that let me fight off the humid evening air by feeding a bit of Current into the garment.

"Y'know you really could have given us a heads-up, man," Viz said with a half-hearted scowl in my direction. I put on my best innocent face, which I knew for a fact wasn't very convincing.

"A heads-up? What about? I find it appalling that you didn't have full faith in our friend," I said happily, earning a rude hand gesture from the malcontent mutant.

"You're lucky I like you, and Justus isn't my friend. At best the Boy Scout is now an expensive acquaintance," Viz said with a mock solemnity, discreetly looking about to check for eavesdroppers.

"Don't get too riled up, buddy. Xavier is obviously itching to bet all this plunder he just won on something that will put it right back into our pockets. What's your poison? More fights? Maybe some sports? There's another few astral races and a shapeshifting competition coming up as well," Freq said after giving Yona a quick hug in greeting.

"He's got another sure bet in his back pocket. At least he seems to think so," Yona interjected. "Are you two forgetting something?" the young witch said, smiling and holding a hand out in expectation.

"Kids these days, no patience," Viz said to me, grimacing as he pulled out a wad of bills and briefly disappearing from sight to count out her winnings. "No such thing as a sure bet," his disembodied voice grumbled cynically. "A month of training against one of the class's top students under the tutelage of the most savage Sage there is. That's how you got these odds. The fact that Justus's too righteous to brag or bet definitely helped," Viz explained matter of factly, reappearing to hand Yona a nice stack of neatly folded bills.

"Not that Viz is being a sore loser," Freq said with an easy smile, earning a chuckle from everyone present, including Viz.

"Justus really threw himself into the work. It was only last minute that I realized nobody else would know about the progress he'd made," I admitted easily, wondering how Viz had figured things out so quickly.

"I always found it odd that Alpha made you come to every class but not participate. Nobody even really knows what kind of teacher she is besides you two," Freq added, taking out a small notebook and making quick notes as he spoke.

"She doesn't have a distinct teaching style like the other Sages," I explained with a slight grimace. "She attacks, and you just get better at surviving it." A shrug was my only addendum as my statement drew more curious stares.

"Never mind, you might see for yourselves later. Anyway, I'm the sure bet. Once Viz gets around to visiting that invisible piggy bank of his, I'm putting it all on myself for first place in the Battle Royale," I revealed grandly, only to realize quickly the grandiose flavor of the reveal had fallen flat. Searching from face to face I found only Yona willing and able to meet my eyes.

"I'll be betting mine on myself to win too. No way I'm letting you show me up," she said with a fiercely competitive glint in her eyes.

"We've been meaning to talk to you about the whole Battle Royale, or whatever they're calling it," Viz said uncomfortably, glancing between the others for support. "Sure you wanna dance with this particular Devil?" he asked evenly, picking at his nails with a knife rather than meet my gaze, and before I could answer, Freq rushed to elaborate.

"Everybody knows that you're a badass, despite not seeing you show off since the start of the year," Freq began, pausing significantly to search for a particular way to word the sentiment.

"You've got more people teaming up to crush you than anybody else. The amount some of the Conduits have thrown out to put people on your tail could probably birth a small nation," Viz interrupted enthusiastically, all in one long breath like he'd been waiting to let it out.

"That's really tactful, buddy. Seriously though X, I've got an entire bracket of people and teams that are as focused on who takes you out as they are on who wins," Freq explained, to my surprise.

"K.K.Kenneth and Ophelia haven't forgotten how you crushed them at the start of the year," Yona added thoughtfully, processing the news next to me. To my surprise, she seemed more amused than concerned about the news.

"They haven't forgotten the fact that you're still getting private lessons and are the Champion of both sides of the Gifted as well," Viz interjected almost cheerily, flipping one of his daggers high into the air and catching it repeatedly.

"Being the undefeated Champ would be enough of a spectacle by itself. Add in your wealthy enemies and the fact nobody really knows how you've progressed...." Freq let the statement hang in the air poignantly.

"I was expecting to get targeted, but not like this," I admitted finally, quelling the overwhelmed sensation trying to flood my mind. "It doesn't change much in the end," I said, trying to project a calm reservedness that I didn't feel.

"I appreciate the heads-up guys, honestly, but if I'm late to my next class, Alpha might kill me," I lied nonchalantly and teleported away. I didn't have any other classes planned, but apparently, there were preparations I needed to make.

Chapter Sixteen

It was easy to forget that nearly fifty students other than myself and my friend lived on the Mountain. Between varied class schedules, private lessons, spread-out housing, and never being invited to any big parties, I had all but forgotten the size of the class overall. I'd made sure to study those at the top of the pile, but that was a rather narrow perspective in hindsight.

A jittery current of nervousness was all but palpable in the air as the congregated contestants habitually checked weapons, armor, and various spell components on their person. I noticed more than a few items crafted by my own hands sprinkled amongst the crowd and felt a fleeting tinge of pride in my craftsmanship. If I'd had the foresight to make some of the more dangerous items incapable of acting against their creator, I'd be much more confident about the upcoming free-for-all.

"Ok, whelps, gather around! Any minute now the field will be charged up and ready for action. Who's ready to bust some skulls?" Pixie riled the crowd up with genuine excitement shining in her eyes.

Cheers and raucous laughter answered her as the throngs paced at the edge of what would soon be our own personal killing field. An opaque wall of power stretched for miles in front of us, forming a barrier around the battleground. Akin to my duel with Kenneth, but on a wildly larger scale, a portion of the verdant lands was being magically altered so students could go head-to-head without causing massive casualties. I couldn't fully wrap my head around the Druidic magic that Sage Atticus was using, but he'd assured me that even I couldn't break it. Apparently crossing the barrier would not only let us into the no-death zone but also randomly distribute Apprentices so that we didn't begin the brawl in one consolidated lump.

"Dead man walking!" cried an unfamiliar voice hidden in the crowd behind me. A lot of people laughed at the jab, but I was more worried by the silently hungry glances that many quieter groups cast my way.

For maybe the hundredth time, I scanned the crowd, though not for enemies as most people probably assumed. On the far edge of the crowd I spotted Yona and Mal along with a handful of other familiar faces. Each person was equipped with a black backpack on their person in addition to whatever other gear they'd equipped. It had been a pleasant surprise to have a handful of classmates reach out and offer secret alliances to me, even knowing the forces arranged against me.

The idea of ruining their chances to better my own wasn't something I could easily stomach, though, so instead, I'd made separate goodie bags for everyone who'd been willing, and purposefully made sure no one entered the fray alongside me. There was no way of telling exactly who had joined the coordinated effort to take me out of the running and who was simply sizing me up as a prospective opponent. The preemptive thrill of battle nerves gripped me by the spine as a flare went up in the distance.

"*Thirty seconds!!!* We'll be watching and judging every move you make! Make us proud," Pixie said with uncharacteristic gravitas to her words.

The crowd surged around me as people pushed forward to enter the Battle Royale. I let them pass in favor of doing an in-depth check of my own backpack and gear. There wasn't much enchanted armor I could make that offered more protection than my naturally mutated skin, so I'd decided to travel as light as possible. With a mob of enemies set on taking me out, mobility was key.

My shoes were spelled for silent movement, the hoodie I sported would help me fade into foliage at will, and both arms sported sharpened metal circles called chakrams stacked like raver bracelets from wrist to elbow. The deadly projectiles were each a powerful attack that only I could use, sharpened on the inside and outside so that anyone attempting to wield them against me would likely lose a finger. A few other surprises waited in the black backpack strapped snugly to my form, but I didn't want anyone seeing them until it was too late.

"Go! Go! Go!" voices cheered all around as students rushed forward to disappear into the barrier.

I moved forward slowly and deliberately, not wanting to be caught up in the initial chaos of people dropping into the competition. Pulling my hood up, I could feel the gentle tingle of the camouflage spell washing over me as I walked through the barrier. Crossing the barrier itself surprisingly felt like nothing at all, but the contrasting environment was shock enough. It had become a blazingly hot summer day without a cloud in the sky between one step and the next. A string of curses escaped my mouth as I realized I hadn't been dropped into this part of the forest alone.

"Looks like today is our lucky day, boys," a nasally voice called out merrily from the trio in front of me.

I recognized the speaker as an Illusionist who'd made sure to laugh at my expense in every class we'd ever shared. Specializing in deceptive spells and abilities, I'd always assumed he made a show of belittling me because of his own insecurities at being able to conduct strong offensive attacks.

"Or our unlucky day, depending on the perspective," said the first boy's friend, standing at the Illusionist's side with an apprehensive look on his face. Taller and more muscular than his friend, I recognized the voice as Moe's, a reserved Conduit I also shared several classes with.

"Oh, come off it, you do what he can do… only better," said the final member of the trio, his curly hair framing his face of sharp angles that glared at me with contempt.

The comment confused me at first, but then memories of Moe showing off in class came to mind. The Apprentice had always been one of the top performers when it came to throwing offensive hexes and delivering explosive results with his magic. I'd thought more than once that I would happily trade powers with him in a heartbeat, though it was a wish that crossed my mind quite often about other students.

"Either way, boys, it's time to earn that reward" commanded the initial speaker, who I decided to refer to as Larry in my head.

Part of me was thankful to only be facing Larry, Moe, and Curly, while the other half of me was annoyed to start off against a unified trio of magic users right away. As the thought of running away crossed my mind, each member of the trio began casting magic in tandem. While they were still forming the magic with hand gestures and muttered incantations, I ran for cover. Unlike many modern fantasy conventions spouted, hitting a target that you couldn't see with your eyes wasn't impossible. Rifling through memories of Larry and Curly, I knew they were respectively an Illusionist and Warding Specialist, so running head-on at them would likely be the least effective strategy I could use.

The battlefield had no mercy for my introspective pondering. There was no way of truly knowing, but at least two out of the three offensive spells hit their mark, and I was tossed like a rag doll into the air before landing hard against the nearest tree. My aching shoulder confirmed Moe's aim had struck true with a pure, concentrated blast of kinetic magic. As one of Sage Solomon's star pupils, I'd seen the blossoming Battle Mage build and perfect quite a few different spells into his arsenal.

I knew Moe found fireballs and other elementally based attacks trivial and preferred to concentrate his raw Flow into destructive blasts. Early on, people had begun to compare his abilities to my own mountain-breaking entrance to the school, so I wasn't surprised he would take today as an opportunity to prove himself the superior mage. I had seen him reduce boulders to pebbles with the attack. Thankfully, I was a bit tougher than the average stone.

The second attack from the trio caught me in the small of my back, barely registering as painful. I hadn't done much spell slinging in class still because of my lack of control, but I knew how to take a hit. Gravity was kind enough to help extricate me from the decimated tree trunk, and I used the awkward moment to teleport behind some foliage just thick enough to block the sight of my falling body. A trio of curses and the sound of more spells hitting where I'd lay seconds ago made me smile. They'd caught me by surprise but hadn't done any real damage while they held the advantage.

Peeking through the shrubbery, I could see they remained clumped together, shoulder to shoulder in their formation, each one sweeping the area for any sign of where I'd gone. My teleportation skills were almost laughable compared to Pixie's, but my ability to cross short distances was perfect for enclosed encounters like this. After studying my surroundings a bit longer, I found a tree limb that stretched almost directly above the trio. With a gentle push of willpower, I found myself looking downward at my opponents, and the branch held my weight as I had hoped.

A diabolical grin stretched across my face as I pulled out my backpack, careful not to make a sound. The first surprise I'd built was completely untested but was guaranteed to be entertaining, if not effective. Nostalgia of walking barefoot in a verdant backyard garden swelled up in my chest as I pulled the first lawn ornament out from the sack's depths.

"Today we go to war," I whispered into a tiny porcelain ear that stuck out from a pointy red cap. A pair of painted blue eyes blinked up at me as the enchanted figure activated.

Immediately taking stock of its surroundings, the foot-tall figure gave me a salute and wordlessly awaited instructions. I handed him a small gun and whispered a set of simplified instructions. I'd realized early on the simplistic golems I could animate were extremely limited when it came to following instructions and learning skill sets.

Teleporting in quick succession, I went in a wide circle around my three opponents in less than a minute, most of which they spent trying to find me through magical means. If I hadn't spent half the year being attacked by people using magical and mutated methods to surprise me, their efforts would probably have yielded exactly the answers they wanted, and I would've been hit with their combined spell craft half a dozen times. Knowing there was a price on my head had convinced me to use every countermeasure I'd ever cooked up this year, layered on top of each other, though.

My shoes had been enchanted with a set of runes, and silver filings worked into the soles helped obscure my presence from divination while leaving no trace when they were empowered. The hoodie on my back had been treated to so many levels of enchantment it was almost disorienting to study the miasma of runes and energy tied into the fabric directly. I'd recently found a dealer of rare and unusual animal resources and found a way to neutralize my scent trail and dampen my distinctive aura. It wasn't enough to fully mask me from a determined Conduit for long, but I was willing to cobble every advantage available to me together.

"Come out you coward!" cried Moe in frustration, taking his emotions out on several nearby trees by either lighting them on fire or exploding large chunks out of the forest around him.

I cursed as one of his tantrums randomly managed to hit a tree I'd left one of my gnomes in. I'd stalled for as long as I could get away with. I carefully dumped the rest of the bagged soldiers and reached out to teleport about thirty feet from where the trio stood defensively.

"Who just randomly blows up trees? Do you need a hug or something, Moe?" I said, doing my best to come off as sincere.

For the briefest moment there was a slack-jawed look on all three of the arcane assassins' faces at my sudden appearance and bizarre declaration. I used the moment to trigger a spell that echoed around the forest from all sides. Their surprise bought me enough time to finish an activation spell before I was hit by the first of three attacks that came when they reacted. This time I was a bit ahead of each strike, able to lean into the blow so that each could be shrugged off for the most part. None of them were strong enough to knock me through a tree again unless I couldn't see the hit coming. Sage Alpha had pushed me hard enough that the two fireballs and cone of ice that came my way were no more than jabs that I could absorb easily.

While soaking up magical damage and drawing the attention of the Conduits, my plan went into action all around us. Red hats no higher than my knee and much of the high grasses spread about the woods began to swarm towards us from all angles, pumping their little legs for all that they were worth. I made a point to move towards the encroaching force at a slow retreating jog, feeling bruises form under my skin as I took repeated hits from the spell slingers. My epidermal mutation didn't make me immune to magic, but I was almost as durable against most magical attacks as I found myself resisting physical ones. A surprised yelp came from Larry, not a pained sound but disturbed all the same. A mix between a tiny war cry / cheer of joy rang out from the two dozen or so animated garden gnomes as triggers were pulled with reckless abandon, exactly as I'd instructed.

Nearly invisible walls sprung up around the trio as Curly began using his magical specialty. The glowing liquid from the gnome army's squirt guns was already splashed on Larry and Moe, but Curly could create shields in midair with such ease that he was never struck. Feeling the effects of the prepared serum, Larry and Moe also attempted to bring their talents to bear on the current conflict. Larry shimmered with gathered Flow until unsteady doubles of each member of the threesome began running in random directions.

Normally, as I'd witnessed before from others in our class, the illusory characters would be indistinguishable from the original subject. Right now, the inebriated stumbling forms were clearly not the fabricated constructs as Larry drunkenly tried to hold onto the spell. I knew the ruse wouldn't be sustainable as the gnome army's squirt guns soaked through cloth and skin, moving straight into the bloodstream. I'd developed the recipe as a birthday brandy at first, then weaponized it later when it had been a riotous success. Moe made a show of causing several sloppy emerald explosions that ended maybe half a dozen of the approaching statuettes. Curly was the most competent of the group left, making multiple opaque barriers that blocked most of the aggressive little things from coming closer.

I silently thanked whatever gnomes had drenched the Illusionist in the aptly named "drunk juice" as I ignored the stumbling twins of my enemies. Becoming drunk didn't make a magic user incapable of casting or weaving spells, but it affected one's concentration and wreaked havoc on the brain's higher functioning. Hence, if the Illusionist is suddenly inebriated, his illusions came out reflecting his mental state. Unfortunately for me, Moe's destructive powers weren't as complicated as weaving Illusions, so besides making his aim go to shit, the arcane demolitionist was largely unaffected. I wondered briefly if he had some kind of heavy drinking problem as I channeled power into my Strength tattoo.

Earning the attention of both the trio of Conduits and their illusory doubles, I ran straight ahead towards Curly. Throwing myself forward with Flow-enhanced momentum, I busted through wall after wall of barely visible magic. The jarring impacts shaking my body were the only evidence of my struggle. The closer I got, the thicker and more specialized the obstacles became. Some obstacles felt like punching lava that stuck to my skin, and others numbed the body parts they came in contact with completely. By the time I had made it within ten feet of the trio, Larry was staring drunkenly off into space, likely trying to stop seeing the world in doubles as he swayed nauseously. Moe turned his attention to me, going shoulder to shoulder with Curly to face me down.

Moe could manifest magic Current and excite it to the point of instability and combustion. People liked to compare the two of us, and though it was mostly out of ignorance, I knew that it was a type of stain on his otherwise respectable reputation. If I was capable of such fine control I wouldn't have burned a hole in the mountain. A rueful voice in my head pointed out I wouldn't have to close in on enemies like I was currently doing now to attack if I had that control. Curly was drenched in sweat as I punched my way through the last barrier of solidified air and magic between myself and the trio. I pulled two of the razor-sharp chakrams from around my forearms and faked a sprint straight ahead at the last two who were still coherent.

A rebellious cry turned into a wet gurgle as I grabbed Curly's hair, pulled back, and efficiently slit his throat from behind. Having teleported right behind him while he was preparing for my frontal assault was a gamble, but it had paid off. Without the shielding provided by Curly, I knew the others would fall much easier than if I tried to pick them off with him controlling the battlefield.

As his simulated body began to fade to nothing, I took an explosive gut punch from Moe, who'd been standing next to the now vanquished Conduit. I heard Sage Alpha's admonishing voice in my head: if I hadn't just stood there fascinated by the body's disappearance, his friend would never have had enough time to get a hit in. I slid back at least five or ten feet while doubled over from the opportunistic blow, feeling at least one rib bone fracture after the wind was knocked out of me. A grunt of pain escaped my lips as I rerouted the Flow of magic to my Healing tattoo rather than the one for Strength, a cold itch birthing where I figured the internal damage was worst, and magic began putting me back together again.

By the time I got to my feet both Larry and Moe had been massacred by the garden gnomes that had only been restrained by Curly's barriers prior to now. Larry lay in the fetal position, having tossed his lunch on the ground while I faced the remaining opponents. I felt a mixture of sympathy and joy as the gleeful gnomes ran circles around the downed men, who thankfully couldn't die of an alcohol overdose through the simulation.

One of the magically sharpened chakrams took Larry out of the competition with a flick of my wrist and a quiet gurgling death rattle. Part of me wondered if a drunken memory of death by neck slashing was one of the more merciful options available today or worse. I was consoled by the idea that I probably would be served a much worse fate if I let anyone else here have a hand in how my overall day ended. Knowing the disc would return later on its own due to the enchantments, I moved to Moe with more confidence than I'd started the battle with. The guy was definitely intoxicated, using the last of his willpower to swat lazily at garden gnomes and remain upright to glare at me.

"Y'know.... shml enonlee ford gol... golddd," he said, with all the eloquence of the town drunk three days into a bender. Before I ended his life with another flick of the chakram ready in my hand, he managed a coherent statement.

"Y'know, we alls only came after ye for the gold. So much gold...." Moe went silent before I tossed the last disk of death into his larynx, then, unfortunately, had to go in and rip it out by hand.

With my mutation I could handle severely sharp items without worry of injury, so I'd altered the traditional rings of metal lining my arms. There were silent gurgles of agony as Moe attempted to instinctively grip the metal sticking out of his neck, only to cleanly sever the grasping fingers from his hand. I wasn't especially proficient with a bow or ranged spells so the throwable discs had quickly become my weapon of choice today.

With all three enemies down, I sent the gnomes out to cause as much mass mayhem as possible. By intoxicating and pranking as many students as possible they would help create the maximum amount of chaos possible. That essential element would make it easier for me to hide because it was inevitable that someone would look over whatever part of the forest I sought refuge in.

Chapter Seventeen

My small army of troublemakers leaving obvious trails from my first fight was enough to make my series of delicately aimed teleports almost untraceable. Activating the enchantments I carried with a bit of extra juice helped me martial my courage as I stuck to the midlevel canopy of the battleground, watching for any sign of the other Adepts in the competition.

The aftermath of people with powers fighting was distinctly different from other violent scenes, like a shootout or bank robbery. A crime scene struck by magic or mutation often stood out quite noticeably to anyone with experience outside the normal ranges of illegal acts. I felt grateful that I'd only landed with Larry, Moe, and Curly to fight against as I passed fields of carnage where dozens of students had clashed en masse. The landscape became a patchwork of different environments as I traveled further out, surprising me with everything from forests, tribal villages, modern city blocks, and more.

I reached an impromptu perch that seemed to rest at the far Eastern border of the battlefield. Despite the fact that bodies disappeared in this reality construct, plenty of signs of blood and violence stained the area. To my surprise, a mage about my age was focused on trying to heal his leg while an ally in plate armor stood guard. It seemed unlikely the pale blond Conduit would be able to fix the mangled mess his leg had become from the knee down. With my hood up I tried to suppress my magic signature by focusing on my dampeners, and in less than a minute, I felt confident I wouldn't project my presence to everyone nearby with a drop of magic.

"The contract said I only had to stay with you until your participation in the battle concludes," the hulking figure said without bothering to look directly at his maimed accomplice. "Are you really going to say that you're still participating by sitting there bleeding out?" His voice grew cold as he posed the question, and the already pale face looking up at him blanched further.

Without waiting for an answer, he began marching away from the dumbstruck Conduit who'd probably just wasted a small fortune based on the loophole in their magical contract. To my luck, the tank of a man ran directly under me in his heavy armored shuffle to abandon his ex-employer. I decided to literally drop myself on him, as I could shake off the near forty-foot drop easier than he could handle getting hit with it... hopefully.

With a mental effort, my suppressed magic rerouted into the rune script for Healing, and I curled up into a ball as the wind whipped around me. When I landed on the unsuspecting warrior, an overwhelming series of crunches and snaps filled my ears with a horrid mix of breaking bones and rending metals. I rolled off from the initial point of impact and felt a collection of painful tearing and rupturing of internal organs and connective tissues.

The cold itch of healing magic within my innards emboldened me to the point I could steadily get to my feet, whereupon I took my time studying my pancaked victim. My skin was so much harder than his plates of armor had been that I'd shattered them on impact and pushed the broken pieces to penetrate the treacherous guard. With little effort I went back and killed off the injured mage with a deftly thrown chakram to the neck. He was still struggling to piece himself back together and hadn't even noticed his approaching death.

Hoping to avoid the larger confrontations, I stayed on the move from then on. The few rare occurrences I would come across others, I would take enemies out, run tactics, or just hide until they passed. To my dismay, most people were fighting in predetermined units by now, and most were united by one thing. Unfortunately, that one thing happened to be me. Or, more specifically, my destruction. I'd be rich if I got a dollar every time I heard someone mention the price on my head. Many of the groups had been paid in advance for their participation in hunting me.

This motivated me some but, to my pleasure, it also had the effect of making people viciously mock Kenneth's desperation. In his hurry to build an army against me he'd spent resources on a large group of people that were only vaguely motivated to do more than keep an eye out for me. The next few hours passed with me taking lone figures out of the competition in quick and quiet moves. Regrettably, the upper canopy I had begun to favor while teleporting through the forest left me exposed to people at the same altitude or higher.

"There he is!" cried an excited voice from above me.

I groaned in dismay and turned to see a girl in a purple leotard pointing at me while floating casually in midair. She was only half paying attention to me as her arms waved wildly to what was sure to be the rest of her team. Not wanting to stick around and find out, I teleported to ground level and threw myself into an all-out sprint. Pouring on speed by channeling magic into my tattoo, I was sure I could lose the airborne enemy that had found my perch.

After spending most of the year working in a similar environment to the one we were in now, I knew how to weave in and out of the foliage and shake off a pursuer better than most of my classmates. The persistence of the purple costumed Mutant who was on my tail quickly shook the confidence from my mind, however. Franny was one of the contenders for top of the class, her psychic powers allowing her to fly at dazzling speeds and attack enemies up close with the violet warbling energy that her psionic energy produced.

After going half a mile without spotting any bodies in the sky over my shoulder, I thought I may have lucked out until I caught sight of a distinctive navy-blue blur out of the corner of my eye. With barely a thought I dove to the side so that I could stand with my back against the closest tree, the unnatural gust of wind pulling at my coat, revealing how close I'd just come to being ejected from the competi-tion. Abandoning the tattoo for Speed, I began pumping my adrenaline-fueled Flow into the sigils for Strength around my forearm, knowing I wouldn't have to wait long to put the power to use. A blinding spray of dirt and another brief gale accompanied the arrival of the blue blur.

"Well, color me impressed, half-breed. You've survived this long by yourself unless you count that horde of lawn ornaments," said the mutant Adept nick-named the Blue Blur, who had stopped his inhuman sprint with genuine sincerity in the backwards sort of compliment.

His spandex suit was a formfitting deep azure number that was designed to reduce friction as he zipped around at ludicrous speeds. The Blur was one of the few people I'd genuinely been worried about going up against while preparing for today. My tattoos were good in a pinch and were enough to make me competitive in most circumstances, but in some cases, I still couldn't stand toe-to-toe with my Gifted classmates. Even at my best, I'd learned that I couldn't keep up with the speed of the guy standing across from me. From within what had to be the world's skimpiest pocket, he whipped out a familiar looking gun and fired it into the air.

"I know you have to hate me right now, but seriously those gnomes were genius. Dozens of Apprentices rendered too drunk to function in the biggest event of the year? Priceless." The cerulean speedster had an odd habit of speaking faster than any human could manage when excited. This time he managed to say everything before I'd even finished lamenting his actions.

The gun was nearly noiseless, producing nothing much more than a loud click when fired. Unfortunately, this was a gun I'd personally enchanted and handed over for sale to the general student population. The rest of the bumbling Blue Boy's group had a handy blend of enchanted maps and compasses arranged to lead them to our location.

A jumble of excitement and jitters filled me as I flexed the growing power in my muscles, trying to work out a new strategy in my head. Outrunning my opponent wasn't an option, and assuming the Flyer was working with the Speedster meant trying to hide in the trees would be near to impossible. To buy a bit of time I carefully teleported in short bursts from the base of one tree to another, verifying that I couldn't jump far enough in any direction to shake him. The bonus info gained from testing my opponent's limits proactively like this let me in on the fact that the Blur wasn't confident enough to attack me one-on-one.

Technically, he could run circles around me, but he probably had no idea what I could or couldn't do to him in return. So far, my best idea was to try and take him out before his team arrived. How was I going to do that? My only idea wasn't a great one. Instead of trying to dodge or outmaneuver the Blue Blur, I started a slow and determined jog straight at him. At first, I was barraged with stiff arm attacks to the chest and even half a dozen slaps to the face. Without any magic or enhanced fortitude behind the blows, I could almost completely ignore all the damage.

This plan wouldn't let me outpace the other mutant, but it wasn't meant to. If I could build up an unstoppable momentum from my enhanced Strength, then hopefully, I could use it to crush the Speedster and evade his team. Only a dozen feet from my starting point, a purple streak broke through the canopy to hover above the struggle between the speedster and myself. In frustration at Franny's arrival, I grabbed onto one of the Blue Blur's attacks. In his haste to halt my momentum, I felt more than saw as my hand gained a solid purchase around his thin wrist.

"Stop playing with him, Blue! Sampson is close," the airborne woman snapped at her companion as she watched me halt my struggle to move forward.

To her dismay, the teammate only answered with a guttural scream of pain as I crushed every bone from his fingertips to the elbow joint. With my super strength it was as easy as breaking a bundle of sticks. I switched my Flow from Strength to Speed as I released the desiccated limb and continued running, only having slowed down for the moment it took to address Blue's arm. Glaring up at my airborne annoyance I threw up a one-finger salute and she, in turn, began tossing colorful bolts of energy in shades of yellow and purple akin to bruises.

The psychic blasts were like a subdermal shock as they hit, my enhanced skin offering no protection in this case. Soon, they weren't as much of a threat, my growing Speed making the act of dodging them child's play. Aiming carefully, I plucked half a dozen chakrams from my wrists, but to say they were ineffective would be a gross understatement. The aerial assailant looked acrobatic with the ease she wove around the metal discs of death, even batting one away with a power infused swat of the hand like dealing with a pesky fly. The chakrams were effective at close to medium range, but I regretted not packing a gun like Sage Alpha had suggested. My magical repertoire didn't include any long-distance spells, so my best option seemed to be engaging in this mobilized stalemate until one of us got in a lucky hit.

This plan fell to shit as a series of earth-shaking thumps heralded the third member of their team. I'd heard them mention Sampson earlier but hadn't processed the fact until I felt the irregular rumblings echo through the forest. Having only experienced it once before, it was no surprise when a dreadlocked man in tattered jeans fell out of the sky like a wayward cannonball. The grinning face that popped up and looked around had an almost childlike innocence about it as he jumped out of the crater he'd created as simply as I would take a step up onto the sidewalk from the street.

To my horror, he also carried an item I was intimately familiar with. The smoothed custom grip could make the knobby length of wood easy to handle with one or both hands, and the runes etched into the business end of the weapon had been hidden in the dark grooves by working with the grain of the material. In anyone but Sampson's employ, the weapon would have been dangerous. Seeing him swing it easily as he walked towards my position made my blood run cold.

The enchanted sheleighleigh had been one of the more impressive creations that I had released for sale to the general public. Every inch beyond the handle had been treated over several weeks with a series of imbued oils and layering of enchantments for reinforcement. The overpowered club was primed with nearly every force transference and enhancement effect I knew, which meant it not only hit hard but also that the power of each blow was altered upon impacting the target.

My eyes shifted between the recovering Speedster, the elusive flying Franny, and the confidently approaching Sampson with growing desperation. Between the Blur covering the ground and the purple figure in the skies, escape was now not only impractical but impossible. I had only tested Sampson's club enough to be sure that it would work as advertised, but the memories of decimated trees and boulders flooded my mind.

"Hey dude, been having fun so far? I just left the craziest bash between...." Sampson began with what was usual friendly candor but was interrupted by a navy-blue blur that had stopped inches from his face.

"How many times do we have to go over this? You can't be friendly and chatting up enemies on the battlefield! Look at what the bastard did to my arm!" The speedster admonished his teammate like an ill-behaved toddler, brandishing his partially healed arm like a limp flag. His shoulder down to his elbow had already reformed, but the forearm and hand hung at bizarrely drooping angles that clearly highlighted the lack of solid bones.

"Oh, not cool, man! Let's rumble!" Sampson bellowed, giving an incongruously gentle pat to his injured teammate before stomping angrily in my direction.

On a whim I wrapped a chakram around my knuckles and carefully teleported directly behind the Blue Blur, throwing all my strength behind a blow to the back of his head. Even though his body crumbled like a paper doll, I knew he'd only be out for minutes instead of hours, and both of his teammates called out indignantly at the cheap shot. My whole body spasmed as a mauve bolt of power struck me from on high, like a god smiting a heathen. The pain from the psychic blast immobilized me just long enough for Sampson to use his mutant Strength to leap the distance between us and line up a two-handed swing that caught me right in the gut. If not for the sadistic training of Sage Alpha, the series of pops and cracks I felt as I went airborne would've been too alien to recognize. After many extensively painful sessions, the feel of ribs breaking like dry twigs was familiar, if not a welcome experience.

A normal wooden club would be more likely to shatter against my skin than do any damage, but the weapon in Sampson's hands was packed full of enchantments. Quite a few of them were for enhanced durability and resistance to damage, but the genuinely dangerous magic was in the Force Transference and amplification effects I had built in. It had begun as an experiment, one which was proving to be far more successful than I had realized. The magic was meant to make purely physical attacks more effective in a fight against magic-wielding enemies. Many of my classmates had improved their ability to cast shields made of pure Current, burning lots of energy but leaving them untouched by most physical attacks thrown their way. The force transference was set up so that wherever the club struck, the power of the blow was carried through the initial barrier and released on the other side.

"Oh shit! Looks like that took the wind out of his sails Sammy. That prize money is ours!" the Blur said, and as I began pouring power into my Healing tattoos a few suspicions I had been harboring clicked into place.

To put it gently, Sampson had shown himself to be no strategic mastermind during our time together at Sage Mountain. In addition to that, this was my first time seeing him wielding a weapon at all. The fact that the sheleighleigh was a perfect fit for a matchup between the two of us, out of the dozens of unconventional items I'd created over the year, was an impossible coincidence. I filed that revelation away in the background of my mind and took stock of my dire situation anew.

Broken bones took time to heal, and I had at least six to fix up, so I'd have to fight smarter than my opponents for now. Making sure the space was clear, I teleported behind Barry again. Whether it was the fact he'd just recovered from my last sucker punch or the broken ribs were slowing me down, the speedster dodged the blow easily and dashed away before I could blink.

Fighting while injured was a definite disadvantage, but one that my teachers had made sure I got plenty of experience with. In my case it was almost ridiculously hard to break a bone, but Sage Alpha had drilled internal injuries into my weekly lessons through a myriad of unpleasant methods. My lung wasn't punctured so I only had to worry about the constant shocks of pain that broken ribs and reckless movement brought. Looking to push the advantage, Sam leapt forward and went through a series of clumsy swings aimed solely at my head.

Muscle memory saved my life as I used the most economical movements to avoid each strike. A quick duck, a well-placed sidestep, and dropping to one knee at the last second left me untouched by the relatively oafish attacks. Each narrow escape rocked my body with pain mercilessly as the broken ribs were jostled and the edges ground together. Even with all the magic dedicated to Healing, I would need time to stitch the ribs up and get back to any real fighting shape.

While I'd watched Sampson triumph over countless classmates with overwhelming force, no combatant fought flawlessly. The super strength the mutant used meant that he telegraphed most of his attacks, so dodging them would normally be an easy enough task. A blur of movement was all the warning I had before my legs were swept out from under me, knocking the wind out of my lungs as the fall sent a fresh wave of torture through my nerves and filled my vision with stars.

Feeling as much as seeing the next incoming blow as my vision returned, I was already rolling to one side. A second later, the slam of a sheleighleigh birthed a not-so-small crater where I'd just been. While the spray of dirt and debris was still in the air, I teleported to the branches of the closest tree, landing clumsily on a branch that nearly snapped under my weight. Surveying the field revealed the

Speedster stretching out his healed arm, like he'd only bumped his funny bone earlier, while Sampson hit the earthen patch I just vacated in frustration. My reconnaissance was cut short as I received a blow in the back of the head. While I fell to the earth, I realized who had been missing from the picture.

"Over here idiots! Keep it together Sampson, don't forget the prize for smashing in his head!" the airborne Francis called shrilly. Compared to the broken bones, her psychic blasts were more like bee stings than knife wounds, but the surprise of her blow mixed with the pain was enough to dislodge me. I had known about the price on my head before the event started, but something in Flying Franny's tone set the repressed rage in my guts bubbling and rising to the surface. Sure, this was a free-for-all battle, and I knew all along I'd be facing my classmates, but Kenneth and his ilk had poisoned everything enjoyable about the challenge. No one was fighting me to see who the best was. No other warrior had stepped up, hoping to become stronger by honing their mettle against my own. A ridiculous bag of gold had been leveraged over my head, and these greedy pigs all dove in headfirst to take a stab at winning it.

Determination ran anew through my body as I straightened to face the rallying trio. If they wanted to earn that blood money, I'd make them earn every cent. I pulled a dozen chakrams from each arm and began tossing them around the clearing at random, empowering different runes on each one before they sank into the dirt. Tossing a few into the air and whispering a trigger word birthed a harmless explosion of oily smoke, the quickly expanding cloud perfect for keeping the purple menace at bay for a bit.

"Come and try your luck, you greedy bastards! Tell me... do you three only kill for money? I'm sure Kenneth would be willing to drop trow and let you earn a few more coins when you fail to get the job done here," I crowed, staring Sampson and then Barry down meaningfully. "I actually respect sex workers, so if you admitted to being a whore for money, I'd actually respect you much more than I do now." I finished the afterthought by striding confidently towards the momentarily dumbstruck pair.

The Healing magic hadn't been idle, but it was still majorly an act of willpower to appear uninjured as I strode forward. As I'd hoped, the unexpected blow to their egos drove Sampson and the Speedster to charge me recklessly with half-formed curses on their lips. With a grimace, I ripped the Flow from the Healing runes on my right shoulder and shoved the bitter bile-like rage into my left forearm, tossing supernatural recovery aside for a burst of Speed.

The Blur and Sampson were two of the few Mutants at school that I couldn't beat at their own game. Simply put, my mutations didn't match theirs, and my magic was too weak to compensate for the fact. Opposite to what I had assumed at the start of the year, this fact had nothing to do with whether my overall skills could overcome theirs. My time watching Sage Pious' classes paid off more than the living statue's weight in gold would be worth.

Stretching my Sight and Speed to the limit had given me ample time to study how the two different Gifted fighters handled most battlefields. The Blue Blur, as expected, took the most direct route and came straight at me, as this was the most logical way to maximize and capitalize on the speed advantage. Though I'd tried to make the chakram tossing seem frustrated and haphazardly done, the straight line between the man in spandex and myself was laden with over half a dozen of the enchanted ringlets. Before the strongman even managed to take his first lumbering step forward, the Speedster had run half the distance to me. As my first bit of luck today, the Blue Bastard managed to step on damn near every one of them.

A cascade of lights and sounds filled the small expanse between me and the Blur. At the speed the mutant moved, the pain of the first chakram lodged into his feet reached his brain at about the same time as the sixth one. Ice, fire, electric shocks, and blasts of kinetic energy racked the blur of a figure in immediate concession without time for more than a flinching reaction from the rest of us. Knowing the damage wasn't enough to kill the guy, I took what joy I could from the howls that rang out as he was sent cartwheeling backwards through the air.

Sampson largely ignored the fate of his teammate and continued the off-kilter sprint that was his way of getting around. Each loping step covered the distance of half a dozen regular footfalls, and he only needed a brief halt in the locomotion when switching legs. I hadn't tried to throw any traps in his way, though he came close to stomping on several all on his own. Looking to the sky, I figured the last of the smokescreen would be gone in a few minutes and now was the time to make my move.

The hardest part was forcing myself to stand still and let the big bruiser get in close. Both hands gripped the enchanted club overhead as the brute leapt boldly through the air to cover the last ten feet between us. My enhanced Speed slowed the world around me to a fraction of its normal pace, allowing the blow to almost connect before tucking and rolling to the left. The real trick was escaping the blast radius the sheleighleigh birthed upon striking the ground where I'd stood less than a heartbeat ago.

As the Earth shattered and erupted, I was already shifting to a side angle that would be most efficient for the blow I planned to deal. Everything felt real, but these were only illusory bodies, meaning tactics normally prohibited against my classmates were viable options for the first time. Having practiced the move count-less times on Sage Alpha, I kicked out with all my strength and speed to shatter Sampson's left kneecap. Feeling the cartilage, bursae, bone, and other important bits fracture as desired, I was already pivoting back and to the right as the behe-moth of a man crumpled to the ground with a wail of pain.

Leveraging his flailing descent to my advantage, I quickly latched onto his left arm and locked it into a modified arm bar. Before the mutant had even fully processed the pain he was in, I used all my strength and his own momentum to snap his elbow and wrench it until the arm was bent firmly opposite from how the Gods had designed it. The mewling yelps of pain that escaped the big man's lips were a few octaves higher than expected, but I couldn't judge him for it. The sounds I had made when Sage Alpha systematically broke every bone in my body had undoubtedly been worse. She'd been unwilling to teach the brutal arsenal of moves to someone with no clue what their victims would experience.

Eyes, wide with shock, locked onto mine as Sampson tried to remain upright on his remaining knee. With Herculean effort his knuckles showed white with strain as the wooden club in his left hand made a half-hearted swing in my direc-tion. The blow didn't come close to connecting, but he managed to throw himself off balance and face plant with a sense of finality to our conflict. Choosing my moment carefully, I lined up a kick to his bobbling head that would make any soccer star weep with jealousy. Grim satisfaction settled in my gut as the kick connected, and the light in Sampson's eyes went out, going completely limp on the grass before me.

Unsure of how the finer details of the construct worked, I wondered if I should land a definitive killing blow now, not wanting him to wake up in agony if he woke up after I'd left the scene. The luxury of compassionate thoughts for my enemies was apparently more than I could afford, however, as a violently violet figure broke through the diminished smokescreen and shot me in the dead center of my back. Rolling forward with the blow, I shamelessly used Sampson's bulk to get partial cover as the enraged woman hurtled towards me from above.

"You asshole! That smoke smells like something that died, shat itself, and then died again! Barry? Where the hell are you?" Franny bellowed, flitting about the now decimated area looking for her other surviving teammate. A tight grin snuck its way onto my face because I'd used a plethora of dead and rotting components in the particularly nasty mix of smoke she'd just fought her way through. If I'd said I was surprised when the Blue Blur skittered back to meet his irate partner I would be lying, but a string of curses came out under my breath when he did so anyway.

"Let's end this, brainless," she declared, tossing a pair of sickly green glowing daggers to the ground.

Within a blink, the Speedster had the obviously magical weapons grasped ready in each hand, though he took the time to slow down and give an insult in return with a rude hand gesture to the Flyer. Inwardly groaning, I recognized the enchanted gear as more of my own work and realized how much more of a threat the Blur would be with them in hand.

"Where the hell have you been? This asshole has been blowing me up and tearing our big guns muscle man into tiny pieces with his bare hands! What were you doing? Being the world's most useless night light again?" Barry said rapidly, in that fast-forward manner that happened most often when he was frustrated or annoyed.

"It's not my fault you two fell to pieces while I was stuck in the black cloud of stank! Are you ready?" she retorted testily as Barry zipped through an odd series of slashing and stabbing motions.

It was obvious he wasn't proficient with the deadly tools, but the magic woven into them assured him he didn't need to be. For the millionth time I wondered how so many of my personal creations had ended up directly in the hands of people aiming to put me down.

"Let's kill the bastard," Barry said resolutely, and his words were my only warning before the two came at me.

All out of smoke screens and stink bombs, my mind raced through all the good ideas I'd had about fighting flying opponents and then settled on a terrible one. Milliseconds before the Speedster would've taken a stab at me, I teleported into midair and immediately began to free fall. My plan to surprise Flying Franny crumbled before my eyes as I teleported above the violet psychic, failing completely at landing on her back as intended. My target flew by beneath me, completely unaware of my presence, though I could hear my opponents howl in frustration at having lost sight of me.

Tamping down the instinctual reflex to scream, I refocused and teleported again, this time reappearing only a few feet above Franny. With a primal scream escaping my lips, I gripped onto the glowing body as she shot through the sky like a pissed-off missile. I wasted no time in throwing wild haymakers into the back of her head while trying to lock my legs around her body. The violet energy shield she projected took the brunt of the first handful of blows I dished out, but visible cracks and fissures blossomed quickly under the up-close onslaught.

In an effort to dislodge her unwelcome passenger, the mutant went to maximum velocity, alternating between dive-bombing the ground and pulling intricate twists and turns that nearly dislodged me every few seconds. Keeping my eyes shut to try and push down the overwhelming vertigo and the blinding bioluminescence of her aura, my desperate attacks ranged from completely ineffectual glancing blows to solid strikes that further broke her protective shell into loose pieces. In a last-ditch attempt, she did the one thing I'd never expected out of her; diving straight into the ground to hurt us both.

Between one breath and the next, the world switched from a dizzying blur to a concussed and slightly whirling sensation. Having lost my grip on the enemy, I tried to get to my feet, stumbling and falling like a dizzy toddler in the sandbox. I only realized I was being attacked when I tried again to stand up and accidentally knocked the incoming Speedster off balance. Shaking my head to summon coherency, I could see that he'd forgone attacking my body in favor of chipping away at the power dampeners on my wrists. An incoherent yell made it out of my lips as I fell to a crouching defensive stance and began trying to protect the already scraped-up bracers. What the hell was this guy thinking?

"If these break, you all die!" I shouted vehemently, but with the world still spinning, I managed to emphatically slur the consonants into an unintelligible mess.

Smelling victory in the air, Franny had recovered enough from her kamikaze tactics to begin blasting me again. Three bolts struck me in quick succession, violent stabs of pain each somehow finding my spine. A guttural howl of pain escaped my lips, the new agony reminding me that my ribs were still in need of treatment under all the other aches and pains the day had brought me.

The Blur took my moment of agony as the perfect opportunity to keep at his odd task. The dampeners were strong enough to even be used as weapons or to deflect most projectiles, but they weren't indestructible. The Speedster's Gift meant he could strike hundreds of times within a handful of seconds, and he'd had much longer than that.

A flareup of raw magic sprang from the depths of my being and I was blinded as the power tore out of me unbidden. Feeling suddenly drained, my vision gradually came back in spots until I could once again make out the scene in front of me. It was like someone had taken a flamethrower to everything in a thirty-foot cone in front of me, starting at my feet and widening as the carnage extended outwards. The stark blue uniform of Barry had been charred almost beyond recognition, but his decimated body still held the smoking daggers in each hand. Whatever magic hit him had moved faster than the Speedster could react, turning him to frozen ash and charred bones instantly.

Keeping an eye out for Franny, I began picking up the jagged chunks of enchanted stone Barry the Blur had carved out of my power dampeners. If anyone had been around to notice, my face was likely burning with shame at the outbreak of power. It was no type of victory in my mind to win by losing control. There were dozens of small shards scattered about, but I focused on the largest fractured pieces strewn over the blast radius. Less than a dozen paces out, I uncovered the next lifeless body, just enough of Sampson's face left to show the mix of agony and horror his last moments had been. My guilt only intensified as the memory of leaving him lying there crippled and broken, but still very much alive, came unwanted to the forefront of my mind.

Chapter Eighteen

After another few minutes of tentative exploration with one eye on the sky, I decided she'd either been scared off or gone for reinforcements. Without the surveillance, I immediately began sprinting and teleporting in a deliberate manner that would throw off any trackers who found the decimated bodies I'd left behind. A large part of me knew that trying to hide with all this magic leaking out of my system might be a fool's errand, but I had to at least try.

Back into a comfortable and obscured tree perch, I began frantically pouring power into the shards of my power dampeners. If I went too quickly, the Flow would grow overly excitable and explode, and more than a few times I had to halt the process entirely as blue flames came to the surface and danced across my fingertips. Going too slowly promised similarly disastrous outcomes as the forced calm I tried to project over the unbound energy felt increasingly false, with small spasms of anxiety and fear regularly breaking through.

More out of surprise than pain, the bullet that found my throat knocked me from my perch to fall fifty feet or so to the solid ground. Before I even had a chance to process what just happened, another lead round struck the back of my shaved head. Despite being bulletproof, the rounds still stung, and it felt a bit like one had managed to rattle my brain about a bit. Rather than try to stand right away, I thought about the angle the two shots had come in at and teleported to lay in a plot of dirt to my left. The shooter likely wouldn't have any angle on me there.

Finally getting to my feet to look for better cover, I at least heard the next shot before the flattened metal bounced off my chest, only inches from my beating heart. Guns weren't exactly unusual at Sage Mountain, but I found it surprising that someone relying on their sniping skills had made it this far in the game. Not all the Apprentices were bulletproof like me. In fact, very few were. Most had Gifts that would make short work of the average shooter.

I ducked in time for the next shot to lodge itself into the tree bark where my head had just been, confirming either the shooter could bend bullets or teleport to find me again so quickly from their previous angle. A red glow was all the warning I had before an explosion busted the trunk of the tree in half from within. Protecting my eyes from the millions of rough toothpicks now in the air, I began to put power into my tattoo for Speed and ran towards my best guess of where the shots were coming from.

At the start of the year, I'd learned that despite Conduits having a hearty disdain for guns, there was still a thriving market for enchanted bullets. Again, I cursed myself and thought over all the items I'd created and handed over to be sold. It didn't take long to remember the large cache of enchanted rounds Mal had requested I try my hand at, and even less time to realize one of those bullets had almost just done serious damage to me. No enchanted guns came to mind, thankfully, so plowing forward still seemed to be my best course of action.

A steady barrage of large caliber bullets continued to find their way into my path, managing nothing more than to harass me as my magic empowered my movement. The sniper's nest wasn't hard to find, though it did appear the jerk could bend bullets far outside their traditional trajectories. I pulled up short and took several rounds to the chest as I was stunned by the scene before me.

Standing cooly without a care in the world was Freq, shimmering eyes locked onto me as he spoke softly but urgently into a walkie-talkie. His presence explained not only how they'd found me but also how they'd kept track of my attempts to hide from the Gifted sniper. The instinctive hesitation upon seeing a friend on the battlefield cost me sorely, a trio of rounds landing like an elephant's kick straight to my diaphragm. My ribs were still broken in a few places, and I groaned in the realization that I'd made a decent number of enhanced kinetic rounds. A burning sensation knocked me from my reverie as I realized that not all three shots had been the same. A corrosive acid frothed and bubbled as it ate through my body armor and tried to dig into my skin. The pain was manageable. My rising temper? Not so much.

Pushing the pain aside, I focused on enhancing my Speed yet again, making a beeline for Freq. Almost immediately I became aware of a tarp on the ground that blended into the green surroundings and covered my friend's prone accomplice, with just a rifle's barrel peeking out into view. I realized the Flow of magic was tearing my dampeners back apart as I veered wildly to dodge the next volley of shots that erupted from under the tarp. To make matters more difficult, I was moving just fast enough to see each bullet seem to change its mind mid-flight to better aim my way.

At the last second, one of the bewitched rounds managed to whizz by my ear, causing an instinctive flinch that brought the round in direct contact with one of my dampeners. As the pieces of stone sparked and fell to the ground, I groaned inwardly and sought cover behind a small ridge of stone and earth between myself and the deadly accurate duo. Despite the pressure inherent in the death match, I had time to realize that Freq must have planned this out in advance. He'd been one of the few to warn me about the teams coming for me, but he also undoubtedly had some of the most useful tools to brandish against me. With the power to visually track everything from teleportation to specific magic users' imprints I was a bit surprised I'd evaded them this long. Even if the last team hadn't ruptured the camouflage I'd built into my power dampeners, Freq was guaranteed to be able to track me through almost any battlefield.

The betrayal began to bubble and mix with the adrenaline in my veins when the unexpected happened. With my back to the earthen wall, I was at the perfect angle to watch as a volley of heavy-duty rounds ricocheted off the rocks and trees ahead of me, expertly causing them to rebound and strike me either in the face or chest. Up to four metal jackets crumpled against my enhanced skin, activating the enchantments I'd imbued them with.

By no means one of my areas of expertise, I was still regretting the level of efficacy my skills had reached while the magical effects I'd created wreaked havoc all around me. A shot of elemental magic covered half my body in a layer of frost, and the next shattered the ice while painfully pushing the shards into me like a superhuman pincushion. Before I could even flinch, the third round released a fresh bout of raging flames that erased all the moisture from the air, leaving me feeling dried out and gasping at the superheated air.

The last bullet ended up being the worst: a generous spray of emerald acid smashing over my unsuspecting face and body. A mix between a howl and a whimper escaped my lips as I pushed magic into healing my unbroken but ravaged skin. Wielding the magic became an awkward balancing act as turquoise flames danced into being when I used too much power, but reigning in the same energy too hastily left me in the full agony of the caustic gunk. Standing upright with a mix of frothing acids and magical flames dancing from head to toe, I stared at the sniper nest with fresh malice pumping through my veins. Before I could begin a rampage centered on the duo, an all too punchable face dropped out of the sky to stand before me.

"You're looking a little crispy there, Xavier. Why don't you let me help you out with that?" the lilting voice reached my ears, a perfect mockery of how a friend would react to the sight.

"You really think I'll believe you arrived at *this* very moment to offer *me* help?" The words slipped from between my teeth with more venom than a herd of black mamba.

Blue magical flames had engulfed the half of my face coated in acid, making the inherently hateful words come out with a gruff grit I had never heard from my own lips before. The boy's shaggy halo of curls shook with mirth as large chunks of Earth began to orderly gravitate around his body, each one nearly the size of my torso. Sparks of lightning began to dance between his cupped hands as he made a show of taking his time before answering me.

"Sometimes, the best thing a friend can do is put you out of your misery." He gave a genuinely maniacal laugh before the first Earthen missile shot my way.

In the split moment I had to decide between taking the boulder to the face or teleporting away, I decided to face it head-on. Compared to dealing with trajectory-bending acid bullets, brute forcing my way through these obstacles was child's play. As the blue flames and the spray of dirt rendered the last of the acid on my face inert, I gave a mirthless chuckle.

"Isn't it kind of sad the guy using bullets under a tarp worries me more than the big bad Elementalist?" I called out while starting a jog straight towards the cocky Conduit.

From observing my classmates, I knew he was proud of the well-earned moniker of Elementalist. I also knew he specialized in more than just Earth and Lightning magic. The next few human-sized stones he threw at me had some extra gusto behind them, showing that my distracting jab at his ego had struck home. I was too furious and well-trained for such straightforward tactics to work on me. Using quick bursts of Strength coupled with my mutated constitution, I could more or less just punch my way through the string of boulders. The fair-haired Conduit revealed surprise before recovering his slightly slack-jawed expression, but he was not taken off guard enough to refrain from unleashing currents of lightning to dance from between his hands to strike at me.

I tried to teleport out of the primal power's way but wasn't fast enough to escape. Fresh agony swept over me as every muscle clenched and spasmed to a rhythm that had no regard for the way my body was built to move. Near the end of the horrific experience I received two more acid-laced bullets to the back of my head, a barely discernible pain that blossomed as my faculties returned. Overall, this still hadn't reached the level of pain endurance Sage Alpha had subjected me to, but I had zero intentions of letting things get worse.

The gold locks of the Elementalist framed his widening smile as he began hastily constructing walls of earth like a maze around me, waving his hands like a mad maestro in front of an orchestra. More than being a true hindrance, I was happy my opponent's move gave me time to think. I could easily teleport or brute force my way through the construct, but I had an inkling my opponents already knew that. If I teleported atop the walls, Freq and the sniper would be waiting. If I made a beeline towards the sniper's nest, I was guaranteed to eat another thunderbolt or two before getting there. A grimace split my visage as the final remaining power dampener crackled tenuously on my right wrist. The patch job I'd done had basically used raw magical flow as a welding tool to reassemble the intricately enchanted item. I wanted to beat these assholes before a surge of power I couldn't control turned them into crispy bits.

Instead of bursting through the walls or teleporting atop them, I began sprinting and teleporting at random. Soon the childlike layout of the hastily constructed maze was memorized in my head, and a plan formed that seemed as much for entertainment as it was for strategic advantage. Forgoing more delicate implements, I used my bare hands and excess magic to carve enchantments into every wall I passed. My prior experience with Freq let me know he would be able to see the magic being loosed but had no clue about discerning its function or intent. That meant that they'd either give the potential booby-trapped labyrinth a wide berth or try and set it off with me inside.

Finishing the last touches of rune script on a wall at the center of the maze, I sat down with a contented sigh and held a calming hand over the barely functional dampener still clinging to my wrist. A grin split my face as the thundering crack of a rifle firing filled the air, hoping that the bullet-bending Apprentice would take the bait. Just moments later, a scream of horror that was barely recognizable as Freq rang out, and I knew the improvised wards had worked. Looking at the spent magic on the wall at my back, I knew the bullet that had been meant for me had successfully been returned to sender, so to speak. For now, there was no way of telling what type of enchanted bullet had been aimed my way, but Freq would only have let out a squeal like that if something truly horrid had been blown up in their faces.

Remaining seated, I waited on my opponent's next move, thinking of the ways my traps could be avoided and what I'd try next with my dwindling time. At the edge of my senses, I heard a yelp of pain, and my mood brightened another few shades. I'd saturated most of the walls with my unrestrained Flow and stamped a type of feedback loop into every other earthen panel. It kept me from doing more elaborate magic but ensured the next person to touch them would magically get a direct zap from the retained power. Using my rough mental map of the grounds, I hurried over to the wounded Elementalist, a few teleports and a short sprint covering the distance easily.

"Any last words? I'm getting tired of speaking to people who think I'm some kind of animal," I said brusquely, noting that the Conduit was less hurt than I had expected him to be. Locking eyes with me for a long moment, the proud man seemed to be choosing his words carefully for the first time.

"How much did it cost to get Freq to turn on me? Five? Maybe ten bucks? I hope you got your money's worth before I took out your sniper." My voice came out with a ground-rumbling bass that I realized was part of the magic being loosed in my system. With a frown I tried to reign the energy in as the enemy mage lifted one fist wreathed in roiling flames and another that crackled with small bright arcs of power and smelled of ozone.

"Freq actually bet on you to win, despite everything. Unlike your other friends, he was smart enough to get paid before the event started." The Elementalist's eyes grew wide in anticipation as he spoke, and the barest flick of the bulging orbs was the only warning I received.

Less than halfway through turning my head, I caught the silhouette of an all too familiar figure as they walked through the earthen wall behind me and shoved both fists into my back. Distantly familiar to the first time it had happened, the sensation of another person's body overlapping with mine surged from skin to soul. In moments I could distinguish the insubstantial arms of another shoved through my core, and then the unique layers of agony birthed in the wake of their transition into solidarity. Just like our meeting on the first day of school, I was sent flying at the juxtaposition of matter, and I wondered if he had trained the move every day since then.

Rather than full-on crashing into a tree, my reflexes had been honed through the months of training so that I caught onto the tree in my path more than collided with it. Instead of feeling some sort of pride at the improvement, I braced myself as both lighting and fire bathed me from head to toe as a follow-up attack. As my cells spasmed from the brush with the semi-incorporeal attack, the trifecta of damage descended upon me differently than any individual one had before.

Lightning bolt? Minor annoyance. Fireball? I'd grown up shrugging them off. Combining those familiar elements while my body recovered from the fists that had gone from intangible to solid while mixed up with my own cells? Not even Sage Alpha had the tools at hand to desensitize me to this cocktail of pain. How long had they been planning this highly specialized attack? As the pain grew more bearable, I found my fingers had dug into the bark and stabbed into the living wood underneath it down to the second knuckle.

"Well, Mal, can't say this is expected, but that's my own fault." I was gasping in great lungfuls of air as my body seemed to settle enough for words to be strung together.

"Come on, X. Don't be unreasonable about this. There is enough gold hanging over your head that we could retire straight after school. Who better to cash in on the prospect than your friends?" Mal wheezed. I noticed both of his arms hanging useless and possibly broken with a tinge of satisfaction. "Besides, what is there for you to do without either of these on?" he crowed, awkwardly brandishing the broken power dampener he'd slipped off my wrist during his attack.

"Closest friends bought by my worst enemies. All loyalty stamped out by the promise of a quick buck? You couldn't kill me on your best day. Remember this moment," I said, thoughts racing a million miles an hour as raw magic built up in me. Without the power dampeners and in the face of such betrayal, I didn't have an ounce of willpower left to deny my magic.

"Hurry! We don't get paid unless we get the kill!" Mal shouted to everyone, but I found myself indifferent to his voice.

Instead of the fear and anxiety that built up in my dreams, I felt a grim peace fill me from the depths. We'd forged a pact of friendship and business over the year. Every item I made was handed over without a second thought, establishing trust between myself and my housemates. As I'd seen time and time again today, the items most likely to hurt me had been curated and sold to those best able to wield them against me, probably at a premium.

Beyond rage, beyond forgiveness, beyond kinship, the will to wipe the slate clean through pure destruction radiated through me. The blue flames flared out and steadily mutated in a cornucopia of ways I'd never seen before. Light from the setting sun was swallowed and reflected only in the cerulean flood that escaped me. Some flames blackened with added light and drew themselves into skeletal hands, digging eagerly into my enemies. Armed with sharpened digits like daggers reaching towards the sky or ensnaring my opponents, nothing seemed beyond the grasp of the manifestations escaping my control.

Other flames became prismatic kaleidoscopes of vibrant color that seemed to crystallize and shatter everything the light touched, different colors freezing, solidifying, and breaking solid matter in seconds. I felt like I was watching events from some remote distance as the maelstrom of magical manifestations spread to consume all I could see. The grass and shrubbery withered in the wake of the flames, and Mal was the first living body I saw be affected.

Pangs of betrayal and satisfaction seemed to bellow through my core like competing church bells ringing out as the mutant retreated in fear, flickering in and out of solidity without hope of escape. Turquoise flames turned into wicked hooks that latched onto his body and grew like sharpened barbs from under his skin. Blood, tears, and screams gurgled from him as he became encased in the fiery tethers, shifting to black and emerald flames as he was fully encased.

A voice in the back of my mind reminded me this was all just an elaborate construct. Despite being viscerally appealing, I was well aware that my actions would only be a frustration for people in the real world. At the same time, it provided the first chance I'd ever really had to indulge the dark and destructive impulses that had been kept carefully dormant all these years.

The longer I left the floodgates open, the more the deadly torrent seemed to build momentum. I could feel each life snuffed out intimately as my sphere of influence grew, like the forest was being soaked in jet fuel. Soon, people I'd never even run across met my tidal wave of magic, and the steady crumpling of lives made me feel like a child rolling down a hill over crunchy piles of leaves with joyful and wild abandon.

The sensation of freshly turned leaves sifting gently between my fingers was the last thing I felt.

Chapter Nineteen

It was dark when I opened my eyes next. Sitting up and getting my bearings, I was surprised to find myself uninjured except for a throbbing headache rooted at the base of my skull. An unworked earthen ceiling hung high above me as I lay upon some kind of stone-hewn altar, eventually realizing that this was likely one of the multitudinous caverns beneath the mountain. I'd heard rumors that generations upon generations of Sages had made their homes down here long before any modern culture had solidified its identity. I had spent little time in the subterranean housing, however, and this portion was bigger than any other chamber I had seen.

Beyond the altar, there was a vast expanse of statues sculpted to resemble exotic creatures and unfamiliar shapes that I'd never seen before. I could make out two or three dozen different indecipherable forms from the stone dais I sat on. Beyond them, the floor seemed to slope until reaching the center of the room. A placid body of luminescent turquoise water provided the entirety of the cave's light. The visible surface was at least a football field in length and width, and I couldn't begin to fathom its depth due to the brightness. As I stared at the oddities around me, an outline of a man rose from underwater and swam towards the lake's edge. An expressionless face with milky white pupil-less eyes breached the surface, and I recognized the bald-headed man as Sage Marequin.

"You've only been out for an hour or two, X. You recovered quicker than I expected," Marequin called out to me casually.

"What are we doing down here?" I asked as he approached.

I knew I had probably made it to the final part of the competition, but there had also likely been others squaring off in other portions of the woods. It was possible that someone had snuck up on me while I was distracted. I wasn't enough of a spell caster to have practiced watching my back properly while unleashing giant torrents of magic.

"Actually... it was me that put you down. I know you must be mad at the match being cut short, but I tend to step in if people are going to die. A lot of people in this case," the teacher said lightly, as if he had simply stopped me from walking about with my zipper undone. Looking back on the match, from an outside perspective, I knew it must have seemed that I had barely escaped being snuffed out under the weight of my opponents' coordinated efforts.

"Why did I get knocked out then? I was hoping to be the last one standing." I immediately regretted sounding ungrateful but being coddled was one of the few things that could really piss me off.

A lot of the people I've met with powers could be dangerous, and I was no exception. I was still learning the extent of my Gifts, and I was even farther behind when it came to the students I studied formal spell work with, but I had proven myself just passably competent. Marequin shook his head lightly, tracing a slight figure eight with his hand and pulling a cane out of thin air. I realized then he had come out of the water dry as a bone, and there hadn't been as much as a single droplet trailed behind him.

"Actually, you were seconds away from killing the entirety of your remaining class. I can't decide if it's more of a relief or deeply worrisome that you seem to have no clue. The amount of power concentrated in your outburst would have torn a hole through each and every Apprentice on the field." My blood ran cold at Marequin's words, the old man's face growing serious while he looked me over appraisingly. I'd never been anywhere near that strong before, though just a few years ago, it would have been a stretch to consider me an overall unremarkable inhuman.

"You're the Baron's son, aren't you? I haven't had a chance to talk to you about the subject privately," Marequin asked, in the tone people use when they already know the answer to their question.

I felt the slight pang of an open wound at the mention of the name, accompanied by a dull anger that I had grown used to keeping in check. It still felt odd how the man was suddenly an important figure in my life somehow, now that he had died. He had never once attempted to meet me, which would be fine if he hadn't signed me up with a group of weirdos running a secret school. Managing to stay off the radar of the weird side of the world hadn't been easy, especially once I grew strong enough to sense others with abilities that normal people only dreamed of. Apparently, all the Baron had cared to do for me was expose my identity to the exact kind of people I'd been avoiding... and pay for some classes at their fancy mountainside school.

"That's what they tell me, but I never met the guy," I responded through gritted teeth. Marequin had been one of my favorite teachers so far, in large part because he had been kind enough to not force me to have this conversation. The Sage seemed content enough to change the subject for now, sensing my reticence to continue.

"Do you remember what ley lines are?" The teacher pulled another smile as he posed the question.

A more theory-based teacher had gone over the phenomenon, but I embarrassedly had already known the concept from reading one-too-many fantasy novels. I nodded to Marequin as I recollected ley lines being ancient geographic convergences of magical energy that occur in rare places throughout the world. I'd learned at Sage Mountain that not only are ley lines real, but that some powers are stronger when active upon them and that certain beings are inherently drawn to them.

"Well, this mountain rests on one of the strongest overlaps of ley lines in the world. Many think that's why the Sages gathered here so long ago, and that's why many Practitioners still gather here today. You've gotten stronger here, haven't you? More than just what your training would do?" Marequin probed, and I was starting to realize I couldn't discern where all this was going.

I was harboring fears resembling every cheesy horror movie I'd ever seen. Have you ever considered how much creepier every serial killer and murderous cult would be if they had supernatural abilities? It had crossed my mind every other day since arriving, and I was starting to feel like a character in one of those films now. I shook the paranoia off and remembered the older man had saved me from committing mass murder only a few hours ago, which was hardly an act of evil.

"I thought all magic gets stronger by ley lines. What are we doing down here Marequin?" I said, trying unsuccessfully to dodge the question with the subtlety of a pipe bomb in a pillow fight.

In the past year, my powers had more than doubled. Since I'd gotten to this school, they'd started growing like wildfire. None of the other Adepts were going through the same awkward growth spurt as me, and the few facts I had garnered asserted that an individual's depth of power should more or less have solidified around puberty.

"Seeing as how you were declared the winner, I think we've reached the part of the year where this talk becomes necessary." Marequin seemed amused by the situation as he dismissed my concerns and ignored the question.

The teacher waved for me to follow and began walking back the way he had come, using his cane as he wove through the carved figures. I couldn't help but feel some childish frustration at winning by losing control. The good news was that I may have become a very wealthy man.

"Forget the competition for a moment. We're here to test the waters, so to speak. How would you like to go for a swim?" Marequin asked with another worrisome smile.

Once we dove in, the water became crystal clear, allowing me to see all the way to the bottom. It was a bit daunting from where we were, to say the least, seeming like miles of water lay ahead of us. An ivory sand floor sloped downward away from the shore; its smooth surface interrupted with stalagmites worn into rounded mounds. Marequin swam at a downward angle, apparently not worried in the least about breathing. For me, the concern was becoming increasingly pertinent.

I could make out some kind of unnatural rock formation in the deepest fathoms of the lake, and it appeared to be where we were heading. The old man had put away his cane and looked nimbler and at ease in the water than I had ever seen him on land. His strokes were relaxed and confident, strong enough that he easily outpaced me. My lungs were burning for air by the time we had gotten halfway down, so I broke off from Marequin's path and kicked towards the surface. I was a hand's breadth away when a hand latched onto my leg with a grip like iron.

"My apologies Xavier, you've advanced so quickly that I forget you're basically self-taught. Most Practitioners learn a method to sustain themselves below water while they're young. Let me show you." The teacher's voice carried unnaturally in the water, though I knew this was no typical lake. He'd also traveled faster than I would have thought possible, covering the distance between where I'd last seen him and the surface so quickly it would have been impossible for any normal person.

Marequin's eyes began to glow the same electric blue as the water, and I felt a tingle in my bones, signifying that magic was being cast nearby. I fought the instinct to kick the teacher's face as an almost feverish heat crept over me, then dropped to an almost pleasant chill wrapping around my body as the spell took hold. I gulped oxygen down greedily until the air cured the ache that had built up in my chest. After I acclimated to the feel of the magic, I asked the obvious question.

"With all due respect, sir, can you cut the mysterious act out? A little transparency would be nice at this point." My voice didn't travel nearly as well as Marequin's in the water somehow, but I had completely run out of patience.

A lot of the lessons that I'd been taught since coming here stressed the importance of patience as a virtue, and a lot of the Sages preferred to maintain an aura akin to the inscrutable mystics of old. Even with that in mind, it was getting hard to imagine what lesson would be worth the effort the Sage was currently putting into this scenario.

"Focus your Sight at the bottom of the lake; that's where we're going. It's where the power of ley line convergence is strongest under the mountain," Marequin said, the way he emphasized the term implying magical Sight.

I closed my eyes and focused on awakening the power, trying to attune myself to the world a layer beneath what I was normally aware of. I opened my eyes and experienced the rare sensation of having one's jaw drop underwater. At the lowest point of the basin there was an intricately carved stone building ahead of us, something between a fancy house and a temple. I started to pose a question but found the Sage had already pulled ahead of me, so I followed.

A few minutes later, we reached the building. Somehow, it looked even more ethereal and alien than I had expected up close. The whole thing consisted of a thin, porous material that had been worked to an unnaturally smooth state, except for interspersed chiseling of rune script spaced around the walls. Marequin went inside immediately while I gawked at the stylistic rounding of a tall roof that felt reminiscent of ancient Arabic architecture with a dash of bastardized Gothic influence by the time one's eyes reached the ground floor.

I followed hesitantly, and as I crossed the doorless threshold, my heart began beating so heavily that my whole body shook. The water abruptly felt heavier somehow, and the weightlessness normally associated with being underwater disappeared. At first, I thought the heaviness might be a method to aid those who lived on land with walking down here, but moments after my feet settled on the building's floor I worried about how strong the growing sensation would become. The entire room was one open space, and the closer I looked, the more everything seemed to be carved from one solid piece.

Marequin stood stoically in front of me at the center of the room without seeming to experience any of the same discomforts. There was some type of warding circle worked into the ground at his feet, and he seemed to be waiting patiently for me to step into it with him. I only recognized a handful of the symbols, and that nagging paranoia in the back of my head came blasting to the forefront in full force. I tensed against the internal fight or flight reflex telling me to run, caught between curiosity and caution.

"What the hell is all this?" I demanded, more dumbstruck than angry.

"This place was carved from the spine of a dear friend of mine quite a long time ago. When I came to live up here, I couldn't bear the thought of leaving them behind. I brought this all the way from our place at the bottom of the ocean. Isn't it beautiful?" The old man looked around wistfully as he spoke, his face pulling a bittersweet smile.

My heart pushed painfully against my ribs as I felt it strain harder with every contraction. I opened my mouth to demand answers, but my tongue had grown too heavy to lift. I reached in vain to try and swim, but my fingers could barely respond to my commands. As I panicked, the blood in my veins seemed to thicken into some heavy viscous solution of molasses and oil. My eyes fixed on Marequin in desperate hope that whatever was happening to me was some kind of accident, but he only watched expectantly like a shark patiently circling a shipwreck. A strong effect of guilt saturated his voice as he spoke next.

"Julian, whose bones we're standing in, was almost a millennium old when we first met. He was the last of his race, carving his people's history and stories into the deep tides. We spent several centuries together before he passed. I would watch avidly as he perfected spells so powerful they enchanted the very ocean itself. I say all this because his final lessons were about unweaving powerful magics and that if any of his spells caused harm in later years, I was to right the balance. Your father helped Julian find rest at the end of his days with his power, and that aid came with a debt that I may now finally repay." Marequin's tone grew melancholy as his hands beckoned me towards him, telling his odd tale like it held significance for me personally.

My body drifted helplessly through the water as a gentle wave dragged me forward in response to his gestures. My heartbeat grew progressively cacophonous in my ears as all I could do was watch the scene develop. My body passed over the edge of the circle, and the numbing paralysis turned almost instantly to overwhelming pain. My throat ached to scream, but even my lungs refused to answer the call to action. Marequin loomed over me impassively as I drifted down with my back against the floor.

"I hope you can forgive me," Marequin said.

The old man began chanting and singing in a language that flowed like steady raindrops on a tin roof, sitting next to me in the circle as he did so. I couldn't even utter a whimper as his hands reached down to cover my eyes. Right before the world went dark, a crowd of luminescent faces gathered to watch from the edge of the circle. I felt a blade press firmly against my neck, and everything disappeared.

Chapter Twenty

Somewhere between a dream and a memory, I found myself reliving scraps of a patchwork life. The wobbly feeling of taking my first steps as two giants, Mom and Dad, watched me, full of pride and apprehension. The tottering steps turned to slow and purposeful movements as I began to learn how to silently hunt prey. Again, I was vividly aware of my Mother and Father watching, perched on all fours, ready to pounce at the first sign of trouble.

The scene shifted again as I leapt upon my unsuspecting dinner, and with a lean, I was balancing the new bike Dad had surprised me with. He did a funny half-jog while Mom held a camcorder, and I pedaled. Before I knew it, I was riding all by myself! The jubilation was cut short as my view of the world gently began to tilt until memories of pain washed over me and changed the surface of the world again.

Both living inside the recollection and watching as a detached outsider, I felt the rain of tears begin at the sight of him. I didn't know why, but everything in my gut said his presence was a promise of pain and loss. Grasping at straws, I tried to retain some detail of the man in black that elicited such a reaction. Frustratingly, the man remained a vague shadow of a concept, seemingly inserting itself at will into the backdrop of these other memories.

The shiny new bike disintegrated as he took me from that home like he had done with each before it. Only now did I realize the myriad of memories I'd floated through each belied more families and homes than I could coherently count. The man in black came each time to make me forget, make everyone forget about me, and bring me to a new home. Over and over, this happened until I reached who I now regarded as my parents, the Earth Witch and the Winged Warrior.

To my horror, Anansi's familiar face accompanied the man in black more often than not, her stern features next to the man in black as they sat us all down in the living room. Years passed in a slide show of memories, familiar where only our three faces were a constant. Anansi's voice came as a distant echo that lingered in my mind, "These are your parents. They have loved and raised you from birth." Her voice rang out not just as a memory but as a living demand on my mind that it still reflexively bent and twisted to accommodate.

The longer I looked at my Mother's wild mane of curly hair and the hunched-over figure of my Father with his voluminous wings bound, the more familiar their details became. This process stretched until their features were almost as familiar as the back of my own hands, and I felt how every memory preceding these two was neatly folded and hidden away until now. Scraps of memories floated to me more coherently now in the wake of this most recent upheaval. Mom's voice coming through clearly as the freckles appeared on her face, like familiar constellations gracing the night sky.

"Sink into your breathing, deep enough to feel it rise and fall within you like ocean waves gently rocking a boat. Relax. Breathe. Relax more." Mom's voice came to me from nowhere and everywhere at once, guiding me through the steps of the meditation like she had a million times before.

"Now feel the pulse of your magic. How the power flows through your body and washes from head to toe. Both your breath and your magic are under your control. Tie them together so that the magic flows peacefully and ceaselessly inside of you." Her steady trail of instructions had a musical lilt about it as I followed her instructions to the letter.

My lungs felt like steady bellows pumping in a smithy, and only when I was sure of their rhythm did I reach out to the errant Flow within me. For possibly the first time in my life, the power heeded my will, coming to life at my summons. Long-held fears over being drowned in the Flow were quickly pushed from the forefront of my mind as the power acquiesced immediately. Feeling the magic course through my body in accord with my breathing may have been the most satisfying experience of my life. Years upon years dealing with the disharmony had left me utterly unprepared for the synchronization of frequencies, like my soul resided in my body properly for the first time in my life. Stars and embers crossed my mind's eye as a host of new senses awakened for the first time.

The new energy seemed to stretch my field of awareness wider despite my eyes being closed. Even asleep, I could feel Marequin nearby, and whatever magic he worked shone like a beacon in the darkness of my mind. In the span of another two breaths, I felt a host of dim lights that seemed to pulse as one, like unicolored Christmas lights putting on a show as they warbled and shimmered to my senses. Another pump of the bellows and I could feel... something alien but inviting.

A moment of clarity sent excitement rippling through my body, recognition of the Atlantean waters and the strange powers they were imbued with. Some instinct pulled my senses inward rather than delve further out into the depths of the lake. My mind's eye narrowed and then inverted in a sense, focusing on my own body but viewing it like a microcosm of the universe. Every muscle felt brand new but ached like I'd spent days pushing them to the limits in training.

I took my time letting my consciousness run through the familiar but foreign sensations of experiencing my body with new senses. The beating of my heart consumed my focus next, the peaceful drum complimenting the puffing of the bellows at work. I felt how the Flow of my magic wasn't limited to being woven into my breathing. It was tied to my heartbeat, laced intricately through my bones, sinew, flesh, and soul. Tendrils of magic reached all about me like a new set of sensory organs, and something felt decidedly wrong. My unease grew as I adapted to the new senses. Out of habit, I pulled at the Flow within me and sent it to the runes for Healing on my right shoulder. At least, that was my intention.

"What the fuck?" I said out loud as I snapped fully awake, reaching for my missing ink.

It was impossible to tell if I'd been floating in the dream state for moments, days, weeks, or longer. Inspecting my shoulder revealed a blank canvas of skin, and by the time I'd ripped my shirt off, it was apparent every trace of ink had disappeared from my arms, hands, and torso. Instead, my skin had darkened so much that the previously brown hue was black enough to be tinted blue, and sorting through my confused pile of memories only left me drowning in confusion. Jumping to my feet, I spotted Marequin, and our eyes immediately locked, his wide with horror while mine were a wild mix of confusion, loss, and anger.

As I looked down at Marequin from a new height, my jaw dropped in surprise. My newly empowered magical Sight and senses were so keen it as was if the world had grown new layers of vivid detail. I'd never imagined before that the Sage's aura was a shifting miasma of impressions of colors that were difficult to decipher. Blue and a mottled silver dominated the color scheme, the turquoise hue immediately making me think of the ocean depths from whence he came. The way the hazy aura shifted and snapped about him seemed to convey an inner anxiety his stoic poker face aimed to conceal.

"You had me worried there for a minute, boy. I'm glad you survived," Marequin said, and my mind snapped back into focus.

"Did you bring me here? What is this place? What happened to the competition?" I gained confidence and momentum as I strung the words together.

The unbound energy in me responded to my burgeoning anger and confusion by forming coiling bolts of dark energy that danced back and forth from my elbows to my fingertips. In a flash, memories played out like a movie in my mind's eye, watching a young boy learn the basics of battle magic from a harsh father who had a fondness for sparring his son until the boy was bloody. My ire ratcheted up a few notches as I confusedly realized that I was the beaten boy from my memories, and reflexively the destructive energy adorning my arms grew thicker and pulsed faster. With my new senses, I both felt and saw the magical energy Marequin summoned to form a defensive barrier around himself.

"Please, Xavier, calm yourself. This is not a simple matter. It will be harder to explain your father's instructions if you unleash whatever the hell that spell is against me," the Sage deadpanned as he eyed the malevolent magic. My mind involuntarily shuffled through a myriad of memories at the mention of my father, a dark silhouette among the countless faces that flitted in and out of my life like twisted clockwork.

"Did you implant these memories in my head? Are they real?" I demanded, part of me enjoying having the upper hand for now.

My mind swam within the deluge of new information until I was able to marshal my focus on the present moment with a heap of willpower. Regardless of whatever chrysalis I had just bloomed from, the Sages of this mountain were all profoundly powerful beings. No Apprentice truly had a clue to the extent of their teacher's powers.

"No, if this worked according to plan, you're being allowed access to periods of your life that you had no previous awareness of. This is only the first of several safeguards in place within your mind," Marequin explained, still eyeing the death bolts brewing in my hands. With a small flash of insight, the details of the spell came back to me, concentrated and amplified necrotic energy that would drain an enemy's vitality with every blow.

"My father... why can't I remember his face? How many times did they tear me from one family just to plant me in another? Are you going to try and unlock the other memories?" My mind raced as I babbled to the point of near incoherence.

The Sage held a hand up, and I took a few deep breaths, holding back the countless questions that ran through my mind. With a thought, the offensive magic I'd summoned dissipated into mist, and I sat back on the stone table in weary resignation. A stab of pain right above my ass made me jump back up, and a bigger surprise than my missing tattoos presented itself.

"You can't be serious." The words escaped my mouth of their own volition. Awkwardly furling and unfurling was a spade tipped tail that was rooted near the base of my spine, a mix between reptilian and feline in appearance.

"Do you have any memories of your Mother? It may help you understand more of what is going on," Marequin offered, seeming to enjoy my discovery of the new appendage more than I did.

"I think I'm due more answers than questions at this point, Marequin. How many times?" I nearly collapsed from the emotional whiplash on the seat, my tail firmly lifted and wrapped around my torso in several coils.

Faint memories of this body being my own once upon a time tickled the edge of my awakened repertoire of memories: enough to believe that this wasn't a freaky experiment under Marequin's thumb, but not enough to overpower feeling like a stranger in my own skin. The Sage eyed me for a long moment, and in an unusual display of staunch rebellion, I didn't relent. The somewhat alien feeling of my tail in my hands helped fuel my resilience, and his aura seemed to deflate noticeably before the Sage broke first.

"I don't honestly know. The goal was to keep you hidden from The Baron's enemies. Do you remember anything about them?" Marequin prodded, and though desperation colored his words. I didn't hesitate to believe him. A shiver ran down my spine and, oddly enough, my tail, as I was treated to another flood of repressed memories.

"Stay hidden. Grow strong. Be safe. Their eyes are everywhere." I recited the mantra under my breath, abruptly feeling very small and vulnerable. My father had made me repeat the phrase every time he'd surgically torn me from one life and injected me into another. A message burnt so absolutely into my psyche that even when I was without memory of hearing or speaking the phrase, I found myself living by it.

"Marequin... what do YOU know of my father's enemies?" I demanded with more of a growl than intended. The rumble from my chest was more bestial than any noise I'd ever made. The magical defenses that had been slowly relaxed around the Sage flared back up in my Sight as the man reacted to my tone.

"Xavier, what do you remember about the Cult?" Marequin probed, his voice clearly enunciating the capital C with the significance of that faction.

My mind went into an involuntary shuffle of memories, and though I felt assured I had never lived a life free of enemies, nothing resonated with his query. It was going to take a while to cobble my sense of self back together again and rediscover the patchwork timeline of lives that made up my history. Until things were at least coherent in my head, I realized I needed to be careful. Very careful.

"Tell me all about them, Sage Marequin. I'd like to start with what you know," I responded meekly, using his formal title in hopes it would make him view this as just another teaching moment with an Apprentice. Whatever reaction the milky-eyed mage had been expecting, this was clearly not it, his aura radiating uncertainty before speaking.

"By the gods... where to start? At the very least, Prometheus and Dionysus were involved with founding and shaping the group, but nowadays, they're not even the main focus. As often is the case between mortals and immortals; the latter made miracles possible for their short-lived and loyal subjects. Of course, the truly amazing thing about humanity is how they can bastardize such miracles into tragedies." The Sage seemed to let the rush of words out as one long lament, closing his eyes and massaging his temples as he spoke.

The sudden name-dropping of two figures from the Greek Pantheon was jarring, but I was already so overwhelmed that I just accepted the information for now. I'd been exposed to enough demonology and holy magic to surmise that Gods may exist in various degrees, though my imagination had never strayed to their potential abilities to run a modern-day cult.

"Both of those bastards have reason to want revenge on the status quo, to murder the divide between the damned and the divine. Make Zeus and every other asshole like him leading a cadre of gods obsolete or obligated to bend their knees. I'm sorry if none of this is making sense yet," Marequin explained, equal parts enthused and frustrated somehow.

"So... you're saying what exactly? That all the gods are real, and two of the mix decided to try and throw a coup over the rest... and I've spent my entire life hiding from them so that I could fight? How can a man that spends so much time teaching explain something this important so poorly? None of this is making sense Marequin." Truthfully, I'd questioned the Baron's motives ever since arriving here, and the first person to offer me any insight into the man's motivations was talking about Gods and Cults that I had no real frame of reference for. It would be absurd to think the Mutant Underground could hide me from the Gods, and though I had no idea of the extent of their powers, I felt certain that Sage Mountain was as dangerous as anywhere else on the planet.

"What do these people know about you other than the façade the Baron carefully constructed over the years?" Marequin posed rhetorically, the hint of a mischievous smile pulling at the edges of his lips.

"You literally had no memories of the man and appeared to carry a seriously detrimental curse cast by him, making you appear to be the polar opposite of the beloved son thirsty for revenge. The very fact you were accepted into an Apprenticeship at Sage Mountain means that they don't think you're a threat," the old man said with a tone of wry admiration.

"You were strong enough not to get eaten alive by the other Gifted in your life but not notable enough to accidentally draw the attention of a higher power. The

Baron set things up so that you could hide in plain sight at the end of the world," the Sage surmised, looking intently at me to try and read any reaction. When I stubbornly refused to give him one, he grumbled curmudgeonly before adding, "It's too late to defeat the Cult, Xavier. The Baron knew that long before the rest of us. You're only meant to survive what's about to happen."

"What does that even mean? It's too late to defeat the big bad mystery gang that apparently has wanted to kill me since I was born... and I'm just supposed to keep on chugging along? What kind of Cult is this, anyway? Electric Kool-Aid? Manson family style? Or maybe more L. Ron Hubbard flavored?" I said, utterly failing to inject humor into the situation. A dry chuckle was all the older man gave me before signaling that I should follow him, setting off at a docile pace.

"The power that puts you in such direct opposition with these cretins is the Gift they value over everything else," the Sage replied cryptically, watching my unsteady gait as I accompanied him back through the cave. They were new limbs with odd lengths to adjust to and different power stored within the muscles.

"You mean my uncontrollable murder-everyone-in-an-explosion power? While I can see how it could be used for evil, I'm pretty sure people would do better to just build old fashioned bombs. A collection of nuclear material would be less complicated and more efficient than what I do." My response rolled off the tongue, though I didn't fully believe my own line of reasoning. Images of being strapped to a rocket and shot from a plane were filling my mind as the gently glowing lake came back into view.

"Nothing so trivial as murder, or even mass murder, is the goal of the game at this level. Now that the first binding is released, it's time for you to think a bit... deeper," Marequin said, stopping at the crest of the hill for me to catch up.

My body didn't hurt anywhere, but the unfamiliar way things fit together gave me a slight limp as I tried to walk like I would have in my previously remembered form. Slowing down to try and sort myself out thankfully triggered some sort of muscle memory. What started as an upper body stretch turned into a comfortable lean forward until I stood on all fours more comfortably than any human man could.

Instead of following Marequin I played with the mechanics of going from standing up to down on all fours repeatedly, knowing somehow that the action had been as easy as breathing in a distant memory. The speed and smoothness of the altered cadence in the lowered stance was counterintuitively more like gliding over the ground than making double the number of steps. My hands were now the size of trash can lids, and my longer arms instinctively knew how to function as locomotive limbs. It sunk in slowly that getting adjusted to my new form would be a longer process than I'd initially thought. Approaching the Sage made me realize that I now came up to his shoulders, even remaining in my new lowered stance.

"Now tell me, what do those brand-new eyes see?" Marequin said, gesturing grandly to the nearly fifty yards between us and the lake.

Jumping back slightly in surprise, I stood on two legs and drank in the spectacle in amazement. What had been an unremarkable expanse of stone riddled with stalagmites was now a mix between a refugee camp and a graveyard. Over a dozen glowing souls loitered incorporeally in the space, waiting with unnatural stillness for us. In the back of my mind, it clicked that these beings were the field of lights my senses had touched upon while I was still half asleep. Long buried memories began unraveling in the recesses of my mind and the answer to the Sage's question came unbidden from my lips.

"Dead souls, more than thirty, bound and kept to this plane," I uttered emotionlessly.

Apparently impressed with the response, Sage Marequin began a parade-like stroll to the ghostly apparitions awaiting us. The man waved for me to hurry forward like a proud child excited to show off his favorite toy collection. The camp of unliving souls didn't bother me, which inherently bothered me on some level. A vague instinct told me that I'd essentially be leaving myself defenseless if I chose to plunge into the convoluted web of memories where answers lay waiting, so I firmly decided not to for now.

"Necromancy is a practice that only the most powerful and gifted of magic users can achieve," Marequin lectured as I followed him dazedly. "With power over death, practitioners are often deemed taboo and unnatural regardless of whether they produce harm or good. None of the other Apprentices are capable of learning it, and few Sages other than myself can teach you anything substantial on the subject. To offset this inevitability, your father spent several lifetimes curating a collection of knowledgeable sources. Of course, the safest place your father could think to store them was here. The Cult is so powerful that hiding things in plain sight is often the best stratagem left," Sage Marequin said, back to his lecturing and slightly pompous tones I was used to.

As we closed in on the congregation of dead souls, it became clear that there was a wide spectrum regarding how well-preserved each specimen was. The spirits whispered fervently amongst themselves, a few in the front holding dignified stances while others floated at the end of their restraints with a mix of fear and resentment. There were at least four dozen, each with unique death wounds and in varied states of decay. In the first row of three, there was a robed skeleton missing an arm, a bearded man with a ragged noose hanging around his neck, and a diminutive figure with two gaping stab wounds to the chest.

Marequin walked up to the skeletal shade whose one good arm was shackled to the statue's base. The Sage pointed his right hand palm outward at the apparition and closed both eyes tightly in concentration. I gasped in awe as the ghost's figure began to regenerate at a visible rate, layers of muscle and skin growing into place like a horrifically reversed time-lapse video of a rotting corpse. The loose robe filled out as the body rebuilt, everything except the left arm's stump at least. I stared in shock back and forth between Marequin and the reformed deceased.

It looked like the process had taken a lot out of both of them. The Sage was drenched in sweat and a fair bit paler than usual, only a few shades more vibrant than the ghost now. I waved at the freshly fleshed man, who looked like he was sick from pain but still managed to grimace a polite smile in return.

"This is Nikolai, one of the rarest occurrences in my collection. When we were young, your father often summoned him as a sort of consultant on different matters. I'll be loaning him to you for short spurts to act as a type of reference material," Marequin explained, fighting to speak normally between gasps for air.

"Hello, it's a pleasure to meet you. I can't wait to begin working together," Nikolai said, grimacing as he went through a painful-looking bow.

I awkwardly bent forward deeper in response, hoping it would translate to a proper level of deference to the poor guy. To be honest, part of me was a bit in awe that the man had been regarded highly enough by people for resurrection. It irked me to hear Marequin refer to a soul that obviously still had thoughts and feelings as if he was simply an object like a coin or a trading card.

"Nice to meet you, sir. I don't want to seem rude, but is there anything I can do to ease the pain?" I asked, reaching my hand out to shake his out of habit.

A warmth blossomed in the pit of my stomach and flowed like lighting out through the arm I'd extended. Before I could react, tendrils of turquoise light blossomed on my fingertips, shooting straight into the ghostly apparition's chest. The flash was gone as quickly as it had sparked into being, but the difference in Nikolai was intense and instantaneous. All I realized initially was that his arm had grown back in the brief moment, but when the ghost looked at his new limb in astonishment, I realized the colorless effect that afflicted all of the lifeless members of the vale had lessened drastically.

"How in the hell did you do that?" Marequin exclaimed, pushing me roughly away and studying the vibrant ghost from head to toe. Nikolai regarded me with a pleasantly surprised grin, flexing and stretching his reborn appendage.

"Like with all great magic, it was born out of desire and intention. Thank you, Xavier, you've greatly alleviated the pain," the spirit answered in an almost reverent tone.

I kept quiet because I genuinely had no clue how I had done it. Thinking back a few moments, I only knew I had wanted to ease his suffering and then reached out to shake hands, which was nowhere near enough effort to make use of magic in my experience. Normally I had to set an intention, martial lots of focus, and put in practice to be able to make things happen.

From the skeptical look I was getting from Marequin that was exactly what he was thinking too. A chorus of whispers brewed among the dead as I self-con-sciously realized how many sets of eyes were now trained in my direction. The only other living face in the cavern regarded me with thinly veiled fury. I could feel the intensity of the magic-enhanced Sight as Marequin glared at me. From the look on his face, the Sage thought if he stared hard enough he could shake loose any secrets from my head.

"Necromancy 101. Ignorantly playing with forces you don't comprehend will get you killed," Sage Marequin said, relenting when I didn't quiver under his gaze.

The admonishment was something I'd take to heart despite regarding the Sage as a less-than-trustworthy source.

"You have no idea how dangerous some of these men were when they were alive. Some are even more dangerous now that they've shucked their mortal coils." Feeling properly chastised, I looked over the morbid crew and admitted to myself he had a point.

My instinct to empower and free the beings in front of me was ultimately naive. Until the Sage's warning I hadn't even considered the ghosts could be dangerous when regarding them, which was foolish. People were always dangerous... whether they had a heartbeat or not.

Chapter Twenty-One

"So... what now? I go back to my regular classes and sneak into your secret cave at night to learn necromancy? I'm having trouble envisioning how things play out from here," I admitted to the older man, flexing my hands as we walked away from the cemetery.

The new magic was a constantly shifting sensation that I had to try and acclimate to. It felt like I'd had my insides hooked up to a nuclear battery causing a new sphere of awareness to extend past my old senses, connecting me in intricate ways to my surroundings.

"Do you hear that? It's like TV static building up in the air around us." I looked at Marequin apprehensively and watched as the color drained from the Sage's face. His cloudy eyes searched all around us as he began to usher me away from the graveyard.

"I thought we'd have more time. The other Sages are coming for us, and if they learn a single word of the truth... we will both face fates worse than death." The dread rolled off the Necromancer in erratically rippling waves of murky emotion to my new Sight. "When she arrives, pretend that you've just woken up and...."

The rest of the Sage's desperate plea was cut short as Pixie appeared in the middle of the graveyard with a gun in each hand and fury in her eyes. The tiny popping sound that I'd come to associate with her teleporting was more like a large balloon popping and put an immediate end to the background static.

"No sudden moves you fish-brained fuck!" Pixie roared. The venom in her voice immediately froze both of us in our tracks.

The normally lighthearted and playful individual was clearly itching to pull the trigger as her eyes slowly took in the cave all around us. To my astonishment, her gaze swept over the undead horde without even the slightest hesitation, not once but at least a dozen times. The Sage slowly swept her guns around while double-checking for hidden enemies, and I held my breath as she once again appeared blind to the glowing phantasms.

"Don't you...?" The words had slipped out of my mouth seemingly of their own volition before both barrels barked explosively. The bullets struck with impressive accuracy on my chest and would've shredded the heart beneath its surface if they had penetrated.

"I didn't say you could talk," was her only reply as a bit of smoke drifted up from the twin pistols, the Sage obviously annoyed that I hadn't died. "Marequin... is that who I think it is? Move your head for Yes or No... and remember, I know you're not fucking bulletproof!" she growled, apparently skipping over confusion and straight into angrier-than-before.

Sage Marequin, more shaken than I had been by the violent outburst, seemed to freeze for far too long before nodding slowly and deliberately in the affirmative. Pixie's eyes went wide with surprise before she let out a growl of frustration, rubbing the butt of the weapons against her temples to relieve stress.

"By all that's holy... X is that you in there?" she said skeptically while staring at my new form.

The notion she would've offhandedly given a stranger a chest full of lead just for speaking out of turn made my pulse quicken, and my blood run cold. If the kindest and friendliest Sage of them all was actually a cutthroat murderer, Marequin's warnings no longer seemed like mad fairytales, and I'd have to trust him for now.

I raised my hands slowly to show I meant no harm and nodded yes to Pixie's question. The gears in her head began to turn as she looked back and forth between us and, with a surly glare at Marequin, she released her grip on the pistols. To my surprise, they disappeared with a pair of familiar-sounding pops. Pixie walked right up to me, doing a surprisingly good job of getting in my face despite being close to a full two feet shorter.

"Where did we first meet?" Her voice was calmer now, but I could still detect the steely undertone of barely subdued violence.

"The basement safe house after the Fight club. You were waiting in the dark like a creep. I thought to myself, you didn't seem like a teacher, but I also thought it didn't seem likely you'd try to kill me. So, apparently, I'm only good at making the wrong assumptions," I said nervously, each moment she didn't respond by shooting me again, emboldening my babbling.

"Let it go already! You're still standing, no harm, no foul," the Sage said dismissively, easily falling back into the playful persona masking the no-nonsense killer from only moments ago. "So, do I have to start shooting again to get some answers out of you two?" she inquired in a lilting singsong manner, getting an immediate rise out of Marequin.

"I saw that his bindings were close to breaking during the tournament... and decided to help the boy break the curse once and for all. As you can see, things are a bit more complicated than I anticipated," Marequin offered feebly, gesturing to the giant hulking monster I'd become.

"What happened to his tattoos?" the Sage asked, almost as if dismissing Marequin's explanation. Pixie walked a few quick circles around me with a hand on her chin, like a patron studying a new statue installation in an art gallery.

"You were already big but now...." She paused her trek directly in front of me, searching for the words. "It's like if you had to wrestle a bear, I'd feel bad for the furry beast," she speculated aloud, and I reached for the familiar sensation of my enchanted ink.

My first true experience of phantom limb syndrome struck home as my senses combed through the layers of each arm and found no Speed, Strength, Healing, or Growth tattoos. More magic than ever before was freely flowing through my body, but my main outlet for the power had always been to channel it through the runic ink. As a pit of despair began to unfold within me, I felt the most delicate resonance, like glass bells tinkling in my thudding chest. Somewhere buried under the new configuration of muscle and viscera, the tattoo representing the Old Way remained intact.

Practically speaking, it had been the least useful tattoo of the set, but I cheered internally at the breadcrumb of familiarity. The only benefit of its resilience is that it could let others know my soul was unstained by massively evil influences. Regrettably, the only people who were likely to recognize the mark were people like the old Druid Atticus and my adopted Mother, schooled in the ways of Old that were... well, ancient and mostly forgotten.

"Is that a tail?" Pixie squealed with delight before grabbing ahold of the appendage.

A yelp escaped my lips as I'd grown so introspective that I had forgotten the new limb even existed. The heavy tension that had hung in the air dissipated as the recently murderous Sage chased me in circles while giggling maniacally as I spun and danced to keep the tail out of her overly eager hands.

"So, you're going to stay put to answer questions for me? I'd hate to have to blow out the last pair of Atlantean kneecaps left in existence." The voice, like frostbite, sharpened into a dagger returned in a blink.

The woman was standing almost nose to nose with the bald Sage, her pistols back in hand and steadily pointed towards Marequin's knees. The sheet of sweat running down his face streamed into his beard as he nodded vigorously in acquiescence to the demand thinly disguised as a question. Before I had time for the whiplash from the bubbly Sage's mood swing to kick in, she had turned away from Marequin and poked a finger into my chest.

With the simple point of contact, the Sage teleported herself and me away. Pixie's powers had always felt distinctly different from mine in ways I couldn't begin to explain. For the first time, my senses were heightened enough to discern some of the more nuanced details of the experience. With the simple touch, she was able to share her own genetically altered bio-electric field, and though my knowledge of quantum physics was inadequate to properly quantify and qualify what occurred, I understood it on a more visceral level.

Pixie existed on a different frequency from most states of matter. She could hone in on her personal frequency and apply her own unique bioelectric field, teleporting herself and others. While I felt the Pixie-specific energy around me, I grew claustrophobic, no longer trusting the Sage. The sense of familiarity with her presence battled with the instinct to buck against the sense of confinement. If the Dreamcatcher and warnings carved into the walls were any indication, Pixie had teleported us from the cave straight to my dorm room.

"Well shit, do you think you could shrink a little or something?" came the Sage's muffled plea, and I realized she was stuck between my widened shoulders and the wall.

Instinct kicked in at the thought of crushing the woman to death, and I had the distinct sensation of sucking in my gut but then folding it intensely and holding it in. Soon my new form had somehow shrunken enough that Pixie had room to move about, though she had to push or hop over my limbs to do so.

"Xavier, what the *fuck* did that crazy bastard do to you? Are you OK? I mean we're all assuming Marequin has gone mad... so I can only imagine the shit he may have said," Pixie said, trying to appear lighthearted as she checked the inscribed runes by my door with a purpose.

When she leaned forward to check a section of sigils, I realized they were the only runes that dealt with instantaneous manifestations, otherwise known as incoming teleports. Somehow, she'd ignored the protections completely, which shouldn't have been possible unless I'd engraved them improperly.

"It literally looks like he fed the old you to... well, a bigger and badder mutation of yourself? I'm trying hard not to give you a complex here, kid." She continued to talk as she took out a pocketknife and confidently carved a series of modifications to the magic.

"I don't know what he did. One minute I was the prize in a school-wide manhunt, and the next, I was waking up a lot less human than when I went to sleep. Can you turn me back?" I asked hesitantly, small things standing out as my skepticism warred with the desire to become human again.

Well, to get *closer* to being human again. It wasn't her immediate acceptance of my transformation that set off warning bells in my head, though I'd only accepted it due to the flood of memories the change had come with. It also wasn't the incongruous switch between friendly neighborhood Sage and a remorseless killer that puts two bullets in someone's chest just for talking out of turn. Honestly, what had gotten my wheels turning was her offhanded yet utterly apparent familiarity with runes, which she further hammered home by making a small cut on her thumb and applying it to the updated sigils for activation. Like most mutants, the teleporting Sage had shown so little interest in Enchanting that it bordered on disdain. A small pulse of magic birthed from the spot rolled over the entire room, feeling like an oppressive weight settling over me and sinking into my bones.

"I'll be back once we finish interrogating Marequin. Maybe one of the other Sages will know more about fixing... your new condition. I've got to say, I actually think it's a pretty solid upgrade, though! You've got to stay in your room for a bit now, 'kay? Don't want to send the other kids into hysterics thinking the same thing will happen to them." Pixie delivered the news in a half-joking and half-serious tone, slowly shuffling herself towards the door. The Sage's erratic aura was in a state of nearly constant flux, but this was the first time I could clearly see that she was lying.

"Wait, I'm just supposed to stay in my room? For how long?" I shouted in a panic, realizing belatedly what a horrid situation I'd walked into willingly yet again.

The only audible answer she gave was the sound of several locks clicking into place from the outside.

"Well fuck," I whispered to myself, moving carefully to the door but still managing to knock over a chair with my tail.

The door was indeed locked from the outside, which I hadn't known was possible before now. Feeling the static build up until a light pop ended the sensation, I received a wordless affirmation on the finality of the situation.

Chapter Twenty-Two

The scent of fresh blood struck my nostrils like a bucket of gasoline was being held right under my nose. For some reason I knew immediately that the smell had been memorized upon inhalation and that my new nose could recognize and follow Pixie's scent like I could never have dreamed of before. There was likely much less use for the new ability with a teleporter like Pixie, but the ability seemed far more helpful than a hindrance.

When I followed my nose to the altered rune script splashed with blood, the feeling of dread that had been building grew from bad to nearly unbearable. I'd spent most of the year building up and enhancing the magical protections around my room. Looking over the symbols with my new magical senses hurt my pride more than being outmaneuvered by the wily Sage. The first thing to stand out was that over half of the warding magic in place wasn't fully functional. The problem with having access to the theory and power but possessing no finesse or ability to genuinely analyze my work was that I'd spent months adding layers of power that were now obviously detrimental to each other.

The next few hours went by in a blur as I examined and built new designs for the room's arcane defenses. My Sight was now able to clearly observe how the raw power in the magic symbols reacted to each other. In many areas around the room, the different weavings of power hampered the functionality of the others surrounding it. Flashbacks of my Mother's gardens floated pleasantly to the surface as the kinship to a poorly organized plot of vegetation became apparent. Just like if one could observe the root systems of the flora and make sure each plant got enough space and sunlight, the enchantments needed to be arranged harmoniously so the magic could flow properly throughout the whole environment.

The trickling floodgate of memories also began reminding me of runes they didn't teach at Sage Mountain. In small bursts, the rare and outlandish magical alphabets firmly reasserted themselves into my knowledge base. It was a queer sensation to have information move back into one's conscious mind and memories, knowing I had learned the magic long ago. Part of me worried that if a stiff breeze struck I'd be overwhelmed by a lifetime of suppressed memories. Another part of me desperately wanted to start banging my head against the walls until I'd knocked loose every stolen moment of my many lifetimes.

The lock on the door was no ordinary item, as even hitting it with my new body's full strength didn't cause a scratch when it should've reduced the door to splinters. Time continued to lose meaning as I sank into the work. The thin trickle of memories that accompanied the reemerging Runic lore further mangled my grip on the hour that passed, blurring my sense of past and present. The flashbacks made it clear I'd spent more time than was healthy locked in some sorcerer's library, but the tutelage was paying off handsomely now.

The name and face of the grouchy elderly woman who had been Caretaker to both the library and me eluded my grasp, which was ultimately more depressing than I'd anticipated. She hadn't been kind, but I also didn't feel like she had ever been cruel to me on purpose. As appointed guardian to the wealth of knowledge contained in the arcane library, she had been trained to protect, maintain, and perform upkeep for magical books, not magical children. The dissociative hindsight that came over me when I thought about her was possibly one of the most uncomfortable facets of my current plight. Instead of the lingering taint of resentment towards her parenting skills, I only felt guilty that she had been forced into watching me like all the rest.

Was I the prisoner of a potentially murderous supernatural cult? Yes, it seemed more than likely at this point that Sage Marequin had been telling at least part of the truth. Furthermore, yes, it did seem likely that Marequin was being tortured by the cult members for information that would lead to the group either wanting to kill me or use me like a disposable pawn.

Could I ever go for a walk in public again because of my obviously inhuman physique? Not unless I was ready to outrun a pack of Purists and regular townsfolk bearing pitchforks, shotguns, and torches. It was all literally more than my brain could handle at once, so I did my best not to be crushed underneath the weight of it all.

As my thoughts continued to spiral, someone knocked at my door with three polite taps. In the moment it took to snap out of my dark ruminations, a flood of feelings overwhelmed new magical senses that I didn't even have names for yet. Without seeing the entity on the other side, I knew with utter certainty they were dead. I could feel the presence of their unnatural state of Undead more acutely than half of the magic inside the room with me.

Now that I was focusing on the aura, details began to spring out as if I'd done this a million times before. The vampiric heart had stopped beating over 400 years ago, and the vibrancy around the edges of her aura meant that she had fed recently. The only thing more startling than my abruptly intimate knowledge of the being was that their aura rapidly shrank and seemed to tense as if flinching away from the scrutiny of my gaze. Still having to crouch to avoid hitting the ceiling, I spoke through the polished wood.

"I'd invite you in Sage Lilith, but last I checked, my door was locked from the outside." I forced a bit of levity into my voice as I approached the waiting vampiress. Without responding verbally, the Sage began what sounded like a lengthy and complicated series of unlocking elaborate metal bolts and tossing aside chains heavy enough to shake the floor beneath us when dropped.

The entryway slowly creaked open to reveal a mystifyingly vulnerable-looking, blood-drinking predator. Seizing the chance, I tried to push myself through the empty doorframe but ran into an invisible wall that didn't budge in the least. Lilith looked at me with a mix of apprehension and a hint of "what did you think would happen" clear on her face. A long sigh escaped my chest as I walked away from the door and the waiting Sage, getting as comfortable as possible in preparation for whatever dire news would be delivered next. To my surprise, the ivory-skinned figure remained a statue at the room's entrance. She had been the one to teach me that a vampire with prior permission to enter a domicile would not need a separate invitation for each room within, so I waited. As if expecting me to pounce, the Sage moved with exaggerated slowness and delicacy upon entering and closing the door.

"So... How much do you know about Necromancy?" Her tone managed to convey a type of brittle strength keeping the Sage afloat right now.

The question caught me so off guard that I just stared at her for what must have only been a minute but felt like hours. A coy smile ghosted across her face as she stood by the door, seemingly reluctant to move any closer to me. At least half a dozen lies reached my throat and died on my lips before being spoken, and finally, Lilith took pity on me.

"Your room is currently warded from auditory scrying… and I am far closer to Marequin's side of the equation than the Cult's. You remember from our lessons that Vampires fall into the Undead Category?" Lilith prompted, leaving me to ponder the truth of her words while my mind recalled the Hunter's lore she'd drilled into me over the past year.

The Sage's species was not a fully dead body reanimated by magic like a zombie, ghoul, or various reanimated thralls. Having started their existence as living people and later turned into undead creatures, being reliant upon the blood of the living made vampires unique among the spectrum between the Dead and Undead. As if she could feel the wheels turning inside my head, Lilith continued,

"Well, Xavier, just as I have special abilities and senses to use upon the living, Necromancers possess special abilities and perceptive powers keyed towards my kind," the Sage relayed nonchalantly, allowing me to dig further with my new senses into her presence.

Though her body tensed, my instincts told me that she was actively letting me scrutinize her aura with my power, and I decided to reciprocate the kindness by not digging too deeply. It was obvious, even to my ignorant fumbling, that I could have grabbed ahold of the Death magic running through her body and used it to my own ends, but I had no clue to what extent I could leverage it.

"Yes. As you may be able to tell, necromancers have a level of inherent power over undead beings such as myself. This is not enough to bend the knee of our entire population as the older vampires can shrug off any attempts at control and provide protection to any under their lineage." She paused and took a reticent step towards me and away from the doorway.

"Did you ever wonder why a school that so desperately makes claims of excellence has so little diversity?" Lilith's eyes locked with mine and seemed unsurprised by the confusion she found there.

"A handful of spell casters, Pixie, Sage Pious, Alpha, and I represent an objectively narrow knowledge base of instructors. The entire student body consists of First- or Second-Generation mutants and the spoiled spawn of rich, but not particularly Gifted, families. We have no fey, elves, dwarves, or even half-blooded kin of any other races. There are dozens of practically identical daycares like this, set up by the Cult, across the world. Apparently, lots of inspiration was derived from the modern college institutions in place among the Regulars." She paused for a long sigh, which was purely for show since the vampire had not needed to breathe in centuries.

I stubbornly kept quiet throughout her big reveal, partially waiting for a trap to be sprung or a hint of a lie in the tapestry she was laying bare before me. To my dismay, everything she was saying seemed all too likely to be true, and my fixation on her aura only confirmed it. Part of me felt joy in having Sage Lilith as a potential ally, but I realistically knew it was far too early to be certain.

"Others will undoubtedly come talk with you, using various concocted tales designed to lower your defenses and find you guilty of knowing too much. They will say that they are working with Marequin and your dead father and insist that you tell them everything," she continued when it became clear I wasn't going to contribute anything.

"As we speak, Marequin is being scrutinized by the Cult. It was a clever lie to claim that he'd meant to put an end to your potential as a threat... and only mistakenly empowered you further. I can only hope his ruse holds up under the investigation. Either way, you'll need to escape sooner than later. I'm going to release his crew of ghosts so that you won't have to do everything on your own," she said with a note of finality, and her hand had almost reached the door before looking back with a mischievous smile.

"I almost forgot! It's not all bad news. After your abrupt conquest ending the contest and then your subsequent disappearance, it came to light that one of your classmates spent an ungodly amount of money to set a bounty on you. We may turn a blind eye to Apprentices betting, but this was deemed utterly unsportsmanlike. Therefore, you shall receive not only the winnings already due to you but a significant amount of gear and other items confiscated as recompense. I must admit that a few of us were disappointed you didn't win in a more... deliberate manner, however. Use it well, X." The Sage tossed me a simple leather satchel that made an incongruously loud thump upon landing.

By the time I looked up she was gently closing the door behind her retreating form. During the raucous metallic clanking of locks and chains being affixed to my door, I used my senses one last time to try and magically probe the Sage. To my surprise, my Sight was able to pierce through the door and dig deeper into the vampire outside than I had delved before.

The inherent instinct to grab the power at play in keeping her animated and twisting it to my own ends was strong, but I resisted the urge with pictures of Lilith's body dropping truly dead outside my door. Instead, I approached the bag with all the caution of a bomb squad technician, noticing the item shimmered with layers of magic like the exotic scales of a tropical fish were slowly shifting across its surface. The unnatural awareness I retained of the Sage's vampiric aura retreated at supernatural speeds after the last chains were fastened to my door.

Did she risk a final death just to trick me into revealing my secrets? The mix of hard truths and harder-to-believe potential truths was certainly a viable tactic. Imagery of the Atlantean mage undergoing enhanced torture tactics to repay his promise to my father. My mind invoked the names and faces that had been unlocked in my memories, each one only accentuating the negative space where my genuine parental figures should have occupied.

Some people accepted the stewardship as an honor, others as repaying a debt, and still more had taken me in as an unwelcome burden that could not be refused. Maybe when I escaped this place, I could visit one of the foster homes that had helped raise me. Something in the back of my head seemed to think this was a bad idea, and I could come up with half a dozen reasons why that would make sense without trying hard. For one thing, only a handful would recognize me in my current inhuman form, and I couldn't clearly recall which faces and names that would be. Out of those few, though, how many would rather kill me on sight than catch up over a cup of tea? I had no way of really knowing.

Another hour of spiraling thoughts, and I found myself at rock bottom of an existential crisis: If my entire life as X had been a lie. Did I even know who I was anymore? Would I be incomplete without a recollection of the life I'd lived? What if these memories returning were just another layer of misdirection planted by Pasithea? It was time to stop thinking like the creature I used to be. With every memory, I learned more from who, where, and what I'd been in the past, literally.

The cloying yolk of trying to pass in human society and build my identity as a mutant in the most unoffensive manner evaporated. I was now able to grasp and manipulate the magical energies that had eluded my control all my life. I wanted to run out of my room and show off to the world, rubbing my energies in my enemy's faces in the way I could weave intricate spells that they likely hadn't even heard tell of yet. I found through accident and experimentation that I could gradually shrink down to proportions that made my room usable again, though I was still somewhere between seven and eight feet tall.

I developed a single-minded focus on learning and consolidating my abilities as they came to me, trying to make sure none of the memories that I could grasp went to waste. There was a general theme to the specialized skills I had spent my real childhood developing. Battle Magic, Enchanting, and Necromancy were the foci, as far as I could tell at this point.

Despite Marequin's assurances that Necromancy was falsely viewed as a dark art, the majority of my childhood lessons attached to it were grim affairs conducted by even more grim teachers. The Baron had messed with a lot of people's lives by implanting and removing me, and I had no idea how any of them handled the ordeal once I was gone. Were my father's associates skilled enough to not leave scars while ripping out and altering years' worth of memories over and over?

My ability to sense life and general auras outside my bedroom was becoming more refined by the hour as I began picking up extra details more consistently, like energy levels and emotional states. The range of my blossoming domain grew from people walking past my door to those on the nearby pathways and trails immediately surrounding the house. Mal had almost knocked on my door four times, full of nervous energy, and one time mostly alcohol-fueled courage, but he always kept his distance in the end.

Instead of calming myself, I found the extra stimulation only made me increasingly restless as everyone went about their lives as usual. I hadn't realized I'd begun pacing until my foot hit the untouched satchel on the floor. It had been more like stubbing my toe on a boulder than a bag meant to hold a few notebooks and a laptop. Lifting the bag by its worn leather strap, it felt empty. Shaking it set off a muffled cascade of echoes that only grew more confusing the longer I listened. For the first time in what felt like forever, my mind touched back on the competition. It would seem sweet that they'd punished the little creep whose name I could barely recall now, but knowing they might come to murder me any minute somehow hollowed the gesture.

Before I could open the bag, however, my whole body froze. At the very edge of my magical senses, something new stirred or was released unintentionally. The manifestation was less than a mile away, but I could feel its ghostly aura as if a skeletal hand had tickled the back of my neck. My hackles rose as another dozen just like the first appeared, belatedly connecting the dots that this was part of the proof Sage Lilith had promised to deliver regarding her true allegiances.

The auras felt distinctly different than how the vampire's had less than a day ago, though there were similarities. It was hard to explain the sensation, but the actual aura of death seemed to become more familiar the longer I stared into its depths. What if this was how they killed me? Marequin had led me by the nose until I literally followed him into this whole mess, willingly and fully unaware of the consequences.

The approaching horde of ghosts surprisingly slowed until only a small fraction of them continued to approach me. Unlike in the past, the Flow that roiled up in my core was somewhat familiar, more like dealing with a subconscious surge of muscle memory than being assaulted by a stranger from within. Memories I'd spent time digesting kept my mind only a step or two behind the instinctual responses, but I was barely able to keep up with combining the thoughts to action.

My right hand began to glow light and project patches of absolute darkness in intricate patterns that seemed ultimately balanced while an icy hot sensation grew in the left. My left hand's fingers began glowing a gentle white like pure snow while my palm became a pulsing latticework of black veins wreathed in silvery mists. As if performing a half-remembered dance, the right hand went through a series of intricate gestures as less viscous, almost syrupy mana suffused the limb all the way up to my shoulder. The spell on my left hand would ward off direct attacks on my soul or attempts to inherit my body... and another protective effect I couldn't fully remember. The spell readied in my right hand was for pure offense, but once again, I found myself at a loss for the specifics rattling around my head.

All the finished enchantments worked into the walls flared briefly as a slightly luminous figure came in through the wall. A dead man strode confidently and casually into the room, seeming to take in the runes on the walls and my readied spells like he'd walked into the most utterly mundane scene in existence.

"If you banish me now, centuries of planning will go to waste... and you'll be dead in three days. Ultimately, the choice rests with you," the specter said, seeming so certain of every word it gave me pause.

Every muscle tensed as I waited for the trap to be sprung. The mass of ghosts waiting outside remained where they were, and the face patiently observing me didn't even move to blink.

"To help put your mind at ease, there is a binding spell," the spirit I now recognized from Marequin's cave calmly offered, causing me to subconsciously shiver.

Not all the memories being returned to me were names and faces. At times there was magic I'd been taught or used before, reasserting itself like having a new arm bloom. The way this spirit offered himself for binding made it clear that he wasn't talking about the kind of magic that had kept me hidden in the past.

In the necromantic arts, there was a binding spell that could only be entered into freely by both parties. It was used so rarely because, if broken, the offending spirit would face total annihilation. Most binding spells required either one party to soundly overpower the other or resort to ludicrously detailed pacts where spirits are held to a meticulous set of instructions. Messing the tone of these up was most often a death sentence for the necromancer, as the worst thing most practitioners could do to a spirit was send it back to the afterlife.

"May I please ask the name of the soul offering itself for binding?" I asked hesitantly, recognizing Nikolai from Marquin's grove of ghosts while remaining unsure of what to expect. There was no wiggle room, no loophole, and no tactical advantage to giving me allies that would literally be destroyed if they betrayed me. Maybe the vampiric Sage had been telling me the truth.

"You may call me Nikolai. I am glad to see the good manners that skipped your father's generation have been imparted upon yours. It is understandable that you are wary of an alliance, and this is why the rest of your people wait outside," Nikolai explained with a deep bow, and I bit back the list of questions that arose at the mention of my father. Hesitantly, my right hand was offered to the glowing phantasm as the details of the ritual came easily to my mind, as if I used it every day.

"I hope you're telling the truth, Nikolai, for both of our sakes," was all I said as the ghost from the cave wrapped both hands around mine.

Chapter Twenty-Three

Less than an hour later, and the magic was in place. Stronger by far than the relatively recent sensation of having a new body was the thrumming feedback of the new bond. Since the fabric of Nikolai's soul hadn't unraveled immediately upon surrendering himself to the binding spell, I knew he had been telling the truth all along. Honestly, I was as unsettled by the Necromantic Ritual as reassured by the solace of having a trustworthy companion.

"Now that that's out of the way, would it be ok to bring a handful of those waiting outside here to meet you? We only have days to reorient your soul and replenish you with Death Energy," Nikolai said hopefully, his smile incongruous with his words.

A spike of anxiety rang through me, not just at the thought of more ghosts but also because of my current ignorance. Large chunks of memories had been coming back to me, but the ghost's mention of my soul combining with Death Energy didn't yet ring a bell. Nikolai's sense of amusement seemed to reverberate across our new bond, almost like hearing laughter from another room and smiling along without knowing the joke.

"It is understandable that you still have gaps in your memory. There's bound to be scarring and injury after the barbaric way the unbinding was conducted. I'm just thankful you're not a brain-addled pile of goop. As a necromancer, you have the unnatural ability to heal such soul-based damages by absorbing specific... frequencies of Death Energy. In this case, you have access to a hoard of loyal ghosts that can save you years of time on the mend," Nikolai explained easily, as if it was as simple as the sun rising and setting daily.

"Why don't I remember that? All these new memories and magics fluttering around my head, you'd think some healing magic would've been on the list of things to retain." My voice came out as a whine instead of the distrusting tone I'd meant to project. If I was going to be dealing with large groups of the living dead, it wouldn't do to be perceived as a petulant child.

"Have you ever stared into your own soul? I'm looking at it now and… things do not look as they should, to put it mildly. At a guess, your mind may still feel as if you've had a series of disjointed and unrelated lives that you're starting to get glimpses of. Part of what the deathly essence will do for you is help you become a singular and coherent consciousness again. We need to get you healthy and whole if you're to escape anytime soon," the ghost said while staring at me with a piteous gaze normally reserved for abandoned baby kittens. I looked down at myself in alarm, knocking everything but my bed and desk over with the urgent movements as I spun in a circle.

"What scarring? What wounds? All I see is a healthy human, well, a healthy body at least. You're right about the rest, though. All these people, these families, the magic… It's more like knowing the stories of a dozen strangers and trying to recall them all at once." My voice was almost a whisper at the end as the more we referred to the other lives I'd led, the more they forcefully pushed their way to the forefront of my mind. The scent of the ocean filled my nostrils, and I felt the floor sway gently just for a moment. Had I lived on a ship at some point?

"It might be easier if you allowed us to show you. On my soul, I promise these two hold no ill intent and will open themselves to binding as I have," Nikolai said, his ethereal hand on my shoulder, somehow centering me in the moment through the magical connection.

"Only two? I thought there were a lot more outside waiting." My senses instinctively stretched out again, the differences in what I could sense almost more jarring than I was able to handle.

Every person in the house gave off a beaming heat and light that signified their living soul, wrapped with intricately detailed auras that reflected everything from current moods to their unique Gifts, making each one distinct. Still waiting together as an eerily immobile mass, the silvery outlines of the ghost horde was easily distinguishable from any living beings.

"The Thief and The Killer should come before the rest of our ilk. Due to our direct work with your father, we are the strongest and safest options available," Nikolai explained as nonchalantly as one would while discussing the weather.

"My safest option... is to bind with a thief and a killer next? I'm starting to wonder if following my father's insane plan is any better than seeing what the Cult has in store," I quipped back, trying to push my senses further to reveal individual ghosts from the overall mob. To my surprise I received a hard slap to the back of the head.

"Your insane father gave everything he had to this plan. The only plan where you survive, where your eternal torment isn't used as literal fuel for the Apocalypse. The only scheme mad enough to keep his son out of the hands of an ancient cabal that has hunted you for longer than you've been alive? I will pardon your ignorance for now, as your mind quite literally can't put the pieces together yet." Nikolai showed more emotion than ever before as a hint of steel and fire crept into his voice. I rubbed the back of my head in astonishment. It didn't hurt but it raised a few questions.

"Can you just choose when to be solid or immaterial, then? That could come in handy. I can respect that you trust the Baron, and I definitely need help... but I've never even really met the man. How about we focus on the whole 'keeping me alive and getting free?' Do you know how to get me back into a more... human shape?" I walked a circle around the now taciturn figure, curious if he'd strike again.

Instead of lashing out, he began incanting softly to himself, a rosary appearing in his hands and chiming like a string of bells as magic rippled out. I'd heard religious magic discussed in theory, as any faith one truly took to heart could be incorporated into your magical life quite easily.

"You have got to be shitting me. This is the kid?" a new voice said, causing me to turn away from Nikolai and regard the dead man sitting perched on the edge of my bed. I couldn't place his accent but felt a thunderous growl rumble through my chest in response to his tone.

"You mistake this wolf for a sheep, old man," an almost bored voice said as a third ghost with a gaunt face walked through the front door.

Their unusually spindly frame was wrapped in the most elaborate weaving of leather strips and buckles from head to toe that I'd ever seen. My hackles raised instinctually; this last ghost was visible, but I could tell it was suppressing its aura, unlike anything I'd experienced before. If I wasn't already staring at the androgynous form, I probably wouldn't be able to tell it was there at all.

"I'm not old, you murderous twig! Being dead is a completely different gamble," said the abrasive man, still sitting on my bed but now rifling through the sack of my winnings from the Battle Royale.

The sight was made all the stranger because the nosy poltergeist couldn't seem to make contact with the items inside the bag. He seemed to have thrust his arms into the bag, up to the elbow, and was just enjoying the sensation of moving them around. I looked around at the pale trio and began to seriously consider if maybe joining the Cult willingly might be my best bet.

"It's only been thirty seconds, and you've already got him regretting our presence," Nikolai lamented in exasperation, covering his face comically with both hands in genuine dismay.

"I understand, Xavier. They're a cult that values necromancy, and you have just recently come into your own considerable powers in said field. However, even if your lineage wasn't an issue, which it certainly is, you were simply born too late to the party. With your strength there would need to be room made for a new seat at the big boy's table... and those coveted positions have been set in stone for centuries now. The payment in blood to gain one is quite higher than I would like to think you're willing to go at such a young age." As the wise elder spoke, I half listened and half observed the two new arrivals.

The thin one was shoving their masked face almost directly into the runes I'd begun to redo around the doorframe. While that happened, the slightly rotund spirit on my bed had dove headfirst into the treasures I'd accrued. A sense of anxiety and annoyance came through our bond, and I realized that I was feeling Nikolai's worries. When I paid attention I could sense that chief among those concerns was that his dire message was being undercut by his oddball associates.

"Don't worry, the only reasons I haven't freaked out and run screaming into the woods are that the door is locked and... I'm honestly still not sure which part of this is worst. Not being human? The cult hanging over my head like a wavering guillotine? The soul scars one gains when you're raised as a changeling and have your mind wiped too many times?" I said, starting off steady but going into another panicking spiral about halfway through.

"Stop whining and come fix this," the monotone voice of the ghost at my door interjected.

For some reason, their matter-of-fact tone struck me just right to derail my momentum and redirect it. Implying something was wrong with my Enchantments also grabbed my attention in a way that nothing else could. Trying to glean a closer look at the leather-strapped mummy, I saw that every bit of skin from their toes to the top of their head was covered in the identical straps of black leather and sterling silver buckles. Their eyes were hidden behind a pair of steampunk reminiscent goggles that only reflected my own unfamiliar visage back when I expected them.

Almost indifferent to my open scrutiny, the ghost's leather-clad finger casually pointed to a segment of my half-finished runic rewrite. Having spent most of the sleepless night going over what the magical defenses used to be, I'd almost gone into a fugue state of half-remembered runes while trying to improve the overall effects. It was almost comically obvious where my need for sleep came into play as half-remembered runes and sloppy line work became increasingly prevalent. I reached a hand out to erase the chalk etchings but was interrupted.

"I wouldn't touch any of that yet. You're not even seeing straight Young Blood. Healing first, then we work." The no-nonsense tone from the mummified presence stopped me cold. The spirit hadn't physically reached out, but some of their soul's power accompanied the words.

"First, we bind, then you sleep... then I teach." They reaffirmed the sentiment after seeing I hadn't yet moved from the spot. The touch of this ghost's power had been more clinical, almost chilling despite obviously trying to be helpful.

"Ok... binding first," I replied hesitantly, trying to think through any malicious plans or advantages the spirit might be attempting to get over me.

The binding magic only served to cut off every avenue of betrayal that I could imagine was available. The next few hours went by in a blur of magic and rituals older than the mountains. Once all three bindings were in place I felt truly tired for the first time since I'd woken up in Marequin's Cave. As my eyes fluttered closed for the night, a smile touched the edge of my lips. The horde of ghosts was bright and comforting to my senses, and they were all headed my way.

Chapter Twenty-Four

My dreams were a riotous ocean of memories. The varied lifetimes that had seemed a tattered patchwork blanket when awake were one all-encompassing body of experience. My flailing body was infused with a light dichotomously alien and familiar, pulsing in sync to the waves as an ocean was absorbed through my pores. The flailing slowed until I watched my dream body begin to sink, my viewpoint looking down on the scene now outside my body.

The humanoid form reflected the ravaged and heavily scarred visage the ghosts had shown me earlier. In a beauty pageant, Frankenstein's monster would've kicked my ass, even on his ugliest day. Watching the wounds slowly reknit and bind at a supernatural speed, it seemed I was easily more stitchwork than substance. The light suffusing me sparked and flared erratically as it focused on the raw and bloodied wounds, certain pieces of myself far more resistant to the reconstruction efforts than others. The ocean gradually shrank into a vast lake as my soul veritably shook from the rehabilitating process. As the landless world's light and waves continued to roil, I felt myself floating further and further from the scene.

My eyes popped open as my waking body fell to the ground. The air was a thick mist as dozens of ghostly forms created a whirlwind of energy around me. Unlike the trio I'd bonded with that retained distinctive features, forms, and identities, these dead seemed to operate as one cohesive unit. Standing up slowly, the swirling chaos left me the undisturbed eye at the heart of a tornado of souls. Every breath I drew in felt thicker than regular air, as if I sucked in part of the ghostly essence as easily as oxygen.

"Enough for now, Saint. They'll have to wait until we work him out a bit before the next round," implored an almost familiar voice with a heavy accent, followed by a gentle flex of power that rippled throughout the room. To my surprise the mass drifted away like a gentle morning mist at the motion, passing effortlessly through the walls until only the dominant trio remained.

"I told you not to call me that, Thief," Nikolai said from where he stood by my desk, giving a long-suffering look of agitation at the first man.

"Can we start the morning with an intelligence report? It seems the Killer had an eventful night while you slept." The old man deftly changed the topic, though I could distinctly hear the Thief guffawing in the background still.

"Well… this escape is going to be a bit more involved than we expected. The Atlantean is holding up admirably under interrogation. Thankfully, the other Sages are competing for the most pain-inducing methodology rather than vying for efficacy. The Baron must have him in quite the contract to keep his mouth shut this long," the killer reported, immediately flooding my mind with images of Sage Marequin enduring a plethora of bloody and painful ordeals.

"Oh, by the gods, cut off the sympathetic mewling Young Blood. The man would've been relieved if he'd killed you instead of breaking the binding. That much he's harped on believably and constantly under duress," reproached the ghost, and I instinctively tried to reign in my feelings. It was more than a little uncomfortable that my emotional state was now broadcast between the four of us. The fact that I was the only one of us not well-versed in emotion and aura control made it a particularly one-way street.

"Cut him some slack, Stabby. Not everyone is born a heartless killing machine," admonished the Thief, earning a middle-fingered salute from the otherwise unreadable specter.

"Focus people, we've got less than a day or two to get ready. We'll have to divide before we conquer. How is the door situation, Thief?" Nikolai said, his neutral tone only slightly hampering the playfulness of the others. The diminutive ghost waddled over to the entrance of the room and leaned over so that his head and shoulders casually passed through the locked door. Only a stream of muffled whispers came from the Thief for a few long moments until he stood fully upright again and reentered the room.

"Well, the good news is that the sound-dampening and anti-scrying wards mean no one can hear or see you in here. If we've got to brute strength our exit instead of finessing the locks, they've helped us avoid drawing attention," the rotund ghost explained, comprehensible now that he was back inside.

"I wish I had taken Mal up on learning to pick locks now. Can't you just stick your head out again and pick the locks?" I asked in confusion, picturing my daring and heroic escape happening this very moment.

"You do recall that we're just ghosts, correct?" ridiculed the Thief, giving me a wry once-over. "The good news is I can teach you to break into or out of anything your fiendish mind can get us caught in... given time." His tone went honey-sweet with the final declaration, eyes sparkling with promise.

"Can we get the boy out tonight or not?" interjected the Killer, a bit of tension in their voice for the first time since we'd met. An imagined life as a career criminal vividly flashed through my mind's eye. Teleporting in and out of bank vaults while dodging cops on the open road seemed rather glamorous compared to my current predicament.

"No... he needs at least one more night in the soul soup before he'll have enough fuel in his tank. What's got your straps in a twist, Killer? I didn't think you'd get this antsy until there was blood to spill." The chubby ghost had given me another assessing once over before narrowing their eyes at their gaunt counterpart.

"You'll need to see this for yourself, Young Blood. What they're discussing is your world's future. Can you teach him quickly, or do we do things my way?" The dull tones the ghost used to say everything only failed to lessen the gravity of the words.

I almost spoke up but found the sudden tension between Nikolai and the other two ghosts a tangible oppression in the room. Flaring my power instinctively seemed to instantly sap all the potency from those around me, imbuing my being with power like a sponge in the desert drawing in moisture.

"What the hell is going on?" a voice I barely recognized boomed out from the depths of my chest.

The raw power was a heady rush as I suddenly felt that all three of the ghosts were specks of dust in the palm of my hand. I knew in that moment I could extinguish their existence as easily as blowing out a candle's flame. The overwhelming personalities being rendered temporarily inert left me to analyze and sort all the facts, insinuations, and suspicions I had to go from with startling clarity. Nikolai and the Thief remained frozen in subservient poses with eyes firmly planted on the ground as the moment lingered. The Killer remained frozen but defiant by meeting my gaze and holding themselves neither in supplication nor outright challenge.

"There is no time to waste. Put these on." The skeletal figure pulled off their goggles and tossed them to me, inciting the leather straps around her face and neck to writhe and constrict like agitated snakes covering the spirit's hollowed eye sockets.

"They will let you see through eyes of spirits you hold sway over, which I spread throughout the mountainside. You must witness what happens now... so you may be prepared for what comes next." Their words hung heavily in the air as the goggles hummed with power in my hands.

I only had to briefly look at the Thief and Nikolai's pained faces to solidify the severity of the situation. Quelling my trepidation with a Herculean effort of will-power, the ocular device stretched unnaturally to fit over my monstrous visage. Besides my head being several magnitudes larger than the Killer's, I found that the blacked-out lenses had also grown to the perfect size to accommodate my larger ocular orbs. My entire visual range rippled and was suddenly placed with patches of white, grey, and unreadable static. As I focused my intent, the disorientation and nausea effect from adopting a viewpoint outside of my own body eased.

"Now push your Sight out and try to feel the shade's spread throughout campus. Only stop once you find the Sages. This power is yours, Young Blood. Take it." My stomach dropped away as incoherent blurs flew by, the visual input transcending regular space-time conventions. My whole body snapped to attention so hard I felt my bones vibrate, and gradually I felt my powers grab onto something like magnets snapping my essence into place.

A large party was going on in one of the most lavishly furnished buildings I'd seen all year. Looking about, I found myself hanging in midair, some twenty feet over a group of people who absolutely hated my guts.

"Your yearly stipend for the next five years... up in smoke?" teased a familiar gleeful voice. A tinny quality to the audio reminded me of shaky cell reception.

Ophelia was easily recognizable by her alabaster skin and dull straw-yellow hair, even at a distance.

"Is this how we're going to spend the rest of the year? If anyone but you shoves this failure in my face... *They. Will. Pay.*" An enraged response answered her immediately, the venom in Kenneth's voice cowing everyone in attendance except for his jubilant sister.

"Once the teachers stop protecting that big baby, there will be a reckoning. We will meet in the open, and he will submit. With father's blessing, I will subjugate the oaf with my own hands," crowed the pale scion, heir to his family's vast presence and authority as one of the strongest noble magic houses.

He stroked and coddled a blade that seemed both alien and familiar, possibly a variation on something he'd used on me before. Through the senses of the ghostly body, I was picking up waves of wrathful, destructive, and deathly energies wafting off the item like oily smoke. Briefly, my mind grabbed at specifics of the new danger, but ultimately, I was forced to let go, remembering I was sent to find Sages and not Apprentices.

The sensation of free falling through a nearly featureless void was less unnerving this time. Following my instincts, I focused solely on the in-between world's unnerving inertial sensation. As I did so, I became able to feel the minuscule tugs and pushes that ferried me from one ghost's sensory field to the next. Briefly, my mind tried to parse together where exactly my consciousness was and the philosophical implications of leaving my body so far behind, but I crushed down the tangent when I noticed my wandering mind had a disruptive effect on navigating. With a refocused center, the ebb and flow between ghosts came back more clearly than ever, the killer's goggles I'd donned acting as training wheels to guide me between all the tethered spirits spread about. This time my whole incorporeal being was jarred as my intent honed to a sharpened edge.

"No Atticus, the deadline was months ago to choose new disciples. All those students remaining will be sacrificed, as we all agreed to. Don't want any of the Bosses to think you're getting greedy just days before the blood is spilled." Sage Lilith's familiar alto was filled with malice and backed up by a backbone of steel by the hungry look in her eyes. The majority of the Sages were gathered in a massive underground cavern that made Marequin's hideaway look like a cramped apartment in comparison.

A gentle push of will let me turn the specter's senses away from the heated conversation. With a jolt of excitement that almost made me lose the connection completely, I recognized the tortured pile of tattered robes and manacled limbs that was once the Sage Marequin I had known. The spirit my consciousness was tapping into seemed to briefly buck at the sight of the other Necromancer, but the magic flowing between us seemed to pacify the spirit.

Making a mental note for later, I realized the undead was comforted by the fact it was aligned with the most powerful Necromancer in the room. Would the horde still act faithfully if my enemy had more raw power than I did? As if the ghost could sense my trepidation, a series of images and emotions flooded through the bond to reassure me. Dread, hopelessness, and a near-infinite promise of stagnation were the only constant companions of the horde when they had come under Marequin's thumb for centuries.

In contrast, the spirit almost seemed to resonate with positivity when the images showed a rapid fire of moments that I had only recently become prominent in. In lieu of posing questions, my thoughts latched onto the image that seemed one of the most important to both of us. My human form only stood a few tombstones away in the oddly lit space. The look of open horror and apprehension was almost laughably apparent on my old face, despite thinking I had held a pretty good poker face.

The bond between the ghost and me flared as I got the impression that I was missing the point. Once again, the scene played out in the shared space of our minds, but this time the novelty of observing through senses different than my own was fully appreciated. The magical Sight I still worked to hone and a menagerie of other senses were nothing compared to the details of a ghost in their own graveyard. Each grave may well have been its own magical fiefdom with how what had been bland earth was now vibrant patchworks of color, textures, and less definable features signifying each soul's limited area of influence.

Before I could get lost in the new details fully, my human body's hand reached out to a nearly unrecognizable Nikolai, still dismembered and ragged. The entire cave was blinded as my human body reached to grab the unexacting Nikolai, a shattered kaleidoscope of light bursting out between the blackened cracks of the binding left on my soul. While my vision returned in patches, I saw the raw essence travel like a well-orchestrated meteor shower as the light transferred violently and purposefully from body to spirit.

Astonishment at my selfless act rippled through the crowd as I viewed things from their perspective. No training, no knowledge, no fear would have worked as a potent catalyst like an empathetic desire to help. The emotional response had to reach all the way to his core to manifest so naturally as a novice, different than any conscious thought or effort. Waves of power flowed from the magic's source and shook the undead's senses like they were at an earthquake's epicenter. The physical interaction had only felt like seconds in the moment for me, but to the dead, it had apparently been an almost timeless spectacle; the layers of muscles, tendons, flesh, and whatever special etheric elements lended to the vitality of undead souls were addressed as one.

Before my mind could process everything, a gentle tug came from my conduit ghost. My sight layered in on the Sages around Marequin as reprimanding voices filled my ears. It took me an almost embarrassingly long time to orient myself and realize the other teachers were taking turns beating and berating their former companion.

"Nobody asked if you felt anything, mighty Necromancer," Sage Atticus taunted haughtily, casually punching the taller dark-skinned man to the ground.

I hadn't heard what the prone mage said, but it was shocking to see the normally peaceful Druid be so callously violent. The bedraggled man rubbing his jaw on the ground had a cumbersome power-dampening collar that I recognized all too well. Apparently, they'd taken some of my designs and added them to a previously existing control collar, my Sight picking out bits of rune script I'd written that had been hastily incorporated to a truly ancient-looking hunk of metal.

"You know the rules. I've watched you cast this spell every year for centuries now. So, if you've never had cold flippers before, Atlantean, what's your problem?" Sage Pixie appeared without a sound to hiss at Marequin before seeming to vent her frustrations by kicking the man repeatedly while he was down.

"Just give it up, you spineless toad. What. Is. The. Plan?" she demanded through clenched teeth, accentuating every pause with a steel-toed boot to the man's gut.

"Are people coming to save the boy? Only me and the Druid can bring people in... no way around that without inside help. If you'd just stuck to your job, we'd be done with all the boring stuff. I could be teaching a Freak right now, building their trust, making their power just *that* much tastier." Pixie seemed resigned to complain at their captive rather than kicking him into unconsciousness at this point.

As if thankful for the small mercy, Marequin dutifully returned to his feet with effort. With a shaking set of hands, the bloodied magus began to manifest and manipulate raw strands of magic in a way I'd never seen before. The thickly coiled ropes of power were handled as easily as if the man was tying his shoelaces together, and I realized he had likely been consistently weaving this spell for as many years as Pixie implied.

Mixing the ghostly sense with my own Sight, a tapestry of sinister energy hung in the air in front of the Sages. To my horror, the circular thirty-foot-wide ritual was very close to completion, and if Marequin could be coaxed to work past his current snail's pace, it would be done by tomorrow evening at the latest. I took time to study the complex working that the fallen Sage was slowly but deftly bringing to life.

At my current level of rune Mastery, I could sometimes look at an enchantment and distinguish parts of its function, but only small fragments of the magic in front of me made sense. A perfectly etched section that floated several feet above the Atlantean now was a variation of the runes I used for my Dreamcatcher, but the angles were so heavily distorted that the magic produced would probably be something completely different. Just as one culture's concept of Sky and God are synonymous, or the symbol for Fire in one place meaning Creation in another, this set of runes was undoubtedly not involved with giving the entire mountain good dreams.

"I can't believe we got stuck watching him while the others get to play with *explosives.* I spend all year stealing and brewing up traps and C4 to fill them with...," Pixie grumbled, looking like she was only barely holding back from hitting Marequin more.

Another tug came from my host spirit, and the magical senses that kept me present were drawn towards the ceiling. Totally unbeknownst to those on the ground, they had more company than X and the ghosts.

"This will be their last harvest, and they don't even know," a voice like gravel and smoke said, making me flinch at the noise as if it had been whispered right into my ears. As my attention shifted, the ghostly vessel effortlessly floated above the ground until we reached a dark alcove without a scrap of light or life present.

"Do you pity them, Pious? After all these years of enslavement I'd think your thirst for revenge would be absolute," spoke Sage Lilith's honeyed voice from the same darkness as the first.

Since none of my senses in this form relied on light in any way, shape, or form, I could make out my two mentors easily. The undead essence animating the vampire almost took the shape of a regular circulatory system you'd see drawn out in an anatomy book. The main concentration of vitality was a mix of black tar and vibrant crimson veins in the emaciated heart that would never beat again.

The centuries of consistent feedings had solidified the body's reliance on digesting blood for power. The utter abandonment of any semblance of human anatomy meant the stores of energy followed the best biological framework for the supernatural predator. I'd been taught the heart was an inherent weakness, but new theories ran through my mind at the sight before me. The withered organ was an endearing center for the stolen and digested essence that ebbed and flowed, animating the entire body with energy. The sense of a soul was less distinct around and within her, as if it was just the tattered remains of one.

"Their joy will turn to fear, helplessness, and terror. Exactly how the children have felt every year. I only yearn to end the cycle." Sage Pious' time-worn sense of resolution and weariness bled through every word.

My ghostly host drifted closer, as Pious' body appeared clearly in my soul vision. The stone body looked like an intricate mix of stained glass windows and stardust, countless notes of light violently swirling about and trying to escape. Without warning, Pious' tail whipped out and caught around the waist of my incorporeal form, pulling me close enough to join their clandestine meeting.

"Did you come for a peek at your future? It is a shame you could not hear my voice prior to now. They wish to sacrifice the soul of the Baron's son more than anything else. We hope you survive. Much of the world needs you to grow into your birthright." Pious' eyes bore into mine like a pair of burning kaleidoscopic orbs, making my heart skip a beat as they clearly could not only see but touch me as well. The vampire seemed to have to squint to make me out but was able to vaguely sense me as well.

"Xavier... if you can hear us listen closely. Down there, Marequin is weaving a soul-catching reservoir. Every student killed with their special thyrsus daggers won't pass on but be caught by the Cult and harnessed. They then sell the souls to the actual Necromancers that run all this fuckery in exchange for power and extended life spans. You must escape before they come for you. You must escape the Harvest," she demanded with increasing fervor until her last words seemed as much a prayer as part of the conversation.

The intensity of her warnings, in addition to Sage Pious' grasp, overwhelmed some part of my mind, and I felt the stretched tether between my physical body and this ethereal one. An almost sad smile crossed the animated stone of Pious' face as I was ripped from the cave, retracing my path of peeping all the way back to my room. My soul recoiled against my mortal coil so hard that I was thrown straight through my desk upon reentry. A trio of expectant faces awaited me eagerly, with only a heartbeat passing before the Saint asked,

"So... see anything important?" The question didn't fall on deaf ears, but something in the back of my mind cowered from all the information dumped on me the past few days. With only a vaguely remembered spell, I waved my hands, and the broken desk began to reassemble itself, the splintered fragments rejoining with little to no effort or concentration on my part. It was one of the first times I'd had such an easy and effortless use of magic. Using my tail to right the chair and pull it to me, I sat down heavily and barely blinked when the chair immediately collapsed under my weight.

"They're going to kill everyone on the Mountain and reap our souls," I answered finally and then passed out without further fanfare.

Epilogue Part 1

"I feel like the end of the world is taking forever. Why don't we all just agree to go out together and mop things up?" Adam asked impetuously, managing to sound immature despite his decidedly Old Testament roots. In response, though their number was few, some voices of likeminded thinkers did murmur assent loudly enough to be heard.

"I know you always feel the need to speak first, Adam," an elderly man with a cane in his right hand said, sporting a broad-brimmed straw hat and placing a friendly hand on Adam's shoulder. He sipped a fine glass of rich, dark rum before smiling amicably at both those seated at the table and other innumerable figures utilizing the standing space like himself.

"You know you're at the table, likely one of the first to arrive, out of a wish to save as many powerless as possible." The man dropped a few apple taffy candies on the table with a chuckle. The young and vivacious man let out a gut-deep laugh as he made a show of picking up each morsel and pocketing them for later.

"You know you're not my Papa, right Legba?" said the first man to walk the Earth... according to some.

A trio of women traded places steadily, manifesting in a seat next to Adam's. The Old Crone had skin the shade of powdered ivory and small bones worked into her braided hair of the same hue.

"We did not have much of a hand in shaping this Champion, in the end. What reason do we have for hope?" The Crone finished speaking and immediately melted into a young child with an air of innocence and the vibrancy of youth. It spoke to the pedigree of deities and supernatural entities that no one even blinked at Hecate's transformations. There was, however, the greatest explosion of conversations and whispering since the dawn of time among the deific assemblage at her words.

"Thank you, ladies. As a prime example of a young man who failed to live up to... the expectations of others? Yes, that's how I'll phrase it for simplicity's sake.

As that prime example, I ask, what good is all this hidden potential if the boy has not been forged to withstand the coming flames?" Adam asked, biting into the vein of uncertainty that ran through the congregation. The handsome smile that had stretched across his face was rumored to have been copied by cats when they first caught canaries.

A long and drawn-out sigh from the opposite end of the table seemed to carry the tested patience of millennia. While appearing perfectly to have been an involuntary response, it was as if the exhalation birthed a blizzard in the room so deathly cold that all the flaming conversations of dissent in the room were snuffed out.

"Your hubris surprises no one, but I do find myself naturally stirred to set the record straight." An unnaturally pale woman, sitting directly diagonally from Adam, declared her words as if scraping Adam's sentiments from the bottom of her boots like any other excrement.

"You were built in your Creator's Image and destined for failure. There is another room full of immortals doing all within their power to end everything we value. I was under the impression that those gathered here would be collaborating to undermine this hell-spawn cult taking over the world?" The lithe and curvaceous form of the woman speaking was an odd counterpart to how her fist sent spiderweb cracks across the stone when she slammed it down to accentuate her question. With a quick and consoling hand on Lilith's shoulder, Brigid leaned forward to place a delicate fingertip on the table and heal all the damage instantly.

"Marequin may have failed, but I know when a game is over. There's not just the fight of our lives coming up, there is still adventure to be had! Do you silly adults even know how many childhoods they've crammed into him? I bet...." A guttural growl from the depths of Hell cut off the quick-tongued boy.

Many cowered at the bone-rattling warning that shook the building from floorboards to ceiling rafters. Instead of being cowed by the display of power, the boy triumphantly put his hands on his hips and floated several feet in the air with a crow's call on his lips.

"All is not lost! He is a Lost Boy just beginning to awaken. If you can't taste the great war coming with him at the center... then you're worthless." The unusual boy's confidence swelled in a room of Elders with a capital 'E' as far as any member of humanity was concerned.

"Would the great Hell-Mouth of a Momma Duck really bother grumbling to cut me off if this kid didn't still have secrets worth protecting? Secrets can save the day." With a sprinkle of iridescent pixie dust, he flew upward triumphantly and disappeared through the open skylight.

The abrupt departure of the small figure that carried a dichotomous nature of being ancient and eternally young, the room seemed shocked into contemplative silence. It was a momentous occasion whenever one of the gods, demigods, or other entities showed that they respected one another's judgment or opinions in any way. The quiet was eventually broken by Lilith, speaking up with an uneasy attempt at leading the narrative.

"We have a vote of support from the Lordling of Avalon. As first of my kind, I too vote in support of the boy X. The apocalypse only comes once, people. Don't you want to be standing on the right side when it does?" The steel in the woman's spine had hardened by the time she was done speaking.

Making no effort to hide her elongated fangs and unnaturally pallid flesh, it made Adam recoil with ages-old disgust and anger. He generally had that reaction to anyone not of human descent like himself and his custom-made bride. As Lilith was the un-living epitome of those not born of Adam and Eve's Union, the normally picturesque visage of the first man was graffitied with ugly blotches of red and purple fury.

"I vote against! Marequin's betrayal leaves the whole point moot, no? There is no messiah to rally behind if he's food for the enemy." Adam sat back, letting his rage seem to melt into a long-held suffering patience, but his body language clearly showed the warring emotions.

Moving to stand in front of their seated position together, two brothers, possibly twins, stood and spoke in near unison.

"Peter Pan votes to support the boy, as does Lilith the First Woman. Adam votes against. Dorian Gray accepted the invitation for this evening but has declined to appear, abstaining to vote. We, Romulus and Remus, abstain as well. Not enough is known at this time for us to weigh in." The swarthy bearded brothers traded off talking every few words as if they shared one mind. Speech was not common for the pair, but they managed to come off as both well-spoken and a bit feral. In unison, the brothers matched gazes with every individual in the room before truly seeming to relax.

"Does Marequin's betrayal mean so little to you all? The boy is now at one of the bloodiest sacrificial sites on Earth. Exposed. Alone. What reason is there for hope? Any other child would already be deemed dead," Xolotl said with some difficulty, the canine head atop his shoulders not perfectly compatible with human speech.

The gods went still, and some of the most powerful people in the world flinched in fear as the cawing of a crow rang through the space like the peals of church bells in a belfry. A cornucopia of names was tossed about as people watched the bird bellow at the top of its lungs and take a spiraling descent until alighting on the center of the table. Flashing crimson eyes, the corvid seemed to lazily menace every figure it fell upon as it strutted around confidently.

"Though we were not invited... This is our place. The eve of war is upon us. The enemy is busy. Betrayal was inevitable in the Baron's mind. This is why even allies like yourself have been kept in the dark. Even my sisters Morrigan and Anand are not privy to the details. When even the Gods are clashing to shape the child's fate, no measure of secrecy is truly extreme enough. He will become the Champion of Death when the realms have been sundered, and Necromancers abolish the lines of life, death, and immortality." The bird's voice went directly into the listener's mind, a slight Irish accent with a pleasant lilt to it.

"There will be a river of corpses, blood, and souls like this owl has never witnessed! He will save the world or die trying." Badb extended her wings with this last prophetic proclamation, a magical aura encompassing the room until the black feathered goddess shrieked like a banshee and flew from the room.

One by one, the myriad creatures filtered out. In the end, the closely tied voting was made moot by the prophecy laid out. Even in a room full of feuding transcendent beings, or maybe especially here, a prophecy could not be refuted. Interpreted in different ways? Inevitable. Can prophecies be manipulated to produce unforeseen outcomes? With great skill and cunning, this is feasible. Stopping a prophecy altogether? This is considered the providence of the mad and foolish. No being present carried both traits, thankfully, so by the time a single ebony feather landed lazily on the table, the room was utterly empty.

Epilogue Part 2

Sage Solomon wiped the sheet of sweat from his brow as the assembly grew larger by the minute. In the last 800 years that he'd been a member of the Cult, there had never been a summons of all the cell leaders at once. Pixie stood subserviently to the side and a step behind the elder Conduit, for once not overflowing with impish rebelliousness. It was easy to be humbled as Cultists of every size, shape, and age stood stoically.

Everyone faced inward, standing in allotted spaces around the massive circle. The room quickly grew cold enough that the once King Solomon could see his breath in the air, an omen of the heavy presence of Necromantic Auras at play. Circulating his own magic to try and subtly offset the effect, he felt the roiling of ambient mana long before a tear in reality was ripped open.

"Welcome, loyal Acolytes. Blessed be to the hands working this, the Last Harvest. We will take account of everyone's reports today, and then there will be no contact until the last soul has crossed over," a faceless robed figure at the center of the congregation spoke. The voice was so gravelly with age that the gender was indiscernible, just the weight of time and the unshaken confidence of living through it.

"I should not need to emphasize to anyone how lucky you are to be with us right now. Millenia have come and gone under our strict guidance, and only now, for the first time, is there room for those in the Cult to Ascend. Do not fail us. Come forth Site 34 Acolyte. Present your projected yield and be evaluated." The voice's command fell upon the group like the faithful receiving God's commandments.

An elderly man seemed to crawl his way to the center of the circular congregation. Like the weight of all the scrutiny amassed as physical weight on the man's back, he shuffled forward slowly and with great difficulty. As the uniform black robes everyone wore obscured their identities, the elaborately carved staff the cultist leaned on seemed the most notable thing about them.

"The Bermuda Triangle is on schedule for a full shipment of souls, with no foreseen complications," reported the first Acolyte, engendering only the slightest of nods from the Elder Cultist.

The procession continued like this for hours, with only the slightest deviations. One school had lost half its stock due to a hive mind that began with two siblings and had grown out of control. Another had run into some type of divine intervention after mistakenly recruiting some Nephilim. Even stranger oddities popped up, each deemed easily rectifiable with brutal applications of murder and magic. An enchanted scroll in the Elder Cultist's hands grew longer as he continued to go down the parchment, sparsely jotting the reports given. Sage Solomon was jarred out of his meditative stance as the room grew silent for the first time since the meeting began.

"Will the Acolyte from Sage Mountain step forth?" The Elder sounded like they were interested in something for the first time today, or possibly ever, it was hard to tell. Not seeing the shark's grin form on Sage Pixie's face, he was more than surprised at the not-so-gentle shove he received towards the center of the room. Barely righting himself before falling face first, the man didn't spare a look backwards at his mutant counterpart. Instead, he marshaled his centuries of experience and sank seamlessly into the regal bearing of a man who was once King.

"Elder... Acolyte Solomon reporting for Sage Mountain." His voice was truly that of a ruler, nothing but confidence and projected competence noticeable in the crisply articulated sentiment.

"Acolyte Solomon, it says here that your team was tasked with harvesting the first soul flagged for significance in over 900 years. I expect the gravity of the situation means it has been handled with the utmost care." Dust shook from the cavern ceiling as the Elder's voice rose in volume by magnitudes.

"With regret, this humble one must report there have been complications with the flagged soul. Outside this individual, our harvest is set to move forward flawlessly as usual," the Sage said in a placating tone. Solomon had overseen countless harvests of fresh souls to the Necromancer Elites. As a Conduit that couldn't use

Necromancy, the souls were meaningless to him outside of acting as currency to buy his way into the Cult's good graces.

"Explain yourself and these... complications. Quickly." The temperature plummeted in the center of the room where Solomon stood. The icy chill gripped his spine as the Conduit attempted to maintain his composure.

"Our cell's necromancer, Marequin of Atlantis, was compromised and made a move on the flagged individual. As already reported, the soul of significance received near constant supervision." A long stretch of silence filled every nook and cranny of the mausoleum.

"We had regained control over the boy and placed him in containment to await the Culling. I regret to report, however, that this morning, with betrayers' aid, he has escaped. We are prepared to hand over the Marequin at your earliest desired convenience as we hunt the fleeing soul." Solomon ended with a deep bow that almost let his forehead meet the dirty floor.

"One traitor outmaneuvered your entire cell? Including yourself?" the Elder Cultist responded immediately, their irritation evident in the tone of voice used. "Have you made any headway into our inquiries regarding the boy's parentage?"

"Marequin's actions came as an utter shock to everyone, Elder. The enemy has access to a Mutant possessing the ability to suppress and lock away memories until a very specific trigger releases them. Right now, neither Marequin nor the boy has information on the sire, even less on a mother figure," Solomon explained eloquently to the Elder Necromancer. Sweat began streaming openly down the Conduit's face as there was no discernible reaction from the Cultist in front of him.

"I will pass along the details of your report, despite it being utterly bare of actionable intelligence." The Elder performed quick and concise somatic gestures before holding out a plain scroll of parchment. A duo of previously invisible skeletal torsos flew up through the stone floor, wrapping their bony hands around the paper and carrying it together through the ceiling effortlessly.

"Now that the matter has been elevated, I must take proper punitive actions against the Sage Mountain cell." The Elder Cultist snapped their ancient fingers casually, releasing potent magic that went off like a bomb to those who felt the spell being released.

Solomon's screams were short-lived as he was immolated from the inside out in a handful of seconds. With an efficiency that left even this murderous congregation speechless, the Necromancer's inferno had been so finely controlled that only a freshly cleaned skeleton was left behind. A wheezing cackle left the wizened Cultist's hood as a simple wave of his hand animated the bones. The obedient leftovers of what was Sage Solomon's body walked noiselessly to the lead Cultist's side and stood there subserviently. While even the most hardened hooded Acolytes gathered were recoiling from the pungent aroma of the vaporized old man, a relative newcomer slowly waltzed directly over the burnt spot where Solomon had died.

"Acolyte Pixie, reporting for duty. Unlike my predecessor, I'm willing to bet more than my life on this. For promotion above Acolyte status, I'm willing to personally deliver the boy into your hands. Just tell me when and where." The flamboyant bubble gum hair chopped haphazardly made the charcoal robe on the Sage look all the more absurd. The mad fervor in her voice fully matched the naked lust for power in her eyes. She seemed to shake with excitement in her combat boots as the Cult Elder sat in contemplation of her bold declaration.

"If you're not willing to gamble it all at the apocalypse, then when can you, young Mutant Acolyte?" A smile was revealed on the Elder Cultist as they pulled back their hood to meet Pixie's eyes.

Most were too taken aback to react, but the few who did could clearly be heard retching at the unexpected reveal. Pixie's eyes twitched, but she otherwise held onto her composure as the rotting skull grinned down from above. Skin in varying degrees of decomposition made a horrifying tapestry of healthy flesh, necrotic rot, and exposed patches of bones and teeth.

"Betting more than your life is the only way to get ahead in the New World. Your oath is accepted, Acolyte." The Elder Licht cackled maniacally at the unexpected turn of events. Sage Pixie bowed deeply to hide her equally insane glee, a rictus grin that promised bloodshed and violence.

About the Author

So, you've made it to the author bio... Welcome! Meet Michael Holmes. This will be mostly nonsense, but a famous author once said that their job was to embrace the nonsense. "Only once space has been made for the nonsensical can creativity flourish." Don't fact-check him on that.

Michael has been in love with the art of storytelling since he was a young boy, devouring every tall tale he could get his hands on. He hopes this first book of the series was to your liking and that when the next adventure is out, you'll enjoy it even more.